By the same author:

That Slippery Slope
Making Lemonade

kate langdon

famous

HarperCollins*Publishers*

For Barney

National Library of New Zealand Cataloguing-in-Publication Data
Langdon, Kate, 1975-
Famous / Kate Langdon.
ISBN 978-1-86950-562-2
NZ823.3—dc 22

First published 2005
This edition published 2008
HarperCollins*Publishers (New Zealand) Limited*
P.O. Box 1, Auckland

ISBN 978 1 86950 562 2

Cover design by Sarah Bull, Anthony Bushelle Graphics
Internal text design and typesetting by Springfield West

Printed by Griffin Press, Australia

50gsm Bulky News used by HarperCollins*Publishers* is a natural,
recyclable product made from wood grown in sustainable plantation
forests. The manufacturing processes conform to the environmental
regulations in the country of origin, New Zealand.

Acknowledgements

Where would I be without The Gals? Petra, Atlanta, Becks, Lauren, Bobbie, Clare, Kirsty and Suz, for their ridiculous stories, laughter, and all-round fabulousness. And for constantly popping the cork and putting their bodies on the line in the name of research. Your sacrifices were not in vain!

Thanks to Jo T for the Bikini Wax Story (no, of course it wasn't her).

Thanks to Olivia for the Flaming Handbag and Iron Stories.

My wonderful (although slightly barmy) family — Mum, Dad, Justin, Ben, Haydon, Faye and Waynne. And also Pamela, Anna and Jo.

My amazing grandparents — Charlie, Pat, Frank and Jo — still going strong and showing us all up.

Claire, Laly and Ben, for being my wee reading guinea pigs and for having no qualms about telling me when something was crap (although *always* in a nice way of course).

Ben, who must be the only bloke alive who knows the difference between a beaded and a sequined dress.

Tracey Wogan, for being such a champion editor and ally.

Lorain Day, for her continuing aid and enthusiasm.

The rest of the team at HarperCollins NZ, a top bunch of people.

And Barney, for not putting me out with the rubbish (even when I began to wear the rainbow socks day in and out and have heated arguments with myself). And for being the most supportive partner a writer could ever wish for. You are the bomb. This book is for you.

Life should *not* be a journey to the grave with the intention of arriving safely in an attractive and well-preserved body, but rather to skid in sideways, champagne in one hand, strawberries in the other, body thoroughly used up, totally worn out, and screaming . . . *woo hoo*, what a ride!

Anon

1

'Pull!' hollered Ethan. 'Thatta girl!'

I lay crouched on my knees in a field of muddy grass, eye level with the fanny of a very large cow, my arms stuck up to their pits in it, covered in God-only-knew-what, attempting to grasp the legs of her very-nearly-about-to-be-born calf. The complete and utter irony of the situation did not escape me. Barely six months earlier my thirty-three-year-old life had been coasting along all according to plan. My plan. I lived in the city in my fabulously stylish apartment, I was *this* close to being made a partner at the advertising firm in which I'd worked for the past eight years, I was invited to the opening of every hot new bar in town, and I was relishing every moment of my Single Girl Metropolitan City Life. In other words, as I crouched in the muddy grass, with my arms firmly planted in the cow's colossal femininity, it was glaringly evident my life had been turned upside down.

'Here she comes, Sam!' cried Ethan, as the cow let out one final long groan. 'Pull!'

And pull I did. Then I pulled some more. I pulled until, with one gigantic squelching sound, I was left cradling a tiny brown slippery calf in my bloody arms.

'Great job, Sam!' said Ethan, putting his arm around my shoulders and grinning. 'You're a pro.'

Still hugging the tiny calf in my arms, I grinned back.

Its eyelids were beginning to flutter, about to see the world for the very first time.

'Better put her down by Mum,' instructed Ethan, taking the calf and placing it gently down beside its mother's head, ready for the cleaning process to begin. 'Otherwise she might think that's you.'

'OK,' I replied. My life may have been turned on its own head but I still had no desire to lick the mucus from a newborn calf.

So, how exactly did I get from the big city to crouching in a muddy paddock wearing a pair of farmer's gumboots? I bet you're wondering. So was I.

In retrospect, which is a fine but essentially useless thing, my life had started to go a bit patchy with a phone call from my ex-boyfriend Jerry eight months earlier. I hadn't spoken to Jerry, let alone laid eyes on him for over three years; he was the closest I had ever come to settling down with a man. We'd been together for a year-and-a-half before I let him move his possessions through my front door. He had lived in my apartment for approximately six weeks. Jerry was stylish, he was kind and considerate, and he was undeniably good-looking, but the effect his presence had inflicted upon my SGD (Single Girl's Den) was catastrophic. He'd hardly been there two minutes before he wanted to hang the hideous photograph of his university football team in my living room. He simply didn't understand that my apartment had taken years of shopping and strategic placement to look just the way I wanted it to. And that there was *simply no bloody room in it for some God-awful footy picture.*

But it was his mother's Christmas cake that finally broke the camel's back. Or my back, to be more specific. His mother had sent him her annual homemade Christmas cake and this had somehow wound up sitting in its ugly floral box in my pantry for weeks on end, cluttering what was an otherwise streamlined space. I hate Christmas cake. I hate the smell of it, the look of it, and the fact it just seems to stick around forever and never go away, much like Christmas ham. I told Jerry in no uncertain terms that he either found another home for his Christmas cake, or for himself, and considered the case to be closed. Then one night I returned home late from a work function and walked through my living room to the kitchen, only to trip over the goddamn cake box lying on the floor beside the sofa, fly through the air and land sprawled backwards across my white Conran coffee table. Through the pain of my two cracked vertebrae I still remember my complete shock that Jerry had been eating the bloody Christmas cake while sitting on my white Emporia Italia sofa. He knew very well there was no eating on the sofa! *He'd probably had his God-awful smelly feet up on it too!*

While lying in traction in the hospital the next day, I informed Jerry that he could promptly *take his cake, hideous football photo and smelly socks and fuck off out of my apartment.* It wasn't easy being livid while lying in traction and completely unable to move any part of one's body, apart from one's mouth (ever so slightly) and eyes. He must have got the message though, because when I was released four weeks later he was nowhere to be seen and my SGD had returned to its natural clean, serene state. I promptly vowed never to let another man move through my front door until I

9

had made a complete stocktake of all his worldly possessions and forced him to sign a declaration stating (amongst several other clauses) that his mother did not bake. I strongly doubted any man would pass my stringent new shack-up criteria and I felt strangely secure in this knowledge.

Plus, I liked having my own space and my own routine. The thought of a bloke messing it all up with stray socks, beer bottles and car magazines made me shudder. It was not the look I was aiming for. I liked my white walls, my chaises longues, my Japanese vases and my clean stainless bench tops. They were soothing and comforting, my Zen-like womb. Every piece of art adorning the white walls was either a relic from an overseas trip or a hard-earned investment.

However, it was slightly disconcerting to note that the only men who shared my passion for minimalist clean lines and white Italian furniture appeared to be gay. Although I felt secure in the knowledge that any one of my gay friends would be happy to donate their sperm (should I at any stage feel maternal) and would undoubtedly make a fantastic husband. They would have their own life, I would have mine, and together we would share a stylish space we called home. And a baby of course. The perfect family.

But back to Jerry's phone call. He had some news he just had to share with the girl who'd helped him see the light. He'd had a sex change. A sex change! And what's worse, he wanted to ask me out to dinner.

'What does that make me?' I'd wailed to Mands and Lizzie, my two best friends. 'Some sort of confused lesbian?'

'No,' they replied. 'That makes him the confused lesbian. You're just an innocent bystander.'

'But I shagged him. Lots. And we lived together.'

'Doesn't count,' said Mands. 'He was a bloke then. Wasn't he?'

'Course he bloody was.' I glared at her. 'A blokey bloke too.'

'Unbelievable,' she said, shaking her head in dismay. 'You just never can tell.'

'So, has he gone the full hog?' asked Lizzie.

'God knows,' I replied. 'All he said is that he's now a woman.'

'What if he's a woman with legs like tree trunks and a face full of stubble?' said Mands.

'Now there's a lovely thought,' I replied. 'Cheers.'

'Wonder if he gets premenstrual?' asked Lizzie.

'All men think they get premenstrual,' I replied. 'Nothing odd about that.'

'So, are you going to go?' they both asked.

'I guess I have to,' I sighed. 'Otherwise I'm going to look like some sort of . . .'

'Transsexual hater,' finished Mands.

'That's right,' I agreed. 'A transsexual hater.'

'Not very PC,' added Lizzie, shaking her head. 'Really not.'

'I just can't believe it,' said Mands, for the umpteenth time that night. 'Jerry is a woman.'

'Trust me,' I replied. 'Neither can I.'

'So, tell me,' said Lizzie. 'What's he called now? I mean, he must have changed his name, right?'

'I don't know. He didn't say anything.'

'P'haps he's just sticking with Jerry?' said Mands. 'You know, like Jerry Hall.'

'It probably doesn't say Jeremy on her birth certificate,' I pointed out.

'True,' they agreed.

'Bet he's changed it,' said Lizzie. 'I would.'

'Oh, are you planning on having a sex change too are

you?' said Mands. 'Nice of you to tell us!'

'Very funny,' replied Lizzie.

'Maybe he wants to get back together with you?' suggested Mands.

'Oh, there's a pleasant thought. My ex-boyfriend who is now a woman wants to start dating again. How fabulous.'

'No,' said Lizzie. 'I bet he just wants to confront you and his past, so that he can move on and . . . and be a woman.'

'I'm perfectly happy not to be confronted,' I replied. 'Really am.'

'Bit selfish though, isn't it?' said Mands. 'He wants you to see him as a woman just so he can move on with his life, without any consideration as to how you might feel about seeing him . . . I mean her.'

'Exactly,' I agreed. 'Selfish bastard.'

'Bitch,' corrected Lizzie. 'Selfish bitch.'

'How weird,' said Mands, shaking her head. 'Did he ever, you know, put your frocks on for no good reason?'

'No!' I replied. 'Course he didn't! Although . . .' I suddenly remembered, 'he did wear my knickers once or twice . . . you know . . . in the sack.'

'He wore your knickers?' cried Mands. 'And you didn't think that was slightly odd?'

'Well . . . no. He said he liked wearing them because they were nice and tight.'

'Bryce used to wear my knickers too,' admitted Lizzie. 'Said it turned him on.'

'Oh for God's sake!' said Mands. 'Say no more. Please. You're putting me off my wine.'

'So that was the only odd thing he did then?' asked Lizzie. 'Occasionally wear your knickers?'

What was she insinuating? That whenever I left the house he'd lunged for my red Trelise Cooper dress and the vacuum?

'Well . . . yes. Though sometimes he'd . . . use my skin products too.'

In fact he'd used my eye cream so much I'd started hiding it from him.

'You didn't tell us that!' cried Mands. 'Stealing your skincare, that's a sure sign of a wannabe transsexual.'

'But he was always watching sport,' I protested. 'And drinking beer.'

'Even transsexuals watch sport and drink beer,' replied Lizzie, ever the pragmatist.

Friday night had arrived and I'd made my way to Savour to meet Jerry. I arrived in a taxi, being that I'd recently ingested a bottle of nerve-settling-pre-dinner-with-transsexual-ex-boyfriend champers with Mands and Lizzie.

'Table for Harrison?' I asked the maître d'.

Oh God, what if he's changed his surname too? I thought to myself.

'Right this way,' replied the waiter. 'You're the first to arrive.'

Well, that's a blessing, I thought, promptly ordering a bottle of wine.

Oh Christ, I despaired, as I sat down. *What if I don't recognise him? I mean her?*

Thankfully I could see the front door from where I sat. I anxiously checked every female who entered the restaurant, frantically searching for one who looked like a drag queen. I hoped he wasn't going to look too much like the ones who stood on K Rd. This might have been a metropolitan city, but it wasn't big enough for that sort of caper. Plus, I liked this restaurant and it would be a shame if I couldn't come back.

The wine arrived and the waiter poured me a glass. I quickly scanned the menu, looking up only when a gorgeous ruby-red embroidered suit jacket approached the table, accompanied by long shiny black hair framing one of the most beautiful faces I had ever set eyes on.

Great, I thought to myself. *They've put me at the wrong bloody table and now I'm going to have to move. Typical.*

'Sam,' said the beautiful woman, 'hi.'

Oh God. It couldn't be.

'Jerry?' I ventured uncertainly.

'Well . . . no . . . Jasmine now actually,' she said, giving me a kiss on the cheek.

This beautiful woman couldn't possibly be Jerry? I thought to myself. *My ex-boyfriend? There's no way. She was gorgeous.*

I scanned her face for stubble, but there was none to be seen. Just smooth, tanned, perfect skin. There was the same slim, aquiline nose. The same almond-coloured eyes. But there the similarities ended. I looked at her chest, I couldn't help myself. There, under the outline of the flattering and well-cut suit jacket, was a pair of what had to be, at least, size-C breasts staring back at me. Perky, voluptuous, size-C breasts. *Bloody hell! The lucky cow! Where had the hairy chest gone?* I wondered. *The chest I used to lay my head on?* I glanced down at her hands, expecting to see the familiar trail of dark hairs covering the back of them. But there were none. In fact, although her hands were large, they looked soft and feminine and . . . and she had the same pale pink nail polish on as me. Plus, she smelled lovely. *What was it?* I wondered. *Givenchy? Gaultier? No. It was Issey Miyake. Jerry was wearing Issey Miyake. Hells bells!*

That's just bloody brilliant, I thought to myself. *Your ex-boyfriend becomes a woman and he ends up more gorgeous than you. How completely and utterly pants! Was there anything worse?*

'So,' said Jasmine. 'You look great, Sam.'

'Thanks and . . . well . . . so do you . . . although obviously a little different.'

'I'd hope so,' she laughed, huskily and sexily.

I couldn't, not for one moment, stop gawping at her. This was the same person who had frequently ruined a white wash with his black football shorts. The same person who left the toilet seat up more often than was called for. The same person I'd shagged in my parents' ensuite while the rest of the family ate Christmas dinner.

'Shocked?' she asked, flicking her long shiny black hair behind her shoulders in a way which, well, looked very familiar. *Dear God*, I thought to myself, *he'd been stealing my moves.*

'Just a little,' I replied.

Truth be told, I was beginning to think she was an imposter, sent by Jerry to break the ice, and at any moment now a tree-trunk-legged, stubble-faced cross-dresser would come sauntering into the restaurant.

Perhaps she's got tree-trunks hiding under those beautifully cut trousers? I consoled myself.

'You do believe it's me, don't you?' asked Jasmine, noting my bewilderment.

'Um . . . kind of . . . I guess,' I replied.

'What if I told you that you have a tiny round mole in the middle of your left butt cheek?'

Wow. She was good.

'And that the thing you hate most in this world, aside from Christmas cake of course, is a badly made bed.'

She really was.

'Closely followed by filter coffee.'

Damn.

'And warm bubbles.'

Unbelievable.

'So,' said Jasmine. 'Do you believe me now?'

'I guess so,' I replied.

'And that's not the worst of it,' I said to Mands and Lizzie the following evening, as I recounted my Date with Ex-Boyfriend who is Now a Woman.

'What else?' they said eagerly, sitting on the edge of the sofa, braced for gossip.

'She's absolutely drop-dead gorgeous!'

'No!' they cried. 'You're having us on.'

'Am not,' I replied, shaking my head for emphasis. 'It's true.'

'The bastard!' they chimed.

'Exactly!'

'What does she look like?' asked Lizzie.

'Gorgeous, straight, shiny black hair.'

'Short or long?'

'Long.'

'And?'

'And a beautiful long slim face with the same brown eyes and nose but that's it.'

'No stubble?' asked Mands.

'No, not a whiff. Gorgeous, smooth, tanned skin with full red lips. And the most perfect eyebrows you've ever seen.'

'No way.'

'Yes way. And, wait for it, a pair of size Cs.'

'No!'

'Yes!'

'But you're only a B. That's not fair!'

'I know!' I wailed. 'They were unbelievably perky too.'

'Fake,' comforted Mands.

'How about that,' said Lizzie. 'Jerry has a sex change and ends up outdoing you in the gorgeous stakes.'

'I know!' I cried. 'The arsehole.'

The more I thought about Jasmine, the more irate I became.

'She even dresses well,' I added, giving a detailed rundown of her attire.

'Think I've seen that jacket at Trelise,' replied Lizzie. 'It's gorgeous!'

Great. Now she was even shopping at the same places as me.

'And,' I added, 'she's been stealing my moves.'

I explained the hair-flicking incident, which had happened on more than one occasion throughout dinner.

'Get out!' gasped Mands. 'That's just not on.'

'Bit SWF,' added Lizzie.

'And did she want to get down your pants?' asked Mands, ever a gallant supporter of the worst-case scenario.

'No. In fact she has a boyfriend.'

'No!'

'Yes.'

'Mother of God,' said Lizzie. 'It just gets more bizarre.'

'She showed me a picture of him.'

'And?'

'And,' I hissed, 'he's incredibly foxy.'

'So, it does get worse,' said Mands, clearly relishing the situation. 'Your ex-boyfriend, who is now a more gorgeous woman than you, has a boyfriend, who also just happens to be incredibly foxy. And yet you don't have a boyfriend yourself.'

'Yes. Thanks ever so much for pointing that out.'

'Unbelievable,' said Mands, shaking her head.

'Ignore her, dolls,' said Lizzie. 'She's just jealous.'

Sometimes best friends were a real pain in the arse, I thought to myself.

Lizzie and Mands had been my two best friends for as long as I could remember. So long that we had managed to synchronise our periods decades ago. They were the kind of lifelong friends with whom you could happily talk about the quality of your last shag (if you could remember it, that is) and who had no problem letting you know when your hair or waistline had seen better days. The three of us were PSGs (Professional Single Girls). Or at least two of us were — Lizzie had been having a raging affair with a married man named Simon for the past three months. Lizzie was to a married man as honey was to a bee.

The next morning, post Sex-Change Date rundown, I sat on the opposite side of the boardroom table in a numb daze as Trixie and Davis, the two young creatives, babbled on about their pitch for the latest shampoo commercial. Gareth, my boss, and Erica, my assistant, were sitting on either side of me.

'Fruitawhat?' I asked, not sure I had heard them correctly.

'Fruitavessence. Fruit nutrients for the hair,' explained Trixie.

'What in God's name is fruitavessence?' I asked. 'Mashed banana in your shampoo?'

'Brilliant!' enthused Gareth, oblivious to the ridiculousness of this fabricated word.

'Fruitavessence to keep your hair alive,' expanded Davis.

'But hair's dead cells,' I protested.

'Shut up Sam, no one knows that,' said Gareth, clearly sold on the ridiculous idea.

'I like it,' chipped in Erica.

I flicked her the Death Stare. Sometimes (quite often) I wished she would actually die. Although she was my assistant she had been hired by Gareth, against my better judgement. She was nothing but a young upstart who had her hungry eyes locked on my job, and would do anything to get it. I didn't trust her from a cheap, fragranced bar of soap. I was just patiently waiting for her to slip in her lather so I could whip the job out from under her conniving young feet. And I was confident the time was near.

I resigned myself to defeat and set about outwardly sulking.

What kind of word was fruitavessence? I wondered. I was the one who had to present their Mork-and-Mindy ideas to clients who thought I was responsible for such ridiculous words. I could only smile profusely and hope the clients were stupid enough to swallow the pitch without questioning the logic. After all, it was painfully obvious to me after more than ten years in this career, the last eight spent at Beckett Brown Creative, that there was no logic in advertising.

I was convinced that at advertising agencies all around the world there were groups of creatives who sat around in brightly coloured rooms with tea cosies perched on their hollow heads and made up these words, solely to embarrass us account managers. Words that no one had ever heard of before. Words that had absolutely *no* meaning *whatsoever*. It was very difficult to be proven wrong when you claimed a shampoo had *fruitavessence*. When no one actually knew what the bejesus *fruitavessence* was.

It hadn't escaped me that the advertisements we created

for men's products didn't use these types of words. They seemed to be solely for the benefit, or rather confusion, of women consumers. Men's ads used words like *close shave* and *silky smooth* — straightforward, self-explanatory, no-nonsense kind of words. What I struggled to understand was why we couldn't take away all of these confusing made-up words and just say things consumers could comprehend? Like *if you use this cleanser then you won't have poxy skin anymore*. Or *our shampoo will tame the wild beast that is your hair*. Or *when you feel like a piece of crap, this moisturiser will stop you crying straightaway*. Or *if you use this eye gel you won't look like a wrinkly old hag in ten years' time*. Or even *if you use this night cream, you'll finally get a date*. Things that actually *have* meaning to women. Things they can relate to. This was the sort of information women needed, the sort of information that would convince them to buy the product. They didn't want to know about *pH 5.5* or *aqua-fix technology*. They wanted to know about *bits of leather* and *how to avoid*.

I was convinced that by cutting down on all of these superfluous and gobbledegook words the advertisements would be shorter and we would thereby cut our clients' costs, meaning we'd have a lot more walking through the doors. For example, a tampon commercial that currently used words like *outer-core* and *revolutionary technology* could just say *comes in a pretty packet* and women would be sold. Do they really care about *outer-cores* and *revolutionary technology*? No. They just want the packet to look pretty in their handbags and cheer them up a bit when their stomach feels as though it's eating itself.

And if creatives weren't using words from another planet, they were bandying about words like *fine lines* and *wrinkles* and *miraculously disappear*. We all know things don't *miraculously disappear*, they just move about a bit when you stare at them too long in the bathroom mirror.

I halted my internal rant and tuned back to the inane discussion at hand. Clearly they had moved on from shampoo.

'Bumology,' said Trixie.

'Bumowhat?' I asked.

'Bumology. Y'know . . . getting your future read by your bottom.'

'By your bottom? Tell me you're joking?' I said, although experience told me she probably wasn't.

'Course not, it's all the rage. Just had it done myself.'

'You had a stranger look into your future by staring at your bum?'

'Yep.'

'And?'

'And what?'

'What did they say?'

'She said big opportunities were going to come my way. Big ideas . . . big things.'

'Like cellulite?'

'No, like y'know, fame and stuff,' replied Trixie, completely failing to notice my sarcasm.

I decided to leave the four of them to it and go back to my office and do some actual work. Plus, if Gareth wasn't going to listen to my opinion, then there was no point in having one. Although he was the more senior account manager at the firm, and essentially my boss, it seemed to be me who managed all of our key clients these days. Ever since his wife Emma had run off with her Pilates instructor he seemed to be getting grumpier and grumpier. It had been three months already, you'd think he'd be over it by now. She certainly was. Mind you, she was probably getting more sleep than him, being that she'd also left him with the two kids. Having a one-and-a-half-year-old with teething issues and a five-year-old with sleepwalking issues was apparently not conducive to getting a good night's kip. When Emma first left him I was completely on her side. She wanted him to understand what it was like looking after two small kids without an inkling of husbandly support. But ever since three weeks ago, when I was convinced by Gareth when I was in a rare state of not having my wits anywhere about my person to look after the two abandoned tykes for an afternoon, I was beginning to feel sorry for him. Almost. Although technically I hadn't actually babysat them for the whole afternoon. I had dropped them straight round to my parents' house where my father was overjoyed to have two small boys descend on the place. And I was overjoyed to leave them there. It was more a case of sub-sitting (ie agreeing to look after someone's children and then farming them off to someone else, preferably someone you know).

I opened up my email folder and set about clearing the piles of messages within.

The first one I opened was from my mother. She had sent me a newspaper article from Chile that blamed television advertising for the fact that two thirteen-year-old Chilean schoolgirls had run themselves to death in an attempt to win a local modelling competition with an international contract up for grabs. Apparently they had done one too many laps of the school field and just sort of keeled over, a hundred metres apart.

What about their parents? I thought. *What exactly were they doing while this was happening?*

My mother had added her own caption below the article:

The advertising devil strikes again. He is killing our children!

Fantastic. What an excellent start to the day.

My mother was strongly opposed to my choice in career. She was a women's rights activist, in the loosest possible sense of the words. She was more like the Arnold Schwarzenegger of the women's movement, a female bulldozer out to mow down as many men as she could. She was vehemently and very vocally opposed to what she termed the 'negative and discriminating portrayal of women in advertising'.

'Look at this woman!' my mother had cried just the weekend before, as she pointed at a magazine ad for an electric juicer. 'She's half-naked! What the hell has that got to do with a juicer?'

'She looks nice,' I replied.

'Yes, she looks nice. But she doesn't look like most women does she? Ordinary women who use juicers.'

'Models use juicers too,' I protested, half-heartedly.

'I'm not saying they don't. I'm just saying that it's not a fair representation of women in our society, is it? You can bet your burning bra it wasn't a woman who thought of that ad.'

My mother considered herself fortunate to have borne three daughters, although all three of us were severely lacking in the feminist-icon department. My older sister Vicky, aged thirty-five, was unfortunate enough to be not only married, but also pregnant with her first child. Vicky's long-term goal was to be an at-home mother with absolutely no desire to ever work again. This was incomprehensible to my mother. 'What sort of example is that for your daughter?' my mother would often ask her. The fact that Vicky didn't yet know the sex of her unborn child, and that it could potentially be a boy, did not even register on my mother's radar.

Although not quite as bad as working in advertising, my younger sister Susie, aged thirty, was a beauty therapist.

'You're not exactly helping the plight of women by making them beautiful are you?' said my mother. 'Couldn't you have become a lawyer? Or at least joined the army?' It's not that my mother was openly scathing about myself and my two sisters (apart from our choice of careers, that is), it's just that she was somewhat disappointed at not having given birth to Germaine Greer. And it's not that she wasn't proud of each of us, in her own slightly barmy way, it's just that we weren't exactly firm contenders for taking over the family business.

The happiest I'd ever seen my mother was when Susie confessed she was a lesbian. My mother was over the moon. She even cracked a bottle of champers in celebration, showering Susie with praise and congratulations. I think she was somewhat disappointed she wasn't a lesbian herself, and this was the next best thing. My poor father visibly drooped at the prospect of yet another female joining our family, until he met Susie's new friend Roz, that is. Roz was what my father called a Man's Woman. In other words, Roz was for all intents and purposes a man, but with breasts. I didn't exactly warm to her. There was something about a woman who knew more about the workings of a Ford Falcon engine than my father which made me nervous.

However, six months later, Susie had decided she wasn't a lesbian, it was just a phase she was going through. She was in fact a good old-fashioned heterosexual. When Susie broke the news, Mum had excused herself and gone for a long walk, tears framing her eyes. My father was also visibly disappointed by Roz's sudden departure from our lives, and at being left once again with the three of us, none of whom were remotely interested in donning a pair of overalls and putting their heads under his bonnet.

As a child I'd often imagined that I was adopted at birth.

I still do hold out some hope. *Surely my birth parents were fabulous celebrities or well-respected businesspeople, who spent their days flitting around the world from one incredibly stylish pad to the next?* I'd think to myself. The only holes in this theory were the fact that my sisters and I bore more than a striking resemblance to each other, and that Mum had three photographs of tiny babies covered in revolting matter lying on her very flabby stomach in a hospital bed. Aside from that I was convinced.

I sent a reply to my mother's email:

What were the girl's parents doing while they were running around the field killing themselves?

Half an hour later I got another one back:

Their mothers were probably working at their two-dollar-fifty-an-hour machinist night-jobs, before going home to make breakfast for their ten children. Their fathers would have either been killed by the Red Rebels, or abandoned the family years ago.

Did she have to be such a pessimist and humanitarian know-it-all? She should take an overseas posting with Amnesty International and leave us all in peace.

2

My life had continued its downward spiral when I was invited to a baby shower, a couple of weeks after my date with Jasmine. Laura, who used to work at the firm, was eight months pregnant with her first offspring. She used to be called Legless Laura, on account of the fact she could always be relied upon to drink until she fell off whatever it was she happened to be sitting on. At which point she, or someone else, would invariably pick her body up from the floor, place it back onto its perch, and it would immediately carry on drinking. She was rarely seen without a glass of champers in one hand and a lethally swinging cigarette in the other. I had absolutely no idea what to buy a baby so I bought Laura a very expensive bottle of champagne instead. No doubt she'd be feeling like a drink when the whole hideous birthing part was over and done with.

I was the last to arrive and upon entering Laura's living room it was glaringly obvious I was the only person out of the ten women present who either hadn't given birth or was going to be doing so in the very near future. And who wasn't sporting either an engagement ring or wedding band. The sunlight reflecting off the enormous diamonds on fingers rendered me temporarily blind.

'Oh . . . thanks, Sam,' said Laura, unwrapping the champers and giving me an odd searching look. She wasn't nearly as excited by my present as she should have been.

Lord how times had changed, I thought to myself. Barely a year ago she would have torn the cork out with her teeth and polished off the bottle in a nanosecond, chilled or not, before declaring it by far the best gift she'd ever received.

'Coffee, Sam?' asked Laura.

Coffee? What about a good old-fashioned glass of wine? Wasn't this supposed to be some sort of celebration we were having here?

'Lovely,' I replied. 'Thanks.'

I sat down in the only vacant seat, in the middle of a sofa, sandwiched between two lactating women.

'Hi Sam,' someone called out.

I looked at the culprit, a rather plump woman with short brown hair sitting on the sofa opposite. The voice sounded familiar but I had absolutely no idea who she was.

'Hi,' I replied, stalling for time. 'How are you?'

'Oh you know,' she replied. 'Busy busy.'

No clues there. Who was she?

'How about you?' she asked.

'Oh good. Still working away, you know.'

'You remember Louise, don't you Sam?' said Laura, handing me a cup of coffee.

Surely not? It couldn't be? Louise? Laura's best friend? Louise who was known for her agility and skill at bar-top dancing? Louise who coined the phrase 'cheap bubbles leads to trouble'?

'Of course,' I lied.

But Louise was skinny as a rake with long blonde hair. And stunning. What in God's name had happened to her?

'Lou's little girl's almost one now,' said Laura.

Oh. There we go then.

I had seen Baby Makeovers before. But this was by far the most extreme case I had ever witnessed. From gorgeous, blonde, champagne-swilling girl-about-town to short-haired, plump nappy-hugger in less than two years. *Unbelievable!*

'So, what do you do Sam?' asked Eve, Mother-of-Two, sitting on my right.

'I work in advertising,' I replied. 'Account manager.'

'Oh . . . a career woman,' she said, raising her eyebrows in a manner that suggested being a career woman was akin to having genital scabies. 'Must work long hours?'

'Yes.'

'Married?'

'Pardon?'

'Are you married?'

What kind of question was that?

'No,' I replied, flicking her the Death Stare.

If she sticks her beak out any further, I thought to myself, *I'll lose an eye.*

'Oh,' replied Eve, as though she had just taken a large swig of vinegar instead of coffee.

'Sam's a lucky single girl,' piped up Laura, adding for enthusiasm, 'God how I miss it!'

This comment solicited several *Well yes, of course, but see how complete our lives are now!* smug grins from the others.

Before Eve had a chance to further interrogate me, the talk somehow turned to nappies. I had absolutely no idea how.

'Yes, but disposables are so much easier, aren't they?' said Ursula, Mother-of-One.

'Gosh yes!' agreed everyone else. 'How people coped with all that washing I'll never know.'

'I use cloth nappies,' admitted Jenny, Mother-of-Two.

'What, all the time?'

'Well . . . during the day.'

'God, I don't know how you do it!' chorused the others.

'Bit of a problem lately though, because Tom's poo's all runny. It's really rather yellow too.'

'Have you taken him to the doctor?' asked Rosie, Mother-of-Three.

'Yes. Thinks he might have some sort of stomach bug. Doesn't seem to be worrying him though.'

'Could be dairy,' suggested Rachel, Mother-of-One.

'Sophie had that problem too,' said Louise. 'Turned out she was reacting to the cow's milk I was giving her. Had to put her back on formula.'

'Well our Jack's going through a phase at the moment,' said Natalie, Mother-of-Two. 'Just loves sticking his hand inside the nappy when he's done!'

Oh dear God! Think happy thoughts, I willed myself. *Champers, shopping, Thai takeaways.*

'Before you know it his hands are covered. He's just so quick too.'

'God, how does he manage it?' asked Jodi, Mother-of-One.

'Buggered if I know!'

Ten minutes later and with the conversation still firmly on nappies and poo, I evacuated myself to the bathroom and took my phone with me. It was a SMS emergency.

Stuk n bb hell! Need evac! Ring asp. Prtnd seppy client. x

I found Mands' number and hit send.

I sat back down on the sofa. They were still talking about Jack's uncanny ability to stick his hands inside his own nappy.

Three minutes later my mobile rang and I excused myself from the room to a distance where I could safely be heard to say things like 'Tell me you're joking! and 'When do they

29

want it by?' and 'This afternoon? Bloody clients!' and 'OK. I'll see you there in twenty minutes.'

I collected my handbag and promptly made my excuses.

'On a Sunday?' said Laura. 'God Sam, that's not fair!'

'No,' I agreed, rolling my eyes for emphasis. 'Story of my life!'

'You're going to work yourself to death if you're not careful,' she cautioned.

She was wrong. The only thing that was going to kill me at this point in my life was sitting in her living room listening to ten women talk about nothing but nappies and poo. I flew out the front door and went straight round to Mands' apartment where she and Lizzie were waiting with a chilled bottle of champers.

The following morning I was still unable to get the picture of Tom's runny poo out of my head. It appeared to be stuck there. I arrived at the office, unfolded the newspaper and set about digesting what useless information the country's media had to offer. It was my routine to sit at my desk and read the newspaper upon arriving at the office every morning while simultaneously ingesting my first trim latte of the day, which I bought from the café on the corner. All I had to do was walk through the door and it was in my hands within nanoseconds. I didn't even have to speak. The front page consisted of the usual parliamentary infighting, seabed claims, and more photos of genetically engineered cows, with the headline 'Her Twin Sister is Her Mother'. This story only made me happier than ever that I did not eat red meat.

I threw the sports pages directly into my rubbish bin. The only thing sport was good for, I'd decided long ago, was the ability to get a restaurant booking at short notice while the rest of the country stayed at home and watched a football match on television. I flicked straight to the business section, as I did every morning, only to find a picture of Lizzie's ex-husband, Bryce the Bastard, staring back at me from page two. I quickly scanned the accompanying story. Apparently Bryce was about to start up another e-media company. *And make many more millions doing it no doubt,* I thought. It had been a tough couple of years, said Bryce, especially with the price of divorce and all that he had subsequently endured. 'But it was better to settle and keep the peace,' he said, 'rather than drag names through the dirt. Even if one was undoubtedly being taken for a ride in the fun park.'

What a complete and utter arsehole!

I had always hated Bryce and his analogies. He could never just say something without comparing it to something else that was completely and utterly irrelevant.

Oh dear, I thought. Lizzie was not going to be happy with this.

Lizzie was a hotshot young lawyer, working for one of the largest firms in the country. She was what my father called a *real sweetie* and a *real beauty* and she cut an imposing and alluring figure in her Keith Matheson suit, strutting off to the courtroom. Her parents were both artists. Her mother was a writer and her father a painter. Neither of them could quite fathom how their eldest child could have been born without an artistic bone in her body. In her younger years they had taken Lizzie to see numerous artistic chanellers, in the hope they could coax some sort of child-like sketch or poem out of her. But she just wasn't interested. All she wanted to do was watch *Dynasty* and *LA Law* and look at the lovely suits. Apparently telling them she wanted to become a lawyer had been like telling them she wanted to become a crack dealer.

She often said it was the sight of her parents still in their dressing gowns when she got home from school, busy painting and writing about the house, which turned her against the arts. It may have also been the fact she and her younger sister, Sara, often went without dinner because their parents hadn't actually noticed they were home, or that it was indeed dinnertime. Subsequently Lizzie's house had been a fantastic place for Mands and I to stay over on the weekends. We could safely walk out the front door and casually remark to her mother 'just off to a club in town' and she wouldn't bat an eyelid, even though we were fourteen. She would just look up from her typewriter, cigarette in hand, and smile wistfully at us.

Five years ago Lizzie had made the mistake of marrying Bryce (or Bryce the Bastard as he is now affectionally known), fifteen years her senior and twice divorced, after representing him in allegations of fraud (she got him off and they promptly started shagging). She had also made the mistake of assuming that having an affair with a very-married Bryce was somehow 'different' and that he would never do the same thing to her, primarily due to the fact she was significantly younger. If anything, claimed Lizzie, she would be the one off strutting her stuff while he was busy eating his hot roast dinner through a straw. Lizzie was a smart woman — as one of her two best friends I was the first to acknowledge this — but her sandpit logic in this matter had astounded me. She had forgotten this very simple rule: one could never hope to tame the penis of a rich middle-aged man. Especially when that penis was busy being dragged this way and that by every young hopeful striving to be the next Mrs Bryce Henrickson.

They had tried unsuccessfully for two years to have a baby, with the fact Bryce had previously fathered two love-children (both outside of his marriages) only fuelling Lizzie's desire and unwillingness to accept that her eggs would remain unblemished. It was only Bryce's affair with a South African model-cum-pole dancer that put a halt to Lizzie's first session of IVF treatment before it had even begun.

To rub red-wine vinegar into the wound, Bryce happened to be one of the country's wealthiest businessmen, coupled with being one of the country's biggest tightarses. The 'price of divorce' Bryce referred to had been extraordinarily low, all things considered, and I still harboured deep remorse that Lizzie had not adhered to Mands' and my advice and 'hung his balls out to dry'. Unfortunately, she was too nice for that sort of caper and had no desire to soil her professional reputation. Unfortunately, that reputation was now taking a public beating at the hands of Bryce.

I finished reading the business section and prepped for my first meeting of the day, which was with the general manager of Yummy Mummy, the country's largest cereal maker, and his PR advisor. I was in the awkward position of having to sound enthusiastic about cereal, when in fact I very rarely ate it, or breakfast in any shape or form. Much to my father's disgust I was more of a coffee-on-the-run kind of girl. The fact we were meeting to discuss a media and advertising strategy to deal with the series of small metal chips found in Yummy Mummy's cereal packets made me even less enthusiastic about cereal. As did the fact that a small child had recently undergone surgery to have one of the small metal chips removed from their oesophagus.

The sound of Debbie Harry's 'I Want That Man' interrupted us in the middle of the meeting, which seemed to cause a rather awkward silence. Especially when one was talking cereal with a fifty-year-old, balding, hideous-tie-wearing man, and his virtual clone of a public-relations advisor. It was my mobile.

Must remember to turn the bloody thing off, I thought to myself. *And change that ring.*

'Sorry,' I apologised, as I answered the call.

'Can you believe what the bastard said?'

It was Lizzie.

'I'd like to shove his sterile testicles up his own arse!'

'Aha.'

'And then I'd make him eat them!'

'Aha.'

'He's a lying piece of crap!'

'Aha.'

'Are you in a meeting?'

'Yes.'

'I hope he gets a terminal disease. A sexually transmitted one!'

'Aha.'

'And that it makes his dick drop off.'

'Aha.'

'Ring me when you've finished.'

'OK. Bye.'

As soon as the meeting was over and we had successfully turned small metal chips into 'an inevitable bi-product of the deregulation of health and safety standards on locally made machinery' and Yummy Mummy's predicament into 'Thank God Yummy Mummy carries out its own safety-standard tests and does not rely on our inefficient industry tests, and managed to avert this potential tragedy', I rang Lizzie back. Of course, Yummy Mummy would be paying for the small girl's surgery, hospital and rehabilitation costs, as well as providing her and her family with a year's supply of cereal.

I prepared myself for another onslaught of obscenities.

'Lizzie. Hi sweets.'

'He's a walking slice of syphilis.'

'Yes, he is,' I agreed. 'And an utter arsehole too.'

'Arsehole's too nice. He's not nice! He's a dirty shit-eating arse-licking pig of a man.'

'Feel better?' I ventured.

'No. I'd like to kill him. Very slowly. Hair by grey hair.'

'What are you doing tonight?' I asked, attempting to change the subject.

'I'm in bloody Wellington. Bloody meetings.'

'What about tomorrow night?' I asked.

'Have to stay down here and go to dinner with clients,' replied Lizzie.

'On a Friday night?'

'Unfortunately, yes.'

'Can you cancel it? There's a good party on which will make you feel better.'

'No. I can't. Bugger it.'

'Well, Mands and I will pick you up from the airport on Saturday morning and we'll go shopping. All day.'

Shopping always made Lizzie feel better. In fact, I had yet to meet a woman whom it didn't make feel better.

'OK then,' she sighed.

'Take care, dolls. Get yourself sloshed tonight, and I'll see you on Saturday.'

'I'd love to shove a hot poker up his arse,' she muttered.

'I know.'

Poor Lizzie, thirty-three and one marriage down to a bastard like Bryce. At least the vows could have been wasted with someone who was actually good in bed. Life could be genuinely unfair at times.

I decided to pay my parents a quick visit on the way home from work. My mother came out to say a brief hello and then retreated back into her office to finish the newsletter. The newsletter was a weekly piece of male-bashing propaganda which my mother felt it was her duty to write and send out, being president and all.

'Why don't you stay for dinner, Sam?' she said. 'Your father's cooking.'

'Am I?' said Dad, with a stricken look that suggested he had foolishly thought he was allowed the night off. No such luck. 'Hell,' he exclaimed, running back into the kitchen.

'Hell!' he said again, closing the freezer door and slapping his forehead. 'There's only two packets of mince in the freezer!'

The complete juxtaposition between my father's life and my own did not escape me.

'So?'

'So, they're frozen!'

'Well, can't you just throw them in the microwave or something?' I suggested.

I had no idea how to defrost red meat, seeing as I didn't eat it, but I guessed a microwave would be a good starting point. I hadn't eaten red meat for the past five years. It wasn't that I was against killing animals, I was simply against polluting my body with substances that took far too long to digest. I was also very receptive to bad press.

'But it's just not the same,' he despaired. 'I knew I should have gone to the supermarket today. Bugger it all!'

My father was clearly upset. Tuesday was his weekly supermarket-shopping day and for some unknown reason he had missed it.

'Why don't we pop to the supermarket now then?' I suggested. 'We can take my car.'

'Of course we can't. Have you seen the time? It'll be chokka!'

My father was averse to frequenting the supermarket during the after-work rush. He felt much more comfortable going during the day, with the other housewives.

'How about I go and pick us up some takeaways then?' I suggested.

He looked at me as though I had just stripped down to my underwear and launched into a rendition of 'God Save the Queen'.

It was my father's view that eating takeaways was cheating. They were only allowed on birthdays and in extremely dire circumstances, such as funerals.

'No,' he said, putting his navy apron on. 'Just give me a minute.'

I poured us both a wine and he set about defrosting the mince in the microwave, boiling spaghetti and expertly whipping up a Bolognese, and a vegetarian version for me. I offered to help, but the offer was politely rejected.

'You just sit down and relax there, love. You must have had a hard day at the office.'

The truth was my father simply didn't trust me to help out in the kitchen. Which suited me just fine.

My mother made an appearance for dinner, and then withdrew straight back into her office again. Apparently she was having a little trouble with the newsletter.

I loaded the dishwasher as Dad wiped the kitchen table.

'Have you tried this stuff, love?' he asked me, holding up a bottle of cleaning spray. 'It's brilliant. Good for the environment too.'

'No,' I replied. 'I haven't.'

In fact I'd never seen it before in my life. My relationship with cleaning products being based entirely on me handing money over to my housekeeper MayBelle to purchase them. My mother had forbidden my father from using any cleaning products that weren't biodegradable. He liked to compare cleaning products with anyone who would listen to him long enough without keeling over and dying from boredom. I generally had absolutely no idea what he was talking about. Cleaning was something I happily paid someone else to do. I had offered to pay for my parents to have a cleaner come in once a week, but my father was vehemently opposed to the idea. I think he was afraid this would make him obsolete. Plus, the chances of him trusting anyone else to polish the furniture to the same streak-free standards was out of the question.

'Don't know what we did before this stuff was invented,' he said, shaking his head and marvelling at the spray bottle in his hand. 'Refillable too.'

'Brilliant,' I replied. Someone had to humour him.

Through no fault of his own, my father had vicariously been forced into the clutches of feminism and the role of a dutiful housewife. Many times I had seen him walk into the kitchen in his boxer shorts and T-shirt with *I am Woman, Hear me Roar* emblazoned in pink lettering across the front. *He'd be shaving his legs and going for a bikini wax next*, I'd think to myself.

But he wasn't the only Manwife around. Over the years he had befriended a selection of other Manwives, who were also married to women's rights activists and who also spent their days running the household and making banners that read *Raising Children is a Job Too!* And *Breastfeeding for the Public Good!* in their garages. It was some comfort for him to know he wasn't alone. Three years ago he and his girlfriends had formed a group called Men 4 Women. Their motto was *Men Are Feminists Too*. And this is the motto that was proudly displayed on their T-shirts, caps and bumper stickers. There was no denying the fact they were a minority group. Under pressure from my father I had attempted to secure them sponsorship from FreeAsTheWind, the feminine hygiene manufacturer and also one of my clients. Surprisingly FreeAsTheWind had offered to sponsor the printing of all their advertising material. That was until my mother declared that under no circumstances were they to take sponsorship from an organisation that 'blatantly poses women as sex symbols who like nothing better than frolicking around on sandy beaches in their skimpy bloody bikinis with their over-sized surfboards'.

My father and his girlfriends were understandably disappointed, but they couldn't argue with the boss.

'How do you cope, Dad?' I asked him once.

'With what love?'

'You know . . . being married to a sexist.'

'Your mother's not a sexist.'

'Yes she is! She thinks men are the scum of the earth!'

'No she doesn't, love,' he replied. 'She's just passionate about women and their plight.'

My father simply didn't realise my mother's passion against female oppression was also passionately oppressing himself.

The following night was the much-anticipated opening of Salute, a new bar owned by Samuel Evans and Darcy Simpson, partners in business and pleasure who owned over half of the city's drinking establishments, the good ones anyway. They were legends in the hospitality world and everything they opened turned to gold. Their bars were the epitome of style and sophistication, each one surpassing the one before, and one always felt comfortable in the knowledge that only the stylish were permitted through the front doors. There was no derogatory battling with riffraff for drinks, service or seats. This, combined with the various strands of eye candy who were employed to work the bar, made the whole experience an undeniable pleasure.

I decided to wear my new Franka Kuijlichrachova (only her regular customers, myself included, knew how to pronounce her surname) dress that I had bought the previous weekend. It was red silk with a dangerously low neckline and gorgeous pink and emerald green beads sewn in a flower down the front. It was what Mands, Lizzie and I called a KTF6 dress. A Knock Them For Six. And it went perfectly with my hot pink Patrick Cox heels. I would loved to have bought the open-toed version, but this simply wasn't an option for me, being that the second toe on each of my feet was a good half an inch longer than the big one. In fact, they looked more like fingers than toes. Over the years I had been told this was a sign of everything from intelligence, to wealth, to being extremely good in the sack. I think people were just being kind. What it was really a sign of was ugly toes that for the love of God should not be squashed up in a pair of open-toed heels and put on public display.

I'd met Dan at the national advertising awards a few weeks earlier (where I had won no fewer than two awards). He had phoned me earlier in the week and asked me out for dinner tonight. The advertising awards had clocked an extremely high Knicker Count this year (ie knickers left abandoned in various locations around the venue). Apparently it was several pairs up on last year. However none of them were mine. There was no one there who made me want to sever ties with my underwear, Dan included. Plus, I wasn't wearing any.

I was not in the habit of going out for dinner with any male until I had spent at least a couple of hours with him in a social context, and could be sure that dining with him in solitude for two to three hours would not bore me to tears. This was a rule which had served me well, and one I was not about to break for anyone. Instead I suggested Dan come with me to the bar opening — at least there would be plenty of other people I knew there, should he prove to be a chore. Plus, I thought to myself, being thrown into tonight's environment would be a good test of his character. I agreed to let him pick me up from my apartment and drive us to the bar.

He was a lot better-looking than I remembered. Nice and tall with well-cut wavy dark brown hair, and tanned olive skin.

We arrived at Salute and the décor was unbelievably fabulous, as expected. The bar area was hidden behind plush red velvet drapes, and gold gilded mirrors covered the chocolate brown walls. A row of beautiful chandeliers adorned the ornate ceiling. It was truly gorgeous. I glanced admiringly across the beautiful mahogany bar top, only to reel back in sheer horror. There, on the opposite side of the room, was a woman with long blonde hair, standing in animated conversation with a glass of champagne. Wearing none other than My Dress!

I promptly leaped behind the large free-standing ice bucket before she, or anyone else with twenty-twenty fashion vision, could spot me.

Dear God! I thought in horror. *This was a disaster! What was I going to do?* Unfortunately, due to the fact it was the middle of summer, I hadn't brought a jacket with me. I would simply have to throw myself into a cab, rush home and get changed, I decided. That was all there was to it.

Dan approached me as I cowered behind the ice bucket.

'What are you doing behind there?' he asked, a quizzical look on his face.

'Hiding,' I replied.

'From what?'

'There's a woman standing on the other side of the room with *my dress* on,' I replied.

'So, that's a good thing right? She's got good taste too.'

Oh God! What a plonker! Had he no idea?

'No. That is a *very, very bad thing*,' I replied, explaining it to him like the confused child he obviously was. 'The worse thing that could possibly happen.'

'Right,' said Dan, although I could tell from his face he didn't agree with me.

'Well, what are you going to do? Hide behind the ice bucket all night?'

'No,' I replied sternly, 'I am going to leave.'

'*Leave*?' He sounded shocked.

'Yes. Leave. Go home.'

'And get changed?'

'Yes.'

Unless, I thought, having a sudden brainwave, the shops in the city were still open. I looked at my watch. It was eight o'clock.

'What time do you think High Street closes?' I asked.

'Don't know,' replied Dan, clearly not appreciating the predicament I was in.

'Give me your jacket,' I demanded.

42

He stared at me like a dumb monkey.

'The jacket,' I repeated, holding out my hand.

He took it off and handed it over. I put it on, wrapping it firmly round my dress.

'I'll see you in half an hour,' I said, whizzing past him and bolting for the door, before the woman wearing My Dress had time to bat an eyelid.

Thirty-five minutes later I sailed back through the front doors wearing a gorgeous, fine-knit, sleeveless, very safe, plain-black Karen Millen cocktail frock to the knee, with French embroidered stitching. My taxi had made it to the shop as the assistant was closing the doors. She had looked up at me in my desperate state, as I said, 'There's someone wearing *my dress*,' and the next thing I knew she was firing me into a dressing room, a look of utter empathy plastered across her face, as the other assistant promptly gathered every black dress she could find on the racks and held them in front of my eyes, one by one, for just the right length of time. The service was impeccable. Ten minutes later I was standing in my new black dress, assistant number one was passing me my lipstick, assistant number two was calling me a taxi and my old dress was packaged neatly behind the counter, ready to be couriered to me on Monday. I had tipped heavily and walked out the door into the taxi, feeling profoundly grateful I lived in a metropolitan city.

I looked across the bar and quickly spotted Dan. He was standing on the other side of the room talking to the woman in My Dress.

The bastard! I bet he's told her all about my dilemma, I seethed.

I decided it was best to avoid him from hereon in. This wasn't going to be too much of a problem as I immediately spotted Mands standing beside the bar, talking to some gorgeous dark-haired specimen of a man.

'Dolls,' called Mands, embracing me in an air-hug, lest we bump and displace hair.

'Sweets,' I replied, kissing her on the cheek.

'Where have you been hiding?' she demanded.

'DC,' I replied, rolling my eyes for emphasis. That was short for Dress Catastrophe.

'Oh dear,' said Mands, giving me a real hug. 'I think we should go and talk this over,' she cooed, dragging me away by my arm. 'Scuse us,' she smiled at the dark-haired fox.

'Rundown,' she demanded, when we reached the other end of the bar.

I gave her the rundown and she showered me with just the right proportion of 'Oh nos!' and 'Ohmygods!' before praising me on my shop-dashing initiative.

'Hi,' said Dan, walking up behind me. 'Nice dress.'

'Thank you,' I replied. Unfortunately I hadn't seen him approaching.

'Just wondering if you've got my jacket?' he asked. 'I'm taking off now.'

Hell! The jacket! I must have left it at the shop!

'Um . . . yes . . .' I faltered. 'I brought it back with me and put it on the . . . ah . . . coat rack at the entrance.'

'Righto then,' he said, 'I'll grab it on the way out. See you later, Sam.'

'OK,' I replied, making absolutely no effort to convince him to stay. His response to the dress dilemma had clearly proved he wasn't my type.

Great! I thought. Now I was going to have to leave a perfectly good party and hide in the loos, all because I had lost Dan's jacket. When, if he was any sort of gentleman at all, he would have come outside, hailed a taxi for me, escorted me to the shop and would have kept his bloody jacket in his sights. I decided to drag Mands and a bottle of champers into the loos with me, for some company.

'What're we doing in here?' asked Mands. I explained the lost-jacket debacle and she understood perfectly.

'Best we give him twenty minutes then,' she said, topping up our glasses.

The rest of the night was spent getting sloshed on Moët and flirting with the dark-haired fox and his friend beside the bar. Mands ended up going home with the dark-haired fox after putting in very thorough groundwork all evening. His friend invited me back to his place for a nightcap, but between the time he asked me and the nanosecond before I replied, I had miraculously sobered up and seen the light.

'No thanks,' I replied, and headed home alone. He wasn't that foxy after all.

Needless to say, I didn't hear a peep from Dan all that week. Or ever again for that matter. I did however get his jacket couriered to my office on Monday from the shop, along with my beaded dress. I took great delight in dropping his jacket off at the City Mission clothing bin later that week, along with some of last season's skirts. No doubt some old homeless man would take pride in wearing an Armani suit jacket over their homespun jersey. It served him right for his utter lack of support in a time of female crisis.

The next morning Mands and I picked Lizzie up from the airport in Mands' shiny black Saab convertible. We were taking her straight out for a serious bout of spirit-lifting shopping. It was a gorgeous blue-sky day and the roof was down. The only hitch was that we had Louie on the backseat. Louie was Lizzie's dog. The dog she had brought home straight after her divorce from Bryce was finalised. She called him her substitute husband and 'the only male I would ever love or trust again.' Louie was a schnauzer.

As though in fear of the solitary male role he played in Lizzie's life, Louie was prone to suffering from great bouts of depression. He was now on Prozac. He had been for the past year.

'Cheer up Louie, for God's sake,' I called out. 'We're in the car. You're supposed to like this sort of thing. Why don't you hang your head out the side or something?'

But it was useless. The only thing Louie really enjoyed was watching television. Sport in particular. Car racing, namely any Grand Prix, was his favourite. He'd eagerly sit directly in front of the screen, barking joyously at the cars as they whizzed around the track. The irony of having a dog who was addicted to watching sport on television had not escaped Lizzie. But at least, as she said, he didn't sit on the couch and drink beer (not yet anyway). When he was around one year old, Louie had developed some strange habits. Firstly he began to ignore Lizzie. Not only would he refuse to follow any of her commands, but he would also turn and stare at her blankly, without averting his gaze, as though he was looking straight through her. After a month of being disobeyed and stared at, Lizzie had taken Louie to visit the pet psychiatrist. The psychiatrist had come to the conclusion that Louie was pining for male company. This was understandably devastating for Lizzie. She had bought Louie as a substitute husband and he was already discontented with her company. The whole drama had put Lizzie on Prozac for six months as well.

Mands and I had suggested to Lizzie that perhaps she should give Louie away, to a man, and get herself a nice female schnauzer. But she wouldn't have a bar of it. 'I'm not being fucked about by him!' she'd declare. 'Not again!'

Obviously she wasn't just referring to Louie. The thing was, Mands and I found Louie depressing to be around. He was like a furry sponge, soaking up all the happiness around him. A canine kill-joy. Mands and I often suggested to each other that one of us should 'do a Helen on him'. (Helen was the best friend of Lizzie's sister Sara and had managed to kill her stepmother's prized pet poodle while she was dog-sitting it, accidentally of course. I think it had been run over or something.) I really wished someone would run over Louie.

We pulled into the drop-off zone just as Lizzie walked out of the terminal. It was a seamless collection.

'So,' I said, as she climbed into the backseat and gave Louie a kiss, without even a wag of his sorry tail in return. 'First we're going for brunch at Mink. Then we're going to High Street. And then we're going to Ponsonby Road. And then we're going for a late lunch and bubbles at Prego.'

'OK,' said Lizzie. 'Sounds good.' She sounded about as excited as a boarding call.

'Cheer up, Lizzie,' enthused Mands. 'Bryce is a bastard.'

'Yes he is!' I agreed.

But Lizzie remained mute on the subject. Clearly she was going to require some serious pampering for the torrent of foul-mouthed abuse to begin flowing again.

We walked into an overflowing Mink and a prime table was miraculously cleared and set on our approach. It helped that Mands had used the resident chefs here for various events she had organised, so the service was impeccable every time. It was as though the staff could sense her approach before they actually saw her. Very *Sixth Sense*. We strolled past the various groups waiting for a table and sat down.

'Bugger waiting for bubbles,' said Mands. 'Let's have some now.'

'Roger that,' I replied. My head was slightly foggy after last night and could do with a bit of reviving. Plus, it was the weekend after all.

'Sure,' said Lizzie, although she still looked like the fat kid who wasn't picked for the netball team.

I decided to tell her about my dress catastrophe to cheer her up. It worked and she even managed to crack one of her beautiful smiles. After a gorgeous brunch and a bottle of champers we decided to hit the designer shops. First stop was Karen Walker.

'Absolutely gorgeous!' I declared, spotting a pale pink silk shirt with sequined panelling and holding it up against Lizzie. Any shade of pink was gorgeous on her English-rose complexion, lucky sod. With my slightly olive complexion (aided by the odd sunbed and spray tan) and green eyes it made me look like an anemic who had recently succumbed to an horrendous vomiting virus. We might have been the same five-foot-seven height and size-ten build, with the same straight shoulder-length hair and soft layers framing our faces, but that is where the similarities ended. Where Lizzie's hair was a dark chocolate colour, mine was (with the aid of highlights) a much lighter shade of brown.

We left the shop with three full bags. Each. Lizzie was finally beginning to smile more regularly. We then hit World and Trelise Cooper, to much the same effect. Mands and I made it our prerogative to lock Lizzie in the changing rooms and enlist the assistance of the salesgirls to make her try on fabulous item after fabulous item. She subsequently spent far more money than she intended to. It's just a pity it was no longer Bryce's credit card she was damaging.

Next stop were the home-design stores along Ponsonby Road.

'I cannot believe what an utter wanker he is!' exclaimed

Lizzie, suddenly coming to life. It must have been the post-shopping endorphins kicking in.

'Scum of the earth,' I agreed, as Mands backed out of the car park.

But I didn't quite catch Lizzie's next turn of phrase, as I was suddenly jolted forward in my seat to the catchy tune of scraping metal.

'Jesus Christ!' hollered Mands.

I turned and looked at the culprit. All that was visible was the arse-end of an enormous and incredibly ugly vehicle.

'Are you OK?' I asked Lizzie, who was sitting in the back seat, luckily with her seatbelt on.

'Think so. What the hell *is* that?' she asked.

'A people mover,' I replied. 'I think.'

'Looks like some sort of freaky bloody spaceship.'

'OK?' I asked Mands, who was staring straight ahead, a nasty look engulfing her face.

'Fine,' she replied, opening her door and getting out of the car.

Uh-oh, I thought, deciding it was best to stay put. I had seen that look before.

I peered into the rearview mirror and saw Mands walk to the back of the car, lift her sunglasses, and assess the damage.

'Oh. My. God!' she hissed.

Lizzie, who had bravely hopped out of the car, reported back that there was a crushed bumper and one smashed taillight. I turned around in my seat to get a better view.

A very badly dressed woman stood beside Mands, looking at the back of her hideous vehicle. The sound of several screeching small things emerged from inside.

'Oh dear,' she said, clearly not as upset as she should have been.

'My car's completely screwed!' declared Mands. 'I trust you're insured?' she asked, turning to the woman.

'Yes,' replied the housewife. 'Are you?'

'Of course I am,' said Mands. 'Although I don't know what that has to do with anything?'

Lizzie had wisely decided to get back into the car too. It wasn't going to be pretty. And with the roof down we could hear the conversation perfectly. Plus, the screeching from inside the kiddie coach was getting progressively louder.

'Well, we both sort of backed into each other, didn't we?' said the woman.

'Listen sweetheart,' said Mands, as though the woman obviously needed the situation explained to her. 'I know it's all a little bit confusing, but I think you'll find that *you* backed into *me*.'

Mands is an event manager. She is the most driven person I knew and has an inherent gift for ordering people around and forcing them to make decisions, but in a way that looked as though they'd made the decision themselves. She is a tiny blonde bombshell. Or firecracker if you prefer.

Mands' father had kept all of her school reports (written proof of her driven nature), if only to sell to a magazine one day he claimed. On her twenty-first birthday he had given her, and everyone else at the party, copies of what he considered the two most outstanding ones. They are as follows.

School Report (aged 6)
Green Meadows Primary School

Amanda has frequently shown what I can only term intelligence throughout the year (I am reluctant to admit a six-year-old is capable of deception). There was the toilet incident where she stuck a 'do not use, out of order' sign onto one of the girls' toilet doors, for three weeks straight. Upon questioning I was led to believe her motive was to 'save the toilet for herself to use and no one else'. Apparently she did not want to catch any type of 'germ' from the other children.

Then there was the incident of selling kisses on the lips to the boys at lunchtime. Amanda was not the one giving the kisses — she had convinced a classmate (Sally Ricketts) to sell the kisses to the boys, taking a ninety per cent share of the profits for herself. Once again, I will refuse to believe a six-year-old is capable of acting as a 'pimp'. Although Sally Rickett's parents believe otherwise.

Joanne Halstrop

(Amanda's Teacher)

School Report (aged 16)
St Catherine's College for Girls

In addition to her straight 'A' report card the principal had written:

I must say that I have never in my thirty-five years of secondary school teaching met a student more willing or determined to succeed than Amanda, and at any cost. Nor have I ever met one who has demonstrated more raw ambition or caused more genuine chaos at our school. As you know, she was the driving force behind the Teacher Lock Out earlier this year, with myself and all members of staff being refused entry to the main building due to 'our inability to cater to the needs of modern society and provide a lunch bar for students'. Fortunately the new lunch bar is operating at a profit (similar to that indicated in Amanda's business proposal I am reluctant to admit).

Then there was the Skirt Incident, which you are no doubt aware of, as it was broadcast on national television for several weeks. It was somewhat disturbing for me to see the school's name dragged through Parliament on Amanda's petition — that it is the right of female students to decide what length to wear their school-uniform skirt. It was also disturbing when the Minister of Women's Affairs publicly supported Amanda's petition, announcing that our school, along with others, was blatantly disregarding basic female rights. It was furthermore detrimental to the school's reputation when we were ordered, via a live televised parliamentary vote, to let our students wear their skirts at any length of their choosing. An apparently ground-breaking decision in the history of education and one which, as I am sure you are aware, has received more than its fair share of media coverage.

Luckily this has not as yet affected our allocation of educational government funding for next year. There are several incidents which have occurred throughout the year, for which Amanda was no doubt the ringleader, but unfortunately there is only so much I am permitted to write in a school report.

There is no doubt in my mind that Amanda will one day be running this country. I can only hope I am either dead or living elsewhere by that time.

Yours sincerely
Patricia Blake
(Principal)

Mands was the only student at our school to have a covering letter from the principal added to her report. Apparently she didn't trust any of her teachers to do it justice. But Mrs Blake was very wrong when predicting Mands' future. Mands wasn't interested in running the country: it simply didn't pay enough.

I remembered how her teenage bedroom had always been clean and uncluttered, aside from the collection of inspirational posters covering the walls, that is. Posters with pearls of wisdom as *You are a Winner, The Ten Steps to Success* and *How to Achieve Power*. Her parents had deemed her 'completely insane' and frequently threatened to either set fire to her bedroom or ship her off to boarding school. (It was only their utter fear of her that stopped them from doing so.) Mands found it amusing that what could only be termed as ambition caused her parents such sleepless nights. I can only presume they wanted another demure well-behaved daughter (like her sister) who never caused them a fuss. Mands simply didn't fit the bill. It was interesting to note, as Mands pointed out to them as often as she could, that the one who never caused them a fuss was now an alcoholic life model.

My mother was so impressed with Mands' involvement in the Skirt Incident, I got the feeling she wanted to adopt her. She had high hopes of Mands becoming a feminist icon and running the country. Needless to say both Lizzie and I were eternally grateful we were friends with Mands at school. Being enemies with her would have been disastrous.

'But we both backed out of parks directly opposite each other,' protested the woman, snapping me back to the dilemma at hand. 'We just didn't see each other.'

'Except for the small fact that I had well and truly begun backing out of my park before you had started to leave yours,' corrected Mands.

This claim was not entirely true.

'Uh-oh' said Lizzie, who had turned around for another gawk. A nosy witness was on the approach. It was the worst kind of witness too, an old person.

'When is the government going to round them all up and build one massive retirement home somewhere in the South Island?' I wondered aloud.

'Looks like it was nobody's fault there,' said the old man.

'Pretty much backed straight into each other from what I saw.'

'Thank you for your input,' replied Mands, as politely as one can through gritted teeth. 'But we're actually managing to sort this out quite nicely by ourselves.'

'OK then love, but if you need a witness testimony that's all I'm offering.'

'No. *Thank you.*'

'Yes, I think that would be a good idea,' piped up the housewife.

'What's the name of your insurance company?' demanded Mands, choosing to ignore her. 'I'll be taking the matter up with them.'

'State,' she replied. 'And yours?'

'I really don't think that will be necessary. Although I had better take your phone number for further contact.'

'Don't you think you should both swap names and numbers?' said the nosy old codger. 'Although clearly it was no one's fault. How about I write down the details for both of you?'

'That *really* won't be necessary,' said Mands, retrieving her Palm Pilot from the car and taking the lady's details herself. She then quickly whipped out her mobile phone and took a series of evidential photographs of the back of both cars.

Old people clearly had too much time on their hands if they were willy-nilly getting involved in vehicle disputes, I thought to myself. *He should take up bowls or something.*

The screeching of small children trapped inside Ugly Vehicle was by this stage unbearable and Mands thankfully decided that the washerwoman was not going to admit liability, so it was best to cut her losses and take it up with her insurance company. She picked her tail-light up from the asphalt and threw it into the boot. I glanced back at Louie, who was surrounded by shopping bags and staring straight ahead into space, as though willing himself to be transported elsewhere.

'Great,' hissed Mands, sitting back in the driver's seat. 'Now I'm going to have to drive around town with a ruined car until the insurance company coughs up. How bloody humiliating!'

Lizzie and I declined to comment, for fear of also suffering her wrath. Instead we nodded our heads in sympathetic agreement.

'Prego then?' I suggested, eager to get Mands some bubbles asap.

'Sounds great,' prompted Lizzie, obviously in the same frame of mind.

'Fine,' said Mands, still sporting a rather nasty expression on her dial.

We managed to secure a table in the beautiful shaded courtyard, and champagne was immediately ordered. After two glasses Mands' facial expression softened, her shoulders dropped dramatically, and she no longer looked as though she was going to smack one of us in the face.

There was a beeping under the table. We all lunged under for our handbags but it was Mands who came up the winner.

'Mario again,' she said, sighing.

Who's Mario?' asked Lizzie.

'Mands' stalker,' I replied.

'You've got a *stalker?*' exclaimed Lizzie.

'Yes.'

'You lucky cow!'

'A twenty-three-year-old Brazilian male model,' I added. 'A Man-Child.'

'Get out!' said Lizzie. 'You cow!'

'I know,' I agreed. 'He's a complete fox too.'

'So, how did you manage that then?' asked Lizzie.

'He was in the Trelise show,' replied Mands.

Mands had organised the launch of Trelise Cooper's new autumn range two weeks ago.

'And?'

'And now he won't stop texting me and sending me flowers.'

'Have you shagged him?'

'No!' exclaimed Mands, clearly upset at this suggestion. 'You don't shag stalkers. It's against protocol.'

Until this very moment I had absolutely no idea there was a protocol for dealing with stalkers.

'Show her your text message,' I urged.

'Which one?'

'The one from this morning.'

'Oh God . . . all right then.'

Mands brought the message up on her screen and handed it to Lizzie, who read it out loud: 'Hey sexy lady! You, me and a bottle of Bolly makes three. What do you say? Will warm the spa in anticipation. Kiss, Mario.'

'Lord above!' exclaimed Lizzie. 'He's a smooth texter.'

'But he's still a stalker,' said Mands.

'How do you know?' asked Lizzie.

'Because he rings me approximately ten times a day and sends, on average, twenty text messages.'

'It's not bloody fair!' complained Lizzie, ten minutes later. 'I want one.'

'Same here!' I agreed.

'What are you foaming about?' said Mands, turning to me. 'You've got one too!'

'Have you?' asked Lizzie, looking at me suspiciously.

'Well . . . yes . . . but it's not the same . . . he's not a model.'

'Well at least you've bloody well got one!' she said, clearly very put out that she didn't have her own stalker.

'He goes to her gym,' added Mands.

'And he's a podgy fifty-year-old who wears bike shorts,' I explained.

'That's not what you told me,' said Mands.

I gave her a sharp kick under the table. She had clearly forgotten we were supposed to be cheering Lizzie up today.

'Ow!'

'Why can't I get one?' despaired Lizzie.

'Oh Christ! You don't want one!' I exclaimed. 'They're a bloody hassle'.

'Touché,' agreed Mands. 'Clogging up your SIM card and inbox. So many fresh flowers you suddenly develop hayfever.'

'Sounds terrible,' said Lizzie, although she didn't look convinced.

At that very moment Mands' phone rang. It was Mario again.

'Go on. Answer it,' urged Lizzie.

'No,' replied Mands.

'Pleeease,' said Lizzie.

'No.'

'Oh go on! Or I will.'

'Oh Jesus . . . OK then. Hello? Hi Mario. How are you? I'm fine thanks. Yes, I got the flowers. They're beautiful, thank you. Tonight? Oh I can't I'm afraid, I have plans with my girlfriends. Tomorrow? Ditto, out as well. Monday? You guessed it. Tuesday? Same story. Wednesday? Perhaps. OK then, you too. Ciao.'

'So?' I asked.

'So . . . he was asking me out.'

'Yes. I gathered that. Are you going to go?'

'No.'

'Why not?' asked Lizzie.

'Because you should never date stalkers.'

'Why not?'

'Because they're stalkers, Lizzie! It's against the rules.'

'Oh. Why didn't you just tell him you're not interested?'

'Because,' I explained, 'she likes having a stalker. It's good for morale.'

'Oh.'

'Isn't that right?' I said to Mands.

'Bingo.'

But even stalkers reach a point where they just can't be arsed anymore. Three weeks, 180 text messages, seventy phone calls, and fifteen bunches of flowers later, Mario realised it was time to move on and find himself a new object of desire. Mands was visibly disappointed at no longer being stalked, but was glad to finally stop sneezing.

3

The following Wednesday (with my life lulled back into a false sense of security) I met Mands and Lizzie at Prego for dinner, once again. They were both already sitting at our usual table, bubbles in hand and one waiting on the table for me.

'Rumour has it a certain someone got lucky the other night,' I said once we'd placed our orders.

'Wasn't me,' said Lizzie.

'I know it wasn't you. It was Mands.'

'Who was he?' asked Lizzie.

'David Tyler.'

'The developer?' asked Lizzie.

'Bingo,' replied Mands.

'I thought he was going out with that woman on the orange-juice ad,' I said.

'Not anymore.'

'So, what was it like?' asked Lizzie.

'Like . . . hugging a rug.'

'Eew! Hairy one?'

'Very,' replied Mands. 'Walking carpet.'

'Did you not know he was a gorilla?' I queried.

'Nope. Unfortunately I've only ever seen him in a shirt and tie.'

'That's the problem with shirts and ties,' said Lizzie. 'You never really know what's lurking underneath.'

'Until it's too late,' concluded Mands.

'Hairy hands?' I enquired.

'No, funnily enough. Dead giveaway, those are.'

'Could he not get it waxed?' asked Lizzie.

'Apparently not,' replied Mands.

'And could you not have done a runner?'

'Too late . . . by the time he got his shirt off.'

'Did you touch it?' asked Lizzie.

'Very briefly.'

'Oh thank God for that!'

'Until I got my ring stuck in it.'

'You got your ring stuck in his chest hair?' we cried.

'Yes . . . for about twenty minutes . . . didn't think I was going to get it back.'

'And did you?' asked Lizzie.

'Eventually . . . once I had cut his hair away with a pair of nail scissors.'

'And what was he doing?' I asked.

'When?'

'While your hand was stuck to his chest?'

'I think he was enjoying it actually.'

'Eew!' exclaimed Lizzie.

'I know. I just kept trying to think of smooth surfaces. Bench tops and the like. It was completely horrible!'

'Bet it was,' I said.

'Yuk,' said Lizzie again, screwing up her face. 'You're putting me off my dinner.'

'Sorry,' said Mands. 'It wasn't pleasant.'

'Trust you won't be going there again?' I asked.

'Not unless he's planning a wax attack.'

'Bryce the Bastard had serious chest hair,' said Lizzie.

'Not like this he didn't, dolls,' said Mands.

'How do you know?' asked Lizzie.

'Cause I've seen Bryce's chest on many an occasion, Lizzie. He was always taking his top off for no good bloody reason. Wasn't he, Sam?'

'Yes,' I replied. 'He was.'

'And anyway Bryce's wasn't that bad,' continued Mands. 'Not like David's. I'm surprised he manages to stand upright and not topple over forwards, it's so bloody thick.'

'OK,' said Lizzie, putting down her fork and pushing her plate away. 'Enough.'

'Agreed,' I replied. I was also swiftly being put off my dinner.

'I desperately need a bikini wax,' said Lizzie, attempting to change the subject, but not very successfully. 'Brazilian.'

'Same here,' I replied. 'It's a jungle down there.'

'Had one yesterday,' said Mands.

Mands had a strong aversion to body hair, both her own and anyone else's. She was continuously getting waxed, plucked and lasered. She seemed to thoroughly enjoy the pain.

'Why don't you come to Jewel with me?' suggested Lizzie to me. 'They're fabulous. Best bikini waxers in the country.'

This was quite a substantial claim.

'OK,' I replied. 'Sounds good.'

Oh how I wish, in sweet but useless retrospect, that I'd said something other than 'OK.' Something like 'I think I'll wait another week or so' or 'I think I'll stick to my usual salon, thanks anyway.' I usually went to Flossie, but Esther, my regular beautician, had recently developed the unsavoury ability to drag a bikini wax out until I was sure she had actually stripped me of my womanhood and was going to hand it to me in a small brown envelope on my way out the door, saying something like, 'Here's your clitoris Sam. Terribly sorry about that.'

Oh Christ, I thought to myself, as Lizzie and I arrived at Jewel on Saturday morning, *I've got my period. How on earth could you have forgotten that?*

'Guess what?' I hissed at Lizzie as we sat in the waiting room flicking through old copies of *Vanity Fair*. 'I've got my period.'

'Hell!' she hissed back. 'Oh well, it shouldn't matter. Are you plugged?'.

'Course,' I replied. Obviously Lizzie and I had fallen out of menstrual sync. It happened occasionally.

'You'll be fine then. Don't worry about it.'

Ten minutes later we were called into our separate rooms. I stripped off my skirt and knickers and lay back on the table reading my magazine, as Celeste the technician plastered hot wax precariously close to my womanly core.

Think about the results, I told myself. *Forget about the pain.*

Please God, just let her be quick, I prayed. There was nothing in the world more horrific than a drawn-out bikini wax.

'Here we go,' said Celeste. 'We'll do the upper area now. Just relax, Samantha.'

Impossible. I braced myself for the impact.

'On the count of three,' said Celeste. 'One . . . two . . . and . . . three.'

Shit and bugger. Was there anything more painful in the world?

'There we go then,' she said, looking up at me and smiling. 'That's one side. Well done.'

Hallelujah to that, I thought, looking back at her with an agonised sneer only being bikini-waxed can perfect.

'Other side now,' she said. 'Here we go. One . . . two . . . and . . . three.'

Lord have mercy. It just didn't get any easier.

'That's the top all done,' she said cheerfully. 'We'll do the lower area now.'

'One . . . two . . . and . . . great, that's one side done. Now for the last little bit. Nearly there Samantha.'

I braced myself for the agonising finale.

'One . . . two . . . and . . .'

Two things happened on Celeste's final count of three. One was that the right side of my lower bikini line had all unwanted hair successfully removed. And the other was, unfortunately for all those concerned, that my hair wasn't the only thing to be removed.

'*Sweet Jesus!*' cried Celeste, as my airborne tampon flew past her right cheek and hit the wall behind her, before dropping to the floor.

'Ohmygod!' she gushed, turning as red as a beet. 'I am so . . . sorry!'

Generally in situations of incredible discomfort involving two people there is one person who is more embarrassed than the other. But in this case I think it was fair to say that Celeste and I were first equal.

'It's OK,' I muttered, as I lay spread-eagled on the table, turning far redder than ever before.

'I'll just . . . um . . . get it,' said Celeste, turning around.

'No! I've got it!' I burst out, lurching up from the table.

The last thing I wanted in this world was a complete stranger picking my used tampon up from the carpet. Especially as it had just sailed through the air in perilously close proximity to her face.

I jumped up, still half-naked, and retrieved my travelling tampon from the floor. By its string.

'Have you got any . . . ah . . . paper?' I asked.

'Aha,' said Celeste, still completely crimson.

She handed me a piece of paper and I promptly wrapped the tampon it in and placed it safely in my handbag.

'Are we . . . ah . . . done?' I asked, attempting to regain some form of composure and desperate to escape before she whipped out her tweezers.

'Yes we . . . are,' replied Celeste, unable to look me in the face. Who could blame her?

'Right . . . I'll be off then.'

'OK Samantha, I'll leave you to get dressed. Hopefully I'll see you again . . . sometime.'

This was definitely one of those things people say, regardless of whether they actually mean it or not. I was quite positive Celeste did not want to see either me or my bikini line ever again. The feeling was mutual.

I got dressed quicker than after waking up next to an ugly man after a huge night on the plonk, grabbed my handbag (complete with runaway tampon) and bolted out to the waiting room.

'You know what's going to happen now, don't you?' I said to Lizzie, as we drove home. 'I'm going to be the horror story that's told at beauty schools all around the country. The story that makes beauty technicians everywhere wonder if they shouldn't consider another career, and is it too late to get their course fees back? The story that gets passed down through bikini-waxing generations until nobody's really sure if it actually happened, or if it's just some sort of horrible urban myth.'

Lizzie slowed down and pulled the car to the side of the road. She was having trouble driving while laughing hysterically.

'I am *never* going back there,' I added. 'Ever. In fact I'm *never* having a bikini wax *ever* again. I'm going to go all Hairy Maclary from now on. I'll be an Amazonian woman.'

'Ksssss,' said Lizzie, as she banged her head on the steering wheel.

'And you're not to bloody tell anyone,' I ordered. 'Not even Mands.'

'Oh . . . come . . . on . . . tsss . . .' laughed Lizzie. 'Gotta . . . tsss . . . tell . . . Mands.'

'No,' I replied. 'En-Oh. And stop bloody laughing and start driving,' I ordered. 'I wanna go home.'

Later that week, after Mands had been filled in on the whole sorry saga by Lizzie and laughed hysterically until I was positive she was going to spontaneously combust, the three of us decided it was well and truly time for us to organise a fabulous and schmoozy dinner party. More commonly known as *the prime opportunity to network and openly pillage one's friends' contacts for the benefit of oneself.*

The girls came over to my apartment after work and we set about organising the crucial list of Who To Invite, while devouring several bottles of sauvignon blanc.

The venue, Mands' apartment, could comfortably seat twelve at the dining table, so the inevitable culling began. The three of us were the pinnacle hostesses for the evening and naturally had to be present. That left nine seats to strategically allocate.

I had vain hopes of one day being headhunted by top ad agency Miles & McKay. Therefore we had to invite one of the senior account managers, Sean, who was very conveniently an old university friend of Lizzie's. That left eight seats.

Lizzie was currently defending the managing director of a pharmaceutical company against allegations of misconduct by two of the board members. One of the board members who had raised the allegations was a great tennis friend of Mand's ex-boyfriend's sister Julie. Therefore we had to invite Julie along, and her husband Hamish. Although she was still seething over Bryce, Lizzie was also presently having a raging affair with a very married man named Simon, the head of his own public-relations company. She had been solidly shagging him for the past three months, so naturally he was invited. It seemed Lizzie just couldn't get enough of married men. For some strange reason she also wanted to invite Simon's wife, Lisa. She was quietly hoping once Simon saw her and Lisa in the same room he would opt for the lure of the younger, single woman (ie Lizzie).

'Are you sure you want to invite her along too?' I asked, concerned that this might not be such a wise idea.

'It's the only way I'm going to get him to make a decision,' replied Lizzie. 'Put him on the spot.'

'Aren't you worried that she'll sense something?' I asked.

'Well hopefully,' interjected Mands. 'That's the plan, isn't it?'

'Right,' I replied, unsure what the rest of Lizzie's plan might be.

That left four seats.

Mands was contemplating adding the title Celebrity Agent to her diamante belt. Therefore I was required to invite Jasper Carlson, the actor I had met on several advertisements over the years and befriended. Jasper had many famous friends whom Mands held high hopes of one day putting on her books. No doubt, like him, they would one day end up shagging an underage girl and need the best PR strategy money could buy. I had no qualms about inviting Jasper, he was absolutely gorgeous and ideal table decoration if nothing else. Three seats remained.

Mands had started semi-shagging a Swedish man named Sven, so we had to invite him along. Sven was a lovely piece of Nordic eye candy and also the owner of several fantastic restaurants around town where we'd often end up dining for free. Plus, his networks were untapped gold. For someone who had been in the country barely a year, Sven seemed to know absolutely everyone. That left two seats.

We decided we really needed to have another celebrity persona present, solely for the entertainment factor, and tossed up between Jenna Griffin, who was good friends with Mands' sister and also a scandalous television personality, and Jonty Hill, the country's most famous jockey, who was much loved for his mountainesque cocaine habit (which he had managed to kick eight times) and for breaking up no less than six marriages in the past ten years. It was a tough call but we went with Jenna. That left one seat.

It was a unanimous decision to squeeze another chair around the table and to invite Samuel Evans and Darcy Simpson, the owners of Salute. They were both MATs (Men About Town) and very well connected. They were also the most in-demand gay couple on the dinner-party scene. It was unheard of these days to host a dinner party without having at least one gay person present. Amazingly, although we had set the date for only a fortnight's time, all of our guests were able to come. That meant there would be thirteen of us in attendance. Some people might have thought this was an unlucky number to have at a dinner party. And some people didn't give it a passing thought, but really should have.

There was no point having a dinner party unless you could afford to have it catered for, we all agreed. The very idea of slaving over a hot oven all day, just to produce something that tasted as if it were homemade, sent shivers down our three spines.

On the Wednesday night before the dinner party, Mands rang Prego to see if their head chef Manuel would do the honours. In past emergencies he had hand-delivered food to her apartment, already immaculately presented on white dinner plates. All we had to do was heat the plates in her oven. It was foolproof. Mands put Manuel on speakerphone and he promptly rattled off a menu for the evening.

'See vill ave poompkin en ginger ravioli in er vite vine zauce for see ztar-ter. Vollowed by oney zeared zalmon villet en vild mushroom vice en zpring veg-e-table ex-travaganza for see main. Vollowed by zokolat en boyzonberry zoufflé for see dezzert.'

'Sounds delicious!' we replied in unison.

The man's accent got me every time.

'I vill bring to yer ouse zat five o'clock pm on Zaturday.'

He was just so efficient too, which made me love him even more. If we could have spared a seat I seriously would have considered inviting him along.

The only thing left to organise was the alcohol, and that's where the phone and a delivery service once again came in handy. I ordered a selection of champagne and fine wines to be delivered chilled to Mands' apartment on Saturday afternoon. I had once ordered several bottles of wine for a dinner party, only to have them delivered at room temperature, which had caused complete chaos as I frantically attempted to chill them in my toaster-sized freezer. It was hard enough getting ready for a dinner party, without worrying about chilling bottles of wine.

Saturday evening arrived and with it Manuel ferrying several gorgeous-looking dinner plates up Mands' stairs.

'Zere vee go,' he declared, delicately placing the last plate onto Mands' stainless-top bench, without so much as twitching one of the chargrilled baby carrots.

He had also brought us several delicious platters of hors d'oeuvres to be served upon arrival.

'Thank you Manuel!' cried Mands, flinging her arms around his neck. 'You have saved our lives.'

'Zu are velcome,' beamed Manuel. 'I hope zu bea-u-ti-ful gurlz ave a loverly zevening.'

He was just so sweet, I thought to myself. *I wanted to pop him directly into my handbag and take him home.*

The champagne and wine had already arrived and several bottles were ensconced in well-positioned ice buckets about the place. All we had to do was set the table and place glasses on the drinks trolley. It was quite surprising how long these two tasks took, considering there were three of us. Lizzie and I set the table, as Mands followed us around repositioning the cutlery and napkins. Upon completion it looked gorgeous, especially once the four tall white candles were lit. The three of us stood back and admired our handiwork.

'See! We can be domesticated when we want to be,' said Lizzie.

'Absolutely!' agreed Mands and I, beaming at the beautiful table.

Julie and Hamish were the first to arrive. They appeared to be one of those ridiculously loved-up newly married couples who, although there's no doubt they both used to be fixtures of style in the single world, now appeared to be sliding towards the married wayside. Julie had, predictably, managed to pack on a few post-wedding pounds. It seemed to me that every woman who got married immediately got fat. (Even stick-thin Lizzie had put on a few unwanted pounds.) As soon as they were out of their white frocks and back from the honeymoon it all turned to custard, literally. The personal trainer who had been hired pre-wedding was now unemployed and washing car windscreens at the traffic lights. The macrobiotic diet was replaced with *whatever was in the refrigerator* and those three-times-a-week yoga classes were deemed an inappropriate use of time management. But it was OK to spend all the time in the world sitting on the sofa with the new husband watching Sky Movies and eating crisps. And all this before the first baby came along. It was like married women resigned themselves to the fact their bodies were never going to be the same Ever Again (at best a milk-vending machine) and that its management was simply no longer under their control. Some women blamed it on happiness, that old cliché of eating all the pies in the shop because you're just so happy. But how can putting on thirty pounds and no longer being able to fit your single-girl clothes make you happy? I just didn't understand it. *This was just one more reason to never, ever get married.*

Sean was the next to arrive, followed closely by a very nervous-looking Simon, his wife Lisa, Darcy and Samuel, Sven, Jenna, and finally, looking as though he'd caught a bus directly from the night before, Jasper Carlson.

Although the food and liquids were firmly under control, no thanks to any of us, the evening didn't begin all that well.

'We're having a baby!' announced Lisa, once everyone else had arrived and were mingling in Mands' living room.

Oh sweet Jesus!

'And somewhere a dog howled,' muttered Mands.

Lizzie's face promptly contorted into a silent scream. She dropped the skewered garlic prawn she was holding onto the carpet. I picked it up and put it in a napkin.

'Well,' I replied, breaking the morgue-like silence. 'That's lovely. Just lovely.'

Simon looked as though he wanted the floor beneath to open up and swallow him directly. The fact Lizzie was completely motionless, with fiery daggers shooting out from her eye sockets towards his head, was not helping matters. Eventually she snapped out of her trance and excused herself from the room. Mands and I found her standing motionless in the kitchen, a large stainless-steel carving knife firmly in her grasp.

'Whoa back!' said Mands, attempting to prize the knife from Lizzie's grip, without success.

'Easy,' I said, also attempting to take the knife from her, and eventually getting her to release it with the aid of a Chinese burn.

'Ouch!' squealed Lizzie.

'Sorry,' I apologised. 'But really sweets, what are you doing?'

'Thinking about what would be the best way to stab him. Not the best way as in the quickest death, but the best way as in the most painful, with the most gradual blood loss and slowest death imaginable.'

'Right,' said Mands and I, obviously a little concerned.

'But then you'll have to go to prison,' I reasoned.

'And you'll have to wear one of those hideous khaki jumpsuits,' said Mands. 'You know that khaki isn't one of your colours.'

'And a gorgeous thing like you,' I added. 'You'd be everyone's favourite little cellmate.'

'Do you think?' asked Lizzie.

'Absolutely,' replied Mands and I, nodding our heads with the seriousness of it all.

This made her stop and think.

'How long do you think they'd give me?' she asked.

'Definitely life,' replied Mands. 'Loads of witnesses.'

'Insanity?'

'Not a chance.'

'Will you kill him for me?'

'Not right now, no.'

'OK,' sighed Lizzie, resigning herself to the fact that Simon was going to live, at least for the time being.

'C'mon dolls,' I pleaded. 'You've got to put on a brave face and come back out. You're one of the hosts, remember?'

'Give me a minute,' she replied. 'And a drink.'

I left Mands pouring Lizzie an enormous glass of vodka and walked back into the sitting room, where Lisa was still talking about her pregnancy. Simon was looking even more like a recently caged animal.

'Couldn't be happier,' she said to Julie, who appeared to be bombarding her with a series of my-life-will-not-be-complete-until-I-too-am-pregnant questions.

Well, that's just great, I thought to myself. *The least she could have done was stayed at home and let Simon bring along someone who was actually going to drink and enjoy themselves.*

'We aren't having seafood for dinner, are we?' asked Lisa.

'Um . . .' I tried to remember exactly what it was we were having '. . . Zalmon.'

'Pardon?' she said.

'Salmon,' I repeated.

'Oh dear. I can't eat fish.'

Fantastic! I thought to myself. Now she had the audacity to completely screw up our menu. *The cow!* She could eat two-minute noodles for all I cared.

'Sammy and I are adopting a baby,' announced Darcy. 'A Vietnamese baby.'

Well at least that was more exotic than having one yourself, I thought to myself.

'Fantastic!' enthused Jenna. 'Which agency are you going through?'

Jenna had also adopted a Vietnamese baby, although it was now five years old and more of a small-child type thing than a baby.

Darcy, Lisa and Jenna then proceeded to spend most of the evening discussing the merits of certain baby products.

'This is *not* what we had planned,' hissed Mands, when the three of us finally got a moment together in the kitchen, placing more of Manuel's perfect hors d'oeuvres onto a platter.

'Those three are completely sabotaging this night with their goddamn baby talk!'

'Absolutely,' I agreed. 'We're simply going to have to break them up.'

'Damnshraight!' said Lizzie, who was looking a little less like she wanted to murder someone and a little more like she might be feeling the effects of the vodka.

'You take Darcy,' said Mands, pointing at me. 'I'll nail Lisa and Lizzie can take Jenna.'

'Agreed,' we replied.

The three of us descended on the baby-talkers and strategically disintegrated their conversation before they knew what had hit them. I managed to corner Darcy and get him to change the subject from babies to bars, which was considerably more exciting. He was a valuable source of gossip on the who's who of the celebrity bar-dwelling set, and provided some very useful information on the many uncompromising positions in which they had been found in the lavatories of some of his bars. The night suddenly took a turn for the better when I noticed Jasper return from the

73

toilet sporting traces of white film around his left nostril.

At least someone wasn't obsessed with bloody babies, I thought to myself.

After Mands had successfully ensconced Lisa with me and Darcy, I saw her make a beeline for Jasper.

He truly has the most beautiful skin, I noted, as one would expect with the thousands of dollars he invested in skincare products and treatments. I couldn't help but overhear their conversation.

'Jasper daahling,' cooed Mands.

'Mands daahling.'

'Refill?' she asked, holding up a bottle of champagne.

'Why the hell not?' he replied.

'So, how *is* life in the theatre and when's the next movie being filmed?'

She really couldn't have cared less, but every successful networker knew the inherent value of small talk. Every successful networker was also an expert in subtle facial movements, such as the attentive and encouraging nod of the head, the yes-I-am-listening-to-you wide eyes, the O-shaped mouth, and the trusty raised eyebrows. All choreographed at appropriate intervals and matched accordingly to the speaker's tone of voice. A successful networker did not in fact have to actually listen to what was being said. It was quite possible to apply the various facial movements and approving comments while also listening attentively to other conversations in the vicinity and processing all relevant information, more commonly known as multi-tasking. After listening attentively, or at least appearing to, to Jasper's very indepth and thoroughly boring account of the differences between stage and camera acting, she finally managed to broach the subject of his famous friends.

'Mands daahling, I've told them all about you,' said Jasper.

'Nicole and Russell are waiting for your call.'

With that comment Mands' networking for the evening was complete. But mine was yet to begin. I spotted Sean on the other side of the table, talking to Jenna and Samuel, and made my move.

'So Sean, how *is* the advertising world treating you?' I asked, pulling my chair up beside him.

'You should know, Sam. Working like a bloody dog for fourteen hours a day without the slightest possibility of forming a lasting relationship, or even getting a shag, just because there's a million twenty-one-year-olds out there with more energy than a six-pack of Red Bull waiting for you to yawn so they can pounce on your clients and watch you packing up your office while trying not to cry in front of your staff.'

Bloody hell, Sean had really lost his spark, I thought to myself. *He could do with a dose of Tony Robbins.*

'How about you?'

'Oh, you know, working hard too. Never a dull day.'

'I know.'

'So how's Becketts going then?' he asked. 'Hit the slump yet?'

'No,' I replied. 'Not yet anyway.'

'We have. Going to have to lay off three account managers this month. Bloody disaster.'

Bugger! I'd be hard pushed to be headhunted when heads were rolling.

My networking didn't appear to be working at all. Plus, Sean was beginning to depress me. He really should try to be a bit more positive if he wanted to get himself a girlfriend, I thought. Negativity was a bona fide sex-repellent. Thankfully it was time to serve dinner so I excused myself and moved into the kitchen with Mands and Lizzie. We placed the individual entrée plates of poompkin und ginger ravioli in zer vite vine zauce in the oven and heated them up. While they were doing their thing, the three of stood with our glasses of wine and watched.

'Done,' declared Mands. I thought she was referring to the food.

'What's done?' asked Lizzie.

'My schmoozing.'

'I know,' I replied. 'I saw you. But,' I warned, 'just make sure he remembers that you had the conversation.'

'Why?' asked Mands.

'Because he's off his head. Haven't you seen how many times he's been to the loo?'

'I thought he just had a weak bladder,' replied Mands. 'I'll be sure to follow him next time.'

'How's yours going?' I asked Lizzie.

'Not very well,' she replied. 'All I feel like doing is killing Simon. And his wife.'

'You're not allowed to kill her,' said Mands. 'I want the honour.'

'Me too,' I added.

'Be my guests,' replied Lizzie. 'Just be sure to make it painful.'

'How about you?' asked Lizzie.

'Terrible,' I replied. 'Sean appears to be a manic depressive and the agency is laying off.'

I went to seat everyone in their allocated places and then returned to the kitchen to help the girls carry out the entrée plates.

'Looks bloody delicious gals,' declared Jasper, as we set the plates on the table. 'Well done!'

'Delicious,' agreed everyone else, once they had taken their first mouthful. I had to agree.

'Gosh, you three must have been cooking all afternoon,' said Lisa, who was obviously grateful there was no seafood in the entrée.

Not only was she highly annoying and ruining our dinner party, but apparently she was also incredibly stupid.

'Absolutely divine ladies,' said Jenna, winking at us. 'Tastes just as good as Prego.'

After receiving more praise for the entrée which we had absolutely nothing whatsoever to do with making, we reconvened in the kitchen to heat the dinner plates.

'What the hell are we going to give her?' I asked. 'She won't eat salmon.'

'Arsenic,' replied Lizzie, who wasn't being much help.

'Hell knows,' said Mands. 'You know I don't have any food here.'

'There must be something,' I said, opening the tiny freezer, which contained nothing but a packet of frozen blackberries and a couple of hash browns.

'That'll do her,' I said, pulling out the hash browns.

'Aren't you s'posed to put them in the oven?' asked Mands, as I popped them into the microwave.

'Who cares,' I replied. 'She's lucky she's getting anything.'

'Bloody right,' said Lizzie.

We brought the dinner plates to the table, where they were received with similar accolades to the entrée. (Except for Lisa's, which just got stared at disdainfully as Lizzie slammed it down in front of her.) But before we could begin to eat Simon managed to knock over a full bottle of red wine and splatter me, Jenna and Mands in the process. Thankfully, for his sake, he didn't get Lizzie, who was sitting at the opposite end of the table, as far away from him as she could possibly be while remaining in the same room. Simon appeared to be dealing with the fact he was sitting at a dinner table with both his pregnant wife and his furious mistress in the only way he knew how — by getting as quickly and rottenly drunk as possible.

'Slow down!' hissed Lisa, giving him an evil look.

Jasper appeared to have contracted a very sudden and violent case of verbal diarrhoea and was presently having three simultaneous conversations with me, Lisa and Samuel, all on completely different subjects. Somehow he was successfully managing to juggle all three without either losing the other parties' interest or forgetting what it was we were talking about.

'Bloody boring pregnant woman,' he whispered, turning to me.

'I know,' I agreed. 'The night is being completely dominated by someone who has yet to form arms or legs.'

'What's up with Lizzie?' he asked. I explained the Simon, Lisa and big baby surprise.

'Oh,' said Jasper. 'That'd explain the look then. I was beginning to think she was rehearsing for the role of Margaret Thatcher.'

As I sat talking to Jasper, eating the delicious zalmon, I suddenly felt myself becoming hot. Very, very hot. All over.

'Jesus!' I exclaimed to Mands, who was sitting on my left. 'I think I'm having a hot flush.'

'Bloody hell,' she replied. 'It's a bit early, isn't it dolls?'

I poured myself a glass of water, but it did nothing to cool me down. My body was on fire. I lunged across Mands for another glass.

'Not very Singapore girl,' she muttered.

I was too uncomfortable to apologise.

'You're going a bit red,' she observed.

And then, very suddenly, I was not only hot all over my body, I was also incredibly itchy. Skin crawling, tear-the-skin-off-my-bones itchy.

I excused myself from the table and walked into the bathroom, madly scratching my body all over. It gave me some temporary relief and I made my way back to the table. But not for long.

Within five minutes I was hot and itching all over again, worse this time. I felt like tearing my clothes off and jumping into one of the ice buckets. But that wasn't the worst of it.

'Jesus,' said Mands, looking at me. 'What's happening to your face? It's going all blotchy.'

I reached my hands up towards my face and that's when I saw them. Red welts all over the backs of my hands.

'Fucking hell!' I exclaimed, jumping up and running towards the bathroom.

Mands and Lizzie followed in hot pursuit, watching me fling my clothes off in the hallway and run for the shower.

'Need cold!' I exclaimed, hurling myself into the shower.

'Bloody hell!' exclaimed Mands and Lizzie, staring at me. 'You're covered in blotches!'

And I was. My entire body, from head to heel, was covered in large red and purple welts.

'They're even on your bum!' cried Mands.

'It must be something you've eaten,' said Lizzie.

The cold water gave me some temporary relief and after ten minutes of icy showering I was ready to bring my blotchy body out.

'Jesus! What's happening to your eyes?' said Lizzie, as I gently dabbed my welty body dry.

'Whaddayamean?' I hissed, staring at my blotchy arms and legs.

'They appear to be closing over.'

'And your lips,' added Mands. 'You look like Lisa Rina.'

'Have a look in the mirror,' they instructed.

They were right. Both of my eyelids were so completely swollen that my eyes had become two thin green slits. And my lips were so big they were practically eating each other.

'Oh Jesus!' I moaned, starting to cry. 'Somebody stop it!'

'We're off to the emergency room,' declared Lizzie, swinging into action. 'Mands, call us a cab!'

'I wanna come too,' complained Mands.

'Look,' said Lizzie. 'One of us has got to stay here and it's not me. If I have to look at that poxy spineless git and his nappy-hugging wife one minute longer, I'm gonna kill the both of them.'

'Right,' said Mands, assessing the potential damage and phoning us a taxi.

'I'm coming too,' said Jasper, meeting us in the hallway. 'I'm bored. Bloody hell!' he added, noticing the state of me.

I wanted to hop into the taxi naked, but Mands persuaded me to put on her silk robe.

When we got to the hospital emergency room Lizzie made me peel the robe apart and flash the nurse on the reception desk.

'Lord above!' she exclaimed. 'That's an allergic reaction if ever I saw one!'

After only five minutes of sitting in the waiting room, with Jasper pacing back and forth from the drink machine, visibly wearing a hole in the white lino, I was ushered into the doctor's room, with Lizzie by my side. It was at exactly midnight that I found myself sitting opposite an Indian male doctor, approximately fifty years of age. I was wearing nothing but a pale-pink silk robe, my eyes were all but closed over, and I was covered from head to toe in large red and purple welts.

'Oh my!' exclaimed the doctor. 'How does the other person look?'

He mistakenly assumed I'd been involved in some sort of uncouth bar brawl.

'Actually . . .' I replied, 'I think I've had an allergic reaction to something.'

'Peanuts?' he asked. 'The last time I saw a reaction like this, nuts were responsible.'

'No,' I replied.

'What have you been eating?' he asked, staring at the red welts all over my arms.

'Zalmon and poompkin,' I replied.

'Beg your pardon?' said the doctor.

Lizzie relayed the dinner menu to him, in English, while I furtively scratched my arms and legs, like some sort of scabby town leper. There's no doubt I would have been locked away in the cellar in years gone by, while the rest of the town rejoiced and threw the only key into the moat.

'I see,' he said, nodding his head. 'And may I ask what spices and herbs you used when you were cooking this?'

'Well . . .' replied Lizzie. 'You see, we didn't actually make it.'

'Who did?' asked the doctor.

'Um . . . Manuel did,' replied Lizzie.

'Who is Manuel?' asked the doctor.

'He's the head chef at Prego,' answered Lizzie, adding for the doctor's benefit, 'It's a very nice restaurant on Ponsonby Road. Fabulous food and service.'

'You recommend it?' asked the doctor.

'Yes,' replied Lizzie.

'I see,' repeated the doctor, making a note of the restaurant name on his pad. 'So a chef made it?'

'Yes,' I replied, very close to tears. 'We didn't make it

because we can't cook for shit and we had to get a chef in. Now can you please for the love of God give me something to stop this bloody itching? Or I am going to kill myself. And the both of you.'

'Righty ho then,' said the doctor, and asked me to lie up on the examination table as he closely examined my cloak of welts and swollen bits. 'I think you are having an anaphylactic reaction to something,' was his verdict.

This was confirmed after he consulted all of the medical journals in his office, every other doctor on duty, and some not on duty but at home sleeping.

As I lay naked on the table scratching all over my body and requesting that Lizzie put her French-manicured nails to bloody use and start scratching me too, the doctor told me that I needed an injection of adrenaline.

'OK,' I replied. If he'd said a good rogering from himself would cure me I would have said OK too. Anything to stop the itching.

Lizzie, who had been a pillar of sanity and grown-up-ness, crumbled into a fit of hysterical giggles at the sight of the needle approaching my naked, welt-covered body.

'Ow!' I complained, as the needle pierced the inflamed skin on my right arm.

'There you go,' said the doctor, motioning for me to hop off the table. 'That should take away the blotches and the swelling. But if you have any problems I want you to ring me. And I am giving you a prescription for antihistamine,' said the doctor, writing on his pad, 'which you need to take in a couple of hours.'

'C'mon Rudolph,' said Lizzie. 'Let's get you home. I'll come and stay at your place tonight, just to keep an eye on you.'

On the way out we woke Jasper, who had passed out in one of the plastic waiting-room chairs, and put him into a taxi, before ringing Mands with an update. She said that everyone had finally vacated her apartment, including an incredibly drunk Simon who had managed to smash her favourite pink Nest vase on his exit.

'Fucking arsehole!' she screeched.

'I hope he cut himself?' said Lizzie eagerly.

'Yes, twice,' confirmed Mands. 'But unfortunately nothing was severed.'

'What a crying shame,' said Lizzie, shaking her head.

The next day Mands and I phoned Manuel who deduced (after listing the hundred herbs and spices he had used in the meal) that it was probably Tahitian vanilla beans I was allergic to, which he had used in the vild muzroom vice.

Oh well, at least it was something exotic, I consoled myself, *and not peanuts.*

Monday morning came around and I was undeniably still suffering from the weekend's events. Though the welts and swelling had settled down significantly, I still looked remarkably like a human patchwork quilt. Thankfully the itching had subsided and I no longer felt it necessary to run around completely naked.

To top off my suffering my first meeting of the day was with Trixie and Davis. We were meeting about shampoo. Again.

'Well . . . we've been thinking . . .' began Trixie.

Well at least that was a start, I thought to myself. Lord knew that didn't happen often.

'. . . about the shampoo,' continued Davis.

Bless. It looked like they were really going to be on the ball today.

'We all know that shampoo is silky . . .' said Trixie.

'. . . and soft . . . and blah blah,' finished Davis.

'Agreed,' I replied.

'But that's sort of well . . .'

'. . . been done,' finished Trixie.

'Right again,' I replied.

Why did they always have to finish each other's sentences?
I wondered.

It appeared that neither of them was capable of starting
a sentence and carrying it through to the full stop by
themselves. It was like witnessing a tag-team relay of
stupidity.

'And we know that it's got the fruit,' said Davis, 'y'know
. . .'

'. . . fruitavessence,' finished Trixie.

*Dear God, they had made the word up themselves and he
still couldn't remember it.*

'But . . .' said Davis. 'Wouldn't it be good if . . .'

'. . . if one of the shampoos gave you, like, big hair . . .
y'know, like . . .' said Trixie.

'. . . like volume,' finished Davis.

'And the little bits that gave you big hair could be called
. . .'

'Volumisers!' they both chorused in unison.

Oh dear God, I thought to myself. I appeared to have
somehow been transported into a scene from *A Clockwork
Orange*.

I took another sip of my coffee and stared straight back at
them across the table. They were both sitting there grinning
and shuffling excitedly in their seats, waiting for my response.
I took another sip of coffee, and struggled to think of a simple
way to tell them their idea was complete and utter crap and
no brand manager in their right mind would buy it.

'Well . . .' I said, suddenly realising I simply didn't have the energy to deal with these two today. 'That sounds great. Good work.'

And with that I got up and left the two of them blabbering on about *volumisers*, and headed off to an ad shoot for one of my clients, Sensy Soap.

I pulled up to the gates of the filming studio only to be confronted by several chanting and banner-waving women.

Oh bloody great! I thought to myself, as I spotted my mother at the front of the rowdy throng, leading the chant.

'Ads Don't Work They Hurt! Ads Don't Work They Hurt!' they shouted.

Hell! I had no choice but to drive straight up to the gate and wait for the security guard to open it for me.

My mother had spotted my car and came round to the driver's window, indicating for me to wind it down. She stopped her chanting.

'Hello darling.'

'Hi Elizabeth.'

'What's happened to your face?'

'Long story,' I replied.

'You've got nothing to do with that television ad they're making in there, have you?'

'No,' I lied. 'I'm just here for a meeting.'

'OK then,' she said, although she didn't seem entirely convinced. 'Do you want to come round for dinner tonight? Your father's cooking.'

How very unusual.

'I can't sorry. Other plans.'

'Okey-dokey then,' she said, standing back as the gate opened, and gallantly waving me through before she started chanting again, 'Ads Don't Work They Hurt! Ad's Don't Work They . . .'

I found the filming studio and thrust myself inside the door.

'Christ! Did you see those bloody women outside?' asked Jeff, the director.

'I thought that one at the front with the army pants was going to clock me one when I drove past.'

'No kidding.'

You're just lucky she didn't, I thought.

'I really hope they're gone by the time we wrap.'

'So do I,' I replied, finding myself a seat.

The two female models in the ad were sitting on deckchairs in front of me, waiting for the filming to begin. I couldn't help but overhear their conversation. It appeared they were talking about food. It was all models seemed to talk about these days. It's true that we always want what we haven't got.

'Why? What did you have for lunch?' asked the one with the brown hair.

'Just lettuce,' replied the blonde one.

'What, the whole thing?' asked the brunette, a look of horror on her face.

It was a well-known industry fact that the only entertainment at ad shoots was the models. Without them I would have nodded off on many an occasion.

The most entertaining display I'd ever witnessed was at a three-day shoot for a tampon commercial. There were four female models present, with the average age of twelve-and-a-half (or at least that's what it looked like). By the afternoon of the second day they were desperate to ingest narcotics and nothing was going to stop them, not even the complete lack of a clean flat surface.

'What about the floor?' one had suggested.

'It's white! How're we going to see it?' protested another.

'True,' the other two agreed.

'I've got an idea,' the tall lanky blonde one had said, as she'd walked towards a crate holding a feather duster, a bottle of cleaning spray and an iron.

She had removed the iron and walked back to the other three.

'What's that for?' asked the others in surprise. 'Do we have to press our own clothes?'

'Hold it,' said the blonde one, shoving it into her friends' hands, flat side up, as she reached for a piece of paper to lay on the bottom of the iron.

Aha, I'd thought to myself. I'd had to hand it to her. This showed an initiative I had no idea she possessed. The sight of the five white lines racked up on the bottom of the iron would have been enough to render any good 1950s housewife speechless. I bet the person who invented the iron had absolutely no idea of its full potential.

I looked back at the two models sitting in front of me. The blonde one kept pulling her top back onto her shoulder, only to have it slip straight back off again. There were simply no boobs to hold it up. *My mother would have gladly sold her soul to have five minutes alone in a room with these two*, I thought to myself. At least neither my sisters nor I had qualified as model material. *God help us.*

Thankfully, by the time the shoot finished it was seven o'clock and my mother and her protesting female entourage had presumably gone home to eat the three-course meals their dutiful husbands had ready and waiting for them.

4

For the next wee while (post disastrous bikini waxes and culinary trauma) my life began to coast along relatively smoothly once again, lulling me back into a false sense of security.

'I've had it with men,' declared Lizzie, as the three of us once again sat in Prego having dinner. She was still suffering badly from the Simon-with-foetus news. Thankfully she had decided to give him the flick post dinner-party disaster, and she had also mercifully managed to refrain herself from killing him.

Mands and I braced ourselves for what was coming next. *Perhaps she was changing teams?* we thought to ourselves. Fair play to her. First there was Bryce the Bastard and the whole no-baby drama. Then she'd convinced herself Simon was going to leave his wife and they'd settle down and have a baby together. All Lizzie really wanted was to have a baby.

'I'm having a baby,' she announced.

But how? Was she already pregnant with Simon's child?

'A donor baby.'

Oh . . . stop the clock.

Mands and I put our glasses of champers down on the table and stared back at her.

'So, you're not becoming a lesbian then?' asked Mands, somewhat confused.

'No,' replied Lizzie. 'Not yet anyway.'

'Wow!' I said, unsure of the appropriate response to this type of news. 'That's great, sweets. A baby. Cripes.'

'I've had enough of trying to find the right man to have one with,' continued Lizzie. 'So . . . I'm just going to do it by myself.'

More staring.

'Well, we'll be there to help you sweets,' I replied, breaking the silence.

Although only God himself knew how much help we'd actually be.

'Won't we, Mands?' I prompted.

'Yep . . . course we will,' said Mands, finally coming to. 'When are you going to have it?' she asked.

'Soon,' said Lizzie. 'I'm just trying to pick the donor. From the internet.'

'You're picking a father from the web?' we cried.

Good Lord. I was all for embracing new technology, but surely this was taking it a bit far?

Lizzie told us about the online organisation she was using to purchase the sperm and how the whole thing worked.

'You're getting it from the States?' I asked.

'That's right.'

'Why?'

'Because there's a better selection of donors to choose from. And they give out far more info.'

Obviously Lizzie had done her sperm homework.

'Plus, this country's too small,' she added. 'I'd probably pick a donor just to find out I went to school with him.'

'Or he's your uncle,' said Mands, once again opting for the worst-case scenario.

'How do you get it?' I asked.

'It gets flown over. Frozen,' said Lizzie. 'And stored in a fertility clinic here until I'm ready.'

'It's all very organised,' I observed.

'And pricey,' added Lizzie, disclosing the amount she was paying. Sperm money.

'Fifteen grand for a bit of sperm?' cried Mands and I. 'Bloody hell!'

So, the following night, we found ourselves sitting at Lizzie's dining table, staring at the screen of her laptop as she showed us the three sperm donors she had to decide between. The first donor profile popped up on screen, along with a picture of a very cute smiling two-year-old.

'But he's already got a kid!' cried Mands, understandably confused.

'No,' said Lizzie. 'That's him.'

'C'mon Lizzie,' I replied. 'He's a bit young to be taking himself to a sperm bank.'

'You can't see recent pics,' explained Lizzie. 'Only their baby photos.'

'Really? Bit dodgy isn't it?' said Mands. 'How are you supposed to know what they look like now?'

'You should go for an ugly baby then,' I suggested. 'It's safer. You know what they say about good-looking babies.'

'No. What?'

'Ugly adults, sweets . . . very ugly adults.'

'How old is he?' I asked.

'Twenty-three.'

'Wahoo!' screamed Mands and I, jumping up from our seats. 'You're going to shag a twenty-three-year-old. Fabulous!'

'Unfortunately I don't get to shag him,' replied Lizzie.

'Oh. That's right,' we remembered, sitting back down. 'Shame though.'

'Here's all his stats,' said Lizzie, opening up a file to rival Watergate.

'Bloody hell!' I exclaimed, staring at the screen. 'It's a family tree.'

Indeed it was. Screeds of information on his family — siblings, parents, uncles and aunts, grandparents, and even great-grandparents. Everything from their shoe size to the disclosure of any addictions.

'One paternal great aunt with a drinking problem,' said Lizzie happily. 'That's it.'

'That's it?' said Mands and I in unison. 'That's hardly normal, is it?'

'Doesn't the rest of his family drink?' asked Mands, a concerned look on her face.

'Don't know,' said Lizzie. 'But they're not addicts anyway.'

'You should check,' I suggested. 'You don't want to give birth to a teetotaller.'

'He's at Harvard,' said Lizzie, ignoring me. 'Studying Politics and English Lit.'

'Ivy League sperm,' muttered Mands.

'Oh dear,' I said.

'What?' asked Lizzie.

'Well, do you really want a child who's going to try and debate with you? Plus, politics are boring.'

'Good point,' said Lizzie, making a note on her pad.

'Does it tell you the size of his willy?' asked Mands.

'No!' replied Lizzie. 'Why?'

'Well, think about the kid, Lizzie. If it's a boy, do you really want to inflict it with a small package?'

Lizzie and I looked at her sideways.

'Just a point,' said Mands, getting up and pouring us another wine.

'This one's at Yale,' said Lizzie, opening up the next donor profile.

Another smiling two-year-old popped onto the screen. He wasn't quite as cute as the last one.

'Height?' asked Mands.

'Six foot.'

'Eye colour?'

'Brown.'

'Addictions?'

'None.'

'He's musical too,' added Lizzie. 'Plays the sax and sings.'

'Fabulous,' I replied. 'You might give birth to some sort of musical child prodigy. They're very profitable these days.'

'You could be a stage mum,' added Mands. 'Travel round the world living off the profits, controlling their diet and occasionally yelling things like *Get a grip Harriet and put that banana down! You know what potassium does to your tonsils!*'

'Or,' I added, getting into the swing of things, '*What do you mean you want to go to the movies with your friends tonight? You know you're singing for Prince Charles! Time is money, honey!*'

Lizzie stared back at us, unmoving. Apparently shopping for a baby was serious business. She brought the final donor profile up on screen. This two-year-old had lovely deep-olive skin and a beautiful smile.

'Height?' I asked.

'Five nine.'

'Hmm . . . a little on the short side.'

'Occupation?'

'Student as well. At Stanford, studying Economics.'

'Clearly there's no student allowance in the States,' observed Mands. 'Just sperm banks.'

'Any bad points?' I asked.

'His maternal grandmother suffered from depression.'

'Oh, not good, sweets,' I replied, thinking of Louie.

'So . . . what do you think?' asked Lizzie, once we had scanned and evaluated everything from his waist size to the occupation of his maternal great-grandfather.

'The second ones gets my vote,' said Mands. 'He looks like the kind of baby you'd take home to meet your parents.'

This set both of us off in a hysterical fit of giggles.

More staring from Lizzie.

'The second one too,' I said, regaining my composure. 'He seems very well-rounded, good family background, nice and tall, and clearly not a thicko. In fact, if he was here right now I'd definitely shag him.'

'After me,' said Mands.

'No,' said Lizzie, asserting control over her sperm. 'After me.'

'Right you are,' conceded Mands and I. 'After you.'

'What's his name?' I asked.

'Eight three nine seven,' replied Lizzie.

'Very catchy. Are you going to give the baby his surname?' I asked.

'I think you should,' added Mands. 'And you should call the baby Twenifor.'

'Twenifor Seven!' we screamed, slapping each other on the arm.

Lizzie closed down her laptop, happy with our feedback but not our attempts to name her unborn progeny, and the pictures of the smiling two-year-olds disappeared. It crossed my mind that the three of us had shopped together for years, but this was the first time we'd been shopping for a baby.

'How's Sven?' I asked Mands, turning the conversation away from designer babies.

'Good,' she replied. 'But . . .'

'But what?'

'But he seems to have developed a fetish . . . with my feet.'

'Your feet?'

'Aha. He only likes me to wear open-toed shoes and he's always bloody well rubbing them.'

'Rubbing them with what?' asked Lizzie.

'Just his hands, thank God. And he talks to them too.'

'He talks to your feet?'

'Yes. In bed.'

'Does he look at them when he's talking to them?'

'Hell yes! He spends most of his time at the other end of the bloody bed with them in his hands.'

I looked down at Mands' feet, sitting in her open-toed Spanish red heels. Although I'd known her forever I'd never had a decent look at them. And there they were, small and petite, like the rest of her. But they were just feet, nothing more, nothing less.

'And I'm getting really sick of foot massages,' continued Mands.

'Get out!' said Lizzie and I. What we wouldn't have given for regular foot massages! 'You can't be!'

'I am. As sad as it is,' said Mands, shaking her head.

'A tragedy,' agreed Lizzie and I, shaking our heads too.

'And . . .' said Mands. 'He took a picture of them last night . . . on his phone.'

Granted this was taking things a bit too far.

'Why?'

'To use as his screen saver.'

'Let me get this straight,' I replied. 'The man is walking around with a picture of your trotters proudly displayed on his cellphone?'

Later that week, I lay back on Lizzie's sofa with a glass of champers in one hand and a salmon-stuffed caper berry in the other, having succumbed to a rather severe bout of peer pressure. I stared nervously at the needle coming towards me, thinking about the last time I had a needle coming towards me and hoping it was going to be an entirely different experience altogether.

Well then, here goes, I thought to myself, as I took another big gulp of champers. *I am about to join the other side. I am about to be one of them. I am very nearly about to be officially botoxed.*

This was Mands' idea, not mine. I had planned on at least hanging out until I hit thirty-five before I branched into any form of cosmetic enhancement. However, I also didn't like to be left out of anything and my arms were not so much rubber as very long strips of velcro. They could not only be bent every which way, but also easily stuck fast to that new position.

'Look girls, how will we know what everyone else is talking about if we don't give it a bash?' Mands had said to Lizzie and I, her sales pitch in full throttle. 'It's in our best interests to keep informed. Fingers. Pulse. On.'

Lizzie and I were at a loss to come up with a decent excuse. And Mands was very persuasive. So, that is how I ended up lying back on Lizzie's chaise longue after work on a Thursday night while a nurse who was an old friend of Mands' sister Jessie injected a skin-enhancing chemical into my forehead.

If only I'd had a closer look at that syringe coming towards me I would have noticed it contained far more liquid than those which had headed towards Mands and Lizzie's foreheads. In fact about twice as much, to be exact. But I'd been too busy taking one last nervous gulp of champers to look beyond the steely needle.

After extracting the needle from my forehead and giving my skin several little firm taps about the place, Jenny, the nurse, packed up her botox kit, downed a glass of champers herself, and vacated Lizzie's terraced townhouse. It was much like any other medical house call, except when you had the flu you generally didn't lounge about with your two best friends drinking champers and eating fabulous hors d'oeuvres.

Lizzie and I lay on a sofa each and Mands lay sprawled across several cushions on the floor.

'Can you feel your forehead?' asked Lizzie.

'Kind of,' said Mands.

'What forehead?' I replied. Mine was so numb I was not entirely convinced it was still there.

'Mine feels really tingly,' said Lizzie, getting up and pouring us all another glass.

'Pass me the mirror,' I instructed Lizzie. 'I need to look.'

She handed me the small oval mirror.

My forehead was still there, right above my eyes, but it wasn't responding to any sort of tapping. Or pinching for that matter. I screwed up my face but the only things to move were my lips and chin. I asked Mands and Lizzie to screw up their faces as well, so I could compare my new look. Their foreheads were also completely crinkle-free, but the rest of their faces didn't appear to be frozen in one spot like mine.

'Come and have a look at me,' I instructed, still holding the mirror in front of myself. 'My bloody face is stuck!'

They both hovered over the top of me, assessing my claim.

'Give us a smile,' instructed Mands.

I did as I was told.

'A smile,' she repeated.

'I am smiling,' I replied through clenched teeth.

'Oh,' said Mands.

'And a frown,' instructed Lizzie.

'I said a frown,' she repeated.

'I am bloody frowning.'

'Oh.'

The way they were both staring at me was beginning to make me nervous.

'Are you sure?'

'Yes. I'm sure.'

'See if you can't put some effort into it,' said Mands.

'I *am* putting some fucking effort into it,' I replied, positive that my face must be resembling a crinkle-cut crisp with all of the effort I was putting in.

'Are you angry?' asked Lizzie.

'Very,' I replied.

'Really? You don't look it,' they both laughed, slapping each other on the back.

'Well I am, increasingly. At both of you.'

'Try wiggling your nose,' said Lizzie.

But my nose was having none of it.

'I'm frozen bloody solid,' I despaired.

'It would appear so,' they agreed.

'P'haps we should give Jenny a call?' suggested Lizzie.

'Give it another half an hour,' said Mands. 'You're probably just having a different reaction than us and it'll wear off soon.'

'OK,' I agreed, rather reluctantly. 'Pour me another champers then.'

Half an hour passed and I still looked as though my face had been dipped into a concrete mixer.

'Lord,' sighed Mands. 'Best we give her a call then.'

I lay back on the sofa in my inert state and let Mands do the talking.

'Good news or bad?' asked Mands, when she had hung up the phone.

'Bad,' I said, opting for the light at the end of the tunnel.

'She says she may have given you too much.'

'What?' I cried.

'She's just checked her liquid supplies and it would appear four doses have been used . . . as opposed to three.'

'Meaning she gave me twice as much as you two?' I asked.

'Correct.'

'She's terribly sorry.'

'Can't she just come back and take it out?' I wailed.

'Ah . . . no . . . apparently not.'

'Is there anything I can do to fix it?'

'No.'

'Bloody hell! What's the good news then?'

'It should settle down in about a week . . . or maybe two.'

'You mean I'm going to look like a piece of lead for the next two weeks?' I cried.

The whole disaster was eerily reminiscent of my blotched St Tropez tan the previous summer. I'd been led to believe, after shelling out two hundred dollars, that my whole body would come out bronzed and glowing as if, well, as if I'd been holidaying in St Tropez. Instead I'd come out all blotchy and streaky, as if I'd been lying under a rain cloud. 'Should change the name to Auckland tan,' I'd told the salon owner, as I phoned and demanded my money back. 'That'd be more bloody accurate!'

'I'm sure she's just being cautious,' comforted Mands. 'You know how nurses are.'

'Fucking hell!' I wailed, a tear streaming down my plaster-cast face.

'Oh dolls. It'll be OK,' said Mands, putting her arm around my shoulder.

'Get off me!' I hissed. 'It's your bloody fault. Why couldn't we have just gone out for dins or something?'

'I'm sorry,' she soothed. 'I really am.'

'Pour me another,' I instructed.

For the next ten days I was unable to venture out in public, aside from the necessary places of course, like work. I ferried myself from home to the office and back again. I cancelled as many meetings as I was able, which wasn't difficult once Gareth took a look at my face. 'We don't want people to think we're frigid nationalists,' he'd said. After he'd finished laughing, that is. I was unable to laugh, or cry for that matter. Oh, I could shed tears all right, but I was completely unable to complement them with any of the necessary facial contortions. I was like a crying statue.

For nine nights, I was a nocturnal prisoner in my own apartment. As I completely blamed Mands for my inoculation predicament she was forced to keep me company each evening, and to bring me whatever cuisine my taste buds desired.

Finally, by day ten, my face had begun to show some emotion again and Mands and Lizzie came round to help me celebrate. It was also a consolation gathering. Mands had organised a fashion show the previous night for one of the country's up-and-coming young designers and unfortunately one of the models had tripped up on the catwalk. In fact she had tripped right off the side of the catwalk and onto a row of international buyers.

'Fucking stick insect!' berated Mands, as we sat in my living room having a glass of wine. 'She ruined the bloody show!'

'Look Mands,' I comforted. 'With all of the shows you've

ever organised, isn't it likely a model's going to trip at some point?'

'They don't get paid to trip,' she glared at me. 'They get paid to walk.'

We ordered a delivery of Thai takeaways, which shut Mands' torrent up just long enough for us to eat.

'All of that work,' she cried. 'Sabotaged!'

'I don't think she sabotaged it, dolls,' said Lizzie, embracing the voice of reason. 'I doubt she really wanted to trip up.'

'You'd be surprised,' replied Mands, ever the conspiracy theorist.

Lizzie and I decided to take Mands out to a bar immediately, in the vain hope this would cheer her up. Plus, we both silently agreed, if we were out then perhaps we could talk to other people and not have to listen to her sulking. After a close inspection in the bathroom mirror I was comfortable with the way my face was looking. It was to be my first public outing at night post the botox balls-up.

We walked into the bar. But this wasn't just any bar. This was the chicest bar in the city, aside from Salute, and it was completely white — white walls, white counter, white booths and white bar stools. It was also owned by none other than Darcy and Samuel, and very aptly named Pure.

'I feel better already,' declared Mands, climbing onto a bar stool.

'And you're about to feel even better,' said Lizzie, ordering three cosmopolitans.

The drinks had the desired affect of making Mands forget about the footloose model and move on to more pressing topics.

'The carpet rang me yesterday,' she announced.

'The ring thief?' I asked.

'Yes.'

'And?' probed Lizzie.

'And . . . he wants to take me out for dinner. Seems me getting my ring stuck in his chest hair had the undesired affect of turning him on.'

'Eeew!' exclaimed Lizzie and I. 'You're not going to go, are you?'

'Course not,' replied Mands.

'So, what did you tell him?' I asked.

'That I didn't think my girlfriend would approve.'

'Oh you idiot!' I exclaimed. 'That's just going to turn him on even more. You'll never get rid of him now!'

'Well, he put me on the spot, didn't he?' So now if we bump into him when we're out, one of you has to pretend you're my girlfriend.'

Lizzie and I stared back at her. She'd be bloody lucky.

'And,' said Mands, clearly on a roll, 'the Swedish Stallion rang today.'

Sven, the Swedish Toe Sucker, had returned to his native land last week, after selling up his various restaurants around the city.

'Really?' asked Lizzie and I. This was far more interesting. 'And?'

'And he wants to fly me to Sweden for a holiday. Next month.'

'Fabulous!' we cried.

'Well . . . no . . . not exactly,' said Mands.

'Why not?' we asked.

It certainly sounded fabulous.

'Because . . . I'm pretty sure he's only flying me over for my feet.'

'What?'

'He asked how they were on the phone. And he said he misses them. A lot.'

'He misses your feet?'

'That's what he said.'

'Did he say he misses you?' I asked.

'No . . . not exactly.'

'Well, that's not so bad is it?' said Lizzie. 'So he wants to see your feet? At least it'd be a free holiday.'

'Exactly,' I agreed.

'But I think he's in love with them,' confessed Mands.

'With your feet?'

'Yes.'

'Are you jealous?' I asked. 'Of your feet?'

'Maybe,' replied Mands, shifting in her seat.

Aha. It was one thing to be jealous of another female, but jealous of your own feet? That was something else entirely.

'Chop them off then,' suggested Lizzie. 'Then you'll know if he's for real.'

'And I'll also be a cripple.'

'Small sacrifice,' we replied.

'Fuck off,' said Mands. 'The both of you.'

'Right,' declared Lizzie, at around midnight. 'I'm off. Got to be in court tomorrow morning.'

'I'd better go too,' said Mands. 'Huge day tomorrow, bloody flower show or something.'

'Flower show?' I asked. 'But you despise gardening.'

'Completely irrelevant,' said Mands, who was by this stage swaying on top of her barstool.

'Guess I'm going too then,' I said, finishing my drink.

I walked to the toilet on the way out and literally bumped into Darcy, who had just arrived and was having a few after-dinner drinks with friends.

'Sammy daahling. Come and join us for a nightcap?' he asked. 'We're sitting at the table down the end.'

'Sure,' I replied. 'Love to.'

Just because Mands and Lizzie were leaving didn't mean I had to. His timing was perfect. Plus, I had arranged some downtime at work tomorrow morning, in anticipation of a foggy head. It would be a crying shame to waste it. I gave Lizzie and Mands a kiss goodbye and told them I was staying on. I approached Darcy's table and found him sitting with two men I'd never seen before.

'Sammy, this is Steve and Alistair,' introduced Darcy.

'Hello,' I replied, shaking both of their hands and simultaneously processing their appearance. Alistair was knicker-shatteringly handsome. Dark and swarthy, with a beautiful head of silky sun-streaked brown hair and luminous green eyes. Steve, although nowhere near as gorgeous, was still attractive with a very sexy smile.

'Now, what would you like to drink?' asked Darcy, pulling me out a chair. 'Champers?'

'Sounds great,' I replied. 'Thank you.'

'How's your night been?' asked Steve.

'Good,' I replied. 'Out with the girls. And yours?'

'Excellent,' replied Steve. 'Alistair and I have just been talking bar concepts with Darcy.'

'Well, you're talking to the right person,' I replied.

Perhaps they're a couple? I wondered. *More than likely.*

'I saw you and your friends on the way in,' said Alistair. 'I was trying to work up the courage to come and talk to you but, as it turns out, now I don't have to.'

Guess they're not gay then. He was a bit arrogant though. But, truth be told, I was rather fond of arrogant men. *God knows,* I thought, *if I'd known they were sitting down here I certainly wouldn't have been wasting my time standing at the front of the bar.*

'What do you do, Sam?' asked Steve.

'Sam is the hottest young account exec in town,' interrupted

Darcy, who had arrived back with my glass of champers.

'Really?' said Alistair.

'No,' I replied. 'He's clearly delusional.'

'No argument there,' laughed Alistair, giving Darcy a pat on the back.

As we chatted away I noticed two girls sitting at the opposite table who couldn't seem to peel their eyes off Alistair. There was no denying he was gorgeous, but they really were being a tad too obvious. About half an hour later their curiosity got the better of them and they approached our table.

'Mind if we join you?' asked the brunette.

'Not at all,' said Steve, gesturing to the empty seats.

Alistair shuffled his chair beside me to make some room. He gave the girls a polite nod hello and then leaned towards me to continue our conversation. I appeared to be penned in between Alistair and the wall. Not that I minded — if one was going to be penned in it really didn't get any better than this.

Darcy took the girl's arrival as his cue to leave. Apparently Samuel was at home with the flu and he was supposed to be playing nurse.

By now we were one of the only groups left in the bar. Steve also decided to head home and the two girls followed close behind, once they realised Alistair and I were far too busy talking to each other to bat them an eyelid. When they had left, Alistair leaned even further in towards me.

Ohmygod! I thought in horror. *I've been dribbling down my chin and now he's going to wipe it off.*

But he didn't. Instead he leaned in and gave me a very quick but lovely soft kiss on the lips.

'Wow!' I said, opening my eyes. I had been expecting a brush with a napkin, not with his lips.

He smiled cheekily at me and took another swig of his beer.

The delicious barman brought another champers and beer over to us and announced the bar was closing.

'What on earth are we going to do?' asked Alistair, finishing his beer.

'Well . . . we could always go back to my place,' I suggested, smiling sexily, or at least that's what I hoped it was.

This was not a suggestion I was in the habit of making to a man I had just met. It appeared the champers was significantly affecting my ability to be demure and alluring.

'Sounds like a brilliant idea to me,' said Alistair.

And with that we got up from the table, walked outside, and hailed a cab.

Just so you are aware, it was at this very point in time that my life stopped running smoothly, and instead began to career completely out of bloody control. If you had to pinpoint the precise moment that led me to have my arms up the cow's arse, then it would be this very one.

We were barely inside my front door before Alistair began kissing me ferociously.

Lord, he's a brilliant kisser, I thought to myself, as I ran my hands through his silky hair and down the back of his neck. Our tongues finally met, but not in that horrible kidnapping-your-tonsils kind of way, more of a tantalising brush, which instantly sent warm ripples hurtling down to my stomach. We frantically kissed our way onto the sofa, where Alistair expertly managed to keep kissing me and undo the zip at the back of my dress, sliding it off my shoulders and letting it fall down to my hips, leaving me sitting in what was, thankfully, a respectably sexy lacy black bra. I slid my hands up the inside of his shirt, across his smooth chest and down to his belt buckle, very slowly undoing it. He kissed my neck and ran his tongue along my earlobe, which very nearly sent the flutters out of my stomach and through the ceiling. Then he slid the palms of his hands very firmly down my breasts. And then down my arms to my hands, expertly lifting me up from the sofa. We stood pressed against each other with him still firmly holding both of my hands down by my sides. I loved it when a man took control of the situation.

'Are you going to show me to the bedroom? Or do I have to find it myself?' he asked, a mischievous and very sexy grin on his face.

'Follow me,' I said, stepping out of my dress and walking down the hallway. 'If you dare.'

He dared.

I sat on my bed and watched him unbutton his shirt. It appeared that his chest was not only silky smooth, but also very tanned and muscular. *He was no stranger to a gym*, I observed, liking what I saw. I couldn't have picked a finer specimen to break my drought with. His eyes followed mine down to his crotch, and the tell-tale bulge that strained against his jeans. He slipped them off and sidled up to the edge of the bed in his boxer shorts, pinning both of my arms back against the duvet.

'Now . . . where were we?' he asked, his breath hot on my neck.

I woke the next morning to the sound of rustling beside the bed. I opened my eyes a fraction and saw Alistair standing up and putting on his shirt.

'Off already?' I asked, looking at my alarm clock. It was only six-thirty.

'Sorry,' he replied. 'Early start.'

'You're not kidding.'

'Thanks for a great night, Sam,' he said, leaning in to stroke my cheek and give me a lingering kiss on the lips. 'I'll see you soon.'

'Bye,' I replied, in what I hoped was my very best I'm-still-sleeping-but-aren't-I-just-the-sexiest-little-thing voice. He walked out and I heard the front door close behind him.

I must have drifted back to sleep because the next thing I knew it was nine o'clock and I was not only incredibly late for work but also, I noted with mounting discomfort, incredibly hung over. I walked into the living room and found my dress hanging off the arm of the sofa, one heel in the kitchen and one sitting beside the front door.

Nothing like a bit of frantic lovemaking, I thought, picking them up.

Although, I suddenly realised Alistair hadn't left me a card. Or even a phone number for that matter.

Perhaps he wants to play hard to get? I thought. *Although that wasn't very manly.*

No doubt he'll just get my number from Darcy later on, I decided.

There was no doubting the fact I wanted to see him again. He was simply gorgeous. But he didn't ring me that day, or the day after that. However, when I arrived home from work two days later I received a much more sinister, lovely-life-shattering-into-crappy-little-pieces type of call.

5

'Is this Samantha?' asked a strange woman's voice.

'Yes,' I replied.

'Samantha, it's Mary Simperington speaking, from the *Daily Telegraph*. How are you?'

'Fine, thank you.'

'Samantha, I'm just ringing to have a wee chat about yourself and Alistair Ambrose.'

'Who?'

'Alistair Ambrose. I believe you know him . . . rather well it would seem.'

'Alistair Ambrose?'

The name sounded familiar but I was having serious trouble placing it.

'Yes. I'm just curious to know about your relationship with him.'

What the hell was this woman talking about? I wondered. The only Alistair I could think of was the one I'd shagged the other night and there was certainly no relationship there. I'd slept with the man once. Plus, he hadn't even called me.

'And what relationship might that be?' I asked.

'Well . . . you did leave Pure on Tuesday night with him, didn't you?'

'Yes.'

Bingo. So she did mean that Alistair then.

'And you did go home with him?'

'Well . . . yes . . . to my home. Why?'

Who was this woman? His mother? God, I really hoped not.

'Well . . . you do know Alistair is married, don't you? With his third child on the way.'

'Married?'

Ohmygod! It's his wife! God help me!

'I take it you're not an avid sport watcher then?' she asked.

Sport? What on earth was she on about?

'No. Why?'

'Football in particular?'

Football?

'No. Definitely not.'

'Perhaps you should follow it a bit more closely, my dear.'

What the hell was she talking about? What did me shagging Alistair have to do with football?

'Anyway, I just rang to say that when you're willing to talk to the papers I'm offering you an exclusive front-pager. Your own story.'

'My *story?*'

It looked as though this wasn't his wife. Or his mother for that matter.

'That's right,' she replied. 'And before you ask, yes, we are prepared to pay a significant sum. Providing you don't talk to anyone else of course.'

'Talk to anyone else?'

'Any of the other papers, love. They'll all be after you now.'

'After me?'

'Anyway, you can reach me at the paper. Give me a call when you've had a chance to think it over, and we'll talk dollars.'

I hung up, my jaw gaping, as I stared at the receiver.

What in God's name was happening here?

I attempted to collect myself and dialled Mands' number with my shaking hands.

'*Tell me* you know who Alistair Ambrose is?' I gushed.

'Alistair Ambrose? You mean the footballer? Captain of the national team?'

'*Oh God*,' I moaned. 'Do you know what he looks like?'

'*Phwoar!* Course I do! Sexy, saucy dark stallion that he is. Why?'

'Because . . . because I think I might have shagged him.'

'*You* shagged *Alistair Ambrose? Ohmygod!*'

'Possibly. Does he have olive skin and green eyes?'

'Yes.'

'About six foot?'

'A little over I think.'

'Dark, silky brown hair with sun streaks?'

'Tick.'

'Perfect white teeth.'

'Spot on. The man is sex on sticks.'

'Oh. Dear. God.'

'*Cripes!* Was that the Alistair you were going on about?'

'It appears so.'

'You lucky cow! And you didn't *know* who he *was*?'

'No.'

'Bloody hell Sam! I know you have no interest in sport, but it's Alistair Ambrose. How can you not know who he is? The man's famous, for God's sake!'

'Well, I knew the name. I just didn't know what he looked like.'

'Well, now you do! Rather well too.'

'Yes, it would appear so. Thank you.'

'Shit Sam! He's *married,* and he's got *kids,* and Christ! I think his wife's *pregnant.*'

'I know.'

'You know?'

'A woman from the *Daily Telegraph* just rang me.'

'What did she want?'

'An interview.'

'Did you deny everything?'

'Not exactly.'

'You mean you told her you shagged him?'

'No . . . not exactly . . . but she knew I'd taken him home with me.'

'How the hell did she know that?'

'I have absolutely no idea.'

'Bet it's those bloody paparazzi stalkers. They never leave the poor footballers alone. Hell! What are you going to do?'

'Christ knows.'

'Alistair Ambrose, I don't bloody *believe* it!'

'Trust me,' I replied. 'Neither do I.'

'Well . . . hopefully she was the only hack who got a whiff and the rest will leave you alone.'

'Oh God, I really hope so.'

'Bloody hell! What a wanker! Cheating on his poor wife like that.'

'Mands please!'

'Sorry, guess that kind of makes you the other woman, doesn't it?'

'Oh great! Now I'm a marriage-wrecker.'

'No you're not, dolls! You didn't even know who he was. He's the arsehole! I thought he was such a nice bloke too.'

'So did I.'

'Oh you poor thing! What crap luck!'

'Appalling.'

'That's it. I'm straight round after work for hugs. And wine.'

'You'd better be.'

I arrived home from work to find both Mands and Lizzie already standing in my kitchen, having let themselves in with their keys. Lizzie was opening a bottle of wine. They took one look at the state of me and promptly embraced me in a four-armed hug cocoon.

'He had no bloody wedding ring on!' I cried, collapsing onto the sofa.

'I know. I know,' comforted Mands, rubbing my back.

'How the hell was I supposed to know?'

'You weren't, you weren't,' they chorused.

'Bloody hell!

'Yes,' they agreed. 'Bloody hell.'

It was Lizzie who was supposed to shag married men, not me! In thirty-three years I had managed to avoid doing just this (or to my knowledge anyway). It's fair to say I wasn't high on morals, but not shagging married men was one of them. And I was proud of it. Now it looked as though all of my good work had been undone.

The next morning I woke to my alarm, as per usual, and for those fleeting few seconds of lovely un-realisation, I was under the impression it was just another morning. That I would get up, have a shower, get dressed, and drive to the office. And

112

that I hadn't shagged Alistair Ambrose, the married captain of the national football team. But then I came to.

Maybe it'll be over and done with by now, I thought to myself. Hopefully that newspaper woman was the only other person who knew, aside from Mands and Lizzie of course. I walked over to the window and drew the blinds, glancing out to check the state of the day. But, I didn't get that far because my eyes were somewhat distracted by the sea of bright flashing bulbs which greeted my sleepy gaze. I lunged back onto the bed, temporarily blinded.

God help me! I thought in horror. *There are twenty photographers standing outside my front gate. This cannot be happening!*

I immediately dialled Lizzie.

'Problem,' I said. 'Very, very big problem.'

'Morning,' said Lizzie. 'Forgot to pick suit up from drycleaners?'

'No. Twenty paparazzi currently standing outside gate waiting for me like pack of demented blood-hungry wolves.'

'Jesus!'

'Exactly. Although he won't be helping me to get out of the house. What the hell am I going to do?'

'Let me think a minute . . . Right,' she replied, after a mere couple of seconds. 'You simply have to get dressed and go to work as normal.'

'You mean leave the house?' I asked.

'That's right.'

'Is that the best you can come up with?'

'You have to act normal, sweets. And innocent. Otherwise they'll keep you holed up in your apartment for days. They're not going to leave. They've been known to survive for weeks without food or water.'

I had a shower, put on my grey suit, and stood beside my front door, bracing myself for the impact on the other side.

You are innocent, I told myself. *Innocent! You had no idea who he was. Or that he was married.*

I opened the front door as normally as I could with violently shaking hands and jelly-like legs and stepped outside.

Just act normal, I told myself. *Don't run. Or panic. It's just any other day and you're off to the office. Oh for God's sake, who are you kidding? There are twenty fucking paparazzi standing at your front gate. There is nothing remotely normal about this day. Whatsoever. At least don't forget to smile. If they're going to print your picture you don't want to be left looking like someone's mean old aunt who hides all the chocolate biscuits and just puts out the Vanilla Wines.*

'Samantha!' they called out, as I approached the gate, which was thankfully nice and high and required a security code to pass through. 'Over here!'

'How's Alistair?' called another couple.

I forced a smile. I had no bloody idea how Alistair was. Dead for all I hoped. Killed in some freak airborne vegetable scenario. Cucumber-wedged-through-the-side-of-the-head type thing. I managed a real smile at the thought.

'C'mon Samantha!' called another couple, as I walked out of my front gate and through the bustling sea of cameras. 'Tell us something!'

'No comment,' I replied, as I briskly walked across the footpath to my parked car and hopped inside as quickly as I could, cameras still incessantly flashing at me.

My car was a lovely new silver Mini Cooper. I loved My Car.

'Wow!' Izzy, the receptionist, had declared upon her first sighting. 'It's hot!'

'You think so?' I asked.

'Hell yeah!'

Izzy knew a thing or two about cars. She was a twenty-three-year-old peroxide-headed Girl Racer. She herself drove a modified black Mazda hatchback, which sounded exactly like a Boeing 747 at lift off, and which sat approximately three inches from the ground. It was not difficult to tell when Izzy was running late for work, or if she was leaving early. It had a muffler the size of a small ship's flue.

'It's definitely a fashion statement,' my mother had said. 'If that's what you're after of course.'

'Maybe I want to drive an attractive car?' I'd protested.

'Vehicles are for getting from A to B Samantha. Nothing more. Nothing less. And it's not very practical, is it?' she said, eyeing up the miniscule backseat, as Dad had circled around the car, gingerly touching the paintwork.

'It's not supposed to be,' I'd replied, staring back at her.

Just because my mother drove an old Land Rover, she thought the sole purpose of cars was ugliness and practicality.

Just relax, I told myself, as my heart practically beat its way out of my Karen Walker suit. *Start the car and drive off. Slowly.*

I did as I was told, leaving a blinding sea of flashes in my wake. But I wasn't the only one to hop into my car and drive off. I looked in my rearview mirror only to find two Land Rovers and three motorbikes hot on my heels.

Oh for fucksake! This is ridiculous!

Just stay calm, I said aloud. *Don't let them do a Di on you.* Thankfully there were no tunnels on the way to work, I remembered, so I should be safe. I drove as fast as I could through the city streets, without crashing the car or running anyone over. My little Mini was finally getting the road test it deserved, although I was unable to shake my pursuers. Finally I skidded to a halt outside the car-park entrance and swiped my card as quickly as I could. *Just don't drop the card*, I prayed, as the harassment convoy pulled up behind me. Thankfully I didn't and the grill gate opened up in front of me. With squealing tyres I drove into the basement car park as the Land Rovers and motorbikes were left on the other side.

No time for a latte this morning, I told myself, as I headed for the lift. *Just get your carcass inside that office.*

Sweating and out of breath, I ran into my office and slammed the door. Thankfully the only person I passed was Izzy, who took one look at me and decided it best to say nothing. I collapsed into my chair, the *Morning Sun* waiting for me on my desk.

Oh dear God! I thought, as I unfolded the paper and stared at the front page. *It just gets worse.*

There, under the colossal banner CAUGHT IN THE ACT! were a series of close-up and over-sized pictures of Alistair leaving my apartment building the morning after our rendezvous. The entire front page was covered in them. There he was, post-extramarital-shag-fest, leaving the scene of the crime. Post-coital glow gleaming off his tanned face. *The smug bastard!* And there, under the photos, was a small story about him leaving my apartment. And there, written in the story, was . . . was my name, Samantha Steel. *Bloody hell!*

How? I wondered. *How in God's name?*

'Sam,' said Gareth, poking his head inside my office a short while later, 'do you know anything about the horde of photographers waiting outside the building? They seem to be asking for you.'

'No,' I lied.

Obviously Gareth hadn't seen the newspaper yet, and there was no point in me hurrying along the carnage. I promptly set about cancelling the three external meetings I had that day. There was no way in hell I was leaving the building if they were waiting outside for me.

What was I going to do? I wondered. My phone rang. Unfortunately someone else had seen the paper. My father.

'Love, it's your father here,' he said, when I answered.

For some reason he thought I didn't recognise his voice after thirty-three years.

'I'm just looking at the newspaper and I've seen your name on the front page.'

'Aha.'

I could have lied and said it wasn't me. It was just my name and not my picture on the page after all. I could have pinned it on another Samantha Steel out there somewhere. But there was something about my father which made it very difficult to lie. Impossible even. How many times had I concocted the most brilliant lies as a teenager. Stories with fantastic imaginary characters, brilliant trails of believable events, and a completely blame-free ending for myself. How I'd stood in my bedroom and practised the stories over and over again in front of the mirror and then walked into the living room, only for Dad to ask, 'Samantha, did you take my car and drive into town with your friends today?' and me to answer, 'Yes, we went to the mall. And then to McDonalds for lunch. And then we went to the movies.'

'Is it you?' he asked.

'Yes,' I replied. 'Unfortunately.'

'Are you seeing this Alistair bloke?' he asked.

'No,' I replied. 'It was just a . . .'

I was about to say 'one night stand' and then thankfully

thought the better of it. These were not three words I was in the habit of uttering to my father.

'. . . a casual thing,' I finished.

'I see,' he said.

'Dad, would you believe me if I told you I didn't know who he was?'

If there was one person in this world who grasped the fact I avoided watching sport like the plague, it was my father. How many times had he tried to get me to sit down on the couch with him and feign some interest in the cricket, only to have me profess a sudden love of homework and declare 'I'd really better get cracking'?

'Yes love, I would.'

'And I didn't know he was married?'

'Yes.'

This was an extremely uncomfortable conversation to find yourself in the middle of with your father. I was sure that in some small gold-gilded and white-linen compartment of his brain he honestly thought my sisters and I were still virgins. Even Vicky, who was pregnant. Although it was uncomfortable for both of us, I filled him in on where I had met Alistair, who we were with, and that, yes, he had come back to my apartment. I decided it best not to fill him in on how we tore each other's clothes off all about the place, how he chewed my nipples with his front teeth until I begged him to fuck me, how we had sex twice within the space of half an hour, and how I hadn't had an orgasm like that since the time I had a threesome in a spa pool at the Hilton with two men whose names escape me. Dad filled me in on how Alistair was one of the most versatile and high-scoring football players this country had ever seen. How he was the glue which held the team together, and how he (Dad) was confident this was going to be our best season yet. I pretended to be interested. It was the least I could do considering he'd been so understanding about me shagging him and all.

'He's obviously a bloody rogue though,' added Dad. 'Cheating on his poor wife like that.'

'Yes. Thanks.'

This was not something I really needed reminding about.

'Sorry love,' he added. 'I didn't mean . . .'

'It's OK Dad, I know. Has Elizabeth seen it?' I asked, hoping like hell she hadn't.

When I was fifteen years old my mother had asked the three of us if we would kindly stop calling her Mum. She wanted to be called by her Christian name, Elizabeth.

'Why?' I had asked, 'It's weird.'

'Because the word Mum is synonymous with the stereotype of the homemaker and child-rearer. And I am not just these things. I am a whole person.'

From that day on there was a Mum jar placed on top of the fridge. Where other families had a swear jar, we placed ten cents in the Mum jar every time we called our mother Mum.

'No,' said Dad. 'She left at the crack of dawn this morning. Something about standing on the Symonds Street overpass with a banner. I think it's about the right to breast-feed in public again,' he added.

'I think I saw her on the way to work,' I realised. 'Huge banner with loads of breasts?'

'That's the one.'

'She'd gathered quite a crowd,' I added. 'Was doing a great job of slowing down traffic on the motorway too.'

'It'll be OK, love,' comforted Dad, snapping me back to the present. 'You made a mistake but I'm sure it'll all blow over soon.'

I hoped he was right. But for someone who was annoyingly right a good portion of the time, this premonition was to be his downfall. The only saving grace was my mother hadn't seen my name in the newspaper yet.

I gave Izzy some money and asked her to fetch me a latte and a blueberry muffin from the café on the corner.

'Holy cow!' she exclaimed upon her return. 'I didn't think I was going to get back in alive! It's the weirdest thing,' she continued. 'There's a whole lot of paparazzi out there asking for you.'

'I know,' I replied.

'Oh,' said Izzy, looking rather perplexed. Clearly she hadn't seen the paper either.

'What did you tell them?' I asked.

'I told them to fuck off and let me back in the door or I was going to spill the coffee.'

'Thanks Izzy,' I replied, giving her a smile. 'I think the best tactic is to just ignore them.'

'Bit hard to ignore them when they're rubbing up against your breasts,' she replied, smiling back at me.

'Don't know anything about it, eh Sam?' said Gareth, once again standing in my doorway an hour later, newspaper in his hands. He appeared to be smiling also.

'No,' I replied. 'Nothing at all.'

Once he realised he wasn't going to get another word out of me, he very wisely left me alone. I spent the rest of the day trapped inside my office, with Izzy kindly running the gauntlet and fetching me some lunch. This time one of the paparazzi actually squeezed her left breast.

'If I didn't have my hands full of muffins I would have punched him in the face,' she declared. 'But I could only use my elbow.'

My only solace were phone calls from Mands and Lizzie,

both of whom had of course seen the newspaper.

'He's a bastard,' they comforted. 'A slimy arse-licking pig of a man. But,' they added, 'he's also incredibly foxy and famous and you should be very proud of yourself.'

But I didn't feel proud of myself, at all. I just felt as though I'd made a terrible mistake. I also felt increasingly irritated at being harassed, photographed and chased. Although I couldn't see them I knew they were there, like crouching tigers, just waiting to pounce. I had a horrible feeling this was just the beginning, that the paparazzi were never going to leave me in peace, at least not for a long while yet. The other thing was I just knew Alistair must do this sort of thing all the time, of course he did, but I was the only one unlucky enough to be caught. Somehow this made me feel worse.

At seven o'clock I plucked up the courage to venture home, where Mands and Lizzie were meeting me for a session of crisis management. As I drove out of the underground car park there were four paparazzi waiting at the entrance for me, the same four who had chased me this morning.

Don't tell me they've been waiting there all day? I thought to myself. *Eleven hours? Standing outside a car park?* Lizzie was right, they definitely had staying power. Even the city's beggars gave up after half a day.

'Samantha!' they called out as I sped past and flashes bounced off the car windows. I was unable to cover my face, due to the fact my hands were required on the steering wheel. However, I was confident I would have been nothing more than a human blur.

Within seconds they were on their motorbikes and chasing me.

Oh for fucksake! I thought to myself, looking in the rearview mirror. *Go home and have dinner or something!* Didn't any of them have wives or girlfriends? *Probably not,* I decided.

Who in their right mind would go out with someone who stood outside a car-park building for eleven hours?

I sped home through the city streets with the motorbikes hot on my heels. They were, once again, completely unshakable. As I approached my apartment building I could see a pack of another ten or so waiting outside the front gate for me.

How did they know I'd come back? I wondered. *Who's to say I hadn't suddenly jumped on a plane and hightailed it to Budapest? Presumptuous bastards! Surely there were more newsworthy stories for them to be chasing? Informative stories that people actually wanted to read about? How could this one tiny indiscretion possibly make the grade?*

I opened the security gates from my car device, as they shouted, tapped the glass and flashed their bulbs at me. There was no way I was parking out on the street again and having to walk past them in the morning. I sat with my sunglasses on, staring straight ahead and attempting to ignore the chaos around me, willing the gates to get a fucking move on and open. As soon as there was a Mini-sized gap I sped through. They didn't dare follow me, although I really wished they would, so I could ring the police and have them arrested for trespassing.

Within half an hour Mands was on my doorstep.

'Jesus Christ! Open the bloody door!' she hollered. 'They're going to eat me alive.'

I opened the door and Mands fell inside, a sea of flashing light in her wake.

'Mother of God!' she exclaimed, leaning her back against the door. 'They're unbelievable!'

'Tell me about it,' I agreed, as she embraced me in a big hug.

'Right, first things first,' she said, as she bustled into the kitchen and plonked a bottle of wine down on the bench, opening it straightaway.

As she was pouring us each a glass there was more furtive knocking on the front door.

'Who is it?' I asked, wary of the possibilities.

'It's Lizzie! For God's sake open the bloody door! They're blinding me!'

I swung open the door, careful to hide behind it as Lizzie collapsed inside.

'Bastards!' she hissed, clearly a bit riled. 'If they lay a finger on any of us I'm gonna sue their arses!'

'What am I going to do?' I wailed, as the three of us sat in my living room, wine in hand.

'I don't know, dolls,' said Mands. 'I don't think there's anything you can do. You can either stay holed up in your apartment twenty-four-seven. Or you can go to work, carry on as normal, and wait for them to get sick of you.'

'How long's that going to take?' I asked, suddenly feeling very depressed at my limited options.

'I don't know,' said Mands. 'Probably just until they find someone or something else to latch onto.'

'Or you can jump on a plane,' suggested Lizzie. 'And flee overseas somewhere, only . . .'

'Only what?' This sounded like a great idea, the best so far.

'Only then it'll look like you've done something wrong. Like you're running away.'

'But I haven't done anything wrong,' I protested, sinking my head into my hands. 'I didn't know he was married.'

'We know you haven't, dolls,' said Mands, putting her arm around my shoulder. 'But that's what it would look like. It'd look like you were ashamed of something.'

I didn't want to look like I had something to be ashamed of, when I really didn't. It was just a case of mistaken identity, mixed in with a bit of mistaken availability.

'I guess I'll just have to stick it out then,' I sighed. 'If I don't get fired first.'

'Right then,' said Mands, opening up a shopping bag she'd brought with her. 'I've got something for you.'

I desperately hoped she was going to whip out some valium, uppers, or some other mind-enhancing drug that would make me feel better. Instead she pulled out an enormous pair of dark sunglasses.

'What're these?' I asked.

'These are your new glasses,' she replied.

'My new glasses?'

'Your celebrity glasses.'

Clearly, without either my knowledge or consent, Mands had decided to take on the role of my agent. It looked as though I was going to be her first client. The celebrity guinea pig. There's no doubting the role of Alistair Ambrose Crisis Management would be a sterling addition to her budding CV.

'They're impenetrable,' she added.

I think she was referring to the gigantic pitch-black lenses.

'You're to wear these every time you leave the house, or office for that matter. The maggots might know where you live and work, and recognise your car, but at least they won't be able to see your expression.'

I tried the glasses on. It appeared they wouldn't be able to see much else either. The glasses were so enormous they appeared to have eaten most of my face.

'Very Liz Hurley,' observed Lizzie.

I ran to the bathroom mirror for a second opinion. I looked more like Jackie O.

'You only need to wear them in transit,' comforted Mands.

'You could always dye your hair blonde too,' she added. 'But there's really no point in doing that unless you shift house.'

'Shift house?' I asked.

Why would I want to shift house? I loved my apartment.

'You know,' said Mands, as though I did in fact know, 'if things don't settle down you might have to change abodes.'

'But that is the very, very worst-case scenario,' added Lizzie, noting my distress at this revelation. 'And I'm sure it'll all blow over soon and you won't have to move anywhere.'

The following morning I climbed out of bed and gently eased up the corner of the blind, cautiously glancing out my bedroom window in the vain hope that yesterday was a one-off hallucinatory nightmare and that today my front gate would be clear of all obtrusive persons. But, as flashing lights immediately began exploding, it was evident it wasn't. And to make matters worse, they appeared to have multiplied. I had a shower, put on my suit and enormous sunglasses, and prepared myself for the onslaught waiting for me at the gate.

Surely they'll get sick of taking photos of me driving, I thought to myself, as I waited for the gates to open and sped past the thirty or so bodies clustered in front of them. *It wasn't very exciting to look at.* Once again they fired flashes at the car, tapped on the windows, and yelled stupid questions at me. I was very close to running one of them over, but unfortunately he dove out of the way in the nick of time. Once again I hurtled down the street with vehicles in hot pursuit, this time three Land Rovers and five motorbikes. It appeared they had upped the ante. I drove even faster than yesterday morning, but they were still unshakable.

I hope the lot of them get speeding tickets, I thought to myself, before realising it would probably be me who got pulled over first, since I was at the front. I slowed down slightly. If I wasn't going to shake them, there was no point putting my life at risk. There were three more waiting for me at the car-park entrance. More flashing as I sped through. But I was safe, at last. At least for a while.

I bolted for my office and sat down at my desk, petrified to look at the newspaper which lay before me. Since yesterday morning my relationship with the newspaper had shifted dramatically. Once, not so long ago, I had flipped it open eagerly, keen to digest the day's news and business inside. Now I sat staring at it, afraid of what new personal disasters it may hold. In the end curiosity got the better of fear and I looked at the front page. I really wished I hadn't. There, beside yet another large picture of Alistair leaving my apartment, and yet another story about our rendezvous, was a large picture of me from yesterday morning, enormous sunglasses on and attempting to smile as I walked out my front gate, but instead looking remarkably as though I had just swallowed a large plate of haggis. And there, beside my grimacing face, was yet another picture. A picture of Mr and Mrs Alistair Ambrose, together, smiling and happy.

Obviously not a recent shot, I thought.

I forced myself to take a good look at her, this pretty, blonde, petite, perfectly manicured woman in her mid-thirties. This woman whose husband I had inadvertently shagged. *I didn't know*, I said to the newsprint face. *Honestly I didn't.*

But that wasn't the worst of it. There was another large photo of me on the front of the sports section, right beside a picture of Alistair jumping about on the football field in his tracksuit, clearly not all that happy with having his photo taken either, under the heading 'Build-up to the World Cup'. *The World Cup!* Even I knew what this was. *Oh God, I thought in horror, no wonder the media were having a field day. They were never going to leave me alone now.* Apparently the World Cup was less than two months away and the team had well and truly begun their training. *Two whole months away? Why the hell hadn't my father told me this?* I wondered. *And why couldn't I have shagged him in the off-season?* It just wasn't bloody fair.

Within half an hour my mother was on the phone.

'Well,' she said when I picked up the receiver. 'Looks like someone's been busy.'

I waited for her to finish. I knew only too well there was absolutely no point in stopping her when she was on a roll.

'I can't say I'm exactly proud,' she continued. 'But at least some good might come from people recognising your face.'

Some good?

'You'd be a great person to have on protests. Perhaps you could even handcuff yourself to a billboard for our plight?'

At this suggestion I simply had to interrupt.

'Elizabeth, I will never in my lifetime handcuff myself to a billboard. It is just something I am simply not interested in doing.'

'That's a shame,' she replied. 'You'd really get people's attention now.'

I filled her in on the fact I didn't know who Alistair was, or that he was married.

'Scumbag!' she spat. 'Someone should chop his pecker off!'

She hadn't finished.

'These sportsmen think they can go around sleeping with

whoever they want and cheating on their wives. And you know what?'

'What?' I asked.

'They always get off scot-free. Always! And it's the wives and the women they sleep with who are left looking like whores.'

'Fabulous. Thank you.'

'Sorry. But that's the way it is, I'm afraid.'

'I just wish I'd never met him,' I sighed.

'It's not your fault, Samantha,' she said. 'It's the media's fault. They're sexist bigots and they will always, always, take the side of a famous man. It really gets my goat.'

And it was getting her goat too. Strangling it in fact.

'But it's nice not to be the only one in the newspaper,' she added.

My mother had been photographed leading chanting throngs, attached to billboards, and naked from the waist up more times than it was safe to remember.

Shortly after hanging up the phone from Mum, Susie called.

'Bloody hell!' she cried. 'Well done you!'

It appeared she thought I was to be congratulated for something.

'For what?' I asked. 'Being on the front page of the paper?'

'No, you ninny! For shagging Alistair Ambrose. What a bloody spunk!'

'Oh.'

'I can't believe it,' she continued. 'My sister shagged Alistair Ambrose. Fantastic!'

'It's not fantastic,' I replied. 'Really it's not.'

'Yes it is!' she cried. 'Think how many women out there would just love to shag him, myself included, and you've done it. Amazing! Wish it was me though,' she added.

'But then you'd be on the front of the paper,' I pointed out.

'True,' she agreed. 'It isn't exactly a great picture, is it?'

Susie's one major flaw was her honesty and inability to lie, even when it really was in her best interest to do so.

'No,' I replied, wincing at the picture in front of me. 'It isn't.'

'So?' she asked.

'So what?'

'So, what was he like in the sack?'

I couldn't lie to Susie, even though I now hated Alistair with a vengeance.

'Brilliant,' I replied, remembering the big Night of Adultery. 'Sexy as all hell.'

'Are you going to see him again?' she asked.

'Are you joking?'

'Well no . . . actually I wasn't.'

'No,' I replied. 'I will not be seeing him again. Ever.'

'Crying shame,' said Susie. 'P'haps you could give me his number then?'

'I don't think so,' I replied. 'Now bugger off, I've got work to do.'

'OK,' she said, realising she was pushing it. 'But just remember that no matter what anyone says, you should be proud of yourself for bagging him.'

'Thank you . . .' I replied, although proud was not a word I was currently associating with myself. '. . . I think.'

Vicky was the final family member to ring me that day, in the early afternoon. I was surprised she'd seen the paper at all. Newspapers weren't generally her first choice of reading material. She preferred *Women's Life* and *Modern Woman*, good solid housewife manuals. Subsequently she was a brilliant and bottomless source of celebrity gossip. Of course she knew everything about Alistair, right down to the names of his two children (Joshua, aged six, and Harry, aged four), and his parents (Hugh and Sylvia), and how many months pregnant his wife Virginia was (four).

'Vicky,' I protested. 'You know what?'

'What?'

'I'm really not that interested.'

But she was having none of it. She even knew he had a small scar on the left side of his neck.

'I could have told you that,' I said.

'His poor wife,' she sighed. 'Not that you knew he was married, of course,' she added quickly. Trust Vicky to take the side of the wife, being that she was one herself.

'Who's to say she isn't out there bagging anything that moves?' I said.

'Oh no, definitely not,' replied Vicky. 'I can tell. Plus,' she added, 'it's impossible to bag anything when you're pregnant, believe me.'

I spent the rest of the day holed up in my office, conducting meetings over the phone, with Izzy kindly running the gauntlet again so I didn't starve to death.

Enormous sunglasses on I decided to head to the gym after work, in an attempt to avoid the pack of vultures who would inevitably be waiting outside my apartment. Four motorbikes in hot pursuit I pulled into the gym car park which was, thankfully, also a secure underground car park with swipe-card entry.

Now you can relax, I told myself, taking a couple of deep breaths. I felt secure in the knowledge the gym was not dissimilar to Fort Knox. You had to swipe your card at least ten times from the car park to the treadmill. If your membership fee was overdue by no more than five minutes you were literally pounced upon, handcuffed, and escorted from the premises. I was confident that with the sunglasses off, my hair tied back in a ponytail, a cap pulled firmly down over my eyes and sports gear on I would look unrecognisable to any nosy punters. And, apart from the odd stare (where the person thinks they recognise you then realise they don't and avert their eyes so sharply they almost dislodge their head) I was left in insignificant peace.

After an hour-long work out (made slightly longer by the fact I had no desire to ever leave the building and was contemplating setting up home at the gym) I had a shower, got changed back into my suit and enormous glasses, and headed home.

Much to my relief the vultures were not waiting outside the gym car park, as I expected they would be. Presumably they had come to the conclusion that if they didn't go and get something to eat they would in fact die. But, as I sat in my office two cat-and-mouse (with me being the mouse) days later and looked at the morning paper, it was evident they had left me alone for another reason altogether. Unlike the day before, which showed the usual pictures of me driving out my gates in the morning, ginormous sunglasses barricading my face, and arriving at the office, this morning's paper had a distinctly sport and recreation feel to it. There, on the front page, were two large full-colour pictures of me. At the gym. Inside the gym to be exact. The first one showed me on the treadmill, looking sweaty, beet in the face, and generally in severe pain. And the second picture showed me on the leg-extension machine. With a cluster of cellulite clearly visible on the inside of my upper left thigh. *Mother of God!* Judging by the slightly grainy quality of the pictures it appeared someone at the gym had sold me out, via a video-surveillance camera by the looks of things.

I bet it was that blonde bimbo with the fake tits and orange face, I thought to myself. *The one on reception.* She was always calling me back to re-swipe my card for no good reason.

I slumped my head down onto my desk and realised there was nothing else for it. I began to cry. Proper cry. I cried until a river of mascara washed down over the newsprint. I cried because I didn't even know I had a cluster of cellulite at the top of my left thigh. And I cried because now I was going to turn into a human sized piece of Play-Doh, who couldn't go to the gym because someone would just sell her pictures to the papers. I cried until Lizzie rang on my mobile.

'I am never going to the fucking gym again!' I wailed. 'I am going to turn into a fat heifer!'

'Oh dolls,' she comforted. 'It's not that bad . . . really.'

'Lizzie!' I ordered. 'I am one half of your best friends. Do *not* lie to me!'

'OK,' she replied. 'You're right. It's a fucking disaster, dolls. The absolute bastards!'

More crying.

'Why don't you go home for the rest of the day?' she suggested.

'Because they'll be waiting for me at home,' I cried. 'There's no escaping!'

'Right. Well I'm going to finish up at lunchtime then and I'm going to come and get you and bring you round to my house. Where I'll kick their arses if they go so far as to glance at my front gate.'

6

The next day at work, post national cellulite disclosure, I had a phone call from *Woman's Life*, wanting to write an article about Alistair and I.

'It'd be completely from your point of view,' assured Linda, the assistant editor. 'You could talk about what it's really like to be the other woman.'

'The other what?' I asked.

'The other woman.'

That's what I thought she'd said. If there's one thing I would never be in my lifetime, that was an Other Woman.

'Look Cindy . . .'

'Linda,' she corrected.

'Yes, I know. Look Linda, I will never ever be the Other Woman. And another thing I will never ever do is sell my story to a crappy piece of crack-filler like your magazine. Goodbye!'

Fabulous, I thought to myself, hanging up the phone. *As if it wasn't bad enough the media had my home number, now they knew my work one too.*

Woman's Life wasn't the only trashy magazine to ring up and request an interview. Over the next few days I had calls from all of them. *Women Today, Star Weekly, Her, Modern*

Woman, the lot. All promising an exclusive story, all wanting me to talk about Alistair, and all receiving the same response from me.

In retrospect I possibly should have been a bit nicer to Linda/Cindy at *Woman's Life* because when the following week's issue hit the newsstands there was none other than guess who on the cover? Go on, take a guess. That's right, Mrs Virginia bloody Ambrose herself. Looking immaculate and fabulous and pregnant and more than willing to talk about how I had ruined her life, her husband's life and, naturally, her children's lives too. It was a sob story, in the best hanky-wringing sense of the words. Initially I had felt sorry for this woman. I had even felt guilty for my role in her devastation. But now I just hated her.

Throughout the whole air-brushed four-page spread there was not one mention of how this whole thing was completely her husband's fault. Not one. But there were plenty of comments about why it was entirely my fault. There was no doubt in her mind that I had thrown myself at her husband (he was always getting women throwing themselves at him apparently). I also had 'no respect for the sanctity of marriage' and was just a 'floozy' who was really no different from a 'prostitute' in her books. *A prostitute?* Here was her husband who had knowingly cheated on her (which he'd no doubt done gazillions of times previously) getting off scot-free and I was a *prostitute?* The woman was a logic abyss.

She herself was 'an emotional wreck' and 'trying to cope' and of course, 'devastated'.

She had no idea what devastated was. Devastated was going out to a bar with your two best friends, thinking you've met a foxy available man, taking him back to your apartment and innocently shagging him, only to have your life and privacy completely violated by the country's media and the entire nation hating you. That constituted devastated.

'The bloody fucking cow!' I howled, as Mands and Lizzie sat in my living room that evening, looking at the article. 'I want to beat her pretty blonde head in.'

'We all do,' they comforted. 'With a hammer.'

'One each,' added Mands.

'Let's find a physical flaw and make up a horrible name for her,' suggested Lizzie, in an attempt to cheer me up.

After umming and ahhing and scanning the several photographs for twenty minutes the best we could come up with was Tiny Tits. They weren't even that tiny, it's just that we were struggling for imperfections.

'She's like some sort of human Barbie doll,' I complained. 'She's even got perfect ears.'

'Air-brushing,' comforted Mands. 'I'm sure she's a complete mole in the flesh.'

The next morning the vultures at the front gate were able to expand their repertoire of repetitive and inane questions. Instead of 'Give us a smile Samantha!' and 'Tell us what Alistair's like in the sack!' they were now able to yell out 'What do you think of Virginia Ambrose calling you a prostitute?' and 'What's it like being labelled a floozy?' The sort of questions anyone would just love to be yelled at first thing in the morning.

Later that day, after seething and stewing over being publicly slandered by Tiny Tits, I decided there was only one thing for it. I was going to have to sell my story to the media. But there was no way I was taking my face on national television, or lowering myself to the filthy depths of a trashy magazine. It would have to be the newspaper. I phoned Mary Simperington from the *Daily Telegraph*.

'I'm ready to talk,' I said.

'Fantastic,' she replied, as though she had been expecting

my call. 'We can offer you a full-page section cover and of course there will be a figure to discuss. As long as we have the exclusive of course. You haven't talked to anyone else?' she pressed.

'No.'

'Right then, let's meet as soon as possible to go over the agreement and set a time for the interview. How are you placed today?'

Before I could blink she was on my doorstep, contract in her hack hands. Clearly I was a hot potato she had no intention of letting slip off her dinner plate. I read through the agreement, which seemed fairly straightforward, and then stopped dead at the figure. It was fifteen thousand dollars. I had absolutely no idea whether this was a good figure or not but it seemed ridiculous. I was going to be paid fifteen thousand dollars to talk to a journalist for one hour. One hour. And to have my picture taken. I had absolutely no idea why celebrities hated doing interviews. *How could you possibly hate this?*

We scheduled the interview for two days time.

I decided to phone Jenna Griffin in the hope that with nearly twenty years' experience of interviewing people to a pulp, she might be able to give me some much needed advice. She agreed to come round to my apartment the following evening after work. She also thankfully refrained from requesting an interview herself. She was on my side after all.

'You have to think about your strategy,' she said on the phone. 'You have to know exactly what she's going to ask you and exactly what your answers will be. Ask her for a copy of her questions so you can prepare yourself.'

'Really?' This surprised me.

'Yes,' replied Jenna. 'And if you're not happy with any of them you can choose not to answer. She'll try and push you to answer all of them though, so you need to be ready for this.'

I asked Mary Simperington to email me her question list and eventually she obliged.

'Bloody hell!' cried Jenna, stumbling through my front door. 'They're the worst I've seen. Barely human.'

'You're not kidding,' I replied, pulling her inside and getting temporarily blinded in the process.'

'A hundred bucks says I'll be on the front tomorrow too,' said Jenna, taking off her coat. She was spot on.

'Right then,' she declared, sitting me down on my sofa and taking the chair opposite, question list in hand. 'We need to have a practice run.'

'OK,' she began. 'Tell me what happened between you and Alistair Ambrose that infamous night two weeks ago?'

'We met at a bar in town. We had a few drinks together. And then we went back to my apartment and had sex,' I replied.

'No you didn't,' said Jenna.

'Yes we did,' I replied. 'It was good too.'

We definitely did.

'*I* know you did but that is something which the public does *not* need to know.'

'You mean I lie?'

'No,' replied Jenna. 'I mean there's no need for you to give her every single detail. Your answer should be *I met Alistair Ambrose at a bar in town, we sat down and had a few drinks together after my friends had left, and then we went back to my apartment.* End of story.'

'But everyone knows I shagged him,' I protested.

'No,' said Jenna. 'Everyone *thinks* you shagged him. There's a big difference. How do people know what really went on inside this apartment? There was no camera in here. Sure there are pictures of Alistair leaving the next morning, but who's to say he didn't just sleep on the couch?'

'I see,' I said, starting to get the hang of it. 'But what happens when she asks me if I shagged him?'

'That's when you say *I am neither going to confirm nor deny those rumours, out of respect for both Alistair and myself. All I will say is that he did stay at my apartment on the night in question.*'

I repeated this back to Jenna.

'And you did have sex with him?' she asked.

'What?' I replied, confused. 'I thought you said I hadn't shagged him?'

'I'm just trying to show you what this woman will be like,' explained Jenna. 'So, what's your answer?'

I repeated the neither-confirm-nor-deny line.

'But surely you can understand how it looks to everyone? You meeting him at a bar, him going back to your house, and then pictures of him leaving your house the next morning.'

'Bitch.'

'Incorrect,' said Jenna. 'What's your answer?' she pressured. 'I'm waiting.'

'I understand how it looks but that doesn't mean that it actually happened,' I replied.

'Good answer,' said Jenna, clearly happy with my reply. 'Next one.'

'Do you have any remorse towards Alistair's wife and children?'

'Clearly I am upset this has affected Alistair's wife and children but, as unbelievable as this may sound, I didn't know Alistair was married. In fact I didn't even know who Alistair was.'

'You *didn't know* he was the captain of our nation's football team?'

'No. I didn't. I barely watch television and I certainly don't watch football. When I met him in the bar I didn't recognise him. All I knew is his first name was Alistair, which is how he introduced himself. He had no wedding ring on and he was buying me drinks, so I naïvely assumed he was single.'

'I see,' said Jenna. 'So you don't make a habit of sleeping with married men?'

'No,' I replied. *Definitely not.* 'That's Lizzie.'

'Pardon?'

'Nothing, sorry.'

'How do you feel about Virginia Ambrose labelling you a prostitute?'

'I think she is a stupid bitch who deserves to be run over by a logging truck.'

'She is a stupid bitch too,' said Jenna, who had met her a few times. 'Wrong answer though.'

'I think she is obviously someone who is very embarrassed and desperate if she is having to resort to such low levels of name-calling.'

'So it hasn't upset you?'

'No,' I lied. 'I just feel sorry for her.'

'Brilliant,' encouraged Jenna. 'You're doing great.'

The following afternoon I sat in my office and waited for the arrival of Mary Simperington. What arrived through the door was a fifty-something-year-old woman with short ginger hair, a bad skirt, sans make-up, and round spectacles. She looked as though she'd come straight from cataloging books at the public library, in the natural-history section. Although I was sweating profusely under my steel-grey Helen Cherry suit I was determined not to show it. I sat at my desk, I had Izzy make her a cup of coffee, I listened to her questions and I answered them. And forty-five minutes later, with a close-up shot of my face and a shake of my hand, she had left. She had largely stuck to the questions on her list, with no nasty surprises, and I had answered the questions as I had practised with Jenna. Nice and cagey, without giving anything away. Or swearing, yelling, or wishing Alistair or his wife a speedy and violent death. All in all I was pleased with the way the interview had gone.

I spent the rest of the week being photographed in my huge glasses, chased, yelled at, and largely holed up in my office or my apartment. The two sets of walls were beginning to not only close in on me, but also choke me to death. My only consolation was that whenever a photo of me was printed, there was also one of Alistair. He was obviously being as hounded by the paparazzi as I was and this knowledge somehow made me feel better. I only hoped he was suffering and hating every single moment of it. *Bet he's probably used to it*, I thought to myself, *the bastard*. Apparently the critics were worried about the effects our scandal would have on his performance in the World Cup. I prayed it would render him a one-legged uncoordinated retard, and that he would miss every goal he kicked for and embarrass the entire nation, before being dropped from the team like a burning spud. This would be the ideal outcome anyway. His manager was of course standing by him and supporting him through this very difficult time. I wished I had a manager to stand by me. All I had was a pair of over-sized sunglasses.

I desperately wanted to go out for a nice meal and a glass of bubbles somewhere, like I used to do nearly every single night. But, since I was followed by at least twenty paparazzi every time I set foot outside my front door I didn't think this was such a great idea. Mands and Lizzie tried to convince me to go out for dinner with them, and just ignore the vultures. But the thought of sitting in a restaurant while a cluster of paparazzi stood outside taking pictures of me through the window and the rest of the patrons stared and pointed was less than enticing. Instead I was forced to survive on delivery food and takeaways brought over by Mands and Lizzie.

The papers had even started taking an interest in what I wore. Beside every daily picture they snapped was a rundown of my outfit, including designer, cost, and whether it suited me or not. I was subsequently labelled everything from a 'clothes horse' to a 'trendsetter'. This was the one positive outcome of the whole bloody saga. The only problem was I was swiftly running out of fabulous outfits. However, it was extremely difficult to go shopping when you were being chased. Lizzie had kindly dropped round several gorgeous items, but I was chewing through them fast. The girls were absolute gems. They were round at my apartment nearly every night, bubbles and food in hand, ready to slag off Alistair and his wife at the drop of a hat, and with an endless supply of hugs and soothing words.

On Saturday morning I got dressed, put on my huge sunglasses, and braved the walk to my letterbox to retrieve the *Telegraph*, amid yells of 'Morning Samantha!' and 'Give us a smile then!'

They'd be bloody lucky, I thought to myself, staring straight through my dark glasses into the great abyss of Ignore Land, as the flashes bounced off my forehead. I walked back inside the front door, sat down at the dining table and rifled through the paper. There, on the front page of the *Life* section, was my interview. At the top of the page, in the middle, was a large close-up photograph of me. Sitting in my office and looking relatively demure and innocent, although still smiling slightly (just to show I was a warm and loving person, and not a cold-hearted marriage-wrecking bitch). *Could have been worse,* I thought to myself, not entirely disappointed. And next to the large photo of me was another large photo, of Alistair, in mid-kick, looking rather foxy in his white shorts, I had to admit. But it was the large photo that lay underneath which I wasn't expecting. There on the page, in full colour, was a picture of Jerry, or rather Jasmine, looking as stunning and gorgeous as ever. And underneath the picture, in large bold type, were the words 'Samantha's Ex'.

Oh dear God no! It can't be! I cried aloud, propelling my head into my hands.

Mary fucking Simperington! The absolute two-faced cow! The bloody sodding bad-skirt-wearing bitch! Now everyone will think I'm some sort of bisexual marriage wrecker. Oh sweet Jesus! How the hell did they find her? I wondered aloud.

Half an hour later, as I remained motionless at the dining table, my head still in my hands and a look of utter despair still plastered across my face, my mobile rang. It was Jasmine.

'Sam? It's Jasmine.'

'Hi.'

'Look Sam, I am *so* sorry. I don't know how they got the picture. They must have been following me or something. I had no idea. Honestly.'

If there's one thing Jerry/Jasmine wasn't, it was a liar. Even the smallest, whitest lies had made him stutter like a schoolboy.

'I know,' I replied. 'Half the time you don't know they're behind you until it's . . . too late.'

'How are you coping?' she asked.

'With the fact the entire country not only thinks I'm a marriage-wrecking floozy but also a lesbian? Still coming to terms with it, to be honest.'

'I'm so sorry Sam.'

'It's not your fault,' I sighed.

'Are you going to tell the media about . . . me?'

'What about you?' I asked.

'You know . . . that I used to be a man.'

The thought had crossed my mind.

'It's just that not everyone knows about my past,' she continued. 'In fact, I have a new group of friends now who don't know about it at all.'

'I see,' I replied.

'So . . . if there was any chance at all you could not mention it, well, I'd be most grateful. . . I really would.'

Great. What were my options? Reveal the fact my ex-boyfriend has had a sex change to the entire country and expose him/her to prejudice, as well as outing him/her to all her friends? Or have the entire country thinking I was a now a lesbian, or at best bisexual? Both such fabulously enticing options.

'I won't tell,' I promised. 'As long as you never talk to the media, or anyone, for that matter, about us.'

'I won't,' said Jasmine. 'I promise.'

'Good.'

'Take care Sam, and don't worry, I'm sure it will all blow over soon.'

'I hope so.'

I stayed trapped inside my apartment for the rest of the day. With the new revelation of my lesbianism, the locusts at the front gate had tripled within a few hours. I took the phone off the hook and turned off my mobile. I had no desire to field calls from shocked friends and family. Instead I set about cleaning the apartment from top to bottom. Ever since MayBelle, my Malaysian housekeeper, had stopped coming nearly two weeks ago, the clean, serene surfaces had become few and far between. Pint-sized MayBelle simply couldn't cope with passing the hounds at the gate.

'Day is tewible Zamanfa. Day scare may.'

Even my offer to triple her pay hadn't given her the confidence to run the gauntlet.

'Win day gone, den I comez back,' she'd said. 'Eyez promiz Zamanfa.'

At four o'clock I collapsed onto the couch and admired my handiwork. I'd no idea how long it took to clean a two-bedroom apartment.

How did MayBelle do it all in three hours? I wondered. *And the ironing too?*

I would definitely have to give her a raise, I decided. It was bloody exhausting stuff.

I decided to put my phone back on the hook and as I did, it rang, sending me catapulting back into the wall.

'Well, well, well . . .'

It was my mother.

'I had no idea, Sammy,' she said joyously. She only called me Sammy in situations of extreme happiness. I hated being called Sammy, it made me feel like a Labrador.

'It's not what you think,' I replied.

'So you didn't used to go out with this woman?' she asked.

'Well, yes, but she was . . .'

'I just want you to know I'm very proud of you love. Very proud.'

It crossed my mind I was probably the only woman alive who'd had a lesbian fling (imaginary or otherwise) whose mother was very proud of her.

'Elizabeth . . .'

But she was having none of it.

'You know what the funny thing is? She reminds me of someone in a strange way.'

'Who?'

'She reminds me of Jerry.'

'That's because . . .'

'She's very beautiful, isn't she?'

'Yes, she is, but Elizabeth . . .'

'The only thing I don't understand,' she continued, 'is why you didn't tell me?'

'Well the thing is . . .'

But before I could explain she was at me again.

'Why did it end?'

'It's a long story,' I replied, deciding to give up.

It was far easier having my mother ecstatic that I'd had a lesbian tryst than it was to explain the whole Jasmine thing to her. Plus, I had promised Jasmine I wouldn't tell anyone.

'Anyway, I think it's wonderful. And so does your father.'

I doubted this very much. In fact I was confident he had very little to say about the matter at all.

As I hung up the phone there was a knock at the door. It was Mands and Lizzie, several bottles of wine and gourmet pizzas in tow.

'How on earth did you know I'd be home?' I asked, as I swung open the front door. 'Oh that's right! I don't go anywhere anymore. Ever. I just stay trapped in my apartment, awaiting the odd visitor and pining for social contact. All while I go completely raving bonkers.'

'How're you doing, dolls?' asked Mands, giving me a kiss on the cheek, and a concerned look.

'Just peachy,' I replied. 'Although I think you should both know your best friend is now a lesbian.'

'Hi sweets,' greeted Lizzie, also giving me a kiss on the cheek. 'We know.'

'Do you know what the funny thing is?' I said, as Lizzie

poured the three of us a wine. 'I didn't even know I was a lesbian until this morning.'

'And now you've seen the light?' asked Mands.

'That's right. I just wish I'd known before I slept with Alistair, then I might have avoided this whole bloody mess.'

'Hindsight is a fine thing,' said Lizzie.

'Is it what,' I agreed. 'I probably wouldn't have gone out with Jerry either if I were a lesbian.'

'Well cheers,' said Mands, clinking my glass. 'Here's to you coming out.'

'Yes. Here's to me,' I said, downing precisely half the glass in one gulp.

'Seriously,' said Lizzie. 'How're you coping?'

'Well, I've done the housework.'

'Jesus,' said Mands, realising what dire straights I must be in. 'Can't you get someone else to do that?'

'MayBelle quit,' I explained. 'She's scared of the locusts.'

'Oh, bugger.'

'Did Jerry, or Jasmine, or whoever the hell she is, ring you?' asked Lizzie.

'Are you referring to my lesbian ex-lover?'

'Yes.'

'Yes, she did. She had no idea she was being snapped. I guess someone must have spilled the bloody beans. God knows who.'

'What did she say?'

'She asked me to please not tell anyone she used to be a man.'

'And?' said Mands.

'And what?'

'And are you going to?'

'No, I can't. I promised her I wouldn't.'

'Good idea,' said Lizzie. 'I think it'd just make the whole thing worse.'

How much worse could the whole thing possibly get? I had no desire to find out.

'What's this?' I asked Mands, pulling a rolled-up magazine from her handbag. 'More shocking revelations about myself that I don't know?'

'It's nothing,' said Mands, grabbing the *Woman's Life* from me.

I saw Lizzie pass her a quick but furtive why-didn't-you-leave-that-in-the-car look.

'I think it might be. Go on, give it back,' I urged. 'I'm enjoying torturing myself. I'm on a roll here.'

'Really,' said Mands. 'It's nothing dolls.'

'We'll see,' I said, taking it back off her and sitting down.

I flicked through the pages but there were no obvious stories about me, Alistair or Tiny Tits. In fact, there didn't appear to be any pictures of us either, praise the Lord.

'Maybe you're right after all,' I said, flicking to the last page. It was the Letters to the Editor page.

'God, what kind of sad old bastards write in to the editor?' I asked, glancing at the page.

'Ones who need bullets,' said Mands, reaching for the magazine again.

'Hang on,' I said, suddenly seeing my name at the top of the page. 'Just a sec.'

But my name wasn't just at the top of the page, it was all bloody over it. There were ten letters published on the page and every single one of them was about me. Every One. With such breathtaking headings as *Nothing But a Floozy*, *Shame on You Samantha Steel! Marriage Wrecker* and my personal favourite *Hands off Our Man!*

I paused to take them all in.

'Don't read them, sweets,' said Lizzie, trying to take the magazine from my grasp. But I was having none of it. I read them all. I was labelled everything from a 'gold digger' to a 'good for nothing' to a 'floozy' and a 'prostitute' (again). And that was just the first two letters.

There was not one mention of this whole thing being Alistair's fault. Not one. Virginia Ambrose was naturally a 'hard-done-by woman', a 'wonderful wife and mother' and, according to Old-Fashioned from Gisborne, also a 'beautiful soul'. *A beautiful soul?* Nowhere was there any mention of her tiny tits.

Alistair was 'a national icon', a 'charismatic man' and a 'good role model.'

A good role model? Sure, if you wanted your kids to go about shagging innocent women while they were married, he was perfect. Couldn't have asked for better.

'They all h-h-hate me,' I wailed, tears coursing down my cheeks. 'Why do they h-h-hate me?'

'Because they're stupid,' gushed Lizzie. 'Stupid people who judge someone they don't even know.'

'Stupid people who crochet things,' added Mands. 'And bake.'

'Stupid people who have no lives of their own,' finished Lizzie. 'I'm taking it now,' she said gently, sliding the magazine from my lap.

'I'm never having sex again!' I cried. 'Ever!'

This made them both stop and look at me with a mixture of pity and pure horror.

'Oh, don't go that far, sweets,' said Lizzie. 'You don't mean that.'

'I do,' I replied. 'I am going to get stitched up. Put out of action for good.'

Mands was speechless, for once.

'But you like sex,' protested Lizzie. 'A lot.'

'And look where it's got me,' I wailed. 'Being trashed in trashy magazines by people I don't even know.'

'It was just bad luck,' soothed Lizzie. 'That's all it was. It won't happen again.'

'Here we go,' said Mands, handing me another glass of wine. 'Drink up dolls.'

I did as I was told.

Unfortunately *Woman's Life* wasn't the only magazine to publish my hate mail. Over the next two weeks every Letters to the Editor page in the country was covered in colourful abuse. All directed at me.

Mands and Lizzie comforted me as best they could. They even conducted a trashy-magazine-burning ceremony one night, which resulted in my entire apartment building being evacuated onto the street at eleven o'clock. Although we had managed to put out the fire in the kitchen sink, unfortunately my smoke detectors weren't the only ones to be activated.

We stood out by the front gate, me in my sunglasses with a scarf wrapped tightly round my head and chin, as my neighbours, largely sporting dressing gowns, gave us death stares. Somehow they intuitively knew it was my fault. Thankfully most of the paparazzi, bar three (the graveyard shift), had gone home for the night. Mands and Lizzie flanked me on either side so they were unable to get a good shot.

'Might as well have a drink while we're out here,' said Mands, who had evacuated two bottles of bubbles and three glasses with her.

She promptly popped the cork, which just made my neighbours stare more. They declined her offer of a glass.

'What on earth were you girls doing?' asked the head fire officer, once the truck had arrived on the scene.

'Sacrificing the magazines,' replied Lizzie.

He stared back at the three of us, too scared to question us further. By twelve-thirty we were allowed back inside the building, my neighbours bidding us evil farewells as they and their dressing gowns entered. We traipsed back inside, rather drunk, with two empty bottles of bubbles in tow. Naturally the whole scene was front page news the following day, under the heading 'Samantha Steel's Blazing Trail!'

The following morning my foggy head and I were woken far too early by a phone call from a complete stranger.

'Is this Samantha?' asked a man's voice.

'Yes.'

'Samantha, this is Alexander Carroll speaking. The writer.'

I'd never heard of him.

'I wrote Bindi Leeth's biography.'

Oh God, the book about the underwear model who shagged the Minister of Foreign Affairs. Called *Uncovered* or *Laid Bare*, or some such bollocks.

'Hello,' I replied. 'What do you want?'

'Well, Samantha, I know this must be a very difficult time for you. But I was wondering if perhaps we could meet for a coffee and a chat? You see, I have a proposal which I would like to discuss with you. A proposal which I think will help your current situation.'

'I don't think anything is going to help my situation, Mr Carroll,' I replied. 'And how did you get my number?'

'From directory,' he replied.

Christ! No wonder I was getting so many unwanted calls. I would really have to do something about that.

'Look,' I replied, 'I'm not in the habit of meeting complete strangers for coffee so I think it's best if you just tell me what this proposal is right now.'

'Well, Samantha, I would like to write your biography. I think you have a valid and truthful story which simply needs to be told.'

'And how exactly do you plan on stretching a one-night stand out into a book?'

'Well . . . it wouldn't just be about that one night,' he replied. 'It would be about you . . . your childhood . . . your ambitions . . . and what drove you to sleep with Alistair Ambrose.'

'What drove me to sleep with Alistair Ambrose, Mr Carroll, was the fact I was in a bar, I hadn't had a decent shag for far too long, I'd had a few drinks, and I thought he was a bit of all right. And single. That is what drove me.'

'I see,' he replied. 'Clearly there are many angles we could take.'

'Look,' I spat, 'I'm not interested in having a book written about me. I have enough trouble seeing my name and face in the newspaper.'

'OK,' he replied. 'Perhaps we should discuss remuneration then.'

'I don't think you understand me,' I replied. 'I don't want you to write a book about me and no amount of money will make me change my mind. Goodbye.'

'I see, Samantha. Well, I will send you my card in case you change your mind. I doubt Mrs Ambrose will be as opposed to my offer,' he added.

Great, now he was threatening me. And he obviously knew where I lived.

'So, how much did he offer?' asked Mands, when she and Lizzie were sitting in my living room that evening.

'What?'

'How much was he going to pay you to write the book?'

'I don't care Mands. He could pay me a million dollars and I still wouldn't do it.'

'Really?' she asked, clearly surprised by my response.

'Good on you, sweets,' said Lizzie. 'Don't lower yourself.'

'I just can't believe all the hype!' I cried. 'You would've thought I'd shagged the bloody prime minister!'

'Except she's a woman,' pointed out Lizzie.

'This is worse,' said Mands. 'Way worse. People actually like Alistair Ambrose.'

'It *is* sport that runs the country after all,' agreed Lizzie.

'Oh shut up! Both of you.'

When I was a young girl I had dreamed of one day being famous. A famous actress or a famous writer. Even a famous politician. Never in my most debauched dreams had I imagined I would achieve fame by shagging a footballer.

The next evening at work I was about to pop on my glasses and make a dash for the car park when Gareth knocked on my door.

'Sam, can I have a quick word?' he asked.

'Sure.'

'That's a nice colour lippy,' he said.

'Sunset,' I replied. 'New line by Lancôme. No smudging, absolutely no flaking, lasts *all* day. You would not believe how fabulous it is.'

I pulled it out of my handbag and held it up for him to see.

'Lovely,' he replied, sitting in the chair opposite, although his tone indicated he didn't quite grasp how life-changing this new find was.

'No flaking,' I repeated. 'Not ever.'

'Sam . . .'

'Unbelievable,' I continued, shaking my head for emphasis. 'Must have a brilliant moisturiser or gel in the mix.'

'Sam . . .'

'And it's about bloody time. All those others claim to be non-flaking, then you get to eleven o'clock and they're falling off your lips already.'

'Sam!' shouted Gareth. 'We need to talk.'

'Oh . . . OK.'

The look on his face was anything but welcoming. Somehow I didn't think he was about to invite me out for a post-work drink.

'Look Sam,' he began. 'this media trail of yours is just getting ridiculous. The phone doesn't stop ringing. There are paparazzi crowding the entrance way, and I even saw one trying to shimmy up the bloody fire escape. It's just . . . well . . . it's just not good for business.'

'I see.'

'Look, I don't care whether you shagged the guy, or shagged his wife for that matter, that's not the point. I just think it's best if you work from home for a week or so, until the whole thing blows over. Or at least until the paparazzi bugger off.'

Working from home was the last thing I wanted to do. I was like a large goldfish in a floodlit bowl. At least here I couldn't see the parasites waiting in the doorway.

'Sorry Sam . . . it's just . . .'

'It's OK Gareth,' I sighed. 'I understand.'

I packed up everything I would need from my office for the next week or two, put on my sunglasses, and drove

153

myself home at breakneck speed.

'Ohmygod!' gushed Lizzie, as she fell inside my front door later that evening, Thai takeaway in hand.

'Ohmygod what?'

'Tell me you know?' she implored.

The tone of her voice was ominous. I wasn't entirely sure I wanted to know.

Ah well, I thought. *You've been kicked out of your workplace, the entire country has seen your cellulite, everyone hates you, and you are trapped inside your own apartment, possibly for the rest of your life. How much worse can it get?* I took a punt.

'Know about what?' I asked.

'Tiny Tits.'

'What about her?'

'She's being interviewed. On *PrimeTime*.'

'What? But *PrimeTime* is quality television.'

'I know.'

'She is not quality.'

'I know.'

Clearly there was *always* room in God's little universe for things to get just that wincey bit worse. I have issues with the fact he supposedly created the world in six days and rested on the seventh. Perhaps he should have taken a little longer and not rushed it quite so much? Or perhaps he should have got off his arse on the seventh day? Or maybe even made a couple of prototypes first instead of launching straight into it? There were a few too many flaws with this model for my liking.

'When?' I asked.

'Tomorrow night.'

'You're joking!'

'Fraid not sweets. I just saw the shorts.'

'And?'

'And what?'

'What did she say?'

'Just . . . you know . . . stuff.'

'Stuff about me?'

'Some.'

'Bloody hell! The cow!'

'What shall we do?' asked Lizzie. 'Burn every television in the city? Take down the national grid?'

'If only. I guess I'll have to watch the bloody thing and torture myself instead.'

'We'll bring you round to my house for a change of scenery,' said Lizzie. 'And we'll drink our way through it.'

'And beyond,' I added.

The next night I donned my sunglasses and long coat, pulled the hood over my head and ran outside to Mands' waiting car.

'Samantha, will you be watching *PrimeTime* tonight?' asked one of the young rookies from the *Morning Sun*.

'No,' I replied. 'Quite obviously I am going out for dinner.'

'I'm sure Mrs Ambrose will be disappointed,' added his colleague, the one with the enormous sideburns.

With two Land Rovers and three motorbikes on our trail we drove round to Lizzie's house. We parked on the street outside and made a mad dash for her front door, while my pursuers ran behind, snapping away. I chose to ignore their pleas for a smile and instead we bolted directly through the front door which Lizzie was thankfully holding open.

'Bloody hell!' I exclaimed. 'Those flashes are going to give me cataracts soon. Or premature blindness.'

Lizzie had been flat out in the kitchen, taking some delicious-looking hors d'oeuvres out of their delicatessen containers and arranging them on a platter. She swiftly set about pouring us a wine. And then another.

Mands switched on the television just as the *PrimeTime* intro music began. Then, when we realised the dreaded interview was on second, she turned the volume back down.

'No need to watch it unnecessarily,' she said, pouring us all another wine.

'Here we go,' said Lizzie, turning the volume back up twenty minutes later. 'Ready?'

'Not in the slightest,' I replied. 'But what choice do I have?'

'You know we don't have to watch it, sweets,' she said. 'Not if you don't want to.'

'Turn the bloody volume up . . . go on,' I replied.

'That's the spirit!' said Mands, rubbing my shoulders.

I just couldn't believe Tiny Tits was being interviewed on *PrimeTime*. *PrimeTime* for God's sake. An award-winning current affairs programme! *How could this ridiculous tabloid drama possibly cut the mustard?*

I listened to the voice over intro.

'Virginia Ambrose . . . wife of our most famous footballer, Alistair Ambrose, chairwoman of the Youngfellows Children's Trust, avid campaigner of Computers for Kids . . . and mother.'

And mother? Said as though this was some sort of accomplishment only she had achieved. Tonnes of people were bloody mothers. They were everywhere. I even knew a few.

'Christ! She's a charity cheerleader!' declared Mands.

'Easy to be when you're rich as all hell,' added Lizzie.

The chirpy voiceover belonged to the interviewer, Glenda Goodson, more commonly known as No Neck, due to the fact she had, well, no neck to speak of.

'It's like she's been beheaded and then they just sort of glued it straight back onto her shoulders,' observed Lizzie.

'I wonder what she says when people tell her to pull her head in?' I replied.

'Probably something like "Look I have, see!" ' said Mands.

I looked at the screen and there, sitting opposite No Neck, was Mrs Alistair Ambrose. In the flesh. Well, a cold flat piece of glass type of flesh, that is, but you know what I mean. From her perfectly manicured peroxide blonde bob, to her perfectly manicured toenails. To her perfect round baby bump. Every perfectly manicured and glowing Chanel-smelling inch of her.

'Virginia,' began No Neck. 'You're a busy woman, aren't you? The Youngfellows Trust, Computers for Kids, two small children. Just how hectic is your life?'

'It's unbelievable Glenda, just unbelievable, but I love it. There's never ever a dull moment, that's for sure.'

'Tell me about your work with the Youngfellows Trust. How involved are you?'

'Very involved. I chair the board which controls the funding for the trust, I head the fundraising team, and I help out myself with the rehabilitation of the children and their families.'

'Now, these are children who have spent a significant amount of time in hospital, either with injuries, undergoing surgery, or in some cases with cancer.'

'That's right. And when they are finally released from hospital we help them and their families adjust back into normal life again by providing a support network for them.'

'That's fantastic,' chirped No Neck.

'Oh God, this is sickening,' moaned Mands, faux-gagging for

emphasis. 'She thinks she's Florence bloody Nightingale.'

'Now Virginia,' said No Neck, 'I'd really like to talk about Computers for Kids. You started this charity initiative, almost ten years ago now I believe, and I understand you're still fully involved with the cause?'

'That's right Glenda. I am still the chairwoman and spokesperson for the organisation.'

'What was it that led you to start this wonderful initiative?'

'Well Glenda, it is a sad fact that not every child in this country has ready and easy access to a computer within their home. And this is something which personally concerned me, and something which I really felt I could do something about. We realise how important computer literacy is for children of all ages. How it contributes to their ability to learn, and their ability to succeed. Not only at school, but in their future lives.'

'Hark,' said Lizzie, cupping her ear. 'Is that a violin I hear?'

I really did have to spend a bit less time drinking bubbles and a bit more time doing charity work, I thought to myself. *Or at least starting to do charity work.* She was making me look bad.

Cutaway to Tiny Tits sitting in a chair in her pale-pink Chanel trouser suit, showing a picture of a computer to two poor computerless children as they sat on her knee.

'You just know she hoisted them straight off and brushed down her pants as soon as the camera stopped rolling,' said Mands.

'Now Virginia, I know this must be difficult for you,' said No Neck. 'But I would like to talk about your husband now. People would have had to be living on another planet, or at least in another country, to escape the media furore which has surrounded your husband, and yourself, over the past few weeks. Just how hard has this been for you?'

'It's been an absolute nightmare Glenda, just so very difficult. The media have been hounding us. And the poor children too.'

'Are you angry with your husband for his part in this?'

'Yes, are you?' I asked the television screen. 'Because you bloody well should be!'

'Honestly,' replied Tiny Tits. 'I'm just far too hurt to be angry.'

Oh! Somebody save me!

'What a load of crap!' cried Lizzie. 'Of course she's pissed off. He's made a big tit of her!'

'A tiny tit of her,' corrected Mands.

'Now Virginia,' said No Neck. 'I know this is very difficult for you, but I have to ask. What do you think happened that infamous night, between your husband and Samantha Steel?'

I must have let out a gasp, because Mands was suddenly rubbing my shoulders again.

'Well Glenda, that woman obviously threw herself at my husband . . . as so many of them do . . . he'd had way too much to drink and he made a huge mistake.'

He was hardly rolling drunk, love, I thought to myself.

'This woman has completely ruined my life. And my children's,' she sobbed. 'We were so happy.'

Can't have been that bloody happy if he shagged someone else! I thought to myself.

'Can't have been that bloody happy if he shagged someone else!' cried Lizzie.

'She's full of shit!' declared Mands. 'Course he's shagged loads of women before. It's just that you're the only one the media's found out about.'

'Well thanks, that makes me feel so much better,' I replied.

159

'Just one more in a whole line of floozies.'

'Sorry,' said Mands. 'No disrespect intended.'

'It's not your fault,' soothed Lizzie, 'it's just that these footballers are always having women throwing themselves at them.'

'I didn't throw myself at him!' I protested. 'He threw himself at me!'

'I know he did, sweets,' said Lizzie, rubbing my shoulder too. 'Perhaps he was after a challenge?'

'Well he certainly got that, didn't he?' I replied. 'The bastard!'

'Is it true Alistair has in fact moved out of the family home?' asked No Neck.

'No,' replied Tiny Tits. 'He is just staying elsewhere temporarily, until this whole media circus settles down. With the World Cup just around the corner he really needs to concentrate on training and working with the team. Unfortunately having paparazzi camped out on our doorstep twenty-four hours a day isn't helping his preparation.'

'Bet he's done a runner,' said Mands. 'Hey,' she added, 'if he's single then maybe you can shag him again.'

I flicked her the Dagger Stare.

'Or maybe not.'

'So, the rumours the two of you have separated are untrue?' asked No Neck.

'Absolutely,' replied Virginia. 'Alistair and I love each other very much and are very much together. There is no doubting we will get through this. I intend to stand by him as long as it takes. It's just that . . . that it's so hard living in the public eye sometimes,' she sniffed. 'Constantly having people taking photos of us and the children . . . and having to read the things that are written about us.'

'At least they bloody well like you!' I wailed. 'Try being

completely hated on for size!'

Close-up of watery eyes and dainty white hankie.

'What a blubberguts!' cried Lizzie.

'Really is nothing worse than a sobbing pregnant woman,' added Mands.

'Is there anything else you would like to say to Ms Steel while you have the opportunity?' asked No Neck, attempting to wind it up.

I gripped the arm of the sofa and braced myself for more abuse.

'I just hope she can live with what she has done.'

Mands and Lizzie clocked my reaction and promptly set about pouring me another wine and rubbing my shoulders a bit more vigorously.

What I've done? If only she'd take some of the anger she was firing at me and target it at her cheating husband, where it belonged.

'For God's sake!' cried Lizzie. 'She really does think she's Mother Teresa!'

'Bet she only got with Alistair by throwing herself at him in a bar,' said Mands.

'He must have been plastered too,' I added, deciding to join in. 'Look at the state of her. Bloody great blubbering mess.'

'Bloody straight,' agreed Mands. 'Wringer. Dragged through.'

'Backwards,' added Lizzie.

'By her feet,' finished Mands.

'Thank you so much for talking to us, Virginia,' said No Neck. 'And I wish you and your family the very best for the future.'

'That woman makes me want to vomit,' declared Mands, switching the television off.

'Which one?' asked Lizzie.

'Both of them,' replied Mands and I in unison.

'What a complete drama queen!' agreed Lizzie.

'How are you feeling?' asked Mands.

'Like the devil,' I replied. 'The she-devil home-wrecker.'

'Look . . .' said Lizzie, attempting to comfort me, '. . . if she's that much of a blubbering mess then he's better off living somewhere else. She must drive him bloody nuts.'

'He's probably glad he's finally got a reason to move out,' agreed Mands. 'He'll be eternally grateful to you.'

I highly doubted that, but took some shameless comfort in their lies. I'd be eternally grateful if I never saw either Alistair Ambrose or his perfect little wife ever again.

'There's only one thing for it,' said Mands.

'What?' I asked.

'You're simply going to have to go on telly to defend yourself.'

'I can't do that!' I cried.

'You have to. You can't let this two-bit charity chimp make you look like some bar floozy.'

'You're not a floozy,' agreed Lizzie. 'You have to stand up for yourself.'

'You have to let the public know you're a professional, intelligent woman,' continued Mands. 'And not some toilet-shagging home-wrecker.'

'But then everyone's going to recognise my face, aren't they?'

'Sweets, they already do,' said Lizzie, wrapping her arms around me. 'But at least this way they get to hear your side of the story. Without your words being distorted by someone's pen.'

7

The next morning, with shaking hands, I phoned the office of *One Nation*, the rival current-affairs programme.

'I've been hoping you'd call me, Samantha,' said Cara Jessup, the producer.

She had left a message on my phone two weeks ago.

'Well, here I am,' I replied. 'All yours.'

'Fabulous,' she said. 'I'll be round with a contract.'

And before I could blink, yet again, she was on my doorstep, contract in her hands. I read through the agreement, which seemed fairly straightforward, then stopped dead at the figure. Really stopped dead this time. It was twenty thousand dollars. Twenty grand! This seemed ridiculous. I was going to be paid twenty thousand dollars to talk to a journalist for one hour in front of a TV camera. One hour. I still had absolutely no idea why celebrities hated doing interviews. The interview was scheduled for Friday afternoon, in three days time, at my apartment. It was to be shown on television the following Wednesday. My interviewer was going to be Shari Vijay, a beautiful part-Indian woman who was, thankfully, not much older than myself.

Hopefully she'll have some empathy with me, I prayed.

Once again Jenna kindly came round to my apartment

and helped me prepare for the interview. Television was her speciality.

'Lots of eye contact is the key,' she instructed. 'Make sure you look her in the eyes at all times. And think carefully about your answers. Form your reply in your head before you open your mouth.'

'And,' she added, 'for God's sake keep your hands still and in one place. Put them in your lap and bloody well leave them there.'

Wayward hands were obviously something which annoyed Jenna.

After two more days and nights holed up in my apartment, attempting to do what work I could, Friday afternoon arrived. Mands and Lizzie had come round the night before to help me with the inevitable task of What To Wear. I wanted to look respectable but not prudish, and above all else, I wanted to look confident. We decided on my cream suit, with skirt and high priest-collar jacket.

'It's perfect,' noted Lizzie. 'You look very demure. But with a good smatter of sexy.'

'And it practically screams saint,' added Mands.

I sat on my sofa, attempting to look as relaxed as possible, which was no mean feat, as the two camera operators set up their equipment about my living room and fitted me with a microphone. I crossed my legs, and then re-crossed them the other way. I looked as though I needed to go to the toilet. Shari, who was as stunning in the flesh as she was on the telly, ran through the questions she was going to ask. There didn't appear to be any nasty surprises, but Jenna's words rang strong in my head. 'There always is,' she'd said. 'Always. Just when you think it's nearing the end, they'll slam you with a nasty question and knock you for six. Be prepared!' she'd warned.

'Comfortable?' asked Shari.

No. Not at all.

'Yes,' I replied.

'Don't worry,' she whispered, leaning in close towards me and winking. 'I won't make you look bad. I'm on your side.'

I doubted this was something an impartial interviewer was supposed to say to an interviewee, but it was comforting nonetheless.

'Right. Let's get started then, shall we?'

'OK,' I agreed, taking a deep breath.

Remember, I told myself. *All you are doing is telling your side of the story. This is your one chance to clear the air.*

'Tell me about your relationship with Alistair Ambrose,' said Shari.

Repeat the 'Met in a Bar, Went Back to My Apartment, Left the Next Morning' story.

Keep your hands still.

'Did the two of you have sexual intercourse?'

Repeat the 'Yes He Stayed the Night But No Comment On the Sex' Story.

And so the pattern went. Shari asked: Had I met Alistair before? I didn't know who he was? Had I seen him since? Were we an item? Was I surprised by the media frenzy surrounding me? And how was I coping with it?

And me answering No. I don't watch sport and he wasn't wearing a wedding ring. No. No. Yes, very. Not very well, I'm a private person.

Keep your goddamn hands still.

After a strew of questions that were by and large expected and unsurprising, she finally sounded as though she was winding it up. But not quite yet. *Oh no.* There was just one more question.

'Samantha,' said Shari. 'Tell me about your relationship with

Jasmine Taylor. Is it true the two of you were an item?'

And there we have it, people. The Nasty Surprise.

Do not lunge forward and throttle her about the neck until she turns blue and begs for mercy. Sit back, smile sweetly, and answer the question.

She used to be a man! yelled a voice from within. *Go on, tell her! Here's your chance.*

No. I can't.

'No. Not at all,' I said, laughing. 'Jasmine is an old and dear friend of mine. And we have never been anything more than friends. Ever.'

And with that, thanks be to Christ, the interview was finally over.

'You did well,' said Shari, once the cameras had stopped rolling. Then she leaned in towards me and whispered in my ear. 'He's pretty top in the sack, isn't he?'

'Certainly is,' I agreed.

But how did she know?

'Bagged him last year,' she added, winking at me.

'Oh.'

She had shagged Alistair too? Was there anyone he hadn't shagged?

So that's why she was being so nice to me, I thought to myself. Here I am getting torn to shreds while she got away scot-free. *Lucky bitch.*

The day after my television interview Mands and Lizzie decided to whisk me out of town for the weekend, to Sprouting Fern Health Spa, the idea being that I would be cocooned in the caressing palm of massages and mud-wraps and exempt from public harassment, at least for a couple of days. I wasn't one to protest. It sounded ideal and I was so relieved at finally being able to leave the confines of my townhouse prison. It would be nice to have some other walls to stare at. They collected me late in the afternoon and we drove out of the city, with a convoy of Land Rovers and motorbikes following closely behind. They trailed us all the way to the spa, which was situated two hours north of the city and set amongst native bush and forest. It was also conveniently set behind a large wooden security gate, which meant we could leave my pursuers on the other side as we were waved through.

We wheeled our three suitcases through the front doors and up to the reception desk, behind which sat a woman with long brown curly hair, sans make-up, pale skin, and a long flowing white frock, who went by the name of Wendy. She was the type of person who radiated calmness and serenity. No doubt if we'd wheeled three bombs up to the desk instead, she would have remained calm and serene.

'You're staying in the Cuban Fertility Cabin,' said Wendy, once we had signed the necessary forms stating that if we died while being full-body-massaged or mud-wrapped then, naturally, Sprouting Fern Health Spa wasn't to blame.

'The what?' I whispered to Lizzie. 'What the hell is that?'

'It's just a name,' she replied. 'You won't get pregnant. I promise.'

'I'd better bloody not. That's precisely the last thing I need at the moment.'

Luckily Mands was too busy evaluating her new surroundings to hear the name of our room.

Wendy walked us outside, along a long bush-framed path, and showed us to the Cuban Fertility Cabin, which was all open and *Survivor*-esque with an enormous round spa pool sitting in the middle of the room.

'Bloody great!' I exclaimed, clocking the spa. 'All we need

now is three Swiss skiers and a crate of champers.'

'Too right!' agreed Mands and Lizzie.

Wendy just stared at us. I think she thought we were joking.

'All you need to do now is unpack and relax,' she said calmly, handing us our itineraries and backing out of the room. 'You're each booked in for a full-body spa massage at seven o'clock.'

'There's no mini bar,' noted Mands, frantically looking around the room.

'No sweets,' replied Lizzie. 'I don't think they put booze in the rooms.'

But Mands wasn't giving up until she had searched every Feng Shui inch of the place.

I set about reading our itinerary. The options for tomorrow morning appeared to be either a rainforest walk or a yoga class.

'Who the hell wants to walk in a forest?' called out Mands, still upending everything in the room. 'Where's the sleep-in option?'

'There isn't one,' I replied.

'I'm doing yoga,' said Lizzie.

'Then so am I,' I replied.

At seven o'clock we made our way back into the main building for our spa massages. It felt wonderful lying under the warm jets of water as Helena, my masseuse, massaged my body from head to toe. I immediately began to feel sleepy and drift off.

'Your back's going very red,' said Helena, who had woken me up to tell me this. 'I think you must hold a lot of anger in here.'

'You don't think it's because you've been whacking it solidly for the past half-hour?' I ventured. I really didn't like being woken up, not under any circumstances.

But she wasn't giving up. 'Anger leads to fear,' she continued. 'Fear leads to . . .'

'Hate,' I interrupted. 'And hate leads to the Dark Side.'

But my words fell into the silence of someone who simply Did Not Get It.

An hour later we wandered back out into the reception area, all three of us in a jelly-like state of relaxation.

'Just wondering where we might be able to find a bottle of bubbles?' asked Mands, walking up to the reception desk.

'Bubbles?'

'Yes, you know, some champers?'

'I'm afraid we don't have alcohol on the premises,' replied Wendy.

'Pardon?' said Mands.

Wendy repeated herself.

'Oh,' said Mands, although I could tell she didn't believe her.

'They don't have booze!' she hissed at me.

'I heard.'

'What are we supposed to drink?' asked Mands. 'Spirulina?'

'We have a variety of freshly squeezed juices available,' replied Wendy. 'Plus,' she added. 'I think you'll find you're booked in for the weekend detox package.'

'The what?' I asked. Now I was concerned.

'Detox,' repeated Wendy. 'No food. Or alcohol. You'll only be ingesting fresh juices for the next two days.'

Mands and I stared at her, our mouths opening and closing. We both turned and glared at Lizzie.

'Lizzie, where the hell have you brought us?' asked Mands and I, as we walked back to the fertility cabin.

'To a weekend of relaxation . . . and detoxification,' she

replied sheepishly. 'And no alcohol . . . or food.'

We stared at her.

'They were booked out,' she added. 'It was the only package available.'

'That's it,' declared Mands, as we stepped inside the cabin. 'I'm leaving.'

Lizzie looked dejected.

'No you're bloody not,' I said grabbing her arm. 'If I have to stay here and suffer then so do you. Plus . . .' I added. 'Think about the facial and mud-wrap tomorrow.'

'OK,' she relented.

Twenty minutes later our dinner was delivered to the cabin in the form of two large pitchers of juice. One green and one red.

'Wish we had some vodka to pour into it,' I said with a sigh.

We drank the juice in silence. Mands visibly grimaced at every mouthful, and Lizzie and I tried desperately not to.

The next morning we made our way to the yoga class, which was taken by Helena and was, surprisingly, rather enjoyable and revitalising. Or maybe it was just the rarity of waking up without a throbbing head which was revitalising. Either way, I felt great afterwards.

'There's a self-esteem and life-values class at eleven o'clock, if you'd like to join in,' called out Wendy, as we walked back past the reception desk.

'Bunch of bloody fruit loops,' muttered Mands, under her breath.

'I think we'll give that one a miss, thank you,' replied Lizzie.

'That's fine,' smiled Wendy. 'In that case just be back here at one o'clock for your afternoon treatments. And don't forget there's a library along the corridor if you would like to sit and read at any stage.'

'I didn't pay six hundred bucks to sit in a fucking library,' said Mands, as we walked back to the cabin. 'We could have done that at home. For free.'

There were more pitchers of juice waiting for us in the cabin. It was remarkable how similar the green one looked to what had started being released from my system.

'Anyone else's poo look like this?' asked Lizzie, pointing at the pitcher.

'Dead ringer,' replied Mands and I.

After a little lie down we headed back inside for our treatments. This was the good stuff. Body treatments followed by another full-body massage.

'You can choose between a foot and leg exfoliant, and facial. Or a full-body mud wrap,' said Wendy.

'What are the mud-wrap options? asked Lizzie.

'Well, you can have good old-fashioned mud . . . or seaweed . . . or cow bi-product.'

No. Surely not?

'You mean cow dung?' asked Mands, screwing her face up.

'Well . . . yes . . . if you want to put it like that.'

'Surely you're joking?' I asked.

'No,' replied Wendy, calmly and serenely. 'I'm not.'

'Wow,' muttered Mands and I.

'What do you recommend?' asked Lizzie.

'Well, the cow bi-product pack is new here and it's proving very popular. A fabulous re-hydrator. It's all the rage in LA at the moment, particularly with models and actresses.'

I looked at Mands and Lizzie. They both looked back.

Twenty minutes later the three of us lay on individual padded tables in a sauna like room, completely naked except for the fact we were covered from head to toe in cow dung.

'This better work,' I threatened, through gritted teeth. 'It stinks.'

'No shit!' agreed Lizzie. 'Har-de-ha,' she added.

'Look,' said Mands, who had completely changed her opinion on the cow dung as soon as Wendy had said the words 'models' and 'actresses'. 'If they're doing it in LA, then it must work. So why don't you both shut up.'

'If I wasn't caked to the spot, I'd come over and give you a bloody good slap,' I replied.

'Me too,' said Lizzie. 'A big old crap slap.'

That sent the three of us into a hysterical fit of giggles.

'We look like three giant poos,' I observed, through fits of laughter.

'Giggling t-urds,' laughed Lizzie.

'Laughing l-ogs,' spat Mands.

It was at this point that Suzanne, our health therapist, came back in to check on us.

'Firming up OK?' she asked.

'Ye-esss,' we replied, convulsing on the tables.

'Try not to move too much or you might start cracking,' she advised.

'Did you say crapping?' asked Mands.

'No,' replied Suzanne. 'I said cracking.'

She wisely decided to leave us to our adolescent behaviour. I couldn't remember the last time I'd laughed so hard, at least not in recent weeks, and it felt great. It was such a relief not to worry about vultures outside my gate. I almost felt normal again.

An hour later, by which stage my entire body resembled a large piece of brown cement, Suzanne came back in and gently instructed us to take a warm shower and wash off the dung. She turned the showers on for us and left us to it, telling us to make our way to the massage room next door when we were ready.

'She really is the shit, that woman,' said Mands.

'No, you're the shit,' I said, looking at her.

'So are you,' she said slapping me on the arm with her brown hand.

'Can you scrub my back,' asked Lizzie. 'I want it off. All of it.'

We took turns scrubbing the cow dung from each other's backs.

'God, that feels good!' declared Mands, drying herself with a towel. 'My skin is tingling.'

'Me too,' I agreed. 'I feel positively younger already.'

After another exquisite full-body massage we headed back to the fertility cabin for more juice.

'There's a meditation class beginning in the green room shortly,' called out Wendy.

'Meditation class my arse,' muttered Mands.

'I think we'll just have a little rest instead,' I replied. 'What I wouldn't give for a bubbles. Or at least a latte.'

The next afternoon, after yet more juice and another yoga class, my wish was granted.

It was time for our final treatment. It was enema time. And I was an enema virgin.

'What sort of treatment would you like?' asked Wendy, as she led us into the womb-like waiting room.

I had no idea there was a choice in the matter.

'You can have a plain enema, or a coffee enema, which is a very popular choice.'

'A coffee enema?' I asked.

'That's right.'

Dear God.

'It's huge in LA,' she added, which sold Mands straight away.

'OK,' agreed Lizzie and I, rather nervously.

'I'll have a decaf trim latte,' requested Mands.

'I'm afraid we only do organic ground beans,' said Wendy, giving her a wee smile.

'Oh.'

'Just sit here and relax and we'll have them prepared for you,' said Wendy, as she floated away.

'These people look as though they've taken loads of drugs,' observed Mands, as we rifled through the pile of health magazines on the table in front of us.

She was right. They were all smiling their heads off and jumping about unnecessarily.

'Maybe they're just happy because they've got healthy bodies,' replied Lizzie.

Mands and I stared at her. For someone so smart, sometimes she was just plain thick.

'Course they're on drugs,' I agreed.

Twenty minutes later I lay on a table in a small private room, naked from the waist down and lying on my right side, with my legs bent up towards my chest, all foetal-like. There was something slightly Romanian-orphanage-like about the scene, aside from the fact I was having a cup of coffee, via a tube inserted ten centimetres into my rectum.

'There we go then,' said Suzanne, leaving me and my enema bag in peace. She had attempted to explain the process to me, but I was too worried about having the tube inserted up my bottom to pay much attention. Only odd words like 'portal vein' and 'fifteen minutes' had glanced my ears. If she didn't come back by the end of the day and remove it I would have to take some form of action.

But fifteen minutes later she did come back and take it out. And ten minutes after that she came back again to have a good gander at my depository bag, while declaring in her raw-vegetables-only voice, 'Lots of nasty toxins in here.'

I had to look away. Her holding a clear plastic bag filled with bits of my excrement in close proximity to her face was a little overwhelming.

'Reminded me of Sven,' said Mands, when we met back in the waiting room, livers stimulated and toxins removed.

Exactly what part of having a tube filled with coffee inserted ten centimetres up your rectum was bringing her memories flooding back I wasn't sure. Nor was I sure I wanted to know. Sometimes it was best to just ignore her.

Back to the fertility cabin for more juice and a little afternoon siesta, and then it was time to pack up and head home. My pursuers had given up waiting at the gate, presumably once they realised I was just going to a health spa for the weekend and not a Tantric sex camp.

'I feel wonderful,' said Lizzie, as we drove home. 'All calm.'

'Same here,' agreed Mands and I. 'All cleansed and energised.'

We were new women, we decided. All three of us. Healthy, invigorated, and pure.

'Who's up for a bubbles?' asked Mands, as we approached the city.

'Love one,' replied Lizzie.

'Dying for one,' I added.

Mands promptly stopped and bought two cold bottles, which we took back to my apartment and guzzled back in record time.

'God, how I've missed it!' cried Mands, swigging back as though it had been two years, and not two days.

The next morning there was a picture of me on the front page of the *Telegraph,* arriving at Sprouting Fern Health Spa, with the heading 'Sam's Weekend Escape'.

At least they hadn't mentioned the cow dung, I thought to myself. *Thank God for that.*

After three more days holed up in the confines of my apartment, my *One Nation* interview was aired on television. True to her word Shari Vijay did not make me look like a marriage-wrecking slapper. Instead I came across as reasonably confident, intelligent and misunderstood by the nation's media. Exactly the face I had been hoping to project. Plus, according to Mands and Lizzie, I looked dead sexy in my cream suit, while also radiating a definitive Don't Fuck With Me air. This was the first singularly positive thing that had happened to me in the past five weeks (if you can call having to go on television to publicly defend yourself positive, that is).

Early the next morning, post television debut, as I sat at my dining table staring into Yet Another Day Trapped Inside My Apartment, Mands and Lizzie both arrived on my doorstep, low-fat blueberry muffins and takeaway lattes in hand, for a quick pit-stop on their way to work. As we sat at the dining table and assessed the damage in the morning's papers, my mobile rang.

'Hello,' I sighed, expecting it to be yet another media hack who had somehow got my number.

'Sam?'

'Yes,' I sighed, not recognising the voice, which was always a bad sign.

'It's Alistair.'

Alistair? Oh. My. God. It was Alistair!

'Look Sam, before you hang up, I just want to tell you that I . . . am very sorry for what's happened.'

'*Sorry?*'

'I honestly thought you knew who I was that night.'

Obviously he had seen my screen debut, or my newspaper interview, or something.

'Clearly not,' I replied.

'So, you don't watch much sport?' he asked.

'So, you don't get your nails done then?' I replied.

'Right. Point taken.'

'How did you get my number?' I asked.

'You gave it to me.'

'Oh.'

I wished it was the only thing I'd given him.

'Look Sam . . .' said Alistair. 'I just want to tell you I really am very sorry . . . and I'd really like to take you out for dinner and try to make it up to you.'

Dinner?

'Make it *up* to me? Alistair, it'd have to be the most expensive restaurant on earth with entrées of gold nuggets to make up for the constant daily fucking harassment I have experienced. And the fact there are now twenty photographers living on my doorstep.'

'So . . . no dinner then?'

'I would, quite honestly, rather go to hell. Plus, haven't you got a wife? I seem to recall seeing her on television looking somewhat devastated.'

'She's left me.'

Aha. So the rumours were true.

'Well . . . so would I.'

'Is there anything I can do to make it up to you?' he asked, sounding rather desperate.

'Aside from inventing a time machine and rewinding my

life to that night in the bar and leaving me alone? No.'

'So you don't want to see me again?'

'Are you completely stupid? Or just deaf?'

'Right . . . I must say that's a shame though.'

'You don't know the first thing about shame,' I spat.

'Well, please give me a call if you change your mind, Sam . . . I'd really love to see you again.'

'I don't think so, Alistair. Good. Bye.'

I slammed down the phone, which was possibly a bad idea because it was my mobile.

I looked across at Mands and Lizzie who were sitting at the table, eyes like saucers and bodies thrust forward, begging for information.

'Was that who I *think* it was?' asked Lizzie.

'Yes,' I replied, still in shock.

'And?' pressed Mands.

'And . . . he wanted to take me out for dinner.'

'And you said *No*?' she asked, disbelief resounding in her voice.

'Yes.'

'Oh . . .' they both replied, clearly disappointed.

'Guys, this is the same man who cheated on his wife and who has ruined my life. Remember?'

'Yes,' they replied in unison. 'But he's still bloody foxy.'

'I can't believe he asked you out,' repeated Mands, shaking her head in disbelief. 'Lucky cow.'

'*Lucky?*' I spat. 'My life has been completely ruined by that bastard.'

'True,' said Mands. 'Sorry.'

'Nice of him to ring and apologise though,' said Lizzie, attempting to create a positive spin.

'There is nothing nice about that man,' I said, pointing my finger at her for emphasis. 'He is the devil.'

'So, are you sure you won't go out with him?' asked Mands.

'Get out!' I hollered, hauling them both up from the chairs in which they sat. 'I want the two of you to bugger off and leave me alone!'

'But . . .' started Lizzie.

'No buts,' I replied. 'Piss off! Now!'

I grabbed their handbags and shoved them into their disbelieving hands, opening the front door.'

'Out,' I repeated, swinging my arm for emphasis.

'Don't you think you're . . .' started Mands.

But one look from my fiery eyes was enough to stop her in her tracks.

'Right then,' they choroused, tentatively shuffling past me out the door. 'Bye.'

I shut the door and collapsed onto the sofa, grateful to finally be alone with my sorrows. I took the phone off the hook and switched off my mobile. And then I had a good old bawl. I was sick of the paparazzi. Sick of the hounding. And sick of the friendly advice. And, I suddenly realised in between convulsing sobs, I was also absolutely exhausted. The past five weeks of constant hounding and lack of sleep had worn me out. It felt like a lifetime. I was in dire need of a good night's sleep, and a holiday. Two hours and many tears later I switched my phones back on. There were ten missed calls from Mands and Lizzie on my mobile. Each. Two minutes later it rang.

'Hi dolls,' said Mands, sounding somewhat sheepish. 'Look I'm sorry. I'm an insensitive bitch.'

'It's OK,' I sighed. 'I'm sorry for kicking you guys out. I just needed to be alone.'

'Understood. Are you OK?'

'Yes, the tears have stopped, and I feel much better.'

'Why don't we bring round some takeaways and a DVD tonight?' she suggested.

'Sounds good.'

'And I promise we won't talk about that bastard.'

'Thank you,' I sighed.

'See you at seven. Love ya.'

I put the phone down and it rang again straightaway.

'Hi sweets.' It was Lizzie. 'I've been trying to ring you.'

'I know,' I replied.

'I'm sorry, babe. So is Mands.'

'I know. She just rang.'

'How about we come round tonight with some dins?'

'You already are. I'll see you at seven.'

'And I promise we won't talk about that bastard.'

'Good,' I replied.

'Love ya. See you tonight.'

Late that afternoon there was a knock at the door. I opened it expecting to see a photographer who was prepared to break the trespassing rules, but it was a courier, with a tiny package in his hand.

'Samantha Steel!' he exclaimed, beaming at me. 'I saw you on the telly.'

'Fabulous,' I replied, sarcasm echoing from my vocal chords.

'Pretty popular, aren't you?' he said. 'Got loads of friends waiting outside.'

'They're not my friends,' I replied, signing the docket and taking the package. 'Quite the opposite.'

I set the courier bag down on the dining table and opened it. I pulled out a small light blue box, with the smallest white silk ribbon I had ever seen. I gently undid the ribbon and lifted off the lid. Sitting inside the small box was an even tinier box. A velvet one with silver writing. *Ohmygod!* I thought in surprise, reading the logo. It said Tiffany & Co. *Hell!* I opened the box to find a pair of gorgeous sparkling diamond stud earrings sitting inside. *Wow!* I whipped them out and put them straight on.

They're fabulous! I thought to myself, standing in front of the bathroom mirror. *God! They must have cost a bomb!*

Who on earth was sending me hideously expensive earrings? I wondered. *Perhaps I had a secret admirer who'd been following my media coverage. Some good had to finally come out of it, surely?*

No, I told myself. *I bet it's some rich media tycoon who wants to make a reality TV show out of my misfortune. Be just my luck.*

I decided to put myself out of my misery and see if there was in fact a card in the courier pack. There was. I tore open the envelope and pulled out the card.

Oh no! I despaired, realising I would not be keeping these beautiful earrings.

The card read:

Dear Samantha,
Since you won't let me take you out for dinner I can think of no other way to apologise to you. I truly am sorry.
Alistair

Bloody great! Of all the people who could have bought me Tiffany earrings it had to be him. I took them off and placed them back into the tiny box on the table. Such a shame, they really were lovely.

'Holy Mary!' exclaimed Mands, picking up the tiny jewellery box that evening.

I knew I should have put it out of sight.

'Oh gorgeous!' exclaimed Lizzie, looking over her shoulder.

'So?' said Mands, looking at me for an explanation.

'So, what?'

'So, where the hell did these come from? Or have you just been out spending ridiculous amounts of money on yourself?'

'Of course, that's perfectly OK if you have,' added Lizzie.

'No,' I replied. 'They're a gift.'

'A gift? From who?' asked Lizzie.

'Yes. Spill the beans for God's sake,' said Mands, sitting down at the table, earrings still firmly in her grasp.

'They're from . . . Alistair.'

'*Alistair?*' they exclaimed in unison.

'My God!' said Mands. 'Will wonders never cease? First he's asking you out to dinner and then he's buying you bloody expensive earrings. All in the same day!'

'Beautiful earrings,' added Lizzie.

'Beautiful earrings which are being returned to him tomorrow,' I replied.

'What?' they shouted, clearly alarmed. 'You're not sending them back?'

'Yes. I am.'

'Why, in God's name?' asked Mands.

'Because they're from *him*. And I'm not accepting anything from *him*. *He* is the man who has ruined my life. Remember?'

'All the more reason to take the earrings. There's nothing worse than being shafted by a man and having nothing to show for it,' said Lizzie, speaking from the heart.

'I can't accept them,' I stated. 'It's against my moral judgement.'

'Look, just because you've suddenly got yourself some morals it doesn't mean you can't give the earrings to me or

Lizzie,' argued Mands. 'We don't mind that he bought them.'

'No, we don't,' agreed Lizzie. 'Not at all.'

'Well I do and they're going straight back,' I replied.

'What a shame,' sighed Mands, staring wistfully at the earrings. 'Look how they sparkle.'

'Give them here,' I demanded, putting them safely out of her reach. She was appearing to look deluded. 'The only problem is I don't have his address.'

'Well, you're simply going to have to keep them then,' stated Lizzie.

'No. I'm going to have to phone him and ask for his address.'

'Really?' they chorused. 'That should be interesting.'

'How about you ring him now?' said Mands. 'While we're here.'

'No. I'm not having you two jumping about in front of me again. I'll ring him in the morning.'

'God, I wonder what he'll say?' said Lizzie, looking for all the world like a lovestruck teenager.

'Who cares what the hell he says?' I replied. 'He's an arsehole.'

'True,' agreed Mands. 'But he's an arsehole with very good taste. And there's something to be said for that.'

'Certainly is,' agreed Lizzie. 'Bryce had no bloody taste. He was just an arsehole. A complete waste of money. '

'And air,' added Mands.

We opened a bottle of wine and they both temporarily forgot about the earrings. Until they were leaving, that is.

'Are you sure you won't give them to me?' said Mands. 'It'd be such a waste sending them back.'

'Yes, I'm sure.'

'Positive?' asked Lizzie.

'Yes. Now bugger off.'

The following morning I retrieved Alistair's number from the depths of my mobile and made the call.

'It's Samantha.'

'Sam. Hi. What a nice surprise.'

'I can't accept the earrings.'

'Sure you can.'

'No. I can't. What's your address?'

'Why?'

'Because I'm going to send them back to you.'

'You can't send them back,' he protested.

'Why not?'

'Because they're a gift.'

'No they're not,' I replied. 'They're a peace-token apology so you can delude yourself into believing you've a clear conscience.'

'Sam, I don't feel guilty about what happened. I'm just sorry at what it's done to you.'

'So am I,' I replied. 'That's why I don't want the bloody earrings.'

'Why?' asked Alistair. 'Don't you like them? Because if you don't then I can send you another pair.'

'Whether I like them or not is irrelevant. The point is they will always remind me of you. Funnily enough that is not something I wish to remember.'

'No one's ever said that to me before,' he said, sounding rather dejected.

I bet they haven't.

'First time for everything,' I replied. 'What's your address?'

'I'm not telling you.'

'For God's sake Alistair, you're not five years old, what's your bloody address?'

'Samantha. I. Am. Not. Telling. You.'

'Yes. You. Are.'

'No. I'm. Not. Keep the earrings for God's sake! Please.'

'I'll be flushing them down the loo.'

'Do what you like with them. Just please accept my apology, and try to understand I honestly thought you knew who I was. And that I was married.'

'So, if I knew that would have made it OK, would it?' I asked.

'No. But it would probably mean you wouldn't be yelling at me right now.'

'You're lucky that's all I'm doing.'

'Plus Sam, I don't regret going home with you . . . in fact I'd like to do it again.'

'Well I bloody wouldn't. All I'd like is for you, and everyone else, to bugger off and leave me alone! Goodbye!'

I slammed down the phone. This time it was the landline, so that was OK.

'You told him *what?*' screeched Mands that evening.

'That they're going down the loo.'

'You're not really going to flush them, are you?' asked Lizzie, disbelief pooling in her eyes.

'Tell me you haven't *already?*' demanded Mands, jumping up and gripping me violently by the shoulders.

'Course I haven't,' I replied. 'I couldn't bring myself to.'

'Oh, thank God for that!' she sighed, sitting back down.

'What are you going to do with them then?' asked Lizzie.

'Keep them in a drawer for twenty years or so, until I've forgotten he ever existed. And then start wearing them, I guess.'

'Instead of putting them in a drawer . . . why don't you let us look after them for you?' proposed Mands.

'We'd be like a safety-deposit box,' added Lizzie. 'Any time you wanted to make a withdrawal, you could just come and get them back.'

'OK,' I sighed. Obviously neither of them was going to shut up until I let them wear the earrings.

'Yippee!' they cheered, slapping their hands together in childlike glee.

'Me first,' said Mands.

'Toss you for it,' replied Lizzie.

'You're on.'

After the best of three tosses, Lizzie won the first month with the earrings. Mands was inconsolable.

'That bloody coin's rigged!' she cried.

'Is not!' replied Lizzie.

'Is too! Toss it again.'

'No chance.'

This went on for half an hour, but Lizzie kept hold of the earrings. Eventually Mands forgot about them and the conversation returned to more pressing topics, such as the fact that Sven, the Swedish toe-sucker, was still trying to convince Mands and her feet to fly to Sweden for a holiday. It was nice to be talking about something normal. Something other than newspapers, or paparazzi, or Alistair. Or me.

For the next week I worked from home, stayed holed up inside my apartment and waited and hoped for the daily harassment to stop. But it didn't. It had now been exactly six weeks since I had slept with Alistair and my life had officially hit rock bottom, and was continuing to fall. Not a day went by where my photo wasn't plastered across the papers, or television screen. I had become a household name, although not for something desirable. I was the household Other Woman. The Marriage Wrecker. The Clothes Horse. *If only they knew*, I thought to myself. *He was the first decent shag I'd had in three years.*

As a result of my television interview on *One Nation* and telling my side of the story, some of the magazine hate mail had thankfully transformed into letters of support for me, which was of some relief, though the hate letters still held the firm majority. It was plainly obvious there was no end in sight to this madness. The media would always find a reason to hound me, always find a reason to regurgitate that one fateful night, and always find a reason to print my picture in the paper, long after the furore had settled down. I had seen it done to too many people, too many times before. There were some stories the media would just never let die. It seemed to me I had no other option, no other choice. I was going to have to go Under The Knife. Going to have to undergo some identity-altering plastic surgery, and swap my marriage-wrecking face for a new one.

Instead of working, I sat at the dining table and searched the web for my plastic-surgery options. Unfortunately, when one does a search on 'plastic surgery' you have to take the good with the bad. The results were not exactly reassuring. *When Bad Boob Jobs Happen to Cute Girls*, *Plastic Surgery Hell*, *Chipmunk Cheeks*, *Courtney Fishlips Cobain*, *Why I Look Permanently Surprised*.

Perhaps the web wasn't the most logical starting point, I decided.

Instead I stood in front of the bathroom mirror and scrutinised my face. If I had to have plastic surgery then I at least wanted to make some major improvements.

My nose would be the logical starting point. There was nothing cute and button-like about it at all. It was an aquiline nose, strong, straight and long. There was no doubting Nicole Kidman's nose would suit me better. And the way my ears stuck out just slightly had always bugged me. Surely I could have these nipped to the side of my head? My lips were a little on the thin side too, nothing a bit of collagen wouldn't fix. Perhaps Kylie's lips would look good? And recently I'd noticed a few fine lines appearing at the corners of my eyes. Perhaps a little eye lift too?

I rang Mands and Lizzie to break the news.

'You're going to *what?*' they both cried.

I was surprised by their response. We'd always talked about how we'd have no qualms hopping under the knife when the time arose. But I guess talking about it and actually doing it are two different things altogether. Plus, whenever we'd talked about it, it was assumed age and wrinkles would have something to do with it.

'I have to,' I replied. 'The vultures won't leave me alone.'

'Why don't you just move out of the city for a while?' they suggested. 'Until it all blows over?'

'Because I don't think it is *ever* going to blow over,' I replied. 'There are paparazzi outside my house every morning. Every day. And every night. I can't go out anywhere. I can't even go to work. I am a prisoner in my own bloody home. All I want is for them to just go away and leave me alone!'

'OK,' they soothed, sensing my distress. 'But at least let us come over and talk about it before you make any rash decisions.'

'Feel free,' I replied. 'But my mind is made up.'

That evening they arrived on my doorstep, bottles of wine in hand. Surprisingly they hadn't had to run past hordes of photographers to get to it, for once. The paparazzi appeared to have cottoned on to the fact that, because of them, I no longer went anywhere at night. The chances of a pic were slim to none, and they were far better off meeting their friends at the pub for a drink or going out for dinner. Things I used to be able to do, once upon a time.

Mands and Lizzie tactfully attempted to change my mind. Mands kept referring to the blotched facial peel she'd had last year, which was still firmly etched in her memory. Unfortunately for Mands it all went a bit pear-shaped. The supposed five days of peeling turned out to be three weeks and she subsequently turned into a walking scab. After taking the requisite five days off work, she'd then had to organise the Devonport Wine and Food Festival looking like she'd been dipped in napalm.

'You know this means you're going to have to move house too?' said Mands.

'I know,' I replied, looking forlornly around my living room. 'I know.'

Lizzie desperately tried to recount every plastic-surgery horror story she had ever heard of. Even her story about the woman who went in for a boob job and came out with three nipples wasn't enough to sway me. I was resolute.

After two hours of concerned pestering they finally gave in and we changed the subject. Mands even agreed to give me the name of the surgeon her old boss had used. The woman who never looked a day over forty, no matter how many years went by. Apparently he was very well respected in the realms of Plastic Land.

Three days later, I found myself sitting in the reception area of Dr Richard Hall's surgery ready for my initial consultation. I nervously flicked through the brochure sitting on the coffee table in front of me. There were pictures of perfect noses, extremely high cheekbones, perky eyes and full bee-stung lips. It appeared there was some sort of mix-and-match system available. A little like paint by numbers, or Mr Potato Head. I sincerely hoped I wasn't going to end up looking like Mr Potato Head, bits falling off everywhere and getting vacuumed up by my father, never to be seen again. I flicked to the back of the brochure. 'Have you always felt as though you're in the wrong body?' read the heading. 'Well, you're not alone.'

Oh Lord, I thought to myself, *perhaps I would be needing a sex change to become unrecognisable? Perhaps I was going to have to become a bloke? God forbid! I'd have to start watching sport and drinking beer. Maybe I'd even start dating Jasmine again? And there'd be no shopping for gorgeous frocks or Prada stilettos. It'd be hell.*

The thought very nearly made me cry. At that moment Dr Hall came out into the waiting room to greet me. I frantically closed the brochure and threw it back onto the table. There were some things even a doctor shouldn't be privy to.

'Samantha, lovely to meet you,' he said shaking my hand. 'Please come through into my office.'

He was a tall man, with an imposing presence. Tanned and well-groomed and looking remarkably good for someone who must have been in their early fifties.

He immediately made me feel at ease, which was good, because sitting down to discuss major life-changing plastic surgery was not something I was naturally relaxed about.

'Why do you want to have surgery, Samantha?' he asked, looking me in the eyes.

I'd had a feeling he was going to ask me this. I could have lied and said I was an actress who needed to look a certain way to get roles. I could have said I was doing it as a birthday present for my husband. I could have said it was because I really hated the way I looked. But there was something frighteningly sincere about this man, and I just couldn't lie. Plus, it would be perfectly obvious to him, unless he had been living in a cardboard box somewhere for the past six weeks, why I needed to change my appearance.

'Because the media won't leave me alone,' I replied. 'And because I want my old life back.'

'And you think surgery will succeed in giving you your old life back?' he asked.

'Combined with a new house, a new job, and a new name. Yes.'

'I see.'

'It's either this or volunteering for the Witness Protection Programme,' I explained. 'And unless you've actually witnessed a murder or know a murderer they're not all that interested. I've already phoned them.'

'So, surgery is a last resort for you then?' he asked.

'Correct,' I replied.

'I must say, Samantha, that professionally I don't think your situation warrants such a course of action. You are a very attractive young lady. But ultimately I am the doctor and the choice is, of course, yours.'

'The choice is made,' I replied, although my voice wavered as I spoke.

'Right then,' he said. 'Just how different do you want to look?'

'I want to be able to walk down the street without being recognised. But I don't want to scare myself when I look in the mirror.'

'I see. Well . . .' he said, gently taking my face in his hands. 'I really think only subtle changes will be required. Probably just a nose reconstruction, combined with a lift around the eye area, and some subtle cheek implants. Of course, you will also need a change of hair style and colour. And blue- or brown-coloured contact lenses.'

This was good news on the nose and eye-lift front, but bad news on the contact lenses. I liked my green eyes.

'Could I have Nicole Kidman's nose?' I asked.

'I don't see why not. It's a popular choice.'

He made it sound as though I'd just ordered a chicken deluxe burger, and not a new nose.

'How soon can you operate?' I asked.

'Well, there's usually a waiting list of at least two months for this type of operation, but I realise there is a sense of urgency in your case. So, I am willing to do this on a Saturday. How does next Saturday sound?'

That was just over a week away.

'Good,' I replied. I was confident I could hold out for that long.

I decided not to tell my parents about my surgery plans. There was no denying the fact my mother would be down here handcuffing herself to his scalpel before you could say 'Let go of the scalpel Elizabeth.' There was no way in hell my father would understand my decision either. He was still coming to terms with the fact Love the Earth biodegradable dishwashing liquid had changed its packaging (he had very nearly had kittens after being unable to locate it in the usual aisle). Plus, *plastic* and *surgery* were not two words he was prone to utter in the same sentence. The only people I told were Mands and Lizzie. I was simply just going to have it done and then show up at my parents' house, when there was absolutely nothing they could do about it.

So, the following Saturday morning, after yet another long stretch of solitary confinement, and yet again being chased by a convoy of paparazzi, I found myself sitting once more in Dr Hall's waiting room, flanked on either side by an uncharacteristically sombre Mands and Lizzie. Minutes away from going under the knife.

'Are you sure you want to do this, sweets?' asked Lizzie for the hundredth time that morning.

'Yes,' I replied, also for the hundredth time.

'You don't have to, you know,' repeated Mands. 'It'll all blow over soon, dolls.'

'Like hell it will,' I replied. I didn't think the media were *ever* going to let me have my old life back.

At that very moment a woman walked out into the waiting room with an enormous white bandage covering ninety per cent of her face, looking for all the world like a new-aged Tutankhamen. Mands and Lizzie glanced across me at each other, and then both looked at me.

'Don't,' I pleaded, and they promptly looked back down at their magazines.

Five minutes later another woman walked through the front doors into the waiting room. I made the mistake of glancing up at her. I wasn't alone. It's difficult to describe exactly what she looked like because it certainly wasn't human. The first thing that hit me was her lips. They were like two giant Swiss sausages that had been crudely stapled to her chin, then stung by a thousand bees. They were ginormous and covered at least half of her face. So big they were unable to close. So big they appeared to have a life of their own. So big they would have needed to rent their own apartment.

I looked across at Mands and Lizzie, who were both staring at the woman, jaws precariously close to the floor.

'Oh. My. God,' whispered Lizzie.

'He had absolutely *nothing* to do with *this*,' whispered back Mands.

I looked up at the woman's eyes. They had been lifted so far up that they were now sitting on her forehead, just below her hairline.

I looked away. My eyes were in a state of utter shock and had gone all fuzzy. But still they kept peeling back to her. It was like watching a succession of train wrecks. I knew what was going to happen, but I just couldn't bring myself to look away.

'I've never seen a set of walking lips,' hissed Mands.

I glanced down at the woman's breasts, which sat just below her chin, like two bobbing balloons. They were enormous. Mands and Lizzie were now also blatantly staring at the woman's breasts.

What else could this woman possibly be in here for? I wondered. There was not one part of her being that had not been lifted or blown up. *What else was there to do?*

I could not take my eyes off her.

Ohmygod! I thought to myself. I bet she started with a little nose job and eye lift too. I bet she only wanted to change her appearance, just slightly, and look what happened. She'd been unable to stop herself. *Sweet Jesus!*

'I can't do this!' I wailed, throwing my hands over my face.

'Oh thank Christ for that!' cried Mands, grabbing my arm and pulling me out of the chair with such force that she almost propelled me up onto the reception desk.

'She's changed her mind, thank God!' called out Lizzie to the receptionist, as they both frogmarched me out the front door, one on each arm.

'Right,' said Mands, as we sat back in the car. 'Let's just pretend that didn't happen and go and have a champers.'

'Good idea,' agreed Lizzie.

I would never forget that women's image, it would forever be burned onto my retinas. I would never, as long as I lived or as hard as I tried, be able to erase those enormous lips from my memory bank. I could only assume she had been some sort of sign from above, sent down to stop me having a nose job, eye lift, and subtle cheek implants. Someone really didn't want me to go under the knife. Not yet. It was funny though, I'd always assumed I would jump under the knife at some point in my life. Give things a subtle perking up when they got a bit saggy round the edges. But clearly my body wasn't ready to take the plunge just yet. However, something simply had to happen. Something to stop me hiding inside my apartment twenty-four hours a day like some criminal under house arrest. Something to make the vultures outside leave me in peace. And something to stop me from going completely and utterly insane.

8

You finally get used to sitting at the bottom of the barrel, like a rotten apple, and then someone above thinks it'd be a right old laugh to knock the bottom out of it. *See how she thinks she's hit rock bottom? Well, look a little closer and you'll see she's not quite there. Not yet. There's still a good couple of inches left for her to fall.*

I looked at my picture on the front page of the newspaper, yet again. And then I took a second look.

Oh. My. God! I thought to myself, staring at it in complete disbelief. Printed on the page was a large close-up shot of my face as I reached into my letterbox — my enormous glasses, my mouth, my nose. And also my left index finger. I looked, well, I looked as though I was picking my nose. My head was bent down and my finger was, well, scratching the bottom of my left nostril.

Oh . . . it just doesn't get any worse than this! I despaired. *It just doesn't! With the exception of the cellulite perhaps.*

On the front page of the *Daily Telegraph* with my finger up my nose. Clearly the bastard had waited until I'd scratched my nose to take the picture. *Arsehole!*

I read the byline underneath in horror. 'Perhaps Samantha Steel should pick her beaus more carefully.' *Oh great! That's just bloody fandiddlytastic! I bet the subeditor clapped their slimy little hands together when they thought of that one.*

I slammed my forehead down onto the dining table. It hurt.

That's it then, I told myself. *You will never be able to step foot outside this apartment ever ever again. You will simply have to grow old and die here.*

I banged my forehead onto the table a couple more times for good measure, until it really began to throb. I was still sitting slumped in the chair, head down, when my phone rang half an hour later.

'Hi sweets.' It was Lizzie. 'Um . . .'

'Save the ums, Lizzie. I've seen it.'

'Have you?'

'Unfortunately yes.'

'Looks a wee bit like you're . . .'

'I wasn't picking my nose! I was scratching it, for God's sake!'

'I know, I know. Bit of an unfortunate angle though.'

'The bastards!'

'Look . . . it's not that bad,' she soothed.

'*That bad?* It's a bloody disaster, that's what it is! I look like I'm picking my nose on the front of the newspaper!'

'People will know you're just scratching it,' placated Lizzie.

'I have to get out of this city!' I wailed. 'I can't stand this any more!'

And I really and truly couldn't. I was at my wits' end. At breaking point. It seemed fleeing the city was my only hope of holding on to any glimmer of sanity.

'Hold on sweets,' said Lizzie. 'We're working on it.'

An hour later, after receiving phone calls from my mother, Susie and Vicky, all of whom also thought I was picking my nose, I had a call from Mands.

'Now,' she said, the serious tone of event management resounding in her voice. 'I've found the perfect place for you to hide out for a while. It belongs to my Uncle Sten.'

'Where is it?' I asked.

'Floodgate.'

'Where's that?' I'd never heard of it.

'About four hours south.'

'Is it a city?'

'Ah . . . not exactly. More like a . . . um . . . small town.'

'Does your uncle have a house there?' I asked.

'Ah . . . not exactly . . . more of a cabin-type thing.'

'A cabin?'

'Yes . . . but it's very cute and rustic . . . apparently.'

'Apparently? You mean you haven't been there?'

'Ah . . . no.'

'What does he use it for?'

'Hunting . . . mainly.'

'Hunting?'

'Look,' said Mands, 'it might be a bit rough around the edges, but at least no one will find you there. And there's no phone for reporters to ring and harass you.'

No phone. This was good news.

'There's no television either, so you won't have to look at yourself.'

That was a definite plus.

'I don't even think there are any shops, which means no face in trashy magazines either.'

'No shops?'

Surely there were shops?

'Well . . . perhaps a couple.'

'So, what do you think?'

'OK . . . I guess.'

'Cheer up, dolls,' encouraged Mands. 'You won't be there long, probably only a month. Just until it all settles down.'

'If it ever does.'

'It will,' she promised. 'Don't worry. Plus, Lizzie and I will come and visit you. Lots.'

'You'd better.'

'Course we will. Now, we have to organise getting you out of this city ASAP. I think we can get you out by the end of the week. Can you hang on for that long?'

'Just,' I replied.

'It's tight, but we can do it,' said Mands, sounding even more like resident master and commander. 'I'll start making plans. All you need to do is organise your work. And pack.'

'OK.'

'And remember,' instructed Mands. 'Don't tell *anyone* where you're going. *No one,*' she repeated.

After hanging up from Mands I phoned Gareth straightaway.

'Gareth. Hi, it's Sam.'

'Hello. Just been looking at you on the front of the paper again. Not a very flattering pic, is it?'

Great. Was there anyone who hadn't seen it?

'No,' I replied. 'It's not. Look Gareth, I'm really sorry but I'm going to have to leave town for a while. Until this whole drama settles down.'

'For how long?'

'I don't know,' I sighed. 'A month . . . possibly longer.'

'Really? Where are you going to go?'

'I'm sorry, I can't say. Top secret. But I'll be taking my laptop and phone with me and I'll be contactable. And I'll do as much work as I can.'

'OK,' said Gareth. 'I think it's probably for the best. I assume

Erica can cover your client contact while you're gone?'

'Yes,' I replied, although it worried me just thinking about it.

I was sure my client contact wasn't the only thing she'd have her sticky little fingers in while I was gone. But what choice did I have?

'Just keep in touch Sam,' said Gareth. 'And take care.'

'I will. I promise,' I replied. 'And thank you.'

Maybe Floodgate wasn't that small? Perhaps it was one of those thriving little romantic towns with exquisite restaurants and wealthy tourists. Eventually I dived for the bookcase and rummaged for the atlas. *Small?* I gaped at the page in horror. *It was practically invisible!*

Floodgate consisted of four roads, which were surrounded by green paper as far as the eye could see. I flicked to the front page to see when the atlas had been published. 1999. I hoped like hell Floodgate had undertaken a massive growth spurt in the past six years. I sat with the atlas on my knee and wine in hand.

What the hell was I going to do? I wondered.

I walked to the window and opened the curtain a sliver. Although it was now eight o'clock and dark outside there were still five vultures standing beside the front gate. *You've got no choice*, I told myself. *You have to go.* I glanced forlornly around my apartment. I felt as though I was about to be shipped off to prison. But at least the prison was in the city.

Five more days of entrapment later, the big Departure Day arrived. It had been almost two months since the fateful night I had slept with Alistair. Mands had enlisted helpers for the evacuation mission. Her assistant Charlie, Lizzie of course, my parents and my two sisters. They had all met at Mands' apartment last night to discuss the procedure. I was not allowed to attend, for fear I would attract the media. Mands had drawn up a schedule of duties and no one was permitted to leave her apartment until they could recite it. Blindfolded, backwards, or from any other unnecessary angle. Apparently I was a bit like President Bush surprising the troops in Iraq. They had to make people believe I was heading to Camp David, when in fact I was flying to the other side of the world.

After a sleepless night I opened the curtain a crack and peered out my bedroom window. There were the usual morning crew outside — standing about chatting to each other, coffee and cigarettes in hand, as if they were on a bloody film set and not imprisoning an innocent woman. I got dressed and stashed as many necessary possessions as I could into my floral Prada tote bag. I wasn't allowed to pack a suitcase, Mands had stipulated, as this would give the plan away. Whatever *the plan* was. Instead, she and Lizzie had been gradually removing some of my clothes on their visits over the past few days, putting on extra layers and filling their handbags. These clothes were now somewhere en route, waiting for me to catch up with them.

Mands and Lizzie promptly arrived. Mands was in her event orchestration element. She was wearing diamante-studded combat pants, a black polo-neck jersey and trainers, and looking every inch the Little General. The feminine version.

'There will be no running, no sudden twitchy movements, and absolutely no talking to the media,' instructed Mands. 'Am I understood?'

'Yes,' I replied meekly.

'Yes,' murmured Lizzie.

'Right then,' said Mands.

'Are we taking my car?' I ventured.

'Well, you're not,' she replied.

'Really?'

This was bad news. If I was going to be doing a runner then I at least wanted to be doing it in my lovely new car.

She looked at my face. 'Don't cry. You'll get it back at some stage.'

Puzzled, I watched Lizzie strip off all her clothes.

Surely this wasn't the best time to be getting completely naked? I thought.

But then for some reason she pulled on my black gym leggings and my sweatshirt, before reaching for my white cap and enormous glasses.

'What're you doing?' I asked.

'Dressing like you,' she replied.

'Here, put these on,' instructed Mands, handing me the long cream coat, blue jeans and high-heeled black boots Lizzie had been wearing.

'OK,' I said, deciding it best to follow her orders.

Luckily Lizzie and I were exactly the same height and build. There's no way I would have fitted into Mands' size-six jeans. At size nine Lizzie's boots were half a size too big, but I decided to let that one slip by. Lizzie brushed my hair down, which was the same shoulder length as hers. Then she handed me her sunglasses and black beret.

'Now,' said Mands to me, 'here's what's happening. You're coming with me, in my car, and Lizzie is driving off to the gym in yours.'

The gym? She'd better make sure she didn't go on the leg-extension machine.

'OK,' I replied, finally beginning to fathom what was going on.

'Where are we going?' I asked.

'To the airport.'

'Yay! Where are we flying to?'

'Nowhere.'

'Oh.'

This was disappointing.

'We're off to meet your father.'

I had no idea why we were meeting my father at the airport, or what in fact he was doing there, but according to the Little General we had to get a wriggle on.

We got to my front door and Lizzie gave me a big hug.

'Bye sweets,' she said. 'See you on the other side. Love ya.'

'You too,' I replied, hugging her back steadfastly, not sure when I would see her again.

'Hustle girls!' instructed Mands. Clearly there was no time in the schedule for soppy farewells. I was officially on the escape from Alcatraz.

'Well, here's hoping this part works,' said Mands, driving us out through my gates and onto the road.

This signalled high excitement for the vultures, who had been staring at nothing but my front door for the past week. Lizzie drove out behind us in my car and then headed in the opposite direction down the street, giving us a toot and a wave. I waved back. The locusts promptly clambered into their vehicles and onto their motorbikes and, thankfully, most of them followed Lizzie in the other direction. I gathered this was also part of the plan. All except two that is, both on motorbikes, who were now closely following behind Mands and I.

'OK,' said Mands, glancing in the rear-view mirror. 'That wasn't too bad.'

Instead of driving erratically and at excessive speed in

an attempt to fob them off, as I did, she drove at a constant and controlled pace, steadfastly ignoring them.

'Why are we going to the airport?' I ventured.

'Pretending to catch a plane. Changing vehicles.'

She appeared to have developed some sort SAS speech pattern.

'Will you be coming with me?'

'Not initially.'

'Will someone.'

'Correct.'

Evidently she was a woman on a mission and not about to give anything away, even to me. Half an hour and very little communication later, we arrived at the international terminal, the two motorbikes still in hot pursuit. We parked the car, retrieved one suitcase from the boot (which I silently and desperately hoped was filled with my clothes) and walked inside the terminal, the two paparazzi walking swiftly behind us.

'Hey Samantha!' called out one of them. As I was supposed to be Lizzie, I chose to ignore him.

'Keep walking,' instructed Mands. 'Make it natural.'

'Trying,' I replied.

'You're doing well,' she encouraged.

This was the most she'd said to me in the past hour.

With the suitcase in tow we walked into the terminal, along past the check-in counters, up the escalator, and straight into the Qantas Lounge.

'Hi Mands,' said the woman on the front desk. 'Take a left. You'll find Charlie at the first table.'

Charlie?

'Thanks Cheryl,' replied Mands.

She knew her name?

I heard one of the paparazzi call out 'Samantha!' one last

time, as we walked on and they were left standing on the wrong side of the glass partition. It appeared we were finally leaving them behind.

'Hi,' greeted Charlie, who was sitting at a coffee table by himself, obviously pretending to read the paper. (It was upside down, I noted.)

Mands' assistant, Charlie, had been hired primarily because he was a fine specimen of young eye candy (it is obviously OK for women to do this). And, as Mands had said, 'if I have to pay someone then I'm going to bloody well get my money's worth.' But unfortunately Mands' gaydar must have been out of order at the interview because it was plainly obvious to Lizzie and I, upon our first glimpse of Charlie, that he was gay. Which he was. He was immaculately dressed, groomed, tanned, hilarious, affectionate and riddled with product. Admittedly he was perched on the straighter end of the gay scale, but gay nonetheless. Mands briefly contemplated firing him for misrepresentation. Only the fact that he was completely lovable and a fabulous assistant stopped her.

'They're outside the door at the moment,' Mands said to him. 'Keep them there.'

'Aye aye captain,' said Charlie. 'Good luck.'

'Walking,' instructed Mands to me, as she led me by my elbow. 'This way.'

I followed her to the other end of the lounge where we came upon a woman standing beside a single door, which clearly said in big red lettering Staff Only.

'Hi Mands,' greeted the woman. 'Come on through,' she gestured, opening the door for us.

It appeared Mands was to the international airport what Norm was to *Cheers. She'd have a lot of explaining to do when this was all over*, I thought to myself.

'Thanks Nancy,' replied Mands.

I stared blankly at Nancy as I walked through, lost for words. I felt like a special guest star on the *X-Files*.

We walked through the door, down a long corridor, down some stairs, down another long corridor, past what looked like a staff lunchroom and some offices, and then into what appeared to be the staff toilets. And there, sitting on a changing bench was my sister, Susie.

'Hi babe,' she said, giving me a hug.

'Hi,' I replied, wondering why on earth we had walked all that way just to wind up in a block of toilets with my sister.

'Pit stop,' said Mands. 'Change over.'

I had no idea what she was talking about.

'Time for you to take your clothes off,' Susie enlightened me. 'You've got to put these on,' she said, indicating at a pair of faded blue jeans, a hooded navy sweatshirt and some sneakers.

It wasn't really my style, but somehow I didn't think I was in any position to protest.

'OK,' I replied meekly, and began to get changed.

Whenever I took off an item of clothing, Susie, who was now standing in her underwear, put it on. She appeared to be pulling a Lizzie on me.

'Hair down,' instructed Mands, brushing Susie's hair and handing her the beret. She also had the same shoulder-length light brown hair as me, and was virtually the same build and height. From the back we would have looked identical.

I stood in my new attire of jeans, hooded sweatshirt and sneakers.

'And these,' said Mands, handing me a pair of black wrap-around sunglasses, and a short-haired black wig. I glanced in the mirror. I looked like a prepubescent male skateboarder, lost on his way to the rink.

'Moving,' instructed Mands.

'Bye,' said Susie, giving me another quick hug. 'See you soon.'

Obviously she wasn't coming with us.

I followed Mands out of the rest room and down to the end of yet another corridor, where we came to a security checkpoint.

'Hi Mands,' greeted the security guard.

'Hi Barry. We all OK?'

'Vehicle's ready and waiting,' replied Barry. 'Good luck.'

Oh Jesus! I thought to myself, staring at Barry. This was all just a bit too surreal for words. We walked outside into a small covered car park and there, waiting in the driver's seat of a vehicle I had never seen before, was my very own father.

'Hiya love,' he said. 'Jump in.'

'Hi,' I replied, no longer entirely surprised by each new face that popped into my path. I looked at Mands, who was putting the suitcase into the boot, unsure whether she was coming in the car too.

'Bye dolls,' she said, giving me a big hug. 'You did great. See you real soon.'

Obviously she wasn't coming with us.

'There's some hair dye in the suitcase,' she added. 'Be sure to use it as soon as you get there.'

I looked at her blankly.

'So you're not recognised,' she explained.

Oh.

'Where are we going?' I asked Dad, climbing into the passenger seat.

'For a little drive in the country,' he replied, obviously relishing his chance to talk cryptic.

The country? This sounded ominous.

'Anyone else coming?' I asked.

'Just us. But we'll be meeting up with your mother.'

The day just got weirder and weirder.

We pulled out of the car park and away from the airport. When we were well clear of the terminal Dad's mobile rang. I didn't even know he had a mobile phone.

'Yes,' he answered, obviously aware of who was calling him. 'Roger. Affirmative. All clear to go.'

Lord above! My father had suddenly transformed into an air-traffic controller.

'Who was that?' I asked.

'The captain,' he replied.

I looked at him searchingly.

'Mands,' he explained.

We drove onto the motorway and headed south of the city. The further away from the city we got, the more relaxed I became, as did Dad. There appeared to be no one following us, which was a good sign.

'Can I take the wig off now?' I asked, when half an hour had passed. 'It's a bit itchy.'

'I guess so,' he replied. 'So long as you pull the hood on.'

'Are you driving me to Floodgate?' I asked.

'No,' he replied.

An hour and a half later, and in the middle of the green countryside, we pulled into a deserted rest area. And there, waiting in my little silver car and having a day off from chanting, was my mother. I had no idea how my little car had made it to the middle of nowhere, and without Lizzie in it, but I gathered there were some parts of the plan I just wasn't privy to.

'Hello sweetheart,' she said, giving me a hug.

'Hi Elizabeth.'

'Good to see you made it.'

'Apparently,' I replied.

I wasn't prepared to believe I had made it to home base just yet. *Surely there were going to be more strange and familiar faces to meet and greet me?*

'On the passenger seat you'll find a map to Floodgate,' she said. 'And instructions on how to find the cabin and keys.'

'Guess you're on your own now, love,' said Dad, who had just transported the mystery suitcase into my car. 'Keep the hood and glasses on until you get there will you? And good luck,' he said, giving me a big hug. 'Thatta girl. You'll be fine.'

'Yes you will,' confirmed Elizabeth, giving me another hug.

And with that they drove off in the strange vehicle and left me standing beside my little car. It was now 3 p.m. and I was officially On My Own. Completely alone (I checked inside my car just to be sure). After what was without a doubt the oddest day of my life thus far. Sitting on the back seat of the car was a large box of supplies, food and drink. I also spotted a few bottles of wine in the midst. There was even a Tupperware container filled with homemade sandwiches and fruit slice. The only person who I hadn't seen on my voyage was Vicky. Obviously she was responsible for the supplies. No doubt she'd been up all night baking in my honour. Bless her, I thought, tucking into a sandwich. And then another, suddenly realising how ravenous I was. I didn't dawdle for long though, I was still a fair way from Floodgate and the notion of trying to find a strange cabin in the woods, in the pitch black, was less than appealing.

Three hours later I drove into Floodgate and was careful not to blink, lest I drive straight on through it. I stared at the one main street in horror. It was positively microscopic.

What the hell is this? I thought in dismay. It was like some sort of cardboard cut-out of a town. A deserted village in a Western movie, but without the dusty street or horses tied up outside. The place was smaller than my apartment building.

And what in God's name was I supposed to eat? I wondered aloud, as I drove along.

There were no restaurants, no gourmet takeaway shops, and no sushi bars. Just one shabby café, a pub, a post office, a fish and chip shop, a butcher, a 4-Square and a hardware store. I was going to die of starvation and that was all there was to it, unless I went to the supermarket and cooked for myself. But there wasn't even a supermarket, I soon discovered. And besides, I was the first to admit I really couldn't cook to save myself. *That's it*, I told myself, *you're going to have to survive on toast for breakfast, lunch and dinner, seven days a week.*

This was a living disaster. I was going to turn into one of those gingham-wearing farmers' wives who stocked up with months' worth of groceries at a time and then came home and made piles of wholesome soup, which she then labelled with her own homemade labels and stacked neatly into the chest freezer. Making soup was not one of the ways I had intended to spend my leisure time as an adult. Drinking fine wine, going out for dinner, and casually sipping bubbles at a waterfront café were more my style. I drove through the village centre, which took a criminal twenty-seven seconds, passing only six other vehicles, eight humans and two dogs. *I guess it is after business hours*, I consoled myself, glancing at my watch and finding that it was 6 p.m. Or at least I hope that was the reason for its ghost-like appearance. All eight humans I passed turned and stared at my car as though it were in fact a spaceship and not a vehicle. *You'd think they'd never seen a Mini before*, I thought in horror. Even the dogs stopped and gawped.

I headed out towards the cabin, or at least where I thought the cabin was. Suddenly there were no buildings or houses in sight, just the odd dirt driveway and lots of bush, and sheep. And no road signs. After driving along a very windy and deserted road for what felt like half an hour I decided I'd better pull over and have a look at the map. Some people are good with maps. Some people instinctively know how to hold them the right way up, how to pinpoint exactly where they need to get to, and how to interpret the cryptic scale at the bottom of the page. I was not one of those people. As soon as my eyes came in contact with a map of any description (on the very few occasions they had) they instantly glazed over and were unable to see anything clearly. Even hearing the word 'map' made them go all hazy. It was no different from staring at a page of foreign dialect. I looked forward to the day when GPS was as common as a seatbelt.

I forced myself to concentrate on the page through sheer will, by telling myself I wouldn't be having a glass of wine unless I found the bloody cabin. My eyes suddenly became clear. Not crystal, but enough to see I was currently travelling in completely the wrong direction.

After two more U-turns, twenty minutes more backtracking and as the daylight faded, I finally stumbled upon the driveway. Fortunately this wasn't hard to pinpoint with the name 'Williams' plastered across the letterbox. Every letterbox I'd passed had a surname, presumably so burglars knew whose house they were ripping off. I drove up the long dirt driveway, flanked by thick native bush on either side. After a couple of minutes the bush gave way and I pulled into a small grassy clearing. And just so you are aware, it was at this precise moment in time my life did officially hit rock bottom. The very bottom. With nowhere left to fall. What lay before me, on the other side of the grassy clearing, was nothing more than a very decrepit old red wooden shed.

Dear God! I thought to myself, staring at it in disbelief. *What in God's name is this? Surely this is just the garden shed? And the cabin is safely tucked away somewhere behind it?*

Desperate, I bolted for a look behind the shed. But all I came upon was an even smaller, even more decrepit, red shed. And lots of bush. As hard as I looked, I could not see any other buildings anywhere.

Deflated, I walked back around to the front of what had to be, as heart-shattering a revelation as it was, the cabin. It was glaringly evident that someone, somewhere, was enjoying a big hearty laugh at my expense. The wooden shelter before me was one step away from camping. And I was not, nor would I ever be, a camper. After taking several minutes to overcome my shock, I walked up onto the small wooden front porch and peered inside the window. I couldn't see much due to the dirt caked all over it, and the large crack in the glass. I walked back around to the smaller red shed and found the keys under an old paint tin, as instructed. I tried to open the ramshackle front door. The key turned but the door wouldn't budge. I barged it with my shoulder, but all this did was hurt.

Oh, this is just great, I thought. *I finally get here nearly twelve hours later only to be stuck outside the bloody front door.*

In a state of desperation and pissed-off-ness I lifted my right leg up to waist height and karate-kicked the door. It swung open and I walked through, searching the walls for a light switch. Thankfully Mands had the foresight to have the power connected before my arrival. In retrospsect, the fact the power had to be connected should have been enough of a warning.

Dear God! I thought to myself, when I finally located the light switch.

The pokey living area I stood in was like a cross between a prison cell and *Little House on the Prairie*. I half expected to see Huckleberry Finn crouching in the corner. I glanced around at the rickety wooden floor, decrepit furniture and paint-peeled walls.

'Aarrgh!' I screamed, jumping back against the wall.

There, on the opposite side of the room, four eyes were staring back at me. Mounted on the wall above the fireplace, were two large deer heads, complete with enormous antlers.

Oh Lord! I thought to myself. *I've two dead animals for roommates.*

The only deer I'd ever seen this close up was on a movie screen, and it went by the name of *Bambi*. Off the side of the tiny living area was an even tinier kitchen, complete with requisite old dripping tap. I took stock of the furniture. One shabby sofa circa 1910, one large wooden armchair (same era, although mismatched) and one tiny square kitchen table with four classroom-style wooden chairs.

How could someone as fashion-savvy as Mands have a relative with such appalling decorating taste? I wondered. It just didn't make sense.

The whole scene was a bit like *Antiques Road Show*, but without the road-show part. Or the woman named Mary thinking the hideous floral vase she'd inherited from her grandmother and had kept locked up in her glass-fronted china cabinet for the past fifty years was going to be sending her on a cruise ship to the Bahamas for ten weeks, and not just down to the bowling club for a Sunday roast. I moved on to the bedrooms, of which there were two. One double (in the very loosest possible sense of the word) and one bunk room, complete with two stuffed rabbits mounted on the wall. *This place is a bloody morgue*, I thought to myself. Both beds appeared to be circa 1950, including the mattresses. I peered into the tiny bathroom (if that's what you could call it) in which sat one very old bath, with an archaic shower over the top, one hand basin, and one mirror, complete with large crack.

Where's the loo? I wondered, peering behind the door. *What an oversight! He forgot the bloody toilet!*

Perhaps it's outside the kitchen? I thought, walking back through the kitchen and opening the back door. But it wasn't. All that was outside the door was a slab of broken concrete, grass, and more bush. I looked across at what appeared to be another tiny tool shed standing by itself on the edge of the bush.

Oh no! I silently prayed. *Please dear God no!*

I tentatively walked across the grass, fear resounding in each step. Then I stood outside the old wooden door, holding my breath, and prayed for mercy one last time before very gingerly pushing it open. It was evident our Lord had very selective hearing. I looked through the door and there, before my sad eyes, was a long drop. A very old long drop, judging by the rolls of yellow toilet paper sitting on the ledge. I had only used a long drop once in my life, at school camp when I was twelve years old. The process of sitting on what was essentially a large hole in the ground, with God only knew what inside that hole, while a very large black spider wound its way down from the roof above onto my bare thigh had scarred me for life. The thought of walking out here in the pitch black and cold middle of the night and sitting on this prehistoric filthy contraption did nothing for my flagging morale.

There's only one thing for it, I decided. *You're not to eat. Ever again.*

Dejected, I walked back inside. The entire cabin was smaller than my living room. It was also as dusty as all hell, and cold. And there were literally piles of dead insects residing in each corner.

Couldn't the man find a cleaner? I wondered.

I had no choice but to set about cleaning the place straight away. There was no way I was bringing my possessions into this dusty hovel. I helplessly rummaged through the cupboards for the vacuum. Eventually my rummaging turned up what could only be described as a collector's item. It was a monster! I initially mistook it for the hot-water cylinder.

Here's hoping it bloody works, I thought to myself, plugging it in. It did.

I vigorously pulled it about the place, being sure to poke it into every single morgue of a corner. Perhaps a bit too vigorously.

E-oww! I yelped, my head suddenly and viciously grabbed by something on the wall above.

My God! I realised with horror. *It's the bloody antlers.*

My head was stuck firmly in the middle of a pair of dead deer antlers. It was a vegetarian's worst nightmare. I dropped the vacuum and attempted to prize the antlers apart and wriggle my head out. Finally they let it me go, but not without leaving two large red welts down either side of my face.

Bugger this! I thought, walking into the kitchen to make myself a cup of coffee. Or I would have if there was a kettle or a plunger. After once again opening and closing every pokey cupboard in the vicinity it was evident there was no plunger kettle to speak of.

Mother of God! I thought to myself, cursing Uncle Sten. *Does the man not even boil water?*

I wrote both items onto the list I had taken to carrying around with me and assessed my prehistoric options. I was going to have to turn the stove on and boil some water in a saucepan for my instant coffee. *Easier said than done,* I thought, looking at the primeval oven. It was like no oven I had ever laid eyes on before, although admittedly my eyes had not come in contact with a great number of ovens in their lifetime.

Half an hour after thinking how nice it would be to have a cup of coffee I was blessed with boiling water. Horrible concoction in hand I collapsed onto the sofa, which was the equivalent of a bowl of oatmeal porridge, all lumps and dips. At that moment my mobile rang. It was Mands.

'Hi' she said, or at least I thought she did. All I could hear was crackling and bits of words.

Christ! I thought. *There's no goddamn reception either! This place really was the arse-end of the earth.* And I was sure even the arse-end of the earth had better coverage.

'I can't hear you! I wailed. 'No bloody reception!'

But all I got in reply was another crackle and half a word. I walked outside and climbed up onto the porch railing, which seemed to ease the crackling, and I even managed to make out one or two words. Something about 'safe' and 'hot water.' And then my phone cut out.

Just brilliant, I thought to myself. *Stuck in the wops and devoid of communication.*

I searched inside for a landline. I found the connection (a very old one), but no phone, as Mands had said. *Well at least there's a plug,* I thought, in an attempt to console myself. If there was no mobile reception then I would have to buy a phone tomorrow and get it connected. It was one thing ensuring no reporters could ring you, but it was quite another having no contact with your two best friends. After finishing the vacuuming, while keeping one eye out for dead animals, and wiping every single surface I could find, I brought my bags inside.

Where the hell were you supposed to hang your clothes? I wondered.

The only wardrobe I could find was in the bunk room and it was the size of a bread bin. And to top it off there were only two hangers, along with one dwarf-sized chest of drawers. I decided to leave my clothes in my suitcase and worry about this one tomorrow. Instead I gave the bathroom a thorough once-over, including picking dead insects' carcasses from the plughole. While I was in there I suddenly remembered I was supposed to be dying my hair. I found the bottle of dye in the suitcase and set about reading the instructions. It looked as though I was going to be a redhead. *Red?*

With my slightly olive complexion I did not have a redhead's features. Plus, I liked my hair. It was shoulder-length, perfectly straight and parted down the middle, with soft layers framing the sides of my face. And it was a lovely highlighted brown colour. *Brown.*

Ah well, it's only for a while, I consoled myself.

But when I try and grow it out I'll look like a licorice allsort, myself complained.

You don't have a choice, I told myself. *You have to be unrecognisable.*

I took a moment to consider my options, which didn't take long due to the fact they were incredibly limited, and then I took the bottle of dye out of the packet and set about dying my hair. I had never dyed my own hair before. Highlights were something I happily paid someone else to do. A hairdresser. Someone who knew things about hair.

Surely it can't be that hard, I thought to myself.

One hour, one T-shirt, one sink and two hands covered in red dye (unfortunately I had overlooked the pair of latex gloves) I was done.

I looked into the tiny, cracked mirror. And there I was, for all intents and purposes, a bright redhead. A Gingernut.

I tried my hardest not to cry. But it didn't work. I looked at my reflection and tears streamed down my face. I knew it wasn't permanent. I knew that soon I would be able to dye it back to brown and grow it out. I knew I had to dye my hair if I had any hope in hell of staying anonymous in this town. But still, it just didn't suit me. I looked like a stripper who'd been told she had to go red if she wanted to keep working at The Club. It was all just so very wrong.

I stopped crying, turned on the shower and stepped in to rinse out the dye, but then jumped back out in shock. The water was cold. Stone cold.

Bloody fantastic! I guessed Mands' two words 'hot water' had something to do with this. I hurried back into my warm clothes and set about locating the hot-water switch. Eventually I found it under the kitchen sink, but there would be no chance of a shower tonight. So, with teeth chattering I dipped my head into a sink-full of arctic water and rinsed out the dye as quickly as I could.

Then, after a lengthy session with the hairdryer in an attempt to return my body temperature to normal, I decided to pull out my laptop and check my emails.

Thank God for wireless internet connection, I thought to myself.

But it seemed my thanks were a little too hasty. It appeared that *Swoosh* coverage did not yet stretch to the arse-end of the earth.

Bloody hell! I wailed. *No phone and no internet! What was a girl to do?*

I settled on rummaging through the enormous box of food supplies which Vicky had packed for me. Aside from fruit, bread and cereal, it largely consisted of numerous packets of instant pasta and noodle thingies. The just-add-water variety.

I knew I couldn't cook, but did she have to make it quite so obvious? And to top it off they all said things like 'just for one' and 'en solo' on the front of the packets. Like it wasn't bad enough you were eating dinner out of a packet, and by yourself, they had to rub it in your face. My eyes fixed on a jar of olives which I decided to open instead, along with a bottle of red wine. I opened the kitchen drawers, searching for the bottle opener. Twenty minutes later I was still searching.

There. Must. Be. One. Here. I kept telling myself, rummaging through the same drawers for the sixth time. *There simply must!*

Having searched the kitchen dry, several times over, I was stumped. But I wasn't giving up. Not now. My glimmer of hope was that I found it very hard to believe any relative of Mands was a teetotaler. It just didn't make sense. In a fit of better judgement I headed towards the fireplace and there, sitting on top of the mantel, was a little chipped bowl. And inside that bowl was none other than a Swiss Army knife.

Hallelujah! I cried, prizing out the corkscrew.

Mission accomplished I dragged my duvet, the olives, and the bottle of wine to the lumpy couch and flicked through the stacks of magazines the girls had brought me. I suddenly realised it was a Saturday night, which made me feel even more depressed. The contrast between the pages of *Vanity Fair* and the walls of this dusty shed I now found myself residing in were extreme, to say the least. It was *rustic charm* all right, but without the *charm* part.

I soon realised how cold I was, largely due to the many holes and gaps in the wooden floorboards, and vainly searched about for some sort of heating device. I didn't have to worry about heating devices in my apartment, whenever I was hot it was cool and whenever I was cold it was warm.

Just the way it should be. *Central heating had a lot to be proud of*, I thought to myself, rummaging through the rooms. My search turned up what could only be described as The Oldest Electric Heater Known to Man. I brought it into the front room, wiped the cobwebs from it and plugged it in. It looked like the type of heater that would willingly burn your house down if you left it alone for thirty seconds. In other words, it looked dangerous. Upon turning it on it immediately lived up to its reputation by firstly smoking profusely, and then making a frightening sizzling sound. Then it died.

Just great, I sighed, pulling out the plug and giving it a kick.

After a forlorn gaze at the empty fireplace, and then remembering I had absolutely no idea how to light a fire, I resigned myself to crawling back under the duvet and being cold. I suddenly wished I had paid more attention to my father's efforts to make a Scout out of me. I flicked through a couple more magazines, devoured the rest of the olives (and wine) and then I took my cold and dejected self off to bed. I stood staring at the tiny double bed, willing it not to be as pitted and lumpy as it appeared. Tentatively I pulled back the duvet and climbed in, only to be immediately sucked into its very core. The bed appeared to have eaten me. I found myself lying in a dip so enormous I was sure I'd need a pair of crampons and winching out come morning. Ten packets of frozen peas could have been put under the mattress and I wouldn't have felt them. I tossed and turned in the crevice, unable to get to sleep. There was something missing, but I just couldn't figure out what it was. *Noise!* I suddenly realised. *There's no noise! No traffic. No drunken domestic disputes on the footpath outside. And no car alarms.* It was eerily and unnervingly quiet. I could even hear myself breathing.

It was completely disturbing just how loud silence was, I thought to myself a long time later. Deafening in fact. It was making my ears buzz. I put a pillow over my head in an attempt to block it out. In fact, that is how I spent my first night in rural asylum — sleeping with a pillow over my head, trying my hardest to block out the silence.

9

The next morning was an entirely different story altogether. I was woken far too high on the Early Scale by a God-awful racket outside the bedroom window. Birds. Lots of them. Chirping, loudly. This was not a sound I was accustomed to in the city. I was usually lulled back to sleep by the soothing drone of traffic and rubbish collectors. Nice, constant, reliable sounds.

How could anyone possibly like the sound of birds? I wondered to myself, putting the pillow back over my head. It was piercing. They were all randomly singing their own songs, completely out of tune. I would almost have rather listened to Celine Dion. I said almost. Half an hour later I'd finally had enough of them and dragged myself out of bed. My neck and back ached from having lain all night in a lumpy, saggy hole. I walked into the bathroom and jumped back as I passed the mirror. There was someone else in the bathroom with me. But then I got a grip and realised it was just me and my new red hair. I stood in front of the mirror and let out a long sigh. Unfortunately it didn't look any better today.

Hopefully I'll grow into it, I placated myself. But myself strongly doubted it.

But at least there is now hot water, I thought, dragging myself away from the mirror and into the bath meets shower. But someone had beaten me to it. A massive gangly daddy-longlegs was currently inching its way down the shower curtain.

Oh no! Get out! I urged, attempting to windmill it away. But it was having none of it, clearly glad for the company after all these years of solitude. It was by far the quickest shower of my life as I exfoliated and cleansed my heart out, all the while keeping my gaze firmly locked on the insect. Not the most relaxing morning shower I'd ever had.

Having exorcised myself of dust and mustiness, I got dressed and opened the front door, stepping out onto the tiny wooden porch. I looked around at my surroundings in the bright morning sunlight. There was absolutely nothing to see. Not another house, let alone a bean. I might as well have been living in an igloo at the top of Alaska. Just a patch of grass at the front, a dirt driveway, and bush. Lots of bush. I was surrounded by it on all sides. I walked round to the back of the cabin and there it was again. More bush.

I decided to drive into the village and buy a phone, putting on my disguise — jeans, T-shirt, gym shoes, sans make-up, and of course my new red hair, tied back in a ponytail and topped off with a cap. I was practically unrecognisable. There was no need for the enormous glasses, although Mands had packed an extra pair for me, just in case. It felt strange hopping into my car and driving away without being chased by a fleet of paparazzi.

Twenty minutes and only one wrong turn later I was standing in the tiny main street, outside the post-office-slash-bank-slash-stationery shop, which I deduced was my best (and only) phone-buying option. I had parked right outside the front door, in one of the many vacant spaces. *At least it looked like parking wasn't going to be a problem around here*, I noted, looking around for the meter. There wasn't one to be seen. *Free parking,* I thought to myself. *What an odd concept.* I'd no idea it still existed.

It was eerily quiet with only a handful of vehicles and other people about. I could have sworn I saw, out of the corner of my eye, a couple of tumbleweeds racing each other down the pavement. The post-office-slash-bank-slash-stationery shop was right next door to the solitary café.

Might as well grab a coffee first, I decided, for want of any other pressing engagements. The outside of the café looked like a relic from the 1950s with its black-and-white-checkered tiles and lacey curtains framing the front windows. I looked through the white lace and contemplated the odds of getting a real coffee. Around twenty per cent, I decided. I stared up and down the street, vainly hoping I had missed another café on my drive-by, and that a well-known coffee sign was going to leap out and dance merrily before my eyes. But no, there wasn't another café to be seen.

Oh well, I resigned myself. *You can't stand outside forever.*

I stepped through the doorway. It was a sad, sad sight to behold. Red checked tablecloths on white plastic tables, with white plastic chairs to match. I visibly cringed. Any delusions I had of the 1950s exterior masking an Italian bean roastery, filled with the mouth-watering aroma of various strands of freshly ground coffee were violently shattered. It reeked of lavender and weak tea.

'Hello love,' greeted the peppery-haired lady stacking scones into the basket on the counter.

Any further delusions of getting a decent coffee flew out the lacey window at the sight of her. She was wearing the brightest shirt I had ever seen. Lime green with white flowers and, oh yes, she had the skirt to match. Thankfully I still had my sunglasses on.

'Hi,' I replied. I was standing just inside the doorway, right on the buzzer it appeared.

I stepped forward. It was too late to turn and run now. I was committed to buying something from this time warp of an establishment.

'What can I get you, luvvie?' asked the woman.

'Um . . . a coffee?' I ventured, apprehension echoing in my voice.

'Ooh . . . a coffee?' she repeated. This was not a good sign. Not at all.

'Okey-dokey love, I'll just pop it on now. Anything else?'

'Yes . . . and a scone please,' I said, looking at the basket on the counter top.

'Date or cheese?'

'Date please.'

'Good choice love, those're fresh out of the oven, they are.'

I hadn't eaten a date scone since my sisters and I had been to stay with Grandma Atkins when I was ten. It appeared they hadn't changed much. I took my wallet out of my handbag.

'That's OK, you can pay on your way out. Have a seat and make yourself comfy. A watched pot never boils after all.'

A what? What was she on about pots for? And pay on my way out? What a foreign concept. The only place that let you pay on your way out these days was a supermarket, not a place I frequented often. Although I presumed the lady was confident I wasn't going to do a runner, being the only person in the place. And that the town was the size of a pea of course. The local constable would have me pinned in no time at all.

I grabbed a magazine — there were no newspapers thank

225

goodness — and sat down. *Heart & Home* was a tragic piece of literature for those women who aspired to make a career out of being a housewife. My sister Vicky was no doubt a regular subscriber. I opened it to a page with the heading '101 Ways to Pickle'.

Dear God, I wondered, as I flicked through the millions of pickle recipes. *Where in the hell have I ended up?*

I smelt the coffee being carried towards me before I saw it. It smelt like filter. I was afraid to look.

'Here we go then, love,' said the woman, putting the filter coffee and date scone down in front of me. 'Enjoy.'

'Thank you,' I replied, choking back the urge to cry.

I steadied myself and slowly brought the small white ceramic cup to my lips, while simultaneously trying not to inhale its contents. The Fluoro Woman was standing back on the other side of the counter, sneaking the odd glance at me. I tried not to grimace as I swallowed the foul concoction. It tasted like black tar mixed with more black tar. I tipped half the sugar bowl into the cup in an attempt to make it drinkable and persevered. The coffee was nothing short of hideous but I reluctantly admitted to myself that the scone was delicious, especially as it was still warm and the butter melted right into it. I generally avoided butter like the plague, but I was in desperate need of something comforting.

'Thank you. That was lovely,' I lied, standing at the cash register.

'You're welcome. Just passing through are you?'

'No. I'm staying here for a while.'

If passing through was an option, there's no way in hell I would have stopped, I thought to myself. *Surely people didn't stop in this place of their own free will? If their cars broke down maybe.*

'Are you really? Well isn't that just lovely. My name's Elsie.'

'Jane,' I replied, shaking her hand.

I might have been stuck in the wops, but I wasn't stupid. Jane was my middle name and now also doubling as my Floodgate pseudonym.

'Have you been busy?' I asked, attempting to make conversation.

'Had the morning rush a little earlier on but no, fairly quiet this time of year. Busier round Christmas time.'

Christmas time? That was months away! And the morning rush? In this town? She'd hardly be lynched by the mob. Perhaps more than one customer in your shop constituted a rush in these parts?

'However,' continued Elsie. 'To get eggs there must be some cackling.'

I had absolutely no idea what she was talking about, so I just smiled back.

'Nice to meet you, love. You have a good day.'

'You too,' I replied, walking out and stepping on the buzzer, for old times' sake.

I had no idea at all what I was going to do for the rest of the day.

I walked next door into the post-office-slash-bank-slash-stationery shop and managed to find one solitary phone on the shelves. They always kept one on hand for emergencies, according to the man behind the counter. Apparently it was my lucky day. The phone looked as though the last emergency in this town had been around 1950.

'I met you somewhere before, love?' asked the man.

'No. I don't think so,' I replied. 'I'm not from here.'

'Must look like someone then. Someone very pretty.'

'Thank you,' I replied, grabbing the phone and lurching out of the shop.

227

It was completely unnerving being talked to by shop assistants. And that was the second one in the space of five minutes. I was used to being tactfully ignored. I hurried home and turned the phone on, but of course there was no connection.

Bugger it! I despaired. *What was I going to do?*

In a state of desperation I located a ladder in the tool shed and leant it up against the side of the cabin, gingerly clambering up onto the tin roof. I couldn't remember the last time my legs had found themselves attached to a ladder, if indeed they ever had. I scrambled up to the peak of the roof and turned on my mobile to call Telecom. Thankfully the crackling was minimal and, after twenty minutes of Mariah-Carey-inflicted torture, I was informed the phone wouldn't be connected until the end of the week, being a rural connection.

'Can't you do it any sooner?' I desperately pleaded. 'I'm in isolation here.'

'Fraid not,' said the young man. 'Guess you'll have to sing to yourself or something.'

And that was just the problem with service in this country these days, I thought to myself as I hung up. *There wasn't any.*

Hell! I suddenly realised. That also meant I was also going to be without internet access until the end of the week.

No internet! What was I going to do? I wouldn't be able to work. I wouldn't be able to email friends. This was a bloody disaster!

It appeared I had been unwittingly marooned on an island of prehistoric communication. I was going to have to learn Morse code next. I decided that since I was still crouched on the rooftop I might as well ring Mands and Lizzie.

'Dear God! You're alive!' exclaimed Mands. 'Thought I'd lost you to a bear or something.'

'No bloody reception,' I replied. 'And no internet either!'

'Oh you poor baby! So, how is it?' she asked.

'You mean the bug-infested, dust-coated shed? It's just fine thanks.'

'Oh dear. Guess it hasn't been used in a while then?'

'Not in the past hundred years anyway.'

'What's the town like?'

'I don't think *town*'s the right word. More like campground.'

'Small then?'

'Let's just say that if you happened to buy a new coat, if you could find somewhere to buy one that is, then there's every chance that within the space of five minutes everyone here would know not only how much you paid for it, but also whether the colour suited you.'

'I see,' replied Mands.

I started to get cramp in my thighs from squatting on the roof, so I said my goodbyes and asked Mands to phone Lizzie for me.

Later that evening, in a desperate state of coldness, I came to the conclusion that I was going to have to light a fire, or at least attempt to light a fire. I found a huge stack of dry wood outside the cabin, an old yellow newspaper (dated November 1971) and a packet of matches, which really should have been sitting in a museum display cabinet somewhere.

Well here goes, I thought to myself, once I had piled the scrunched-up paper and wood into the bottom of the fireplace and opened the box of matches.

A short while later I found myself lying on my stomach on the old wooden floor blowing furiously into the fireplace, as the last flicker of flame died before my smoke-filled eyes. Then I stopped blowing and started crying instead.

How was I going to stay warm, I sobbed, *if I couldn't even light a fucking fire?*

Deflated, I put on another jersey and climbed back under the duvet.

The next three days were without a doubt the longest of my entire life. They stretched out before me like an endless piece of frayed brown string. How long is a piece of string? You may well ask. Well, I can tell you it is nowhere near as long as living in a cabin in the bush, in the middle of nowhere, with no mobile reception (aside from the peak of the tin roof), no landline, no internet, no television and no other humans. My only entertainment was a portable CD player which the girls had kindly packed for me. The only problem was they'd only packed five CDs. There was only so many times I could sing along to Norah Jones without wanting to violently murder myself. And her. I'd read all of the magazines they'd bought me from cover to cover on the first day. And then I'd re-read them each five times. I'd stood on the rooftop and talked until both my phone battery and my legs had died. Then I'd re-charged my battery and headed for the roof top again, only to be rained on, hard. I'd found an old yellow raincoat and headed up again, but then I'd come to my senses and realised the peak of a slippery, wet, sloping tin roof possibly wasn't the best place to be standing, especially with one hand locked to my mobile. My only social contact was my morning outing to the café in town and a chat with Elsie. I had swiftly decided to substitute my morning coffee with a pot of tea, in light of the hideous experience on my first day. Elsie was pleased with my switch to Earl Grey.

'A change is as good as a holiday love,' she said. I think she was just glad she no longer had to try and work the filter-coffee machine.

I hated tea. It reminded me of musty woollen jerseys, old people and the war. No, I wasn't in the war, but whenever I was forced to drink tea I felt like I might as well have been. Barely a week ago my morning tea had consisted of a trim latte and a low-fat blueberry-and-cream-cheese muffin. Now it was a pot of tea and a date scone. A pensioner's morning tea. When I complimented Elsie on her date scones she replied, 'Thanks love, but chickens don't praise their own soup.' I think she was trying to be modest.

After my third night of adding boiling water to a pasta packet for one, I decided I had no other choice. I was simply going to have to learn to cook for myself, which meant I was going to have to go and buy some fresh food. I also needed tampons, of all things. With FreeAsTheWind being one of my clients I hadn't bought a tampon in about five years. I had enough to sink a small ship back at my apartment. But that was back at my apartment. Plus, I was desperate to find a newspaper, in the vain hope the media had finally had enough of me. I tied my hair back, put my cap on, and once again refrained from applying any make-up. I was Plain Jane. Incognito. I drove into the village, had my cup of tea and date scone, and then walked across the road to the grocery-slash-dry-cleaning-slash-liquor store.

'Hello love,' called a woman from the back of the shop.

I turned around, slightly startled. I still wasn't used to being greeted when I walked into a shop. It scared the bejesus out of me.

'Hi,' I replied.

'You're the girl who's moved here from the city, aren't you?' said the large woman, bustling her way around the overcrowded counter.

'Well . . . yes . . . I'm just staying here for a while.'

Good news obviously travelled fast in these here parts.

'Well I hope you enjoy yourself,' she said. 'Not much happenin' at the moment though, be a bit busier around Christmas time.'

'So I've heard,' I replied.

Although God himself couldn't help me if I was still in this hellhole then.

I set about walking around the shelves and fridges, and then walked around them again. I was at a complete loss to think of something I might potentially be able to cook. Or what ingredients I would need to cook that something. In the end I decided to throw a mixture of fresh vegetables and a couple of packets of risotto into the basket, along with some olive oil and dressing. Hopefully they would be happy to mix together and form something edible. I took my full basket to the counter and looked around for a newspaper.

'What're you after there, love?' asked the woman, noting my confusion.

'A newspaper please,' I replied.

'Just over there,' she said, pointing at the other side of the counter. 'Help yourself.'

It appeared there was no *Daily Telegraph,* although this wasn't such a bad thing. I might still be on the front page, but at least I wouldn't have to see myself there. The only option was the *Morning Sun,* so I popped one into the basket. There was a small selection of trashy magazines, but thankfully none with either Alistair, myself or Tiny Tits on the cover.

'Do you get the *Telegraph*?' I asked the woman.

'Not usually. Not much interest in it in these parts. More of a city paper isn't it?'

'I guess so,' I replied.

This was good news in the concealed identity stakes, although I'd now have to rely on Mands and Lizzie for *Telegraph* updates. Until I could look at it online of course.

'The other thing I'm after is a coffee plunger?' I ventured.

'A what, love?'

'A plunger. For coffee,' I repeated, making the appropriate plunging motions with my arms.

'Oh . . . ahh . . .'

This didn't sound promising.

'I know what you mean but no, we don't have one. You might want to try Bruce at the hardware store next door.'

'I have coffee though,' she added, leading me to the back of the shop. 'Here we go.'

I assessed my limited options and picked the best of a bad bunch, in the vain hope I might eventually be able to find something to plunge it with.

'I'm Della,' said the woman as she handed me my change. 'Nice to meet you.'

'Jane,' I replied. 'And you.'

'Have a good day, won't you love.'

'Thank you,' I replied. 'You too.'

I walked next door into the hardware-slash-pharmacy store and asked Bruce, a tall Maori man with an enormous beer belly and a large moustache, for a coffee plunger.

'A what, love?'

How can the man not know what a plunger is, for God's sake?

More appropriate arm-plunging motions, then a few more because Bruce wasn't as good at charades as Della.

'Oh . . . no I haven't. Sorry love.' He scratched his head. 'Hmm . . .' he said, '. . . can't think of anywhere here you might find one of those. Might have to go to Misty Creek.'

'Where?'

It transpired that Misty Creek was the closest town, the one with the supermarket. The one which was fifty kilometres away.

How bloody ridiculous! I thought to myself. *Not one goddamn coffee plunger in the entire village. This place was a shopper's living hell.*

I wasn't that desperate for a coffee, at least not yet. I drove back home, made myself another cup of tea, sat down at the rickety kitchen table and tentatively looked at the newspaper. Thankfully the front page was devoid of my picture; this was good news. Relieved, I turned to page two, only to lock eyes with a very large half-page full-colour photograph of my mother — combat pants on, ferocious glint in her eye and arm outstretched in mid-swing clutching what appeared to be, on closer inspection, a large loaf of organic bread. The large bold heading above read 'Sam's Mum Swings Out'. And the byline below: 'Samantha Steel's mother takes a plug after ladies call her daughter a slapper.'

Oh dear God! I thought in horror. *What the hell has she done now?*

With my head in my hands I read the small clump of text below. It appeared the incident had happened in an aisle of Woolworth's yesterday afternoon, while stunned shoppers looked on. My mother had apparently overheard two middle-aged ladies glancing at a newspaper and gossiping about me. She was then quoted by several witnesses as saying, 'No two-bit jam-making housewife will call my daughter a slapper!'

before taking to both of them with her loaf of sourdough (presumably because she didn't carry a handbag). And before the police arrived at the scene. *What the hell was she doing in the supermarket?* I wondered. That was my father's job.

There was only one thing worse than sleeping with a famous married man, being portrayed as a home-wrecking floozy, and being forced to flee your great job and fabulous city apartment for a bush shack at the arse-end of nowhere, and that was seeing your mother on page two of the *Morning Sun* swinging her bread at two middle-aged women in the fruit and veggie aisle of her local supermarket, looking like an extra from *Rocky*. The police had arrested my mother and charged her with assault. She had been released on bail last night.

Dear God above, I despaired. *It didn't get any worse than this. It honestly didn't.*

I immediately clambered onto the roof and rang home, getting my father on the line.

He recounted the sorry details. It was true she had been released on bail last night and was due to appear in court next week.

'Put her on!' I demanded. 'What the hell were you thinking?' I yelled, when she picked up the receiver. 'Just when things were looking like they were settling down, you had to go and do this!'

'What was I supposed to do?' she asked. 'Stand there and listen to those two walking doilies mouth you off?'

'Yes,' I replied, through gritted teeth. 'That would have been the sensible thing to do.'

'Well, I'm afraid that's not in my nature.'

'No bloody kidding!'

'I was just trying to stand up for you,' she protested.

'Mum, I mean Elizabeth, I am thirty-three years old. I have not lived at home for the past thirteen years. I am an adult. I do not need you to protect me, OK? What I *need* is for you to stay the hell out of it!'

And what I also needed was a chair. My thighs were killing me.

'Fine,' she replied, clearly sulking. 'Goodbye then.'

My father came back on the line.

'Take it easy on her love,' he urged. 'She was only trying to stand up for you. You know what she's like.'

'I know she likes getting arrested.'

'Well yes, that's true,' agreed Dad. 'But this was different. This was about you.'

'That's right, this *is* about me,' I replied. 'And I don't want to see *myself* in the paper, let alone my own *mother*.'

'OK, OK,' said Dad, noting my distress. 'So . . . how's everything else going then?'

'Terrible,' I replied. 'There are peas bigger than this town.'

'You'll be back home in no time,' he encouraged. 'Hang in there.'

'Thanks Dad,' I sighed. 'Oh, and can you please email me some dinner recipes?' I asked.

'Some recipes?'

'Yes,' I confirmed. 'There are no restaurants in this place, so it looks as though I am going to have to either learn to cook or starve. Make them easy though,' I added. 'Very easy.'

'Sure thing, I'll send them through tonight. That's great news!'

'Don't get too excited,' I warned. 'I'm sure I won't be able to do anything with them.'

'Don't be silly love, you'll be fine. And I'm only a phone call away if you need any help. At any time.'

I hung up the phone, aware I was possibly one of the only thirty-three-year-old women alive whose father was offering a twenty-four-hour cooking-info line.

That afternoon, much to my delight, the phone line was finally connected. I was even awarded a brief sojourn of social contact with the Telecom man.

'Plug it in and give it a whirl there,' he instructed, once he had done his thing with the cables and bits.

I did as I was told and was greeted with the nostalgic sound of an active line. Gold to the ears. With a 'Bob's your uncle', he hopped into his van and was off again. This meant I could finally, after six days of solitary confinement, log on and check my emails. I was as excited as a Jehovah's Witness on their wedding night. But slow did not even begin to sum up the connection speed. It barely moved. There were tortoises out there with a greater sense of urgency. Ten minutes passed by and I still wasn't connected. Whereas at home I would have phoned the provider and demanded they come round straightaway and 'Make it fast!' I realised there was simply no point in doing that here. There was no way in hell they were going to come and fix it.

When I was finally able to access my inbox, twenty minutes later, there were fifty-six new messages there to greet me. Ticker tape and all. Fifty-six! For a fleeting second I felt overwhelmingly popular, but that was before I realised at least ninety per cent of them were work-related, of the 'Where in God's name have you disappeared to?' and 'Are you still alive?' variety. At least twenty were from Gareth who was very keen to know if I was ready to do some work. The rest were from my clients who wanted to know if I still worked at the agency, or had I set up on my own somewhere? And if so, would I mind very much telling them where the hell that was? The feeling shifted from overwhelmingly popular to just plain overwhelmed in the space of a few seconds. I had only been four working days without communication and my career was on the verge of collapsing entirely.

I switched into damage-control mode and spent the rest of the day firing off emails and assuring everyone that yes, I was still very much alive and yes, I did still work for the agency and yes, we did still want their business and yes, I was only on leave and would be back in the very near future. It was obvious Erica wasn't doing such a great job of looking after my clients for me. *The cow!* I made sure to copy her in on every reply I sent, with the words *and in my absence you can contact my assistant Erica Jordan* clearly spelt out, with her direct dial, mobile and email in bold lettering below. I refrained from adding her home phone number.

What would these people do if I actually had died? I wondered. *Would they be upset? Or would they just be pissed off that their thirty-second television commercial was now going to take six weeks to produce instead of four?* Unfortunately I knew the answer, and it didn't involve fresh flowers and words of condolence.

At nine o'clock I decided it was possibly in my best interests to make myself some dinner. I was supposed to be cooking risotto after all.

I located the old saucepan and put the risotto on the element on a low heat (as instructed). Then I put the diced vegetables into an equally ancient frying pan on a medium heat. So far, so good. And then I sat back down at my laptop. Which was not so good. It wasn't until the smell of black and shrivelled vegetables reached my nose I realised (a) I had forgotten to add the olive oil and (b) I had also forgotten about the vegetables.

If there was a bloody smoke detector they might have been saved, I thought to myself, as I scraped the charcoal remains into the rubbish bin.

I sat down to a large bowl of bare, dry risotto. *I will never be able to cook,* I despaired. It was only the continuous swigs of red wine which stopped the risotto from taking up permanent residence in my oesophagus. Thankfully my father emailed me several recipes the following day. All with headings like *Easy Meals* and *Simple and Delicious*, which gave me some small glimmer of hope. And a couple of days later, although I was still burning things left, right and centre, I was finally able to construct something reasonably edible. It was only the complete lack of any other eating options which made me persevere. I wasn't willing to starve to death just yet.

The next morning I began to feel guilty for yelling at my mother, but there was no point in ringing her to apologise. Whenever she was told off she generally went all silent and uncommunicative. So, I decided to send her an email instead.

Dear Elizabeth,

Firstly, I would like to apologise for yelling at you.

However, can you please try to understand how seeing you belting women with your bread, simply because they were talking about me, might make me slightly upset?

I really don't need any help in the publicity stakes, I seem to be doing quite nicely by myself at the moment. Plus, I think you should understand everyone is talking about me and not all of it is pleasant. All I want is to keep a low profile and for the media to leave me alone, hence hiding out in this hellhole. So, can you please do me a favour and keep your handbag on your shoulder from now on?

Love,

Sam

I got a swift reply.

Dear Samantha,

I have processed your thoughts and will endeavour to keep a lid on my emotions in future. However, there is no denying those two gossiping sock-darners got what they deserved.

Elizabeth.

PS. Your father has made you some boysenberry jam and wants to know where to send it?

Great. I had jam coming out my ears. *When was he going to start making wine?*

I also emailed Mands and Lizzie with my new phone number and within a millisecond they had both tried to phone me. Lizzie was the one who got through.

'We have contact, sweets!' she cried. 'Hurrah!'

'Yes, finally,' I replied. 'I was beginning to think I had died and been deported to the Land of Eerie Silence.'

'How are you?' she asked.

'OK,' I replied. 'Just bored. And lonely. I've even started talking to the spider in the shower. Oh, and I now drink tea.'

'You *what*? But you hate tea.'

'Yes, you're right, I do. I also hate dusty old sheds but that isn't stopping me from living in one.'

'Poor dolls.'

'But enough about me,' I urged. 'Why don't you tell me what the rest of the country thinks about me?'

'Well . . .' began Lizzie. 'There's some good news . . . and there's some bad news.'

Why was there always some good news and some bad news? Why couldn't it be all good news and no bad news at all? It's like the good news got lonely and packed a sad if

240

there was no bad news to keep it company.

'Good or bad?' asked Lizzie.

'Both,' I replied. I had given up believing there was a tunnel, let alone a light at the end of it. There was simply an eternity of blackness.

'Your mother's been beating up women in the supermarket with her . . .'

'Bread stick,' I finished. 'Seen it.'

Good news.

'Right. Well OK, that's good. Apparently there was a picture in the *Morning Sun* as well, but that was only on page two, and it was much smaller.'

Correction. Bad news.

'It looks as though Tiny Tits has overtaken you in the publicity stakes.'

Good news.

'Over the past couple of days there's been more news in the papers about her than you.'

Very good news.

'Her pictures are huge and yours are much smaller and sitting either underneath or to the side of hers, just as a sort of reference point.'

Fabulous news.

'The cow looks immaculate in every picture too!'

Terrible news.

'I think it's because they haven't got any new pictures of you. They just keep printing the same old ones.'

'Not the one with my finger up my nose?'

'Well . . . yes . . . but only a couple of times.'

Hideous news.

'Has she done any more telly interviews?'

'No.'

Good news.

241

'The media seem to know you've skipped town.'

Bad news.

'But they have no idea where to.'

Good news.

'The *Telegraph* seems to think you're lying on a beach somewhere in Fiji.'

'I bloody wish.'

'Oh, and the World Cup's about to begin. The team's leaving tomorrow.'

Bad news. That meant even more news about football in the paper, which meant even more pictures of me. But at least it would be over soon. And perhaps then they might decide to leave us both in peace.

'Well that's about it,' said Lizzie, wrapping up her report. 'They'll soon get sick of you, dolls, now they haven't got anything new to say.'

10

I had my breakfast and flicked through the rest of yesterday's newspaper. *What the hell was I going to do today?* I wondered.

It was Saturday morning. If I was at home I would have been going shopping with Mands and Lizzie. *Shopping*, I thought in faint recognition. I had almost forgotten what it was. *Fat chance of doing that here.*

I suddenly remembered Elsie saying it was market day in the village that day. Whatever that was. Probably some sort of prehistoric food-bartering system, villagers swapping potatoes for fertiliser type of thing. However, God knew, I really did have to get out of the hovel at some stage, the antler-clad walls were beginning to close in on me. *Plus perhaps*, I thought, in a faint glimmer of deluded hope, *there would be something for me to buy? Some local clothing designer yet to make it big?*

I put on my Plain Jane get-up and drove into the village. It appeared the market was in the church car park, judging by the stalls and crowd of people. *People.* I'd no idea so many people lived in this town. I mean it wasn't a city-strength crowd, but it was a crowd nonetheless. A rural crowd. There were a surprising amount of stalls too, largely food, with a few revolting arts and crafts thrown in for good measure.

And people appeared to be paying with money, rather than potatoes.

I really should buy some food, I thought, walking over to the row of produce stands. The first stand I came across was unfortunately the butcher.

'Buggerandhell!' I gushed, jumping back. There, staring up at me from the table, was a pig's head. Not something I was accustomed to seeing. One generally didn't stumble into pigs' heads of a Saturday morning in the city.

'You all right there, love?' asked the butcher.

I managed a nod.

This was closest I had ever been to a pig. My childhood had in no way consisted of quality time on farms or tramping in the bush. Most of my quality time had been spent down at the shopping mall or going to the movies. I attempted to wipe the twisted grimace from my face and quickly moved on. At the next stall there were rows and rows of preserved jams and chutney thingies piled up on the table, with little bits of gingham wrapped over the lids. It looked as though Jenny was the culprit, judging by the way all the labels said 'Jenny's Jam'.

She must spend every waking moment making jam, I thought in horror, staring at the pile of jars before my eyes. The first contender for Jam RSI. She could give my father a run for his money. I bought some strawberry jam and onion chutney and walked on. The next stall along, and unfortunately the only clothing stall I could see, was piled high with ugly homespun jerseys and woollen hats in delightful shades of brown and green.

Please God, I prayed, *no matter how long I have to stay in this hellhole, never let me wind up wearing one of those.*

The next stall was filled with art (in the very loosest possible sense of the word). There were more watercolour paintings than there were old people alive to hang them. Paintings of boats, fields of wheat, vases of daisies, horses, and other predictable watercolour subjects. It's as though whenever anyone painted in watercolour they had to paint one of these things, or there was a good chance their paint brushes would self-combust. I hated watercolour paintings. They reminded me of doctors' surgeries and retirement homes.

'Jane! Jane!' shouted a woman's voice, as I walked away from the watercolours.

I suddenly remembered that was my new name and turned for a look, even though the chances of me bumping into someone I knew at a market fair in the middle of the country were slim to none.

But I was wrong. It was Elsie. There was no hope in hell of missing her. She was wearing some sort of bright-pink-and-black-striped all-in-one trouser suit. She looked like a disco zebra.

'Hello love,' she said, approaching me with several shopping bags and two men in tow. 'How are you?'

'Good thanks,' I replied. 'And you?'

'Marvellous, thanks. This is my husband Bob.'

I shook hands with and smiled at a shortish rotund man with grey hair and a close-cropped grey beard. He looked like some sort of happy Swedish woodchopper, all round, smiley and bearded.

'And this is Ethan,' said Elsie, turning to the youngish man on the other side of her. 'He's my surrogate son.'

Ethan smiled at Elsie and then at me. I had been under the impression that only people aged under ten or over sixty lived in this town. At thirtyish he was definitely breaking the mould. Plus, he was also reasonably good-looking, in a kind of bad-checked-shirt-wearing farmer way.

'Hi,' I replied, shaking his hand.

'Jane's moved here from the city for a wee while,' explained Elsie. 'She's one of my regular customers. And my favourite,' she added, giving me a little wink. 'How do you like the market, luvvie?'

'It's great,' I lied.

Although, to be honest, it felt good to be out of the cabin and surrounded by other humans for once.

'Do all of these people live here in town?' I asked.

'No love,' replied Bob. 'Most of them are farmers or orchardists in the area. They just come into the market each week to stock up.'

'Well, a rolling stone gathers no moss,' said Elsie. I think that meant she was making a move. 'See you on Monday, luvvie, have a tip-top weekend.'

'Bye,' chorused Bob and Ethan, each giving me a little wave and a friendly smile. 'See ya soon.'

I walked on and did a loop of the remaining stalls, coming across one piled sky high with fresh fruit and vegetables. I was ecstatic. In my euphoria I purchased a far greater quantity of fruit and vegetables than one person could hope to eat in a month.

The last stall I came across was a bookshop, of sorts. More like a table stacked with piles of ratty hundred-year-old books and well-dated and worn magazines.

I really did have to get something new to read, I thought to myself. I could now recite my copies of *Vanity Fair, Tattler, Harpers Bazaar* and *Style* word for word. I aimlessly foraged through the piles of books.

I picked up a battered copy of *Anna Karenina*, which I had failed to finish when I was at university.

'You know only fifty per cent of people who start that book ever finish it,' said a voice next to me.

'And I'm one of the pikers,' I replied, turning to look at the voice, which belonged to Elsie's friend, the youngish man.

'Are you planning on torturing yourself again?' he asked.

'Apparently,' I replied. 'I'm feeling a bit self-deprecating at the moment. Just can't seem to get enough of inflicting pain on myself.'

'Perhaps you should read something a little lighter then. How about this?' he suggested, holding up a battered copy of *Treasure Island*. I'd never read it.

'I guess I'm reading this then,' I said, taking the book from him.

'I think you'll enjoy it,' he said, picking up his food-laden basket, smiling at me and walking off.

Never in my life had I seen a man carrying a woven cane basket in such a leisurely manner. He was completely and utterly at ease with it.

That afternoon I curled up on the lumpy couch with my duvet and opened *Treasure Island*. With much rejoicing I even managed to light a fire, which stayed alight. Before I knew what was happening, I was immersed in the classic adventure story. How I had managed to miss this gem when I was a child I had no idea. The book itself was almost eighty years old, and was filled with beautiful full-page colour illustrations. The dust covering each page only added to the magic. I couldn't remember the last time I had curled up on a couch for an entire afternoon, reading a book from cover to cover. I contemplated turning on my laptop and checking my emails, but I was just too cosy to move. *It can wait*, I told myself, turning back to the book.

My only interruption was the phone. It was Mands.

'Guess what?' she said.

'What?'

God, what else has happened? I thought to myself.

'Lizzie and I are coming to visit you next weekend.'

'Really?'

'Yes. Really.'

'Really really?'

'Yes. Really really.'

'Fabulous!'

Yay! I was finally going to have some human company!

'You'll need to bring several duvets,' I instructed. 'One to sleep on and one to smooth out the lumps in the mattresses.'

'Sound peachy,' said Mands.

'It's a shithole,' I reiterated for the tenth time, lest she have any romantic log-cabin-in-a-field-of-daisies-with-a-hunky-in house-woodchopper notions. 'There hasn't been any human activity in this place for at least forty years.'

'Probably why Uncle Sten had forgotten he owned it,' said Mands.

'There's a lot to forget,' I replied.

'So, what do you need?'

Half an hour later Mands had a concise list of what to bring: Clarins moisturiser, fresh magazines, a calendar (so I could mark off each day, just like a real prison), CDs, a selection of wines and a pair of long-forgotten running shoes.

'What are those for?' asked Mands.

'To run in.'

'What do you want to be doing that for?'

'Because, there's no gym and I'm rapidly turning into a porker. Oh, and I need some tracksuit pants too.'

'Some what?'

'And I don't own any so you'll have to buy me some.'

'I should hope you bloody don't! Where the hell do I get those from?'

'A sports shop . . . I guess.'

'Spose you'll be running in those too?' she asked.

'Correct. It's too cold for my gym leggings.'

'I'll make Lizzie get those. I'll buy the moisturiser and wine.'

'Fine. Just *please* don't forget anything. Or plan on picking any of it up on the way through the village. There is nothing there. It is the shopping Antichrist.'

'OK, OK,' said Mands, noting my desperation.

'Oh!' I suddenly remembered. 'And I need my coffee machine too.'

'What? That bloody great thing sitting on your kitchen bench you've never used?'

'Yes.'

'How the hell am I supposed to carry that?'

'OK,' I relented, realising I might be pushing it. 'Just buy me a plunger then.'

'Gotcha,' said Mands, adding it to the list.

'Update,' I pressed. 'Just how much does the world hate me today?'

'Actually,' replied Mands, 'I think the world is beginning to get sick of you. There was only one picture in the *Telegraph* today and nothing in the *Sun.*'

'What picture was it?' I asked.

'Um . . . the nose one.'

'Oh for fucksake!' I cried. 'When are they going to lose that?'

'P'haps you should send them a new picture of yourself?' suggested Mands. 'So they've got something else to print.'

'Not a bad idea,' I replied. 'So, what was the story about?' I asked.

'It was about Alistair at the airport, leaving for Italy with the rest of the team. Looking very foxy too,' she added.

Good, I thought, ignoring her. *So the story wasn't actually about me then.*

'Well here's hoping the plane crashes,' I said.

'And that a few of them survive,' continued Mands. 'Including Alistair. But they have to resort to eating each other to stay alive.'

'And that Alistair gets eaten first,' I added. 'Because he's got the most protein.'

'Exactly,' finished Mands, who was always brilliant at playing along with imaginary tales of death and destruction.

The following morning I headed off for a walk, which was intended to be half an hour but ended up being slightly longer. With the help of a farmer on a four-wheel motorbike I managed to find the cabin again, over two hours later. Navigation, in any way shape or form, had never been my strong point and this was only accentuated in the country, where every paddock, fence and grassy ditch looked like a clone of the one before. There were no shops to clock as reference points. No traffic lights, pedestrian crossings or buildings to judge my distance from home.

'Might want to carry a compass next time,' suggested the nice farmer, as he dropped me back at the bottom of the dirt driveway.

A compass? All I wanted to do was go for a simple walk. I'd no desire to take up orienteering.

I had a shower and drove into the village for my morning tea. There was absolutely no one in the village, at least no other humans to speak of, and all the shops were closed, including the café.

'What the hell's going on?' I wondered aloud.

It looked as though the entire township had been abducted by aliens.

I looked up and down the street for any other sign of

life but there was nothing doing.

What day is it? I asked myself. *Sunday,* myself replied. *Oh.* I suddenly clicked.

It appeared that Floodgate was one of those prehistoric towns where retail life ceased to exist on a Sunday, presumably so that everyone could bugger off to church and other pressing familial engagements.

Had they never heard of seven-day-a-week service? I was used to being able to purchase whatever I wanted and on whatever day I chose. There was no blatant discrimination between Sunday and weekdays in the city. It was all just one big happy seven-day shopping week.

What if I'd no food left? I thought in horror. I did, but I was just taking a moment to exaggerate the situation. *I'd starve, that's what. And then I'd sue this town!* Providing I was still alive of course.

From now on I was simply going to have to make a better effort to stock up and be prepared for The Closing. It'd be like preparing for some sort of civil emergency, cans of baked beans stacked sky high on every shelf. I was just annoyed there'd be no date scone for me today. I had come to love them. I stood on the footpath for a few more minutes and definitely saw a couple of tumbleweeds roll past this time. Then I drove back home and made myself a cup of tea, sans scone. I spent the rest of the day reading, lazing about and generally recovering from my morning hike. I contemplated checking my emails, but for some unknown reason decided against it. They could wait.

I spent the next week working at the tiny kitchen table, interrupted only by my morning-tea excursions to Elsie's café and a daily walk. It was surprising how much work one could accomplish when one didn't have numerous people asking one a succession of stupid questions. I felt as though, for the first time in over a year, I was finally getting on top of my workload. It helped that I didn't have to leave my laptop for time-consuming meetings or ad shoots.

Friday evening took far too long to arrive. I couldn't wait to see the girls. I had now been living in rural isolation for exactly two weeks and I was beyond the point of loneliness. I had even begun to converse with myself, on a regular basis.

I picked some wild lilies from the roadside and scattered them about the cabin, in a pitiful attempt to make it more feminine and welcoming, and less like the hunters' trophy shack it was. Then I opened one of my two remaining bottles of wine in anticipation and rustled up three mismatched glasses.

I had polished off the bottle by the time they finally arrived. They were two hours late when I spotted Mands' headlights inching up the driveway and went outside to greet them.

'Bloody road signs!' cried Lizzie, climbing out of the car. 'We got lost.'

'Gathered that,' I replied, giving her a huge hug.

'I need a drink,' sighed Mands, collapsing into my arms.

'She hit an animal,' explained Lizzie. 'Not coping very well.'

'You mean I *killed* an animal,' corrected Mands.

'Sorry, correction, killed.'

'What sort of animal?' I asked, hoping like hell she hadn't run over one of the neighbour's farm dogs.

'A brown furry one,' said Lizzie. 'Something nocturnal.'

'Where?' I asked.

'Back there . . . somewhere,' said Mands, waving her

hand. 'It all looks the bloody same to me. Pitch black and no houses.'

'It wasn't very pretty,' said Lizzie. 'It just sort of sat down in the middle of the road and stared up at us as we ran over it.'

'With its big scared eyes,' wailed Mands.

'And then it sort of went bump under the car,' added Lizzie.

'So I pulled over,' continued Mands, 'and we went and had a look with the phone.'

'The what?'

'My phone's got a little torch on it.'

'I see.'

'And . . .' faltered Mands.

'And it was mashed all over the road,' finished Lizzie, clearly enjoying herself. 'Like a can of guavas.'

'*Please!*' said Mands.

'Sorry.'

'OK, come in and let's sit you down with a vino then,' I said, leading Mands by the hand. 'And don't forget the dog,' I said to Lizzie.

Louie was sitting solemnly in the back seat, looking every inch the condemned prisoner. He continued to sit there even when Lizzie opened the door to let him out. Eventually she grabbed him by the collar and hauled him inside.

'Jesus Christ!' exclaimed Mands, when we got inside under the lights. 'Your hair!'

After two weeks I had become immune to my red hair. In fact, I'd even become rather used to it.

'Crikey!' cried Lizzie, also seeing it for the first time.

They both touched it, to make sure it was real, and then they stepped back.

'It just looks . . . well . . .' said Mands. 'A bit wrong doesn't it?'

'You're the one who bloody well picked it,' I reminded her.

'I don't think so, sweets,' said Lizzie, cocking her head to one side. 'I think it suits you. It's just different, that's all.'

I couldn't tell if she was being honest or just kind.

'You look a bit like Nicole Kidman,' she added.

Obviously she was just being kind.

I watched as Mands and Lizzie evaluated their new surroundings.

'Bloody hell!' declared Mands. 'He said it was basic but he didn't say it was a shack!'

'A little on the rough side,' agreed Lizzie, although the look on her face indicated it was quite substantially on the rough side. 'A real fire!' she exclaimed, noticing the blazing fire in the hearth.

'Yes,' I replied.

'Who lit that?' she asked, looking around. 'Have you got a bloke living here already?'

'No,' I replied proudly. 'I lit it.'

Against all odds I had managed to light a fire every night for the past week.

'Get out!' said Mands, suddenly cheering up. 'No you didn't!'

'Yes. I did,' I confirmed.

'Hell!' said Mands. 'Unbelievable! Who taught you then?'

'No one. I taught myself.'

'Go on! You're having us on!' said Lizzie.

'No, I'm bloody not,' I replied.

Did they really think I was incapable of lighting a fire? Well, OK, a couple of weeks ago I was. But nothing enhances your ability to learn like freezing your tits off.

'It's just a fire,' I added. 'It's not that hard, you know.'

I had a sudden flashback to my second night in the cabin,

lying on the floor, furtively blowing into the fading embers, tears streaming down my face. Well, maybe it was a bit hard.

They glanced sideways at each other, a strange smirk on both of their faces.

'She's going all *Survivor* on us,' said Mands. 'She'll be voting us out of here next.' She stared at the antlers on the living-room wall. 'Christ alive! The man's a mass murderer!'

'And you're related to him,' I added.

'I had no idea,' said Mands. 'He always seemed so normal.'

'That's not the worst of it,' I said, showing her the stuffed rabbits in the bedroom.

'I'm not sleeping with those,' she wailed. 'Get them the hell down!'

I lifted them off the wall and shoved them into the bottom of the wardrobe.

'Is that a bunk?' she asked, noticing the bedroom furniture.

'Yes.'

'And I'm sleeping on that?'

'Yes.'

'I'm gonna fall off and kill myself.'

'Why don't you put the rabbits on the floor to break your fall?' suggested Lizzie.

'Very funny,' said Mands. 'I'd like to see you sleep on that thing.'

'I'm sleeping with you,' whispered Lizzie in my ear.

'I heard that,' said Mands. 'Which is fine by me because we all know you snore.'

Lizzie and I laughed. We both knew it was Mands who snored when she'd had a few. Like a trooper. Over the years we had both thrown various cushions, pillows, and anything else within arm's reach which wasn't going to cause serious head injury at her, in a vain attempt to make her wake up and shut up. Invariably she stopped for about two minutes before roaring straight into it again. It was astounding how something so small and petite could make so much noise.

'Where's the toilet?' asked Lizzie, popping her head into the tiny bathroom. 'Absolutely busting.'

'Um . . .' I replied.

They both turned and looked at me.

'Um what?' said Lizzie. 'Have you broken the toilet already?'

'No, it's just . . . um . . .'

'Spit it out!' cried Lizzie. 'Or I'm going to pee on the floor.'

'It's outside,' I replied. There was no easy way to say it.

'Outside as in outside the back door?' asked Lizzie.

'Yes . . . sort of.'

'Please,' said Mands. 'The suspense is killing me.'

'You're not the only one,' said Lizzie.

I grabbed the torch and took them outside the kitchen door and pointed across the glass clearing, at the small shed.

They both stared back at me, eyes wide with disbelief and jaws agape.

'But . . .' started Mands.

'. . . it's a shed,' finished Lizzie.

'It's a long drop,' I corrected her.

'Is that the only toilet?' she asked, looking very much like a wounded child.

She was obviously hoping I was telling a big fat lie and somewhere back inside the tiny cabin there was a spanking new porcelain amenity waiting just for her.

'Yes,' I replied solemnly. 'It's the only one.'

'That uncle of mine's got a lot to answer for,' declared Mands, walking back inside.

Lizzie stood staring at the long drop for a few more minutes, too scared to take a step towards it.

'Come on,' I urged, grabbing her by the hand. 'It's not that bad, and I've even cleaned it for you.'

And I had too, wearing rubber gloves up to my armpits while dry-retching. Truth be told it wasn't actually that dirty, it was just the concept which made me feel ill.

She didn't look convinced.

'OK,' she reluctantly agreed. 'But you have to do a check for rats and wait outside the door for me.'

'OK,' I agreed, swinging open the old door.

With a little shove she was inside, torch at the ready.

'See, it's not so bad, is it?' I called as I stood outside.

'It's fucking horrific,' replied Lizzie, who sounded as though she was trying to squat above the toilet seat rather than sit on it. 'I am going to voluntarily constipate myself.'

Upon our return and after the girls had calmed their shattered nerves with a couple of wines, we set about unloading the car. I was as eager to get my supplies as a deserted ship rat. They had done extremely well. Even the pair of track pants were decidedly unrevolting for, well, a pair of track pants. The girls had gone completely overboard on the liquid front. There was a crate of hand-selected wine, and a crate of champers.

'Just to get you through the next couple of weeks,' they said, as we lugged them inside.

'And the moisturiser?' I asked.

'In the bag,' said Lizzie.

'*Oh thank God!*' I exclaimed, pulling it out. 'You don't know how happy I am to see this!'

'Settle down dolls,' said Mands, looking at me sideways.

I had run out of moisturiser nearly a week ago, and had since had to resort to using what I could find at the local pharmacy-slash-hardware shop, the cheap concoction a shock to my poor pampered skin.

As a succession of goodies piled up on the table, it appeared the girls had done better than just extremely well. They had outdone themselves.

There were gorgeous cheeses; smoked salmon; a selection of antipasto delights — marinated olives, artichokes and mussels; fresh berries; croissants and baguettes; and chocolate liqueurs. And piles and piles of magazines. I lunged across the table at the latest *Vanity Fair* and gave the cover a smooch.

'Easy,' said Mands, taking the magazine from me. 'One thing at a time.'

Louie spent the first hour sitting in the corner of the cabin, staring at us.

'Shouldn't you be sniffing around or something?' I encouraged him. 'Marking your territory?'

'Ignore him,' said Mands. 'He's just pining for attention.'

But he didn't look as though he was pining for attention. He just looked like he was, well, depressed.

'He's been Mr Morose the whole bloody trip,' said Mands. 'A real sack of sad.'

'Come on Louie!' urged Lizzie. 'At least make yourself look comfortable,' she said, leading him to the tatty rug beside the couch and making him lie down. 'That's better, isn't it?'

But Louie just looked up at her blankly, with no change in his expression or desire to roll over and have his tummy scratched.

Once all of my goodies had been unpacked I set about opening several delicatessen containers and whipping us up a delicious antipasto platter. Mands set about updating me on my gossip.

'Well,' she started. 'It's far better than last week. The *Telegraph* are convinced you're in Fiji now. Apparently there's been a couple of sightings of you there.'

'They even printed a picture of you lying in a bikini on a sandy beach,' added Lizzie.

'How did I look?' I asked.

'Lovely and skinny,' they replied. 'And brown.'

'Fabulous. Can I see the papers?' I asked, as we sat down at the rickety table.

'Here we go,' said Mands, passing me the last two weeks' clippings from the *Telegraph* and the *Morning Sun*.

'Some days they don't even mention you at all,' said Lizzie.

'The very odd one,' I replied, staring at the stack of paper clippings before me.

'Oh,' said Mands. 'And there's . . . this.'

'But perhaps you don't want to read that right now,' cautioned Lizzie.

'Give it here,' I instructed.

And there, on the cover of this week's *Modern Woman* was Mother Teresa herself, Mrs Alistair Ambrose, with the words 'My Pain and Agony' emblazoned underneath her Mona Lisa-like photo.

Not again, I thought to myself. *Please God.*

'Steady,' cautioned Mands.

I took another gulp of wine.

'The woman has absolutely no shame,' comforted Lizzie. 'None whatsoever.'

'She's a publicity-hungry slapper,' added Mands. 'Just creaming it while she can.'

'Don't worry,' consoled Lizzie. 'They'll soon get sick of her.'

I turned to the article, which was spread over several pages. And there, with their arms wrapped tightly round the neck of their immaculate, pregnant and wounded doe-eyed mother, were Alistair's two small children. The boys who were now living without their father.

'Don't do it,' pleaded Mands. But it was too late.

A tear had already left my eye and was heading down my cheek towards my wine glass.

'Oh sweets,' soothed Lizzie, standing up and wrapping her arms around me. 'It's not your fault.'

'No dad-dy,' I sobbed. 'Tis my fa-ult.'

'No it's not,' repeated Lizzie. 'It's his fault and no one else's.'

'And his wife's for making such a big bloody deal out of it,' added Mands.

'No dad-dy,' I repeated.

'We're putting it away now,' said Lizzie, taking the magazine from my grasp. 'It's not good for you.'

'There there,' said Mands, rubbing my back as the tears began to subside. 'Have another wine.'

I did as I was told.

Snap out of it, I told myself. *You're bigger than this. Pull yourself together for God's sake!*

The truth was, newspaper and magazine articles aside, I was actually feeling incredibly happy. Happy to finally see the girls at last. I'd really missed them. There was no denying that the past two weeks had been the longest two of my entire life.

That night my deep, several-empty-bottles-of-wine-induced slumber, was interrupted by something shaking my arm, gently at first, and then annoyingly frantically.

'Wha-at?' I moaned.

'I need to go toilet,' hissed a little voice.

It was Lizzie.

'So grab the torch,' I hissed back. 'It's on the dresser.'

'But I want you to come,' she whimpered. 'I'm scared.'

'Oh for God's sake,' I sighed, sliding back the covers. 'OK then, c'mon.'

I had trained myself to go to the toilet just prior to climbing in bed, meaning I could generally hold out until the morning and avoid any middle-of-the-night cross-country excursions.

'Where are you going?' hissed another little voice as we walked out the bedroom door.

It was Mands.

'To the loo,' I replied.

'Hang on,' she instructed. 'I'm coming too. Bloody busting.'

So, with me and the torch at the helm, the three of us traipsed across the grass clearing in the freezing cold, in our pyjamas, with Mands and Lizzie squealing like a couple of thirteen-year-old Girl Guides.

'Wait for me!' called Mands, tripping over the trainers she had hurriedly slid her feet into.

'What's that?' hissed Lizzie, grabbing my arm as a morepork let out its nightly hoot.

'Just a bird,' I replied. 'Relax.'

'I can't relax,' said Lizzie. 'Don't you remember *Blair Witch*?'

'Yes. And it was just a movie,' I replied. 'Now get in there,' I instructed, pushing open the old door. 'And hurry, its freezing.'

'Come in with me,' pleaded Lizzie. *'Please.'*

'Just hurry up,' I replied, standing half-inside the door and shining the torch. 'Or I'll leave you here.'

'Bloody noisy insects,' said Mands, clinging to my elbow.

'I thought the country was supposed to be peaceful.'

'It is,' I replied. 'It's just there's no traffic to drown them out.'

'Give me traffic any day,' she muttered. 'At least you can see it coming and it doesn't land in your mouth.'

Several squeals and one traipse back across the long grass later, the three of us were safely tucked up in bed once again.

I woke up the next morning to find Lizzie spooning me. This wasn't unusual. On the few times we'd shared a bed since her divorce she invariably latched onto me like a human limpet. Apparently she thought I was Bryce, and that she was still married. I invariably woke up thinking I'd been blessed with a one-night stand, and was understandably disappointed to look down and see a pair of pink silk pajamas hugging me. When her hand began to rub the top of my thigh I decided it was time to get up. I put Louie outside for his morning pee and started to make some breakfast. I put the coffee on the stove and set about carefully poaching some eggs.

'Morning,' said Mands, stumbling into the kitchen a short while later. 'What the hell's going on?' she asked, taking in my apron and the frying pan in front of me.

'I'm making us some breakfast,' I replied.

'But you can't cook,' she said, very matter-of-factly.

'I can poach eggs,' I replied.

'Since when?' It was evident she wasn't giving up.

'Since two weeks ago.'

'Who taught you?'

'No one,' I replied, proudly. 'I taught myself.'

'What's going on?' asked Lizzie, as she too walked into the kitchen.

'Sam. Is. Making. Us. Breakfast,' hissed Mands, turning to face her.

'No!' said Lizzie.

'Yes,' I confirmed. 'I am just poaching some bloody eggs for God's sake.'

'My God! She is too,' said Lizzie, staring at the frying pan.

'Look, let's get one thing straight,' I said, holding my wooden spoon up for emphasis. 'Yes, I can now poach eggs. But that doesn't make me Martha Stewart, all right? I have had to learn to cook if I want to eat anything while I'm stuck here at the arse-end of the earth. It's as simple as that.'

'Gotcha,' said Lizzie, ever the pragmatist. 'And I think it's great, sweets, really I do.'

'Is that your apron?' asked Mands, as she searched for some coffee cups.

'Yes. I bought it.'

'You *bought* it?' she asked, clearly in shock.

'Well I don't want to get my clothes greasy, do I?'

'No, that's right sweets, you don't!' said Lizzie, forcefully elbowing Mands out of the kitchen, with a shut-the-hell-up look on her face.

'So . . .' said Lizzie, attempting to change the subject as we sat down to breakfast. 'What shall we do today?'

'Do?' I replied. I wasn't sure I'd heard her correctly.

'Yes. Do. You know, like activities?'

Obviously Lizzie had failed to hear me when I'd reiterated for the umpteenth time that there was absolutely nothing to do in this place. *Nothing.*

'Well, there's a fabulous restaurant in town that does a gorgeous salmon salad, with a wine list to die for. So perhaps we could go there for lunch? And then I thought maybe we could go and see a film, before we pop back into one of the bars for a few drinks tonight.'

'Really?' said Lizzie. 'Sounds great!'

'I think she's kidding, dolls,' said Mands.

'Oh . . . so there isn't a restaurant?'

'No.'

'Or a wine list to die for?'

'No.'

'Well, what can we do? There must be something.'

'We can go for a walk, and we can go to the pub, and that is about it,' I replied.

'I'm on for a walk,' said Mands. 'As long as it doesn't involve cow dung.'

'Don't hold your breath,' I cautioned.

'Same here then,' said Lizzie. 'And why don't we go into the pub tonight?'

I looked at her sideways. She had absolutely no idea what she was lining herself up for. 'Sure,' I replied. 'Let's.'

'Roger that,' agreed Mands. 'Never know, might be some talent.'

This night was going to be fun, I thought to myself. *A lot of fun.*

After breakfast we set straight out on our walk.

'Are you wearing those?' I asked Mands, staring at her shoes.

'They're trainers,' she said. 'What am I supposed to wear?'

'Yes, but they're Prada trainers.'

'Well I don't have any other ones, do I? And yours are too bloody big. I'll just walk carefully.'

We set off down the dirt driveway, dragging an unenthusiastic Louie behind us, and headed along the grass strip at the edge of the roadside, past green paddock upon green paddock. We returned one hour later, Mands' white designer shoes completely covered in cow dung.

'I can't fucking believe it!' she cried. 'Six-hundred-dollar shoes plastered in crap!'

We spent the afternoon tucked safely inside the cabin, reading magazines and nail-painting. Mands was very reluctant to set foot outside again. For want of anything else to do, we decided to head to the pub at seven o'clock. I watched in amusement as Mands and Lizzie fussed over what to wear.

'Diamantes yes? Or diamantes no?' said Lizzie, holding up two identical black silk shirts, save for the diamante flowers on one.

'Yes,' answered Mands.

'No,' I replied, knowing full well we were already going to attract undue attention.

'I think yes too,' said Lizzie, putting on the shirt with her D&G jeans and black kitten-heel boots.

'I'm warning you for the last time,' I said to both of them. 'Everyone else will be in shorts and tracksuits.'

'Oh come on!' said Mands. 'No one wears a tracksuit to the pub. Not even here.'

'Whatever you say,' I replied, pulling on my jeans and trainers.

It's not that I wasn't desperately pining to get dolled up. It's just that I knew there was absolutely no point in going to the effort. Not in this town.

'What are you doing?' asked Lizzie. 'Off for a run?'

'What I am doing,' I replied. 'is trying my best to blend into this town in which I unfortunately find myself now living.'

'I think your standards are slipping,' said Mands, looking very concerned. 'Jesus, you've only been here two weeks. Get out of the trainers!'

In order to shut them both up I compromised and wore my hot-pink suede loafers, with a fitted white T-shirt and the jeans. Lizzie clearly wasn't happy with the T-shirt. Mands was also wearing black knee-high boots, with her designer jeans, and a jade Chinese-style shirt. They looked like they were off to Parnell Road for the night, not some country tavern in the middle of Hicksville. I opened us a bottle of champers and watched the two of them fuss about putting on their make-up.

'Sten really needs to get some better lighting in here,' complained Mands, as she and Lizzie elbowed each other for the tiny, cracked bathroom mirror. 'It's bloody terrible.'

'Oi!' snapped Lizzie. 'Watchit!'

'Which earrings?' she asked, holding up two identical glittery pairs of long silver earrings.

'Definitely the leaves,' replied Mands.

'Neither,' I said. But she wasn't listening to me.

'Your turn,' said Lizzie, twenty minutes later, once they had finished tousling and were both immaculately powdered, mascara'd, eyelined, eyeshadowed, lipsticked and glossed. With hair perfectly positioned and gleaming.

I hopped in front of the mirror, quickly rubbed some moisturiser onto my face, put on a tiny bit of mascara and lip gloss, and tied my red hair back in a ponytail.

'Done,' I said, throwing the lip gloss into my handbag.

'You what?' asked Mands. 'No you're not.'

'Yes I am.'

'Are you sure, sweets?' asked Lizzie.

'Yes,' I replied. 'Done.'

'All right then,' said Mands, 'but don't complain to me if you don't pull tonight.'

The fact she thought there was going to be anything remotely pullable at the pub made me laugh out loud.

'What's so funny?' they both asked.

'Nothing,' I replied, smiling back. 'Nothing at all.' As we left, I turned to the dog. 'Right Louie,' I instructed, 'you're in charge.'

He stared back at me, not even bothering to lift his head. There was no doubt a goldfish would have made a better guard dog. He'd be lucky to raise his eyebrows at a burglar, let alone bark.

'How're we going to get home?' asked Lizzie, as we hopped into my car. But not before Mands had a SC (shoe catastrophe) and ran back inside to swap her black high-heeled boots for her chocolate-brown high-heeled boots.

'We can't wear the same bloody shoes!' she declared, having just noticed Lizzie's black boots.

'One of us will have to stay sober enough to drive,' I replied to Lizzie.

'Can't we just get a taxi?' she asked.

I looked at her. She really had no idea where she was.

'No,' I replied. 'There are no taxis here, Lizzie.'

'Oh.'

While driving I briefed the girls on my Floodgate pseudonym, lest we bump into anyone I knew at the pub, although it's fair to say the chances were slim to none.

'Jane?' said Mands. 'Couldn't you have come up with something a bit more fabulous, like Scarlett?'

'Jane's my middle name,' I reminded her.

We pulled into the pub car park, which was brimming with Ford Falcons, old four-wheel drives and farm utes. We parked next to a farm ute, complete with farm dog chained to the back.

'Eeeek!' screamed Mands, climbing out of the car and coming nose to nose with the excited dog.

We walked through the front doors of the pub and were immediately glared at by all inside. It was a sea of shorts, tracksuits, ripped jeans and jandals. A heartbreaking sight to behold.

'Don't they know it's a Saturday night?' whispered

Mands, walking straight up to the bar and ordering a bottle of bubbles.

'Yeah?' said the young man behind the bar.

'Bubbles please,' said Mands. 'A bottle.'

I tried kicking her in the back of the calf as I hissed 'vodka' but she was completely ignored me.

'Bubbles?' replied the man, searching her face for more clues. 'You mean something fizzy like lemonade?'

'No. I mean something bubbly. Like champagne.'

'Oh. Sorry. Nope. None of that stuff.'

'Well,' said Mands, clearly dismayed but also wisely remembering this was the only drinking establishment in the entire village. 'What can you recommend then?'

'The beer's good,' he replied.

She turned round to face us. 'The beer's good, girls. Did you hear that?'

'Yes,' I replied, very keen to remove myself from the scene we were already causing at the bar and find a dark and dingy corner table. 'I'll have a beer then.'

'Right. Three beers please!' said Mands, turning back to the barman. 'Make them large.'

I went and found us the most inconspicuous table I could and watched as Mands and Lizzie carried over three buckets of beer.

'I'm not sure whether to drink it or strip off and have a swim in it,' said Lizzie, putting hers down on the table.

The people at the table next to us were staring at Mands and Lizzie as though they were a couple of Martians.

We sat and watched the group of people playing pool at the table in front of us. It looked as though the middle-aged Maori woman with no front teeth and her burly partner had just won, judging by her gummy smile.

'Who wants a game?' asked Mands. Lizzie and I stared

back at her mutely. 'Of pool?' she added.

'Har-har,' said Lizzie.

'Very funny,' I added.

'I'm putting a coin up,' declared Mands, jumping out of her seat.

Lizzie and I passed each other a furtive has-she-finally-gone-completely-barking-mad look.

'Mands, what are you doing?' I hissed, when she sat back down. 'All these people do is play pool. Every single day. And night. You are going to get your tiny arse kicked.'

'Bring it on!' she replied.

Dear God, I despaired. She'd only been in the pub for twenty minutes and she was already chugging back the beer and talking like a bogan.

It appeared Mands and her partner were going to play the winners, toothless Cass and tattooed Jimmy. Jimmy even had a tattoo of a fin with the words 'pool shark' engraved on his right forearm. Mands tried to pry me out of my seat, but I wouldn't budge. So she picked on Lizzie instead.

'Oh come on!' she encouraged.

'I don't think so,' replied Lizzie. But she wasn't as strong and feisty as little Mands, who had pulled her out of her seat and up to the pool table before she could utter another word of protest.

'So,' said Mands, once she had introduced herself and Lizzie to Cass and Jimmy. 'Who's breaking?'

'You are,' said Jimmy, handing her the cue.

Oh God! I thought, bracing myself for the painful sight ahead.

But Mands was one of those annoying people who never screwed up anything. Anything. She managed to break the balls evenly and even managed to sink one in the process. I watched in dismay as the four of them embarked on what can only be described as the Longest Game of Pool Ever. It wasn't aided by the fact that whenever Lizzie hit a ball (when she did) she just sort pushed it with the cue, rolling it in slow motion towards the edge of the table.

'Could you at least *try* and aim for the holes,' urged Mands.

'I am,' replied Lizzie through gritted teeth.

Sports had never been Lizzie's forte. At college, during physical-education class, she had managed to take a forehand swing on the tennis court and chip her two front teeth in half. This was no mean feat. In fact it had been deemed 'absolutely impossible' by our teacher, until she saw Lizzie's teeth that is. Jimmy and Cass were clearly taking it easy on the girls too, which wasn't speeding things up.

The only disadvantage of drinking beer, I thought to myself as I sat and watched, aside from the fact I didn't actually like it, was that it turned the bladder into some sort of garden water feature. We had only been in the pub for an hour and I had already peed six times.

Might as well just take the beer and sit on the toilet, I thought to myself.

'Brarp!' burped Lizzie, covering her mouth. 'Oopsie, 'scuse me.'

The propensity to burp was the other issue with beer.

Finally, praise the Lord, Jimmy sank the black and the game was over. Mands and Lizzie still with two-thirds of their balls sitting on the table. Relieved it had finally finished I got up to congratulate him too. Cass, the toothless woman, stood with her arm draped across Mands' shoulders. It appeared she had taken quite a liking to her.

'I think you should move here too,' she said to Mands. 'You're all right, you are.'

That was a big compliment in these parts, and Mands took it well.

'Cass, you know, I'm seriously considering it,' replied Mands, returning her kiss on the cheek.

It was a Kodak Moment. Big, toothless, grinning Cass engulfing petite, immaculate Mands in a pub bear hug.

'Mands,' said Lizzie, pointing over at our table. 'Your bag's smoking.'

'Jesus!' yelled Mands, running back to the table, and grabbing her bag, 'My bloody handbag's on fire!'

And it was too — smoking like a banshee and seconds away from bursting into a very expensive fiery ball. The few people in the pub who hadn't been staring at the three of us all evening definitely were now.

'Water!' yelled Mands, as one of the big-bearded men from the next table over lunged across and tipped his full jug of beer into her handbag.

'That'll sort it love,' he said, very happy with his swift thinking.

'Thank . . . you,' managed Mands, just, as she stared down at the beer-soaked, steaming piece of charcoal leather in her hands. The beer dripped down onto her brown boots.

On closer inspection it appeared she had been ashing into her handbag for a good portion of the evening. It was fair to say Mands had suffered some collateral damage in the country thus far. A pair of Prada sneakers and a Louis Vuitton handbag, all in one day. Lizzie and I made her put down the still-smoking handbag and dragged her up to the bar for some shots of tequila.

'I loved that bag!' cried Mands, slamming down her third shot glass. 'Cost me a week's wages!'

'Insurance,' placated Lizzie.

'New handbag,' I added.

Seeing how upset Mands was over the bag, Cass even came up to the bar and bought her another tequila, before wrapping her into yet another gummy bear hug.

'Shanks Cass,' said Mands, now quite drunk and also having the air consolingly slammed out of her.

By this time the karaoke was in full swing. A woman named Sharee, in a mauve shell suit and with enough blue eyeshadow to sink a small ship, was belting out an ear-shattering rendition of 'I Got You Babe', with a very bearded man named Bill.

'How about a song?' suggested Lizzie.

I pretended I hadn't heard her, in a vain attempt to not draw any more attention to myself.

'Let's!' said Mands, on whom the tequila had worked wonders.

The two of them decided we should sing 'I Will Survive'. A sort of ode to Mands and her handbag.

'It's all right for you two. You're leaving tomorrow!' I hissed, as they dragged me up onto the small stage.

I had no choice but to throw myself into the performance, with the same drunk gusto as the other two. Thankfully, as the three of us had karaoke'd to this song more times than was called for in our younger years, the words came flooding back. We even remembered our dance routine. Standing in a row, hands on hips, turning side on and pointing our arms at the crowd. A formation which was broken down and repeated, many times over. Much to the crowd's unbelievable delight. 'Encore!' shouted Cass, the table of big-bearded men joining in.

'Yeah!' shouted what appeared to be the rest of the pub.

'OK!' shouted back Mands, gripping my arm and stopping me from hopping off the stage. 'You got it!' She appeared to be immersed in some sort of entertainment trance.

Lizzie and I looked across at each other, nervously.

'Stay there girls,' she instructed, walking towards the karaoke operator.

Ten seconds later the opening sequence to 'Material Girl' began.

Oh dear God, I thought in horror. *What on earth was she doing? They're going to hate this!*

But I was wrong. Oh so wrong. We danced in a line with Mands at the centre helm, wiggled our hips, did lots of Madonna-inspired shimmying and arm-pointing, and they loved it. When we had finished the entire pub erupted into claps and cheers, with a series of wolf whistles piercing the air.

'Thank you,' mouthed Mands to the crowd, as she instructed Lizzie and I to take a bow.

'Another one!' shouted several people, as we climbed off the stage.

'Maybe later,' replied Mands, as the three of us walked through the clapping to the bar.

'Jane,' said a voice behind me. 'Great performance.' I turned around to see the man from the market. Elsie's friend.

'Oh hi . . . um, thanks . . . I think.'

Mands and Lizzie, who had suddenly slammed on their brakes, turned around and gave me the elbow.

'Oh, these are my friends, Lizzie and Mands,' I said. 'And this is . . .'

'Ethan. Hi,' he replied, shaking both of their hands. 'Do you karaoke for a living?' he asked. 'Or just when you're on holiday?'

'Just wherever there's the demand,' replied Mands, giving him one of her very best flirty smiles.

'We've only just come out of retirement,' I added.

'That's far too much talent to be hiding away,' said Ethan.

'I think you should take up a regular Saturday night slot.'

'We'll think about it,' replied Lizzie.

'What are you ladies drinking?' he asked.

'Um . . . vodka . . . I think,' I replied.

'Please let me,' said Ethan, as he excused himself to the front of the bar and ordered three vodka and tonics.

'I'm sitting over there with some friends,' he said, handing us our drinks and pointing to a table at the far wall. 'Would you like to join us?'

'Sure,' said Mands and Lizzie, before I had a chance to reply. 'We'll be over in a sec.'

As he walked off Mands and Lizzie stood staring at me.

'Looks like someone won the meat pack,' said Mands, slapping me on the arm.

She obviously thought Ethan was good-looking.

'And?' said Lizzie.

'And what?'

'And why the hell haven't you told us about him?'

'What do you mean?'

'We *mean*,' said Lizzie, 'that you appear to have omitted to mention to us, your two best friends, that you have met a foxy man in this town.'

'Village,' I corrected her.

'Or that there is actually a good-looking person living in this place,' added Mands.

'I hardly know him,' I protested. 'I've only met him once. At the market.'

'At the what?' asked Lizzie.

'The market,' I repeated. 'It happens every Saturday morning in the church car park.'

'I see,' she replied, looking decidedly blank.

'Irrelevant details,' said Mands, dragging me over to Ethan's table.

He was sitting with his friend Mack, and Mack's wife Abbie, whom he promptly introduced us to.

'Outstanding performance!' congratulated Abbie, one of the few women in the pub who wasn't wearing a shell suit.

Fortunately they had only arrived at the pub in time to see our back-to-back karaoke performance, and had not witnessed Mands' flaming handbag episode. Naturally they had already heard about it. After a couple more rounds of vodkas Cass tentatively approached the table. It appeared she wanted to sing a duet. With Mands.

'Hell yes!' said Mands, jumping up from her seat. It seemed you just couldn't keep a good karaoke-er down.

The next minute they were up on stage, big solid toothless Cass with her arms wrapped round Mands' tiny shoulders, belting out 'Islands in the Stream'. One microphone apiece.

'Dear God!' exclaimed Lizzie. 'I knew I should've brought the camera.'

'No kidding,' agreed Abbie, laughing.

I was rendered speechless. Mands was a human chameleon. It didn't matter what situation you threw her into, she'd blend in as though she'd been there all her life. At the end of the song Cass gave Mands another of her bone-crushing hugs, just for old times' sake. Thankfully the call was made for last drinks and we weren't subjected to an encore.

As we said our goodbyes to Ethan, Mack and Abbie and headed for the doors, Mands handed Cass one of her business cards.

'Call me dolls!' she instructed. 'We'll do lunch.'

I dragged myself out of bed far too early the next morning, as Lizzie once again moved in for the spoon-and-thigh rub.

I was sitting motionless at the kitchen table, sunglasses planted firmly over my eyes and strong coffee in hand, when Mands surfaced.

'Hell!' she moaned, as she dragged herself, eyes barricaded also, onto a chair. 'Quite a night.'

'Oh yes,' I replied, unable to string together more than a few words.

'What on earth were we drinking?' she asked.

'Beer, vodka, tequila, rum . . . everything,' I replied.

'That'll explain it then,' said Mands, tentatively stroking her forehead.

'Lord above,' said Lizzie, walking in and stumbling over Louie, who couldn't even summon the enthusiasm to yelp. 'I think someone may have spiked my drink.'

'You should be so lucky,' said Mands. 'Self-inflicted, dolls.'

We spent the rest of the day lying on the lumpy couch and a sea of duvets, complaining about our sore heads, eating chocolate biscuits and reading magazines, while Mands and Lizzie attempted to summon enough energy for their drive back home.

'It's now or never,' said Mands, peeling herself from the couch at four o'clock.

Once we had rounded up all their possessions, which lay across every surface and in every corner of the cabin, and forced Louie into the car, it was time for them to go. You'd think they'd been there a month judging by their depth of spread, not a weekend.

'Bye sweets,' said Lizzie, giving me a big hug. 'Thanks for a lovely weekend.'

'Oh, don't cry,' said Mands, noticing the tears which had welled up in my eyes. 'We'll be back before you know it.'

'And you'll be back before you know it,' added Lizzie.

They both gathered me into a hug cocoon.

'I hope so,' I replied.

I was really going to miss them. Again. The weekend had felt just like the good old days (despite the primitive surroundings of course).

Waving madly they drove off, Louie staring forlornly out the back window. They had left me with the cases of champagne and wine, which I was unable to make eye contact with for a good few days.

11

'How about you come round and have dinner with me and Bob one night?' asked Elsie the next morning, as I sat in the café having my date scone. 'In fact, how about tomorrow night?'

'Sure,' I replied. 'I'd love to.'

God himself knew I didn't have anything else to do. It was slightly strange to be asked for dinner at someone's house I'd only known for a few weeks, but nice all the same. Plus, I doubted that Elsie and her husband were the type to chain you up in their basement and feed you dog roll, before whipping your naked body with a fly swat.

I arrived at seven o'clock sharp the next night with a bottle of wine in tow.

'You remember Bob, don't you love?' asked Elsie, as she bustled me inside and gave me a hug hello.

'Yes. Hi,' I said, smiling.

'Hello love,' said Bob, who got up from the dining table and gave me a kiss on the cheek. 'Come and have a seat.'

'Now,' said Elsie. 'We're going to have a lamb roast. I hope that's OK with you?'

Not exactly, I thought to myself, being that I didn't eat red meat.

Should I tell her? I wondered. The only other option was to sit there and eat it. And I hadn't eaten red meat for over five years. But I couldn't bring myself to say anything. Here she was kindly inviting me for dinner and cooking away. No, I'd just have to grin and bear it. Somehow.

'Sounds yummy,' I lied. 'Can I help?'

'Only if you want to, ducky. You can come and talk to me though. Bob's just reading the paper anyhow.'

Bob looked up from the paper and gave me a smile.

'Brandy and soda or a glass of wine, luvvie?' asked Elsie. 'Brandy's my poison.'

'Oh, wine please,' I replied.

'You can top and tail the beans if you really want to,' she said, handing me a glass of wine.

I had absolutely no idea what she was talking about.

'Sure,' I replied.

'Don't they have beans in the city?' asked Elsie, noting my confusion.

'Yes. But I've only ever seen them on a dinner plate, being carried to me by a waiter.'

She and Bob laughed. Which made me laugh.

'Just like this love,' she said, showing me how to cut the ends from the beans. 'It's very easy.'

And it was too. Even I could manage it.

'Cutting off a mule's ears doesn't make it a horse,' laughed Elsie, who was replying to a question from Bob.

I had no idea what she was talking about.

Then turning to me, she whispered, 'Don't throw the baby out with the bath water, luvvie.'

Apparently I was chopping a bit too much bean from the ends.

Once the roast vegetables and lamb were ready and the beans were cooked (by me), Bob set the table and we sat down to eat. Elsie put the enormous leg of roast lamb down onto the table and Bob began to carve it. I tried to look anywhere else.

Don't think about it,' I told myself. *Just don't think about it.*

'How much would you like, love?' asked Bob, who appeared to be dishing up my plate first.

'Oh, just a little,' I replied. 'I'm more of a veggie girl.'

Just cut it, put it into your mouth, chew it, and swallow, I told myself. *Cut. Put. Chew. Swallow.*

I did as I was told and contrary to gagging, as I seriously hoped I wouldn't but anticipated I would, I was pleasantly surprised by the taste. In fact, I liked it. It was warm, juicy and tender. And, well, delicious. In fact it tasted so good I had another helping.

What on earth are you doing? I asked myself. *You don't eat red meat, remember?*

I know, but it tastes good, I answered. *Real good.*

'Delicious beans,' said Bob.

'Thos're Jane's beans those are,' said Elsie, giving me a wink.

I smiled back.

'Great beans, Jane,' Bob said, smiling.

'Thank you,' I replied; even though I'd only top and tailed and steamed them, I was relatively proud.

After dinner, I did my best to field questions about why I was living in Floodgate, without either giving anything away or sounding rude.

'Just taking a break from the city for a while,' I explained. 'Getting some country air.'

Elsie and Bob remembered Sten and I explained he was my friend's uncle, hence I was staying in his cabin. I asked them all about Floodgate and how long they had been living here, which was forever, apparently. They were both lovely and friendly and it felt just like having a normal family dinner with your parents. Providing your mother wasn't a ball-crushing feminist and your father wasn't a housewife of course. And it was nice not to be eating dinner on my own for once.

The next morning I had a call from the post-office-slash-bank-slash-stationery shop. They had a parcel for me to collect. High excitement. How on earth a parcel had managed to find its way to this Lilliputian village in the middle of nowhere I had no idea. But I was itching for some social contact so off I went.

'Your lucky day, love,' said the man behind the counter, who also happened to be Elsie's husband, Bob.

How exciting, I thought to myself, driving back to the cabin, placing the box onto the kitchen table and tearing into it. It was glaringly obvious that my views as to what constituted exciting had shifted dramatically in the past few weeks. It was from either Mands or Lizzie, judging by the handwriting.

Dear God, here's hoping it isn't more champers, I prayed.

I opened it up and was immediately overwhelmingly glad I'd waited until I was back in the confines of the cabin to do so. Sitting inside the box was an enormous black vibrator, a set of Ben Wa balls, two hot-pink vibrating nipple clamps, several copies of *Playgirl* magazine, and two purple fluffy things (purpose unknown). And a card.

Dear Sammy,
Enclosed are a couple of city implements to stem your country boredom. Have fun & don't do anything we wouldn't.
Lots of Love,
M & L xx

I had to laugh. Here I was in a hut in the middle of nowhere and my two best friends had sent me a box of sex toys. Clearly, post visit, they were worried about the state of talent in the vicinity. And with good reason. I put everything back into the box and put it down on the floor, beside the kitchen table.

The following day I had another burst of high excitement, a surprise visit. It appeared I was rapidly turning into some sort of lonely rural pensioner whose week was defined by surprise visits and the like. Nothing was a surprise in the city. A butt-naked three-legged pierced-all-over Hare Krishna could turn up on your doorstep and it'd be just another day in the big smoke. There were two surprise visitors, both wearing police uniforms.

Oh God! I thought to myself. *Now they've gone and sent me a couple of strippers.* This really was taking it too far. *Although surely they could have organised some better-looking ones? And possibly a bit younger?*

'Hiya love,' said the silver haired one. 'My name's Constable McRae. You can call me Des. And this is Constable Grant.'

'Denny,' said the younger one with the moustache, holding out his hand for me to shake.

'Hi,' I replied. 'Jane.' I wondered when they were going to stop the formalities and start stripping.

'Elsie said you were living in Sten's cabin,' said Des. 'We were just driving past and thought we'd pop in and make sure everything was OK. There's been a couple of squatters found living here in the past, so we just wanted to check that you hadn't had any unwanted visitors.'

'No,' I replied, 'I haven't.'

Who in God's name would want to squat in this hell-hole? I wondered.

'Good, good,' said Des.

'Would you like a cup of tea or coffee?' I asked.

I'd never had two police officers turn up unannounced on my doorstep before but I gathered, now it was clear there'd be no discarding of kits, that offering them liquids was part of the protocol. Grandma Atkins, had she been alive, would have been very proud of me.

'That'd be grand,' replied Des.

'Sure would!' agreed Denny.

'Have a seat,' I said. 'I'll just put the kettle on.'

Oh Lord! I thought in dread. I had just uttered the never-to-be-spoken words. *I'll just put the kettle on.* I had officially morphed into a 1950s housewife. The only thing missing was a husband.

The officers followed me inside. I noted the row of empty champagne and wine bottles sitting on the kitchen bench and cringed. I had yet to clear up the remnants of the girls' weekend visit. Recycling wasn't quite so straightforward in the country. My eyes flicked to the full case of champers sitting beside the kitchen table, just in time to see Des peering at it too. *Hell!* The place had boozehag written all over it.

Oh well, perhaps they'll just think I'm a hoarder, I hoped, quickly making us a pot of tea.

They sat down at the table and I brought the tea over. I even had some of Elsie's chocolate afghans at the ready.

'So, what are you doing living in these parts, Jane?' asked Denny.

'Oh, just taking a bit of time out,' I replied. 'You know . . . getting away from the hustle and bustle of the city for a while.'

'Too right!' said Des. 'I don't know how city folk cope with all of that noise and pollution. It can't be good for the soul.'

'Well . . . yes.' I replied. 'It does get a bit much after a while.'

What I wouldn't give to be back in that noise and pollution right now, I thought to myself. He was making me homesick.

I glanced across at the box of champagne, willing it to miraculously disappear. And it was then that I saw it. On the other side of the table, right beside Denny's left foot, sat the box of sex toys. Wide open. *Oh dear God, no! No!*

All he had to do was glance inside the box and there'd be a huge black vibrator staring straight back at him.

Please no! I prayed, my skin suddenly prickling with nerves. *Don't look down!*

I couldn't lunge for the box. That would only make him look at what I was reaching for. I drank my hot tea so fast I was left with third-degree burns on my bottom lip. Then I started ferociously glancing at my watch.

'Well . . .' said Des, noticing my overwhelming desire to wind it up. '. . . guess we'd better be getting on the road then. C'mon Denny.'

'Righto,' said Denny, standing up. 'Thanks for the cuppa, Jane.'

'You're welcome,' I blurted, jumping out of my seat.

Denny put his chair back in and edged around the side of the table.

Please don't look down! I prayed. *Anywhere but down!*

He didn't look down. But this was the catch-22. Because, by not looking down, Denny subsequently managed to trip over the box of sex toys at his feet and send them scattering out across the wooden floor. Vibrator, Ben Wa balls, nipple clamps, purple fluffy things, *Playgirls*, the lot.

'Whoopsie,' said Denny, stopping in his tracks and turning around. 'What a clumsy bugger.' He suddenly noticed what items were now scattered across the floor and promptly began to go bright red in the face. But nowhere near as beet as I suddenly found myself turning.

'S-s-s-s-sorry,' he aplogised, reaching down.

'It's OK, I'll get . . .' I said. But it was too late.

Denny was now standing with the large black ribbed vibrator in one hand and two hot pink nipple clamps in the other.

'Wh-wh-wh-wh-wh . . .' he stuttered. Obviously he only stuttered when he was embarrassed. I guessed that standing with an enormous vibrator in one hand and two nipple clamps in the other qualified as embarrassing.

'Fa-fa-fa-fa-fa . . .' he continued, as I stood rooted to the spot in anguish.

'Just pop them back in here, shall I?' said Des, taking the vibrator and nipple clamps out of Denny's hands and placing them back in the box.

'That'd be great,' I replied, as Des also picked up the purple fluffy things, examined them closely, and put them into the box.

'Present from my girlfriends,' I explained, picking up the Ben Wa balls and *Playgirl* magazines. 'Bit of a joke between us.'

'Must have some interesting friends,' said Des as they walked outside.

'Yes,' I replied. 'They certainly are.'

'L-l-l-l-lovely to m-m-m-meet you J-J-J-J-Jane,' stuttered Denny, staring intently at the dirt driveway.

'And you,' I replied.

'Take care and . . . ah . . . enjoy your stay here,' said Des.

'Thank you,' I replied, just wanting the whole hideous moment to be over.

'And th-th-th-thanks for the c-c-c-cuppa,' said Denny, again.

And with that, thanks be to God, they hopped back into their police car and drove away. I walked back inside and slumped down at the table. The one time I had been paid a visit from the police in my lifetime and they wound up holding my vibrator and nipple clamps in their hands. Grandma Atkins would not have been at all happy with this outcome. It had all been going so well with the chocolate afghans too.

I spent the next few days working, interrupted only by my morning-tea breaks and runs. It appeared I had unwittingly constructed myself some sort of a routine. It wasn't the most exciting routine known to woman, but it was a routine nonetheless. I found that my morning-tea break and daily chat with Elsie was the only thing that stopped me from going completely barmy from the loneliness. Elsie had decided to take me under her wing. Exactly why, I had no idea. It seemed she needed a project, and I was it.

'How about you coming along to our dancing class on Friday night?' she asked, as I sat with my pot of tea and date scone.

'Dancing?' I replied.

On a Friday night?

'Our dancing class in the school hall. Mrs Holyoake takes it.'

'What sort of dancing?'

'Just dancing for fun, you'll see. Nothing serious. It's a blast!'

I must have looked entirely unconvinced.

'You'll enjoy it!' encouraged Elsie. 'I promise.'

'But I can't dance,' I protested.

'Don't worry love, neither can I. There's not much skill involved, trust me.'

'Are you sure?'

'Positive. It's a date then!'

'OK,' I replied, completely stuck for an excuse.

'Seven o'clock sharp,' added Elsie.

Bloody hell! I worried. I hadn't been to a dancing class for over twenty years. Somehow I didn't think that grade-one ballet was going to cut the mustard.

I tried my hardest to get out of going. I even strapped up my ankle and limped into the coffee shop the next day, but to no avail. Elsie was determined to drag me along, even if it was on my hands and knees.

'Well, what else are you going to do, love? Go to the disco? Har-har-har.' She thought this was positively hilarious.

The fact I would have rather sat in the freezing dusty cabin by myself and stared at the walls did not even register on her radar.

What else are *you going to do on Friday night then?* I asked myself, realising she simply wasn't going to take no for an answer. *Go on a hot date with some gorgeous man who suddenly sweeps through the village only to have his BMW break down in the main street and finds himself at a loose end? That'd be nice*, myself replied. *Get real!* I shouted back at myself. *You'll be sitting in the cabin staring at the bugs. You should be taking any social invitation that comes your way. God knows you need it!*

So, Friday night rolled around and there I was, off to a dancing class. *A dancing class!* Whereas I would usually have been found drinking cocktails in one of Darcy and

287

Samuel's fabulous bars, before heading to dinner at some just-opened restaurant with rave reviews, here I was going to a dancing class in a country school hall. What a dive my life had taken, and in such a short space of time.

I wasn't entirely sure what to wear to a dancing class, especially when I had absolutely no idea what type of dancing it was. *Not likely to be salsa or hip hop*, I thought to myself, *more likely ballroom or rock'n'roll*. Just to be safe I opted for black leggings, a long red T-shirt, and slip-on red trainers. I parked outside the old wooden school hall. I was five minutes late and, judging by the cluster of stationary cars and the lack of people getting out of them, I was also the last to arrive. I walked tentatively into the hall. There were about twenty men and women milling around inside, all wearing blue jeans and checked shirts, and all at least a good twenty years older than myself. For some strange reason, about half of them were also wearing cowboy hats and boots. Including Elsie. *Bloody fantastic!* And here I was looking like Madonna's personal trainer. I had no idea there was a dress code. *Bugger it!* I was already having issues blending in and we hadn't even started dancing yet. I spotted Elsie waving madly at me under her huge brim and walked over.

'Hel-lo love!' she hollered, giving me a kiss on the cheek and ramming her brim into my forehead in the process. 'Everyone, this is Jane!'

Everyone turned to greet me, the men raising their eyebrows and tipping the brims of their hats and the women showering me with lots of 'hello luvvies'.

Oh God, I thought in horror as I spotted the two policemen, Des and Denny, on the other side of the room. *Have mercy.*

'Hiya Jane,' greeted Des, sidling up next to me in full cowboy regalia.

'Hi,' I replied, immediately turning bright red and sinking as far back as I possibly could. There was no doubt in my mind he'd told everyone here, and the village for that matter, about my box of sex toys. I would have if I were him.

'Hi J-J-J-J-Jane,' stuttered Denny, coming up also. He was a dead ringer for Lucky Luke. Beige plaid shirt done up to the top button, dark jeans and cowboy hat with cord hanging under his chin.

'Hi Denny. How are you?' I replied, praying for the ground beneath to open up and swallow me whole.

'V-v-v-very g-g-g-good. Y-y-y-yourself?'

'Fine thanks.'

'Right ev-ery-body! Let us begin!' came a blast of voice from the front of the hall, from the mouth of what could only have been Mrs Holyoake herself. 'Assume positions.'

Thankfully this made Des and Denny retreat to the back of the group.

'You know why he's stuttering?' whispered Elsie in my ear. 'It's because he fancies you, love.'

I think Denny's stutter probably had to do with something else entirely, but I saw absolutely no need to enlighten her.

Under Mrs Holyoake's instruction the congregation promptly divided themselves into four evenly spaced lines, with Elsie dragging me into position between her and a man with one of the largest moustaches I had ever seen. It looked as though it was well and truly in the throws of suffocating him to death. In fact there were a lot of moes present, I observed with horror, including Denny's. Perhaps it was a village trend? Even a few of the older women seemed to be joining in.

Dear God, I prayed, *please never let my sight deteriorate to the point where I can't see the presence of facial hair.*

I glanced down our line and saw clean-shaven and

moustache-less Ethan at the end. I returned his wave, relieved I wasn't the only person under forty present. He looked almost as uncomfortable as I felt, I noticed. And then, without warning, some very frightening-sounding music burst out of the stereo beside Mrs Holyoake.

My God! I balked in dread. *It sounded like country!* A cross between Lyle Lovett and the *Deliverance* soundtrack. Sort of a do-si-do, but with lyrics. Bad ones.

Everyone began to move, shuffling from side to side, with their forefingers looped through the belt holes on the front of their jeans.

God no! It can't be! I thought in horror. *They're bloody line-dancing! Christ above! Surely they were joking? This was far too much of a country cliché to be true.*

'C'mon love!' urged Elsie. 'Time to get a groove on!'

I stared back at her, aghast.

'Thatta girl!' she encouraged, as I reluctantly shuffled across to the right. Due to the fact I didn't have any belt holes on my leggings, I had hooked my fingers into the waistband, not the most attractive look I had ever perfected.

Elsie beamed at me, as everyone did some sort of cowboy-style 360-degree twirl. I decided to let that one slip me by and stayed facing forward instead. Now they were stepping forward on their right legs into a bow-type pose, and then stepping back. I attempted to follow suit.

When in God's name will this torture be over? I wondered, as Elsie nudged me with her elbow and gave me a huge grin.

She was clearly having the time of her life. I glanced back at her with what was supposed to be a semi-smile, but no doubt looked much more like the silent scream of childbirth. However, she was far too busy jigging along to notice.

If only Mands and Lizzie could see me now, I thought to myself. *What had become of me?* Line dancing that's what.

I had only witnessed this abomination once on television. I had no idea people *actually* did it. And for enjoyment? I was positive it was banned in the city. And if it wasn't then it should have been.

'How much longer?' I hissed at Elsie, as I shuffled towards her in a ridiculous sidestep.

'Notha forty minutes, love.'

Hell!

If only I wasn't sandwiched between Elsie and the moustache I probably could have sidestepped all the way back out the door without too many people noticing. The twirls and sidesteps seemed to be building up pace now, as the do-si-do soundtrack took on new whining heights. The odd shout of 'Yee-ha!' from anyone who felt like it appeared to be growing more frequent too. Elsie even let one slip, which nearly made me ricochet straight into the side of the moustache.

'Isn't it fun, love?' she hollered, grabbing me by the arm, when we were finally permitted a water break.

Now was my chance to flee.

'Hiya Jane,' smiled Ethan, walking over to me. 'How's things?'

'Great,' I replied, as if being at a line-dancing class was just part of my normal weekly routine.

'So, how are you finding it?' he asked.

'Um . . . good.' This was clearly a lie. But I didn't want to offend him.

'You don't have to lie,' he whispered, with a smile. 'As long as you don't tell anyone I absolutely loathe line dancing.'

'Your secret's safe,' I replied. 'So, what are you doing here then?'

'My uncle,' said Ethan, pointing at a very handsome silver-haired man in a black cowboy hat, 'made me come along.'

'Couldn't you say no?' I asked.

'About as easily as you could,' he replied, raising his eyebrows at Elsie.

'Gotcha,' I replied. 'I even told her I'd sprained my ankle.'

'I doubt that even if you'd lost a leg Elsie would take no for an answer.'

I laughed. How right he was.

Our conversation was interrupted by an announcement from Mrs Holyoake that the second half of the class was about to start. Dwight Yoakum blared from the stereo. It was too late to run now. *Damn it all!*

The line formation got underway again and I found myself standing between Ethan and Denny.

'Hiya Denny,' smiled Ethan.

'Hiya Ethan,' replied Denny, without one waver in his voice.

I guessed he didn't fancy Ethan and he'd never tripped over a box of his sex toys.

'You've got some rhythm there,' said Ethan, turning to me.

'I don't think so,' I replied. 'You're just being kind.'

'Well, you've got more than me anyway,' he said, smiling. 'I'm the antithesis of a black woman. Whatever that's called.'

He had a lovely smile, all dimples and straight white teeth. I smiled back. He was pretty funny too, in a sort of goofy farm-boy way.

'So, what are you up to this weekend?' he asked, when the whole nasty experience was over, and we were finally free to go.

'Oh I don't know, probably doing the crossword or something,' I replied.

Usually when a man asked me what my plans were for the weekend I assumed he wanted to ask me out, and therefore made out I was busy as all hell and it would virtually be impossible to squeeze him into my schedule, even if all I had booked was a facial and massage with the girls. But for some reason I couldn't be bothered lying to Ethan. I'm sure he wouldn't have believed me anyway. I could hardly say I was busy with beauty treatments in this town.

'Would you like to come on a picnic with me?' he asked.

'A picnic?'

A picnic? Did they still exist? And did people really go on them? Surely not these days?

'Um . . . OK,' I replied. 'Where to?'

'How about the river?'

'The river?'

'There's a river about five kilometres out of town. It's very pretty. Trust me.'

Obviously I looked a little unsure. 'Sounds nice,' I replied.

Although a picnic was a bit prehistoric for my liking, it had to be better than sitting in the dusty hovel by myself.

'How does Sunday sound then?' asked Ethan.

'Fine,' I replied. Lord knows I'd no other plans to speak of.

'I'll swing by and pick you up at twelve o'clock. Please don't bring anything, I'll have it sorted.'

'See you on Sunday then, Jane,' he said. He gave me a cheeky smile and a wee tip of his cowboy hat.

At that point Elsie hurried over to me.

'Sooo . . . he's a lovely boy, that Ethan?' she said with a wink.

Apparently she was asking me a question. But I declined to answer.

He was hardly a boy, I thought to myself. *He was at least thirty.*

'Wonderful family.' Clearly Elsie hadn't finished. 'His mother was one of my closest friends. A gorgeous woman she was.'

Was?

'Did she die?' I asked.

'Yes. Ten years ago. Cancer. A real tragedy it was. He was a real mummy's boy too. Loved her to bits.'

Losing a parent in your twenties was far too young, I thought to myself. As irritating as my mother was, it would be devastating if anything actually happened to her.

I said my goodbyes and drove home to my dilapidated habitat.

A picnic with a farm boy? It was a bit 1950s for my liking. *But what the hell else was I going to do this weekend?* Apart from go insane from boredom and loneliness of course.

I walked back into the cabin and immediately poured myself a glass of wine, collapsing onto the lumpy couch. *Line dancing.* I had been line dancing. As I attempted to recover from the ordeal the phone rang. It was Mands.

'Howareya chook? How's life in the whippidy-wops?'

'Oh . . . so so,' I replied.

If only she knew.

'How's the smoke?' I asked.

'Good. Just been to the launch of Kylie's new knicker range. Cocktails, celebrities, undies, the usual.' She paused. 'Whatcha been doing? You sound puffed.'

'Ah . . . nothing,' I replied. 'Nothing at all.'

At least nothing I would *ever* be telling her about.

'Been shagging that foxy Ethan again?'

Foxy? Why did she think he was foxy? Sure, he wasn't ugly. Well OK, he was pretty cute, I guess. But he was still a farm boy. A farm boy who wore plaid shirts.

'Very funny,' I replied.

'Might as well,' said Mands. 'It'd help stem the boredom.'

'How much does the world hate me today?' I asked, changing the subject.

'Not very much at all,' replied Mands. This was a relief. 'In fact the only picture of you today was on page four of the *Telegraph*. And they only put it in because Alistair scored two goals. If he hadn't scored the goals I don't think you would have been in there at all.'

This was very good news, although bad news about the goals of course. Clearly our rendezvous wasn't affecting his ability to play, which was a shame.

'But,' she added. 'It looks like we're out of the World Cup anyway.'

'Really?'

This was fabulous news. I only hoped Alistair was suitably devastated. *Perhaps he would even get lynched at the airport on his return?*

'Although the team did well,' continued Mands. 'Got to the semi-finals. Great effort.'

'Oh.'

I guessed he wasn't going to be lynched then. Probably get a bloody ticker-tape parade up Queen Street instead, the bastard.

'And Tiny Tits wasn't in the paper either,' continued Mands.

'Good.'

Every time Tiny Tits was in the paper they invariably threw in a photo of me for good measure, regardless of what it was she was doing at the time.

'I did a drive-by of your apartment too,' said Mands. 'There were only three pests at the gate. Looks like the rest have given up on you.'

'Fantastic,' I replied. And it was.

Although, there was a *very* small glittering disco ball part of me that missed the attention. That missed being photographed and chased. That missed being recognised. The same part of me that liked being called a 'trendsetter' and a clothes-horse.

'Looks like things are finally settling down,' said Mands. 'You'll be coming home soon,' she added. 'I just know it.'

I decided that if Ethan already knew enough about me not to need to ask my address, then it was in my best interests to find out more about him before Sunday.

So, the next morning I probed the subject, during my morning-tea ritual. It didn't require much probing at all, as Elsie could happily talk about Ethan until the cows came home, which is what cows tended to do in these parts.

'What does he do?' I asked.

'Ethan? Why he's the town vet, love. And not just for our town. He's the best vet for miles.'

A vet? Interesting. I'd never met a vet. I knew they did stuff with animals, but that was about the extent of my knowledge.

'And he was born here?' I asked.

'Born and bred. Apart from his years away at school and university. And travelling of course.'

So young people in this town did travel? I thought to myself. Probably an attempt to get the inbreeding down. Whole town chips in to pay for the plane ticket type of thing.

'Does he have any siblings?' I enquired.

'Just the one sister, Anna. She's married to Marty, he's a farmer.'

'And where does Ethan live?'

'He's got a beautiful little cottage on his parents' farm. Looks after the place for his dad, even takes care of Sally's garden. Sally, that was his mum. Big farm it is too, one of the biggest in the whole region.'

'So why isn't he a farmer like his dad?' I asked.

'Oh, he's a good farmer all right, he just loves looking after the animals more. Plus, they've got a manager who looks after the farm for them these days. Greg, that's his name. Lovely bloke he is too.'

It seemed every bloke around here was lovely, if you took Elsie's word for it.

At twelve o'clock on Sunday, true to his word, Ethan arrived to pick me up. It was a beautiful day for a picnic. Clear blue sky and no wind.

'Nice car,' I said noting his Land Rover. 'My mother would like it.'

'Really?' he replied. 'Then I think I'd like your mother.'

'Don't count on it,' I replied.

'Nice Mini,' he said, looking over at my car. 'A good solid farm vehicle if ever I saw one.'

'I'm actually from the city,' I replied. 'Can you tell?'

'Not at all!' he laughed.

'I'll just grab my bag,' I said, walking back into the cabin.

'And I'll just be nosy,' he said, following me inside. 'Don't mind me.'

I really wished he wouldn't. Although it wasn't a date I still had no desire for him to witness my primitive surroundings.

'Little different to my city pad,' I explained as he glanced around.

'Bet it is,' smiled Ethan.

I noted the case of champers still sitting beside the dining table and inwardly cringed. At least I'd had the foresight to hide the box of sex toys.

We drove straight to the river on the opposite side of the village. It was a beautiful spot, calm and tranquil with crystal clear, flowing water, framed by sweeping trees and green grass. And no other people to be seen. Ethan laid a rug out on the grass and unpacked the gorgeous-looking picnic basket he'd brought. There was smoked salmon, olives, cheeses, French bread and a delicious bottle of pinot gris.

'Where did you manage to find this gem?' I asked, tasting the wine.

'There's a couple of great vineyards about half an hour away,' replied Ethan. 'I usually just go and stock up there.'

'Wow,' I replied, very surprised to learn there were vineyards within striking distance of the village.

'Perhaps we can go to one of them for lunch one day?' he suggested.

'Sounds great to me,' I replied. The only thing that came close to being in the city when you weren't was a good country vineyard. It was a happy consolation.

'Sooo Jaaane,' drawled Ethan. 'White med ya move ta these here purts?'

I had to laugh at his country accent.

'Well cowboy, I just needed a break . . . I guess.'

'From work?'

'From everything.'

'What is it that you do?' asked Ethan.

'Advertising. Account manager.'

'Sounds important.'

He could sense I didn't really want to talk about why I'd left the city, and didn't pressure me with any more questions. Instead we tucked into the delicious spread laid out before us.

'Would it be rude if I had a quick fish?' asked Ethan, when we had finished lunch. 'There's a few trout in this river.'

A fish? In the river? It was a bit of a farm-boy cliché, wasn't it? I wondered when the woodland creatures were going to come out of the forest and dance about on the grassy bank.

'Not at all,' I replied.

I lay back in the warm spring sunshine as Ethan cast out into the river directly in front. The sun felt gorgeous on my skin, and my head felt clear of any thoughts, as I stared up into the blue sky. I was truly relaxing, and it felt strangely wonderful.

'Jane, come and have a look at this,' called out Ethan, a short while later.

I walked to the water's edge just in time to see him winding in a big beautiful fish, flapping wildly. It was the first time I'd seen anyone catch a freshwater fish, or any fish for that matter. It was big and shimmery, and beautiful.

'Have you ever eaten baked trout?' asked Ethan.

'Don't think so,' I replied. 'Perhaps from a packet.'

'Then I think this one's a keeper,' he laughed, hooking it into his net. 'As long as you come round to my place tomorrow night and help me eat it of course?'

'Deal,' I replied, watching him handle the fish with ease. The clear sparkling blue of the river was the exact same colour as his eyes.

Get a grip! I told myself. *Just because there's slim pickings in this rural outpost, there's no need to let your city standards drop.*

We whiled away the rest of the afternoon, chatting in the sunshine, until the sun turned to shade. It felt wonderful to be sitting in the long grass, beside the river, without having anywhere or anyone to rush off to. I couldn't remember the last time I'd spent an afternoon just lazing about in the country sun, if I ever had. I certainly hadn't been on a picnic in recent years, not that I could remember anyway. It was nice chatting away to Ethan about all sorts of things, without any uncomfortable or awkward silences.

I asked him all about his work, and family, and he filled me in on the village inhabitants. The ones who were quirky (but sweet) and the ones you should avoid at all costs.

'Elsie appears to have taken me under her wing,' I confessed.

'I've noticed,' said Ethan. 'That's not such a bad thing. I've been under her wing for years.'

'Have you?'

'Her and Bob couldn't have children, so my sister and I became their substitutes. And when my mother died, well Elsie just sort of took over that role.'

'You don't mind?' I asked.

'Not at all,' he replied. 'She's a wonderful woman.'

'And your father never married again?'

'No. The old codger's too stuck in his ways to turn on the charms again. Plus, he and my mother were together for so long I don't think he'd know how to.'

'Were they both from here?' I asked.

'Yep, grew up next door to each other.'

'My God, that is a long time.'

'So, tell me about your family,' urged Ethan.

'Where do I begin?' I replied. 'Well . . . my mother's a full-time feminist . . . my father's a housewife . . . and my sister used to be a lesbian.'

'I think you should pitch that one to a network,' he laughed.

'Don't think I haven't thought about it,' I replied.

When dusk came along and the temperature dropped Ethan drove me back to the cabin, asking me if it was OK if he invited his friends Mack and Abbie along for dinner tomorrow too.

'Of course,' I replied.

It'd be nice for me to get to know some other people while I was in this rural prison, I thought to myself.

I climbed into bed early that night and slept soundly, unperturbed by the silence. I'd had a wonderfully relaxing afternoon and was glad that I went. Ethan was great company and, although he wasn't shag material, I had a feeling he and I were going to be good friends. Even if he was a farm boy. At least he didn't actually like line dancing.

12

Thankfully some more work came through from the office the next day, which saved me from perishing of boredom, and took my mind off the fact the insects inside the cabin appeared to be multiplying at a frightening rate.

Lizzie rang me in the afternoon for her day-about media update.

'Rundown,' I said.

'Not too much to report today,' she answered. 'Just one shot of Alistair in his white shorts and one small pic of you. Must admit he looked pretty hot.'

'Brilliant,' I replied, ignoring her observation. 'Better than yesterday.'

'Anything exciting to report at your end?' she asked.

'Oh, you know, endless parties, too many cocktails I can't remember the names of, fine dining, gorgeous men galore.'

'Poor sweets,' she consoled. 'But look on the bright side, at least you're not spending any money.'

She was right. I had spent approximately twenty dollars in the past week. Aided by the fact there was absolutely nothing for me to buy, apart from food, and fertiliser (which I had no great need of at the present time).

'Actually, I'm going out for dinner tonight,' I confessed.

'Fantastic!' cried Lizzie. 'Who with?'

'Calm down. I'm just going round to Ethan's house. With some of his friends.'

'My God! This is fabulous news! Is foxy Ethan making you dins?'

'Yes, he is. Trout. He caught it too.'

'He what?'

'He caught the trout in the river.'

'My God! He's a hunter-gatherer! I thought they were extinct!'

'Settle down, Lizzie. It's just a fish.'

'A fish he caught and is cooking for *you*.'

The evening arrived and I hadn't a clue what to wear. Whenever I went out for dinner at home it was to a nice restaurant, and I dressed up to the nines. Somehow I didn't think that turning up to the farm wearing stilettos and a short black cocktail frock was going to cut it.

Should I wear jeans? I wondered aloud. *Or is that too casual?* On the other hand I didn't want Ethan to think I'd made too much effort and get the wrong message.

I finally decided on a red-and-white-striped rah-rah skirt, with white mules and a red fitted top. Comfortable yet still sophisticated. I grabbed a bottle of red and hit the road. Ethan had given me very concise and accurate directions on how to get to the farm, which was a good thing considering my map-reading skills. About twenty minutes' drive from the cabin I spotted the 'Willow Farm' sign on the gate and pulled into the driveway. The long driveway was gorgeous, framed on either side by blooming magnolia trees. The cottage was the first house I came to and Ethan came outside to greet me. It was absolutely beautiful, surrounded by a gorgeous big garden and plenty of large shady trees. A scene direct from the pages of *Country Home & Garden*.

'It's gorgeous!' I exclaimed, hopping out of the car with my bottle of wine.

'I'm glad you like it,' said Ethan, giving me a kiss on the cheek.

'Who's the gardener?' I asked, looking around at all of the colourful, healthy-looking plants.

'Well, my mother was — she planted it. But I guess I am now,' he said, shrugging his shoulders.

'Amazing,' I said, looking around in awe.

It was difficult enough for me to comprehend that some people could grow and take care of plants, but to find out that Ethan, a man in his early thirties, was one of those people was extraordinary. If it wasn't for MayBelle watering the few plants inside my apartment and the couple outside on the balcony, they would have died long ago.

'Come inside and I'll show you round,' said Ethan, interrupting my spot of plant appreciation. 'Mack and Abbie will be here soon.'

The cottage was just as gorgeous inside. It was clearly very old but had been renovated in a way which kept a lot of the beautiful old wooden features and combined them with all the mod cons, and a nice open spacious feel. It felt like a real home. The paint colours were light, soothing and warm. The house was a lot roomier on the inside than it appeared from the outside, with two large bedrooms, an office, a huge open-plan modern kitchen and dining area, and a large warm sitting room with loads of comfy old furniture and bookcases. It was the type of living room that made you want to snuggle up on the couch with a blanket, a good book and a glass of wine. Ethan even had a fairly substantial wine cellar to the side of the kitchen.

'Wow,' I said, standing in front of it and ogling at all the bottles.

'I try to collect a bit,' he said. 'But that's a very difficult thing when you like to drink a bit too.'

'I know what you mean,' I agreed. 'My wine rack looks disturbingly skeletal most of the time. Like it needs a good sandwich.'

Ethan sat me down at the dining table with a glass of wine and chatted to me from the kitchen, where he was busy chopping and slicing, and doing other cooking things. He even had an apron on.

'Can I help?' I asked.

I suspected my egg-poaching skills would be totally outclassed, but it was the polite thing to do.

'No, you just sit back and relax,' was his reply.

He obviously knew what was good for him. Or for the meal anyway.

I couldn't have been more relaxed if I tried. Sitting down with a glass of vino, listening to a soothing blues CD in the background, while a man cooked me dinner.

Mack and Abbie soon arrived, bustling into the kitchen with bottles of wine in tow.

They both greeted me with gusto, yelling out, 'Hiya Jane!' as though we'd known each other for years and not just met one night in a pub. I immediately felt relaxed around both of them. Abbie came straight over to sit beside me with a glass of wine and before I knew what was happening the two of us were chatting away like old school friends, interrupted only by dinner. Whole trout, baked with lemongrass and pepper, fresh asparagus, new minted potatoes and a garden side salad (made with ingredients from Ethan's vegetable garden). And no Tahitian vanilla beans in sight, thank Christ. With a home-baked brownie and cream for desert. It was all, quite simply, delicious. Manuel would have glowed fluro-green with envy.

'How about a game of darts?' asked Ethan, when we'd cleared the plates away.

'A what?' I asked.

'Darts. You know, you throw them at the board.'

'Oh.'

I'd heard of it before but it wasn't something I'd ever played.

'Don't worry,' whispered Abbie. 'I'm crap.'

I had a funny feeling I would be too.

'Sure,' I replied. 'Why not?'

We walked outside into the games room which was attached to the garage — a whole room completely designed for games and drinking. There was a small bar and a beer fridge, a large pool table, a couple of couches and the infamous dart board.

'You have to make your own entertainment in a place like this,' smiled Ethan, as I had a good nosy around.

'Great pictures,' I said, admiring the well-framed large photographs which were mounted around the walls. Photos of old dilapidated houses, sheds and fences, taken in a way that seemed, well, beautiful. Old red sheds against green grass and a bright blue sky.

'They're really great,' I said, walking around them all.

'Thanks,' said Ethan.

'Did you take them?' I asked in wonder.

'Over the years, yes.'

'Wow.'

I wondered just how many other things Ethan was capable of. I suddenly felt incredibly uncreative. The only artistic bone in my body was the one that bought art and hoped like hell it was a good investment.

'You ready?' asked Ethan, darts in his hand.

'Um . . .'

'It's very easy,' he encouraged. 'All you have to do is aim at the board.'

He gave me a brief demo, with all three darts effortlessly making their way to very respectable places on the board, and then handed the darts to me. The first one I threw went half a metre to the right of the board, into the wall. The second one hit the window, way to the left of the board. And the last one just sort of dropped onto the carpet, underneath the board, without even making it to the wall.

'Wow,' said Abbie, giggling. 'I think you're worse than me.'

'Are you sure you haven't played before?' asked Ethan, trying very hard not to laugh.

'Ya, positive,' I replied, breaking into a fit of giggles myself.

'Just a question,' he asked, 'but were you actually aiming at the board?'

'As unbelievable as it may seem, I was.'

After another couple of games, where some of my darts even managed to make contact with the board, and much laughing, Mack, Abbie and I decided to head home.

Abbie and I arranged to go for a walk together the following weekend. I was sick of walking or running the same old route and there were a couple of bush tracks nearby which she was going to show me. She and Mack both seemed like lovely people, and the more friends I had to pass my time with, the better.

As I thanked Ethan and gave him a kiss on the cheek, I felt as though I should return the favour and ask him over to the cabin for dinner. Although there were two rather large obstacles: the first was that the cabin was a dusty hovel, and the second was that, although I had improved in leaps and bounds, I still couldn't cook to save myself.

Ah well, I thought to myself, *I have a week to overcome them.*

I drove home and climbed straight into bed, falling soundly and happily asleep in the dip. But not for long.

I awoke a couple of hours later to a loud crashing sound. There was someone inside. In the cabin. *Ohmygod!* I thought in horror. *An intruder.* Thrashing about in the front room. *Bloody hell!*

I'd always wondered what I'd do in a situation like this and now I knew. It appeared I froze. Completely froze. Solid.

Suddenly the racket stopped. I began to breathe again, as quietly as I could. Until it started again two minutes later. It sounded as though the intruder was having it out with the old wooden furniture.

I looked at the bedroom window in anguish. It was tiny. I was not. Plus, I seemed to recall trying to open it one day, only to find it was stuck in one position, and that was slightly ajar. Even if I starved myself for the next three months I still wouldn't fit through it. I doubted my intruder would be happy just beating up the furniture for that long.

What the hell was I going to do? I fretted.

I couldn't ring anyone. My mobile was beside the bed but there was no reception.

Plus, what if he heard me? Surely I'd be a goner.

All this way just to get raped and murdered in a tiny country cabin.

It just wasn't fair, I thought to myself. *All those nights of living in a crime-filled city, alone. Just to end it here. In this rural dust-hole.*

It was incredible how many thoughts ran through your head, and at such a rapid pace, when you were confident you were about to be murdered.

I even thought about my mother, and what she'd do in

a situation like this. Would she cower in bed, frozen to the spot, just waiting for a stranger to attack her?

Not very likely, I decided. She'd be straight out there, loaded .22 in hand, demanding an explanation why she'd been woken at such an ungodly hour.

Suddenly, and for the first time in my life, I wished I was just a little more like my mother.

What are you going to do? asked the voice of reason. *Sit here and wait for it?*

Yes, I answered. *It would appear so.*

Shouldn't you at least try to stand up for yourself?

Do I have to?

Yes.

And with that, the voice of reason (or complete insanity, depending on the outcome) won. Ever so quietly I slipped out of bed in the darkness and put a jersey on over my pyjamas. If I was going to die, then I at least wanted to be warm.

I lay down on the floor and felt around under the bed. I was positive I had seen an old wooden bed slat laying under there. Finally my hand stumbled across it.

What exactly are you going to do with this? asked the voice of reason, as I stood back up.

I am going to belt the living daylights out of whoever is out there, I replied. *I think.*

You don't sound sure?

I am sure.

Sure sure?

Yes, I replied meekly. *I will not die without a fight.*

That's the spirit!

I stood up straight, pushed out my chest, clutched the wooden slat in both hands and walked as slowly and quietly as I could out of the bedroom and into the front room, stopping when I reached the doorway. Suddenly the banging stopped too. All I could hear was my rapid breathing and my African drum of a heartbeat. I desperately urged myself to breathe quietly. Now I was frozen in the doorway, staring into the pitch blackness of the tiny living room.

Are you going to stand here all night? asked the voice of reason.

Yes,' I replied. *If that's OK with you.*

What would your mother do?

I am not my mother.

Yes, I know that, but what would she do?

Call out something, I guess. In a loud, aggressive don't-fuck-with-me voice.

Why don't you try that?

OK then.

'WHAT THE HELL DO YOU THINK YOU'RE DOING?' I yelled into the blackness.

There was no reply.

'GET OUT OF MY BLOODY HOUSE!' I yelled. Still no reply. Just awful eerie silence.

What now? I asked the voice of reason.

You're simply going to have to switch on the lights and see who's there.

No? Really?

Yes.

Crap.

I felt down the wall for the light switch.

Go on! urged the voice. *You can do it!*

I flicked the light on in time to see something jump down from kitchen table and run across the wooden floor, under the old sofa. Something brown and furry. And large.

Mother of God, I wondered aloud. *What the hell is that?*

It certainly wasn't the six-foot, balaclava-wearing man I'd been expecting. I willed myself to crouch down on the floor and look under the sofa. As I did two bright red eyes stared back at me, without blinking, accompanied by a nasty hissing sound. Clearly whatever it was, it was very annoyed at me having turned the lights on and spoiling its middle-of-the-night jaunt. I stood back up and it scurried out from under the sofa and went hurtling into the kitchen. I yelped and jumped back against the wall.

It was enormous. Some sort of steroid-induced woodland creature. With a bad attitude. I suddenly wished I had watched more nature programmes instead of *Friends*.

Obviously I was relieved it wasn't going to rape or torture me. At least I didn't think it was. But I was completely unsure what to do next. You just didn't wake up to find unwanted wild furry animals in your apartment in the city, thrashing about as if they owned the place.

It's probably making itself a cup of tea now, I thought, still cowering against the wall.

I looked down at the piece of wood in my hands.

You know what you're going to have to do, don't you? asked the voice of reason.

What? I replied.

You're simply going to have to beat it to death.

Pardon?

Beat it. With the wood.

But I don't want to.

Truth be known I was afraid it would snatch the wood out of my hands and start beating me instead. It *was* rather large.

I crept to the kitchen and saw it cowering in the corner, behind the rubbish bin. It began hissing again. I kept my distance.

Good God it was ugly! Not at all like the furry animals depicted in my childhood story books. Not very *Mother Goose* at all. And it had claws too. Long ones.

How the hell did it get in here? I wondered.

I glanced around the room and my eyes rested on the chimney. *Aha.* I doubted it was going to pop back out the same way.

What can you do? I wondered. I had decided that beating it to death possibly wasn't the best option for me. As yet I still hadn't worked up the courage to kill the spider in the shower. Instead I wisely decided to open the front door and leave the light on, in the hope it would run back outside, away from the light. Preferably before I got up in the morning. I crept back out of the living room, and shut the bedroom door behind me, lest it have any notions of joining me in the sack. I climbed back into bed, the piece of wood still firmly in my grip.

I woke up with the piece of wood lying across my chest, my arms folded across it, like a knight who had been buried with his sword. I walked into the living room, praying for the furry monster to be gone. Thankfully it was. But not before it had decided to leave me a thank-you note. There were small brown poo pebbles everywhere. Everywhere. It was at this precise moment that Lizzie decided to ring and wish me good morning.

'Hi sweets. How are you?'

'OK,' I replied, looking around at all of the droppings. 'Bit of a sleepless night though.'

'Still worried huh?'

'No. Had an intruder.'

'A *what*?' she screamed.

'An animal. Not a person,' I explained.

'What was it?' she asked.

'Not entirely sure,' I replied. 'But it's crapped everywhere.'

'Really?'

'Yes.'

'What did it look like?'

'Brown and furry. And big.'

'A rabbit?' asked Lizzie.

'Rabbits don't hiss,' I replied.

'P'haps it was a badger then?'

'Do we have badgers?'

'Hmm . . . not sure actually.'

'A cat?'

'I know what a cat looks like, Lizzie, and this was no household pet. Trust me.'

'Did you give it a key?' she asked.

'Chimney,' I replied.

'Oh dear.'

I went into Elsie's for my morning tea and relayed my night of terror.

'Damn possums,' she replied. 'Always popping down the chimney and never finding their way back out.'

So it was a possum then. Perhaps it was a relative of the one Mands ran over, looking to settle the score.

That night I was rudely awoken once again. I was in the middle of a dream. One of those deep, this-feels-like-real-life-so-therefore-it-must-be type dreams. And in my dream was Jasmine. *Why was I dreaming about Jasmine?* I have no idea. But anyway, there we were, Jasmine and I, living together in my apartment. Doing things that normal couples do. Cooking, paying bills, watching DVDs. Boring, coupley things. And then, as we lay on the sofa one evening, snuggled up together under a duvet, Jasmine suddenly morphed back into Jerry. And then Jerry stood up and pulled down his trousers. And then, well, then he began to pee onto my face as I lay on the sofa. *Why was he peeing on my face?* I wondered (in my dream state). A minute ago he was Jasmine and we were

313

watching a DVD. *Yuk. Stop it!* I thought. *You dirty bastard!* But I was glued to the sofa, unable to move.

Wake up! said a little voice inside my head. *Wake up!*

And so I woke up. Only to find it wasn't Jerry peeing on my face, but the roof. There was a continuous drip landing just below my left eye and rolling in a small stream down my cheek.

For the love of God! I thought, jumping out of bed and grabbing a plastic bucket from the kitchen. It was raining outside. Raining hard.

The next morning, after my date scone, I went to see Bruce at the hardware-slash-pharmacy store. I needed to find someone to come and fix the leak before it began raining again.

'Oh . . . let's see . . . hmm . . . there's Jim. But he's busy working at the Simpsons' farm at the moment. Or there's Dave . . . but I think he's working there too.'

I waited patiently for him to come up with more names. Names of people who might actually be able to come and fix it, at least in this lifetime. But there were no more names forthcoming. And then I waited for him to offer to come and fix it himself, but that wasn't doing either. In retrospect I should have started crying. Back in the city I would have just phoned Hire-a-Hubby and they would have been round in half an hour, leak forgotten.

'What's the roof made of, love?' asked Bruce.

'Metal.'

'You mean tin?'

'Yes, tin.'

'Big leak?'

'Not overly. Just a steady drip.'

'Well how about trying some sealant on it first?' he suggested.

'Some what?'

'Some sealant. Try popping that round the edges of the tin sheets and see what happens.'

'Me?'

'Yes. You.'

I stared back at him. Obviously he was under the illusion I was capable of fixing a leaky roof.

Half an hour later I found myself straddling the top of the cabin roof, directly above the bedroom, squirting sealant into the narrow gaps between the sheets of tin.

This was not something I had ever envisaged myself doing. But what choice did I have? None. It was either this or be peed, I mean dripped, on. One tube of sealant and one rainy night later, it was evident that I, Samantha Steel, had fixed a leaky roof. All By Herself. My mother would have glowed with pride.

All the rest of that week I heard whispers about a fair. Whispers in the grocery-slash-drycleaning-slash-liquor store, whispers in the post-office-slash-bank-slash-stationery store, and whispers in the café.

'What's going on?' I asked Elsie, curiosity finally getting the better of me.

'Why it's the Floodgate town fair, luvvie,' she replied, as if this was something I should have been aware of, or that I would care about.

'When?' I asked.

'This weekend. On Saturday.'

Elsie explained that the Floodgate town fair was an annual event with games, competitions and children's rides. And a cake-off.

'What's a cake-off?' I asked.

'A cake-baking competition love. You bake a cake, any kind of cake, and enter it and a judging panel decides whose is the best.'

Aha, I thought to myself. That explained why Elsie had been substituting my date scone for a different slice of cake every morning for the past week, then standing beside the table until I'd finished it and asking me what I thought.

'Delicious,' I'd replied. Or 'a little more lemon perhaps? Or 'maybe a tad more icing?'

'So you're entering the cake-off then?' I asked.

'Am I what, luvvie. I'm not having that trollop Deidre Watkins win again.'

Deidre Watkins was the reverend's wife. A small, bird-like woman with round spectacles who liked to waltz into the café every morning and say things like *Oooh, scones didn't rise so well today, did they Elsie? Look a bit like they've been run over, don't they?* In other words, Deidre Watkins was a bitch. And it appeared she and Elsie were fierce rivals in the annual cake-off.

'Why don't you bake one too, love?' suggested Elsie.

Bake a cake? Having only just stopped routinely burning things every time I set foot in the kitchen, I didn't think this was such a great idea. Plus, baking was something old people did. And my father of course.

'Go on,' she urged. 'You can come round to my place on Friday night and we'll do it together. It'll be fun.'

It looked as though she wasn't going to take no for an answer. Again.

'Won't I need to practise?' I asked.

'I guess that depends on how well you want to do,' she replied. 'But if you just want to have a go, then Friday will be fine. If the first one's no good then you can just bake another one. We'll have time.'

'OK,' I replied. 'But I'm warning you, I can't cook to save myself.'

First line dancing on a Friday night and now cake baking? God, what the hell had happened to me?

So, that evening I went round to Elsie's house for a glass of wine and to select my cake recipe. I had never baked a cake before and I wasn't entirely sure she really understood this. But before I left the cabin I had a phone call from Mands.

'Guess what, dolls?' she cried. 'We're coming to visit you this weekend!'

'Fabulous!' I exclaimed, amid nasty flashbacks of their last visit.

'Oh but . . .'

'Oh but what? she asked.

'It's the town fair this weekend.'

'The town what?'

'The town fair. It happens every year. And I have to go.'

'Sounds like a blast,' said Mands. 'Count us in.'

'OK,' I replied, nerves suddenly rising.

The idea of Mands and Lizzie loose at the Floodgate town fair was not a relaxing vision.

As soon as I put the phone down from Mands, it rang again. It was my father, with his weekly media synopsis and usual soothing words of *Don't worry love, it'll all be over soon.* I'd told him there was no need for the updates as Mands and Lizzie were keeping me well informed, but he liked to feel as though he was part of the loop. I knew for a fact that his updates were filtered. And he never told me when they used the nose picture.

'Your mother and I would like to come and visit you, love,' he said, wrapping up his rose-tinted rundown.

'Great,' I replied. I was so desperate for visitors that even this sounded like a fabulous idea.

'How's this weekend?' he asked.

'Oh . . . well, Mands and Lizzie are coming this weekend,' I replied. 'Can we make it another one?'

'Of course, love,' said Dad. 'I'll just check with your mother and get back to you with a date.'

After much deliberation and aimless searching through Elsie's stacks of recipe books, I decided to make an orange-and-cream-cheese cake. A slightly ambitious choice for someone who had never baked a cake before. Elsie opted for a blackberry-and-brandy sponge cake. To be honest I think she just wanted to get some brandy in it somehow.

'You know what, love?' she said, as we sat at her dining table, surrounded by recipe books. 'I think it's about time you had yourself some visitors.'

'Funny you should say that,' I replied. 'My two best friends are coming again this weekend.'

'Yippee!' she cried. 'They'll be here for the fair.'

'My parents were going to come too,' I added. 'But I've put them off till another time.'

'Why?' she asked.

'No room.'

'Hang on, love,' she said. 'How about your parents come and stay with Bob and me? That way you've got everyone here together for the weekend.'

'Oh Elsie, that's very kind of you but . . .'

'No buts. Bob and I would love to have your parents to stay.'

And just like that I now had my two best friends and my parents converging on sleepy little Floodgate for the weekend. The thought of my mother descending on the place was enough to disturb my sleep for the next three nights. She was a worse prospect than Mands. Way worse. I just hoped and prayed she would control herself and her tongue. I suddenly realised that if my parents were staying with Elsie, this meant my identity would inevitably be revealed. I had told my parents my name was now Jane and under no circumstances whatsoever should they call me Samantha, but I just knew one of them would let it slip. Plus, I felt like it was time I told Elsie who I really was. I was sick of keeping her in the dark. I knew I could trust her.

'So how long do you think you're going to stay here for, luvvie?' asked Elsie, as she poured herself another brandy and me another wine. 'In Floodgate?'

'I'm not sure,' I replied, taking a sip. 'I'm kinda waiting. Waiting until it's safe to go back.'

'Safe?'

Well, here goes.

'Elsie . . . there's something I really should tell you,' I said, putting my wine glass down on the table. 'The thing is . . . my name's not really Jane.' I paused. 'It's Samantha . . . Steel.'

'Love . . .' said Elsie.

'And,' I continued. 'I had a rendezvous with Alistair Ambrose, the footballer, once. And I was so harassed by the media, with photographers camped out on my doorstep every day and night, chasing me to work, and everywhere I turned, I had to leave the city and escape here. They wouldn't leave me alone. Not for one second.'

'Love . . .'

'It was hell,' I continued. 'I had to leave my job because the vultures were flocked outside the building. They even printed pictures of me at the gym and . . .'

'Luvvie,' said Elsie, gripping me with both arms and staring me straight in the eyes. 'I know.'

'You know?'

She knew?

'But how long have you known?' I asked.

'I had a fair idea on your first day in the café,' she replied.

'Why didn't you say anything?' I asked.

'Why should I say anything? It's none of my business, love. You've come here to escape something and the last thing you need is an old duck like me pestering you.'

I didn't know what to say.

'Thank you,' I replied. 'Do many other people know?'

'Oh, I think a few others have probably figured it out for themselves. We're not completely out of touch here, you know.'

I must have looked shocked.

'But don't worry, love,' she comforted, patting me gently on the arm. 'If they know I can guarantee you they won't say anything. People will respect your privacy round here, as long as you respect theirs. They like their peace and quiet and they're not going to do anything to ruin it. It's not all needlework and gossip, you know,' she added, reading my mind.

'Do you know what the worst thing is?' I asked.

'What, love?'

'That I didn't even know who he was, or that he was married. I thought he was just a nice single man sitting in a bar.'

'If God were not willing to forgive sin then heaven would be empty,' said Elsie. 'In other words, don't beat yourself up about it, love. Plus, smooth seas don't make skilful sailors.'

I think she was implying this whole hideous experience would somehow make me a stronger person. At least I think that's what she was saying.

'And if you ever want to talk about it, you just let me know.

A trouble shared is a trouble halved, remember.'

'I will. Thanks Elsie,' I said, smiling at her. 'For everything.'

'Does Bob know?' I asked.

'I doubt it, love. He's not the most observant man ever created.'

'And Ethan?' I asked.

'I'm not sure. Perhaps you should ask him sometime?'

I went back to the cabin happy and relieved. Relieved I was no longer keeping a secret from Elsie, and happy that she understood.

The following day I invited Ethan round to the cabin for dinner. Now that I had decided I could cook (at least without turning everything into a flaky piece of charcoal) it was time to repay the favour. After consulting one of Dad's email recipes and a visit to Murray the butcher and Della at the grocery-slash-dry-cleaning-slash-liquor store, I decided to make a chicken curry. (With bought curry paste — I hadn't come that far.) It was surprising how well stocked the grocery-slash-dry-cleaning-slash-liquor store was. With Della's help I had no problem finding all of the ingredients I needed, even the poppadoms.

Who would have thought? Me, Samantha Steel, cooking dinner for another person. Without burning either it, or any part of the kitchen for that matter.

Ethan brought along a lovely bottle of white wine to have with dinner.

'Delicious, Jane,' he said, helping himself to more curry.

And it was too. I was as proud as anyone had ever been of a chicken curry.

The only problem was I was bit too nervous to eat much myself. I knew it was time for me to tell Ethan who I really was. To fess up. He had become a good friend, and not one I wanted to keep secrets from. Plus, I trusted him just as much as I trusted Elsie.

'Ethan' I started. There was no going back now. 'There's something I've got to tell you.'

'What's that?' he asked.

'Well . . . the thing is . . .'

God, why was this so hard for me to say? It's not like I fancied him, for God's sake.

'The thing is . . .'

'The thing is?' he prompted.

'That . . . I'm not who you think I am.'

'How so? Are you really a bloke?' he smiled. 'Not that you look like one of course,' he added. 'Although of course it would be absolutely fine if you were.'

'No,' I laughed, thinking of Jasmine. He had no idea just how close to the bone this remark was.

'My name isn't Jane. It's Samantha . . . Samantha Steel.'

Ethan looked at me, apparently waiting for more information.

'And?' he asked.

'You don't recognise my name?' I asked, amazed.

'No, should I?'

'Well no . . .that's good. It's just a surprise, that's all.'

'Are you a bank robber then?' he grinned.

'No,' I laughed.

'That's a shame. I've always wanted to meet a bank robber.'

'It's just that my name's quite well known for . . . something I did.'

He looked at me, waiting for more.

'You know Alistair Ambrose?' I asked.

'The footballer?'

'Correct. Well he and I had a bit of a . . . well a thing.'

Ethan was still sitting there looking at me, calmly waiting for more information.

'Look, what I'm trying to say is that we had a one-night stand. I had no idea who he was, or that he was married. And as a result I was literally set upon the very next day by paparazzi. Tons of them. Chased, harassed and photographed for weeks on end. And that's why I'm here. I'm in hiding.'

'That's why you left the city?' said Ethan.

'Yes.'

'And?' he asked.

'And what?'

'And that's it?'

'Yes.'

Yes. That was it. All of it.

I filled Ethan in on just how horrific the hounding had been. How I'd been set upon every time I walked out my front door. How I'd had to stop going into the office and work from home. How I'd been photographed at the gym. And how I'd made my elaborate escape. He didn't pass judgement, or criticise, or even seem shocked. He just sat and listened to my story and nodded his head, and let me say what I had to say.

And when I had finished he said, 'I'm glad you told me. Thank you.' And that was it.

I slept like a baby that night. I felt relieved, once again. Overwhelmingly relieved, as if some sort of weight had been lifted from my body. As if the guilt I had been carrying since the Night of Shame was gone. As if everything was finally going to be OK.

The next morning I took a break from work and headed into the café, as per usual. Elsie was standing in her well-worn spot behind the counter, restacking the sandwiches and scones, wearing a bright-blue-and-yellow-checked dress, with a headband to match. But for some reason she wasn't her usual bright self.

'Are you OK?' I asked.

'I'm fine love,' she replied, although she didn't look fine. 'Just in a wee bit of pain with the hips. Nothing that won't pass though.'

'Can I help?' I asked. 'How about I look after the café and you go home and rest for a while?'

'No it's fine luvvie, honestly. I've just taken some Voltaren. It'll kick in soon.'

I didn't like seeing Elsie in pain.

'Are you sure?'

'Positive.'

'At least let me make my own tea then,' I said, moving round to the other side of the counter and making us both a pot, before sitting down at my usual table.

I had long ago started to bring my old magazines into the shop for Elsie. I would rather read them for the twentieth time than be subjected to the likes of *Heart & Home*.

Just as I finished my second cup of tea I looked up from my magazine to see a shiny new silver Porsche pull up outside.

Looks like someone's really got themselves lost, I thought to myself.

A tall man wearing a navy cap, jeans and a T-shirt hopped out of the car. As he walked past the café window he glanced inside and caught my eye, just for a split second.

Oh no! I thought to myself, averting my eyes back down to my magazine as quickly as I could.

It was too late. He had already seen me.

'Sam?' he said, walking through the doorway and up to my table.

I toyed with the idea of telling him that no, it wasn't, my name was Jane and I'm terribly sorry but he must have mistaken me for someone else. Somehow I didn't think he'd fall for it.

'What are you doing here?' I asked, as he sat down at the table.

'I've been looking for you everywhere,' he said. 'I arrived last night.'

'How did you know I was here?'

'Believe me it wasn't easy to find out. One of your friends finally gave in.'

It had to have been either Mands or Lizzie. Either way, one of them was as good as dead. (It turned out Lizzie had accidentally let my whereabouts slip to Darcy and he was the culprit, but anyway.)

'Nice hair,' he added. 'It suits you.'

I chose to ignore him.

'What do you want Alistair?' I asked.

'I want to talk to you.'

'Why?'

'I just do.'

'Well, I don't want to talk to you.'

I glanced over at the counter and saw Elsie hovering behind it, stacking sandwiches. She wasn't looking at us but she was within earshot all the same.

'Please Sam,' he said. 'Just let me speak to you. That's all I'm asking.'

Clearly, if he'd driven four-and-a-half hours and spent the night here, he wasn't going to leave me alone just like that. Plus, although he looked as though he hadn't slept in days, he was still incredibly foxy.

'OK,' I agreed. 'But not here. I'll meet you outside.'

Alistair left and I said goodbye to Elsie. She gave me a small smile and said 'The honey is sweet, love, but the bee has a sting.'

'I know,' I replied, giving her a kiss on the cheek.

She was telling me to be careful.

'Where shall we go?' asked Alistair.

'To the river,' I replied, hopping into his car.

We drove in silence, me in anger and shock and him in nervousness. Our only communication was my curt directions, 'left here' and 'right there'.

Alistair parked the car at the edge of the grass clearing.

'Sit on the grass?' he suggested.

'OK,' I replied, getting out of the car and walking along the grass, with Alistair beside me at a safe distance.

'What do you want to say to me?' I asked, turning towards him.

I had no intention of dragging this conversation out any longer than necessary.

'Well . . .' he started. 'I know you're still angry with me but . . .'

'Alistair,' I interrupted. 'I will always be angry with you. *Always*. Lest there be any confusion.'

He looked hurt at this comment.

'But,' he continued, 'I came here to see you and to tell you that . . . that I can't stop thinking about you . . . and that I miss you.'

'Alistair, we slept together once. What's there to miss?'

'I don't know and I can't explain it. All I know is I really like you Sam. A lot. And I want you to know that.'

'Fine,' I said. 'And now I know it. You came a long way just to tell me that,' I added.

'That's not all,' he replied nervously. 'I want to get to know you, if you'll let me. I want to be with you, Sam.'

'Me and how many others?' I asked.

He winced at this remark.

'Just you.'

'And when did you decide this?' I asked. 'While you were still living with your pregnant wife?'

'No. And I don't expect you to believe me Sam, but our marriage had been falling apart for a while, well before I met you. And now it's over. For good.'

'And I'm supposed to believe you?' I asked.

'I know you won't straightaway, but it's true, I swear. And I know it's going to take time for you to trust me again.'

'What if I don't want to trust you?' I asked.

'That's your decision Sam, no matter what I say.'

I stared at the grass beside me.

I hadn't expected this. Ever. Not in my lifetime. Here was Alistair Ambrose telling me he liked me. Telling me his marriage was over. Telling me he wanted to be with me. It was all just a wee bit overwhelming.

'Will you ever be able to forgive me?' he asked.

'I don't know,' I sighed. 'I just don't know.'

He moved closer and tentatively put his arm around my shoulders.

'Will you think about what I've said?' he asked.

'Yes,' I replied. I would give him that.

He leaned in to kiss me.

'Please,' I said, holding up my hand. 'Don't.'

'OK,' he replied, pulling back.

'I need time, Alistair,' I said. 'This is a complete shock for me and I need time to think everything over.'

'If I stay in town for the night will you meet me for dinner?' he asked.

'There is absolutely nowhere to eat,' I warned him. 'Unless you want to go to the pub for roast pork.'

'How about fish and chips back here beside the river then?' he suggested.

'OK,' I agreed. It wasn't as though I had any other plans.

It turned out Alistair was staying at the only accommodation available in Floodgate, a small bed and breakfast on the edge of town.

'Do you think they recognised you?' I asked.

'I don't think so,' he replied. 'I've had my cap and glasses on. If they did, they haven't said anything.'

We agreed to meet back beside the river at six o'clock, Alistair with the fish and chips. I went back to the cabin and tried to work for the afternoon, but I couldn't stop thinking about him. He had come all this way just to tell me he cared about me, and he wanted to be with me. *Why?* It's not like he really even knew me. It had been one night. *One night.* Plus, it was obvious he could get any woman he wanted.

As angry as I still was with him, there was a part of me that was flattered. Flattered he'd come all this way to see me. Flattered he wanted me. And then there was another part of me that said *be careful, be very careful.*

I went back to the river just after six and Alistair was there already, sitting on the grass. We sat and talked, drank a bottle of wine, and pretended to eat the fish and chips in front of us, but really just moved them around on the paper.

We talked about his kids, football, my job and my family. Things we possibly should have talked about before jumping into bed together.

'Will you stay with me tonight?' he asked. He had to drive back to the city early in the morning.

'No,' I replied.

It was hard to say no. Extremely hard. Here was Alistair. Incredibly good-looking, wanting me, asking me to spend the night with him. And here was me, remembering how good the sex had been, lonely, and wanting to be wanted.

'I just can't,' I said. 'Not now. Not yet.'

But every girl is entitled to change her mind. The memory of the mind-blowing sex was just too powerful to ignore. Plus, there was nothing wrong with make-up sex, I decided. It was one of the most common forms of sex known to woman.

It doesn't have to mean anything, I told myself. *It'd just be a shag and that's it: nothing more, nothing less.*

'Really?' he asked, his green eyes lighting up. 'Fantastic.'

We decided to head back to the cabin. Staying at the bed and breakfast would have been like erecting a billboard of our rendezvous in the main street of Floodgate.

'Nice pad,' smiled Alistair, as I showed him into the cabin.

'Yes,' I replied. 'Lovely isn't it?'

And it's your bloody fault I'm living here, I thought to myself, but refrained from saying it.

I opened a bottle of wine and we sat down on the lumpy couch.

'Come here,' said Alistair, immediately putting down his wine glass and opening his arms.

You can still run, I told myself. *This is your last chance.*

Bugger that, myself replied, looking across at his handsome face.

I was pleased to note he was still a brilliant kisser, and an expert at removing layers of my clothing before I'd realised they'd gone. With only my bra and undone trousers remaining we headed to the bedroom, Alistair leading me by the hand. Unlike the frantic sex of last time, this was slower, more sensual, and quieter. It felt, in a passionate way, as though our bodies were actually connecting.

Just think about it as sex, I reminded myself. *Nothing else.*

I kissed his now-familiar smooth and toned chest, as he lay on top of me and gently slid inside. And then I fell asleep with his arm wrapped around my shoulders and my head resting on his chest.

Early the next morning Alistair left to drive back to the city.

'Will you think about what I've said?' he asked again.

'Yes,' I replied. 'But I can't promise anything.'

He looked wounded at this but said, 'I know. But just think about it, Sam. Please.'

'I will,' I agreed.

The sex had been nothing short of fantastic and part of me wanted to forgive him, but part of me was still angry too.

As his silver Porsche headed down the dirt driveway, trailed by a cloud of dust, I phoned Elsie at the café to see how she was feeling.

'Oh I'm fine love,' she replied. 'Thank you.'

But she didn't sound fine.

'Look,' I said. 'I want you to go home and have a rest. I'll come in and run the café for you today.'

'Honestly love, I'm fine.'

'Don't you think I can do it?' I asked, hoping this would make her change her mind.

'Well, of course I do.'

'Then let me,' I said.

Finally she gave in and told me she'd only be a phone call away if I needed any help.

'How did it go with your man yesterday?' she asked.

'He's not my man, Elsie.'

'I know, I was just checking.'

'It went OK,' I sighed. 'I guess.'

'Just remember, love,' she added, as I said goodbye, 'put a silk on a goat and it is still a goat.'

I think this was some sort of warning, and I had a funny feeling Alistair was the goat. I went into the café and, after a thorough rundown, finally managed to shuffle Elsie out the front door and home. It was a steady day, but I coped. In fact, I even enjoyed it. Ethan popped by for some lunch and gave me a hand to serve a few extra customers. And, as unbelievable as it was, I even managed to make an extra batch of date scones without either burning them or making them look like they'd been rolling round in your handbag for a week.

13

Friday arrived and with it Cake Baking Day. Mands and Lizzie weren't going to be arriving until later in the evening, so at four o'clock I went round to Elsie's house for a glass of wine and to, well, bake my orange-and-cream-cheese cake. I was nervous. I just prayed I wasn't going to set any part of Elsie's kitchen on fire. We stood side by side at her kitchen bench in our aprons, mixing our ingredients into two big bowls. I stirred my cake mix, pleasantly surprised at how therapeutic and relaxing it was to stand and stir a cake mix with a wooden spoon. And then, under Elsie's guidance, it was oven time.

'If you keep opening the door and looking it'll never cook,' warned Elsie, as I checked my cake for the tenth time. 'The continuous drip polishes the stone,' she added.

I think she meant I should be patient.

When the buzzer finally went off I lifted my cake out of the oven, too scared to look at it.

'Holy Mary! Get a load of that!' exclaimed Elsie. 'Well done love! All you need to do now is ice it.'

Much to my complete surprise it appeared to have risen perfectly. In fact, it looked delicious. It looked like a proper cake and not remotely like a piece of charcoal. After waiting for it to cool I set about covering it with cream-cheese icing. Forty minutes later (it was my first cake after all) I took my apron off and stood back to admire my handiwork.

'Well, I'll be,' said Elsie. 'That's a cake if ever I saw one.'

I beamed back at her. I, Samantha Steel, had baked a cake. A cake which had not collapsed, or burned. And the funny thing was, I had actually enjoyed baking it. *Who would have thought?*

My parents arrived at Elsie's house a short while later, my mother in the driver's seat as per usual.

'That's Samantha's cake,' said Elsie, as we brought their bags inside. 'Isn't it a beauty?'

'You baked that?' asked Dad, disbelief in his eyes.

'Yes,' I replied. 'With a bit of help.'

'That's fantastic, love,' he replied, giving me a hug. 'Just fantastic.'

My mother stood staring at the cake. And then at me. And then back to the cake. No words were uttered. After having some dinner and settling them in with Elsie and Bob, I made my way back to the cabin in time to meet Mands and Lizzie. Thankfully they managed to arrive safely, without either getting lost or killing any animals.

We immediately set about opening a bottle of wine. And then another. And catching up on long-overdue gossip. Lizzie, after taking our feedback on board, had ordered her sperm. She went with number two, the sax-playing, singing, Yale undergraduate. I think she secretly wanted to be a stage mum. Mands, after much deliberation, had decided not to visit Sven the Swedish toe-sucker. She was in fact (by her own admission) jealous of her own feet.

'I wish they were ugly,' she sighed. 'Then I might get a free holiday.'

The girls informed me that my limelight was definitely fading. This was great news. There were no more magazine articles with Tiny Tits and her poor fatherless children and only a few newspaper articles to speak of about any of us. They had even stopped using the dreaded nose picture, thanks be to God.

'You'll be back in no time, dolls,' said Mands. 'I can feel it.'

I'd made a decision not to tell the girls about Alistair's visit, as hard as this was. I needed time to make up my own mind, without their friendly advice or enthusiasm.

I'd tell them once I had made my decision, whenever and whatever that may be.

The next morning I let the girls have a little sleep-in as I got up to put the coffee on and make us some breakfast. I couldn't seem to sleep in anymore, I don't know why. I think it might have had something to do with how soundly I slept here, no tossing and turning as I did in the city. Here I fell into a deep slumber straightaway, the kind of deep slumber that resulted in a patch of dribble on the pillowcase come morning.

'Rise and shine,' I called out, walking into the bedrooms.

They both groaned and rolled straight over.

'What time is it?' grumbled Lizzie.

'Time to get up and go to the fair,' I replied.

'Mary bloody Poppins,' mumbled Mands, from the other room.

'My head hurts,' moaned Lizzie.

'Nothing a bit of brekkie won't fix. Upsy-daisy,' I urged, pulling back the duvet.

'I'll give you upsy-friggin-daisy,' she muttered.

'You're turning into a bloody morning person,' called out Mands. 'You'll be down at the chicken coup at six o'clock collecting eggs next.'

I decided to ignore her and pour the coffee instead.

Our first stop was Elsie's house to collect my cake. I arrived to find Dad and Elsie standing in the kitchen, aprons on, chatting away like old friends and clearing up from breakfast. My mother and Bob were sitting at the dining table, reading the newspaper in companionable silence.

'What's this?' asked Mands, as we hopped back into the car and I handed her the cake to hold.

I had been dreading this moment.

'It's a cake,' I replied.

'I can see that.'

'A cake that I made and am entering in the cake-off.'

'The what-off?'

'The cake-baking competition at the fair.'

'Let me get this straight,' said Mands. 'You, Samantha Steel, have baked a cake which you are going to enter in a cake-baking competition at the town fair.'

'Yes.'

A long pause while they both finished laughing. And then started again.

'Hells bells!' exclaimed Lizzie. 'What in God's name is happening to you?'

'That's it!' laughed Mands. 'We're going to have to evacuate you soon, before you turn into some sort of lemon-faced washerwoman.

'If you drop it, I'll kill you,' I replied, which shut her up.

The fair was being held on the school football field. I had never seen so many people gather in this town at once, not even at the market.

Where on earth had they all been hiding? I wondered.

First stop was to meet Elsie at the cake stall where we were to deliver and register our cakes, while Mands and Lizzie stood beside the stall giggling hysterically.

I arrived, cake in hand, to find Elsie chatting to a tall girl with long blonde hair, who looked only a few years younger than me.

'This is Josie,' said Elsie, introducing us.

'Hi,' she replied, blatantly giving me the once-over. I was no stranger to the once-over, being that I frequently give it myself.

Josie promptly said her goodbyes, telling us she was off to meet Ethan.

I guessed she must be a friend of Ethan's.

'She's trouble, that one,' whispered Elsie, once she had gone. 'Back in town again. Poor Ethan.'

'Are they an item?' I asked, curious.

'Used to be,' replied Elsie, shaking her head. 'Her parents own the farm next to his. Broke his heart three years ago, poor ducky, and then she went to live in Sydney. A wild goose never laid a tame egg I say.'

We put our cakes down on the judging table. The judging panel was convening at two o'clock sharp to taste and rate the cakes. There was quite a pile sitting on the table already, on a large lace tablecloth.

Please don't let there be another orange-and-cream-cheese one, I prayed.

It was a gorgeous day and we spent the first part of the morning wandering around the various food and craft stalls, meeting up with my parents, Bob, Ethan, Mack, Abbie and Josie.

'Who's the snooty cow?' asked Mands. I gathered she was referring to Josie.

'Ethan's ex,' I replied.

'*Really?*' said Mands, raising her eyebrows. 'I smell a competition.'

I had no idea what she was talking about.

We sat down for an early picnic lunch on the grass, Mands and Lizzie having headed back to the cabin to rescue four bottles of cold champers.

'What's a picnic without bubbles?' said Mands, as the three of us, and Abbie, proceeded to get stuck in.

After lunch we decided to partake in a few of the activities on offer. The first one we came across was a mechanical bull whose sole purpose, it appeared, was to have you innocently sit on it and then throw you round like a sack of potatoes.

'Fantastic!' cried Josie, excitedly. 'Haven't seen one of these for years. 'C'mon Ethie,' she said, grabbing Ethan by the hand.

'No, not this time,' he replied, holding up his hands.

'Oh,' she said, pouting at him and smiling cutely. 'You're no fun.'

He didn't smile back.

'What about you, Sam?' he asked, turning to me.

'Oh . . . um . . .'

'Yes Sam,' said Josie, smiling at me sweetly, as she joined the line. 'Why don't you give it a go? It's fun.'

'Go on Sammy,' urged Abbie.

'You can't let that horsey woman beat you,' hissed Mands in my ear, giving me a little push. 'Get up there, for God's sake.'

'Why?' I hissed back.

'Because she's making you look bad.'

'Whaddayamean?'

'I mean she's clearly challenging you to a competition and you've got to kick her arse.'

'Why? What for?'

'Because, it's a Chick-Off, that's why. Town versus Country.'

A what-off? I had no desire to compete with Josie, especially as I wasn't sure what exactly we were competing for, but (due to the effects of the bubbles) I decided to give it a go and stood in the line behind her.

Josie was up first and she hopped onto the bull like a natural.

'I told you she was a horsey person,' whispered Mands. 'All lanky and freckly. They all look the same.'

She rode the bull like there was no tomorrow, getting bucked left, right and centre, as the speed increased, but clinging on like a pro. It looked as though she was going to ride it into the sunset. After five minutes of violent and furious bucking she was finally thrown off, landing perfectly on her feet on the rubber mat.

Bloody hell, I despaired, knowing there was no way in the world I would be staying on the thing for that long.

'I think we have a new female record,' said the man with the microphone.

Josie walked off the mat towards Ethan, smiling proudly.

I immediately tried to make my way out of the line.

'Don't even think about it,' said Mands and Lizzie, who were blocking my way.

I had no choice but to walk up to the bull and climb on. There was nothing graceful about my mount, as I finally managed to get one leg over.

A mere thirty seconds later, as the bull picked up its bucking pace, I suddenly found myself airborne, flying face first towards the blue rubber mat.

'Crikey,' said Dad, as he came to help me up. 'That was quite a fall.'

'Looks like we might need to organise you some riding

lessons,' said Ethan, also helping me up.

I was too winded to say anything, having had every last breath of air knocked from my body.

'Bloody great effort!' said Mands, as I bade her an evil look. I would have liked to have seen her ride that thing.

'Guess they don't have bulls in the city?' said Josie.

'Stupid cow!' hissed Lizzie. 'I think you should challenge her to a cork-popping competition. Then we'll see who the winner is.'

I was still too winded to reply.

The next activity we came to was the Gumboot Throw. I couldn't remember ever having worn a gumboot before, let alone thrown one. The boys all had a go first, with Mack throwing the winning boot. And naturally Josie was the first to enter the female competition.

'Don't just stand there,' whispered Mands and Lizzie. 'Grab your boot.'

'Oh for God's sake,' I sighed. I was still in rather substantial pain.

There were five females in line to throw, including Josie and my mother. Josie was third to throw, immediately taking the lead.

'Bloody hell!' I hissed to Mands and Lizzie. 'She's some sort of rural Xena.'

'Just throw it,' they urged. 'You can do it!'

I stepped forward and hurled the gumboot, watching as it sailed a good two metres beyond Josie's one.

'Yee-haa!' cried Mands, Lizzie and Abbie.

'Good on ya, luvvie,' joined in Elsie.

'That's one for Town,' added Mands.

But my lead was shortlived as my mother stepped up to the line and hurled her boot another two metres past mine, winning the female gumboot throw hands down.

She was rather chuffed with her prize, which was a T-shirt with the slogan *If You Can't Wear 'Em, Throw 'Em* and the outline of a pair of gumboots.

Toothless Cass was among the spectators and soon persuaded Mands to be her partner in the sheep-herding competition, which was a sight to behold. And it was a relief to sit my body on the bench for a while.

Next up, and the final activity for the day, was Wood Chopping, which was run by Bruce from the hardware-slash-pharmacy store. Ethan, Mack and Dad all lined up for the male competition, with Ethan cleaning up by a long shot. He made it look so easy.

'Well done,' I congratulated him.

'Whaa thaaank ya Saamanthaa,' he drawled.

I had to laugh.

'You'll be having a go then, won't you?' he asked, as the beginning of the female competition was announced by Bruce. 'Oh no, I don't think so,' I replied.

'C'mon Samantha,' urged Josie. 'Don't they have axes in the city?'

She really was proving to be a large pain in the arse, I thought to myself. Her city comments were beginning to wind me up, especially considering she'd been living in a larger city herself for the past three years.

'Course we do,' said Lizzie, giving me a little shove.

'Thatta girl,' encouraged Mands.

It appeared I had no choice. Thankfully my mother had decided to sit this one out.

Dear God, I thought, as I picked up the heavy axe, a completely foreign object in my hands. *I'm going to chop off my bloody leg.*

I put my left foot onto the log in front of me, as everyone else appeared to be doing.

'Three, two, one, chop!' called out Bruce, as I took my first swing at the log.

And what a swing it was. So powerful that it took me completely by surprise. So powerful that the weight of the axe flipped me head first over the log and onto the grass beyond, where I lay sprawled, narrowly missing landing on the axe which, incidentally, had not made contact with the log. My body throbbed, having sustained its second high-impact collision in the space of two hours.

'Upsy-daisy!' called out my mother. 'Thatta girl!'

I hoisted myself up from the grass, quickly realising that (as embarrassed as I was) I really did have to start chopping. I put my foot back on the log and, with arms steady and controlled, managed to make some small dents in the medium-sized log. And I was nearly a good quarter of the way through it when Josie threw her axe down and her hands up, her log neatly dissected.

Bitch! I thought to myself, but at the same time feeling grateful it was over. *Why on earth would anyone want to chop wood? Especially when you could buy it already chopped?*

I looked down at my left palm, which was sporting the beginnings of a red blister.

Thankfully the gruelling physical activities were finally over and it was time to head to the cake stall for the announcement of the results. The announcer, and also one of the judges, was ample Della, from the grocery-slash-dry-cleaning-slash-liquor store. She stood outside the stall, where a small crowd had gathered, with a microphone in hand. After a little speech about how this year had been the toughest competition yet, and with the most entries, she announced the winners.

'Third prize goes to . . . Deidre Watkins!' cried Della.

Yay! I thought to myself. That meant Elsie simply had to be first or second place.

Deidre Watkins looked less than impressed as she walked up to collect her bronze medallion and non-stick muffin tray.

'And,' boomed Della, 'second prize goes to . . . Jane S!'

That wasn't Elsie. I looked around for Jane S, whoever she was.

'That's you love!' cried Elsie, grabbing me by the arm. 'Well done!'

Ohmygod! It was too! I was Jane S. And I had won second prize. *Second prize! Unbelievable!*

I walked up to receive my prize from Della, amid much loud whooping from Mands, Lizzie, Elsie and Abbie. It was a silver medallion in the shape of a layered cake, which she placed around my neck, and a copy of the latest Jamie Oliver cookbook. I was congratulated by my friends and family, even my mother and Mands, who said as she was giving me a hug, 'Just promise you won't make a habit out of it, dolls.'

'And . . .' hollered Della. 'The first prize goes to . . . Elsie Thompson!'

'Congratulations!' I cried, giving Elsie a hug, as she beamed back and went to collect her apron, olive oil and cookbook.

She'd done it! And together we'd cleaned up the competition and left narky old Deidre Watkins for toast.

I promptly cut the remainder of my cake and gave everyone a slice, even Josie.

'Delicious,' they praised. 'Best cake ever.'

Dad was over the moon for me. I think he was a bit miffed at not being able to enter the competition himself though as it was only open to locals.

'A woman of many hidden talents,' smiled Ethan, giving me a congratulatory kiss on the cheek.

'Definitely one for Town,' whispered Lizzie in my ear.

That evening we all descended on Mack and Abbie's farmhouse for a barbeque. Ethan's friends Jamie and Ellen, whom I had met for the first time that day, and Josie, came too.

'Sam,' whispered Abbie, as the two of us stood in her kitchen whipping up some salads. 'I'm sorry she's here tonight.'

I gathered she meant Josie.

'She sort of invited herself along and I couldn't really say no.'

'It's OK,' I replied. 'She seems nice.' This was clearly a lie.

'Oh she can be nice all right,' whispered Abbie. 'But only when she wants to be. Usually she's just a two-faced cow.'

'So why did Ethan go out with her?' I asked.

'Who knows? Mack and I certainly never figured it out. All I know is he deserves better than her. Much better.'

'Do you think she's back to stay?' I asked, just being curious.

'I really hope not,' replied Abbie. 'But she seems to be on some sort of mission. I just hope Ethan smells the smoke before he sees it.'

'So do I,' I replied. He was a good friend after all and I didn't want him to wind up with someone who wasn't going to treat him as well as he deserved.

We all sat down to a delicious spread at the table on the deck outside. Josie wasn't forthcoming with polite conversation, so I thought I'd make the first move.

'Where in Sydney were you living?' I asked.

'North Shore,' she replied.

'And have you come back to stay?' I asked.

'I've just come back to collect a few things,' she replied,

deliberately glancing across at Ethan, who was sitting beside her.

I'd never seen Ethan look uncomfortable before, but that's how he looked at that moment. It appeared Josie was one of those people who didn't feel the need to reciprocate with her own questions and I got the feeling she wasn't all that keen to chat to me. It was glaringly evident she hadn't exactly taken a shine to me, although I'd no idea why, or what I'd done to deserve it.

Perhaps she was jealous of the fact that Ethan and I had become friends? I thought to myself. *But why? What was there to be jealous of?*

Whatever the reason, it was a shame she couldn't be a bit friendlier, I thought. This town was far too small for enemies. However there were enough other conversations and laughs to join in on, so her icy reception didn't bother me. It was wonderful having Mands and Lizzie here again, and my parents too, I thought, looking around. And it was great to see how well everyone got on together. My old friends and my new friends. As completely different as Mum and Elsie were, they were even chatting away like old pals. And I was pleasantly surprised by how well behaved my mother was being. It appeared she was able keep a lid on her opinions after all, when the need arose. And Dad, well he was already swapping recipes with Elsie like there was no tomorrow.

The next morning, with foggy heads in tow, Mands, Lizzie, Abbie and I went for a bush walk, with Mands managing to find the only cow pat en route to stand in.

'Unbloodybelievable!' she exclaimed, wiping her shoe on the grass. At least she had learned her lesson and was wearing gym shoes this time, the Prada trainers nowhere in sight.

That afternoon the girls and my parents headed back home, amid much waving from myself, Elsie and Bob. The cabin felt eerily silent that night, as it had the last time they'd left. I missed them already. They were like a friendly tornado that left an unfillable gap in its wake.

Thankfully the silence was interrupted by a phone call from Ethan.

'What are you doing tomorrow night?' he asked.

'No plans,' I replied.

'How about you come round for dinner then?'

'Sure,' I replied. 'I'd love to.'

I wondered if I was going to be the only one there for dinner, or if Josie would be inviting herself along too.

'If I'm not at the cottage I'll be up at the main house,' he said. 'Come and find me there.'

The next night I arrived and Ethan wasn't at the cottage, so I walked up to the main house. It was a beautiful walk, the driveway framed by rose bushes and sweeping green trees.

Ethan's father answered the door.

'Hello there. He's just out in the front paddock. One of the heifers is having a bit of trouble birthing.'

One of the what?

'Why don't you go and find him? You can borrow some gumboots if you like,' he said, glancing at the pink loafers on my feet. 'Bit muddy out there.'

With a pair of enormous old black gumboots on my feet I traipsed out across the paddock in search of Ethan. I quickly spotted him kneeling down beside what appeared to be, on closer inspection, a very large cow. Which appeared to be, on even closer inspection, in the process of giving birth.

'Just in time Sam!' he called out. 'Come and give us a hand.'

I looked down at the muddy grass, and then I looked down at my clean blue jeans. And then I thought *fuck it* and knelt down beside him anyway.

'Put these on,' instructed Ethan, handing me a pair of surgical gloves. 'And then put your hands up here.'

I looked at him and waited for him to say, 'Ah! Just joshin' with ya.' But he didn't.

'Go on,' he urged.

And so I did.

And that is how I found myself crouching on my knees in a field of muddy grass, eye-level with the fanny of a very large cow, my arms stuck up to their pits in it, covered in god-only-knew-what, attempting to grasp the legs of her very-nearly-about-to-be-born calf.

'Here she comes, Sam!' cried Ethan, as the cow let out one final long groan. 'Pull!'

And pull I did. And then I pulled some more. I pulled until, with one final gigantic squelching sound, I was left cradling a tiny, brown slippery calf in my bloody arms.

'Great job, Sam!' said Ethan, putting his arm around my shoulders and grinning. 'You're a pro.'

Still hugging the tiny calf in my arms, I grinned back.

14

With the help of three members of the national cricket team testing positive for cocaine while playing against the West Indies, and one of them waking up naked beside two models-cum-strippers (neither one his wife), the media furore surrounding Alistair and I appeared to have all but ground to a halt. Finally! Almost five months after we had first slept together. It was rather ironic that sport had got me into this whole mess, and now it was about to get me out of it.

Perhaps I would have to start watching it? I thought to myself. Or perhaps some things would never change.

There were no more phone calls to my work (according to Izzy). No more journalists pressuring Mands, Lizzie, my parents or my sisters to spill the beans as to my whereabouts. No more paparazzi camped outside my apartment. And no more pictures of, or stories about, either me and Alistair, or Tiny Tits. It appeared they had even had enough of her. The frenzy had finally abated and it looked as though I might finally be getting my old life back. At last!

Mands and Lizzy were both confident it was now safe for me to return to the city, as were my family. Although they all recommended I keep the red hair and a low profile, at least for a while. I felt confident too. Ready to return to my old life.

I had been living in Floodgate for just over three months. And what a three months it had been. I had learned how to cook and bake a cake. I could fix a leaky roof, light a fire, and confront wild animals. I had a new-found appreciation for tea and date scones. And I had even delivered a baby calf.

Now it was safe to return home there was nothing to keep me here in Floodgate. So, I planned my departure for three days' time, which would give me enough time to pack up my belongings and say goodbye.

That morning in the café I told Elsie of my plans. She immediately grabbed me by both arms and shouted, 'Oh no, luvvie!' before sighing and saying, 'Ah well, I knew the time would come. A rolling stone gathers no moss after all.'

When I got back to the cabin I phoned Ethan.

'What are you doing for your last night?' he asked.

'No plans,' I replied.

'How about I cook you dinner then?' he suggested.

'Fabulous,' I replied. That sounded like a great idea.

Over the next few days I chipped away at some work, including letting my clients and a very elated Gareth know I was returning to the office.

'Well thank Christ for that!' he cried, sounding more than relieved.

But mostly I spent time packing up all of my things. It was amazing how far I had spread my possessions and how they had become as one with the tiny cabin. I also cleaned the cabin. I don't know why I bothered, seeing that it wasn't exactly clean when I arrived and it would more than likely be vacant for the next twenty years or so. But I did anyway. Then I went round to Ethan's house for my last dinner in this town.

He opened the front door wearing a blue apron with pink flowers on the front.

'You didn't tell me it was dress-up,' I said, walking in.

'Oh, this is nothing,' he smiled. 'You should see what I wear to bed.'

I walked into the living room to find Elsie, Bob, Mack, Abbie and Ethan's dad sitting on the sofas.

'Surprise!' cried Elsie, standing up and giving me a huge hug, closely followed by everyone else. 'We're crashing your goodbye dinner.'

I was pleased to note that Josie wasn't crashing my goodbye dinner too, although perhaps she hadn't been invited.

I just stood there, grinning inanely, suddenly speechless.

'Somebody get the girl a drink!' cried Abbie, placing a glass of wine into my hand.

'The squeaky wheel gets the grease,' said Elsie. I think she wanted me to say something.

'This is great,' I said, smiling at Ethan. 'Thank you.'

'You're welcome,' he replied. 'You didn't think this lot were going to let you go without a proper send-off did you?'

It was a wonderful dinner, the best I could ever remember having. And the only surprise dinner ever thrown in my honour. We laughed, talked, told jokes, drank lovely wine and ate delicious food. We had whole baked trout (for old times' sake), eye fillet, new potatoes, chargrilled vegetables and a green salad. All cooked by Ethan.

As we finished dessert the time came to say goodbye.

'Don't worry,' I said to Elsie, who looked as though she was about to cry. 'I'll come and see you in the morning. I'm not leaving this place without a date scone.'

I hugged them all. Abbie, Mack, Bob and Ethan's dad. These people who had become my good friends. They all wished me well and told me I had to come back and visit them. I told them all how wonderful it was to meet them and of course I would come back. And I meant it, every word.

I gave Ethan a hand with the dishes and then we sat back down at the table with a glass of port each, just him and me. He asked me questions. Was I excited to be going back? Yes, I was. Would I be going straight back to work? Yes. I bet Mands and Lizzie are looking forward to having me back? So they keep telling me. He was polite, he was funny, he was the same old Ethan. I asked him all about his vet rounds, how his dad's farm was doing, and when was he going to start taking photos again. Soon, he promised, soon. It was like any number of the conversations we'd had over the past few months. Interesting, flowing, and without any awkward silences. But there was something slightly different too, something I couldn't quite put my finger on.

'I suppose I'd better hit the road and finish packing,' I sighed, at eleven o'clock.

Ethan convinced me to stay for another small glass of port before I made a final move to go, and he walked me out to my car. We kissed each other on the cheek and then we hugged each other, tight. And then we both stepped back. And then, just for one second, a strange vision flashed before my eyes. A vision of What Could Be. A vision of a life I could have, if I stayed here, in this town. But as quickly as it appeared it was gone again.

'Bye Sam,' he said, stepping back. 'I'm really going to miss you.'

'Me too,' I said. 'Promise you'll come and see me.'

'Of course,' he said.

I hoped he meant it.

That night I went to bed in the little wooden cabin for the last time, soothed to sleep by the sounds of silence. I thought back to my first night, with the pillow over my head, and smiled to myself. It seemed like so long ago.

The next morning I woke early to the familiar and beautiful sound of tui outside the bedroom window, loaded my little car to the hilt and locked up the cabin, standing outside and looking at it for the last time. Instead of looking at it in horror, as I had on that first day, I looked at it with fondness. As old and tiny and rundown as it was, I was actually going to miss it. It had been my home. I hopped into my car and drove off down the dirt driveway. But I had one last stop to make before I left this town. A morning-tea stop.

I sat at my table by the window with my pot of tea and date scone, and Elsie sat with me. We ate our morning tea slowly and together, as they tended to do in this town. There was no need to hurry. As Elsie was prone to say: God did not create hurry.

Elsie cleared away the plates and I stood in the café, looking around at the red-checked tablecloths, the plastic chairs, and the white lace curtains for the last time. At least for a while.

'Will you come back and see us soon, love?' she asked, as she folded me into a huge hug. There were tears in her eyes. And in mine.

'Of course I will,' I said, hugging her back, as tightly as I could, and trying not to cry. 'So much that you'll get sick of me.'

'Never,' she said. 'There'll always be a room for you here.'

'Will you and Bob come and stay with me in the city sometime?' I asked.

'Does the hen cackle?' she replied.

I think this was a yes.

'And remember, love,' she said, letting me go, 'when one door shuts, another one opens.'

And then I was on the road, driving back towards my old life. I felt a whole mixture of things. I felt excited. Excited to see my friends, my family, my apartment and my office again. Excited to get my old life back. I was a bit scared too. Scared of what would be waiting for me, scared of what might happen with Alistair. And I felt sad. Sad because I was leaving behind my new friends — Elsie, Ethan, Bob, Mack and Abbie. People I had come to know and love. I also felt something else I couldn't quite put my finger on. Something which made me feel a little uneasy, almost as though I was driving in the wrong direction.

You're just a bit nervous, I told myself, *it's understandable. You'll be back into the swing of things in no time at all.*

Exactly four-and-a-half hours later, and without getting lost, I had pulled off the motorway and was back in the city. As I was stopped at the lights I looked around in awe. Everything seemed so big and busy. And it was a little bit, well, a little bit overwhelming.

In the process of being overwhelmed I was tooted at, several times, for missing a green arrow.

For God's sake! I thought to myself, as I hit the accelerator. *Take a chill pill!*

As I pulled up outside my apartment I was immediately aware there was something missing. And there was. There was no one waiting outside my gate for me, no one yelling out 'Give us a smile Samantha!' and no cameras firing flashes at me. I walked to my front door, calmly and slowly. It was a wonderful thing to behold.

I stepped back inside my apartment, for the first time in over three months. Initially I thought someone had broken in and robbed the place in my absence, until I remembered this is what it looked like when I left. White, clean, spacious and minimal. The look I had created. The look I relished. For some reason it felt a little strange, a little empty.

Think I'll paint it a brighter colour, I thought to myself. *It's time for a change.* Plus it felt, well, it felt a little cold.

I walked into my bedroom and threw my suitcase up onto my white duvet, suddenly aware this is not something I did. Or used to do anyway. I decided to leave my unpacking until later on and drove round to Lizzie's house for dinner instead.

'The eagle has finally landed!' cried Mands, opening the door and embracing me in a huge hug.

'Yay!' screamed Lizzie, running to the door also, arms wide open.

'So, how is it being back?' they asked eagerly, as we sat down with a wine.

'A bit strange to be honest,' I replied. 'I'm not sure about my apartment, it feels kinda odd.'

'What do you mean?' asked Mands. 'It's a fabulous pad.'

'Yes, I know. But it's just a bit, well, a bit cold and stark I guess.'

'But you decorated it yourself,' said Lizzie. 'Everything.'

'I know, and that's the problem,' I replied. 'I think I might be . . . well . . . a bit anal.'

Mands and Lizzie stared at each other, odd expressions on their faces.

'Of course you are, dolls,' they both said. 'You always have been.'

'In fact, you used to pride yourself on it,' added Mands.

'Plus sweets, being anal's good,' said Lizzie. 'It's just another word for being in control.'

'I'm anal and I'm proud,' said Mands. 'Go on, say it.'

'OK,' I replied, although I wasn't entirely comfortable with the supposed attribute. 'I'm anal and I'm . . . um . . . proud.'

'Wasn't very convincing,' said Mands.

'Where's Louie?' I asked, changing the subject.

Mands promptly shook her head and gave me the don't-ask look.

'He's gone,' said Lizzie, hanging her head.

'Where?' I cried. 'Don't tell me he got run over?'

By this stage Mands was violently shaking her head behind Lizzie's back.

'No,' sighed Lizzie. 'I gave him away.'

'To who?'

God. Who on earth wanted to take a dog on Prozac?

'Pete.' Pete was Lizzie's cousin.

'Really? And how's he doing?'

Mands looked as though she was about to shake her head right off its hinges.

'Great . . . the bastard.'

'Oh.'

'Happy as fucking Larry,' continued Lizzie. 'And he's off the bloody drugs too.'

'Really?'

This was surprising. I thought Louie would be buried with a six-pack of Prozac.

Clearly Lizzie was upset at being deserted by a male, once again. Even if that male was a canine.

'But she's getting another dog,' prompted Mands. 'Aren't you?'

'Yes. A female. A loyal, content, non-sport-watching female.'

'Lovely,' I replied. 'I bet she'll even like going shopping too.'

'True,' agreed Mands. 'And she'll just love going out for bubbles with us as well.'

'What's for dins?' I asked, as Mands poured me another wine.

'Thai,' said Lizzie, shoving a menu into my hand.

'Oh,' I said. 'Takeaways?'

'But of course,' said Lizzie. 'The kitchen's just for show, you know that.'

'How about I fix us something easy instead?' I said.

They both looked at me as if I had finally gone insane.

'But why would you cook when you don't have to?' asked Mands, confusion crowding her face.

'Because,' I replied. 'I kind of like it.'

Another uneasy look passed between them.

'Go on,' I instructed. 'You two sit down and relax and I'll whip us up something.'

'Good luck to you,' said Lizzie, backing out of the kitchen. 'I've absolutely no idea what's lurking in there.'

'I'll find something,' I assured her. Although Lizzie couldn't cook to save herself, she also didn't want to be seen without the right ingredients in her kitchen.

'Have you got an apron?' I asked.

'The cleaner might have left hers,' said Lizzie. 'I'll go have a look.'

She returned from the laundry with her cleaner's red-striped apron and I set about rummaging through the pantry, fridge and freezer. Mands and Lizzie sat on the barstools at the bench opposite, staring at me as though I were some sort of body snatcher who had infiltrated their best friend's being.

'Are you sure you haven't bumped your head today, dolls?' asked Mands.

'Sit, sit,' I motioned, twenty minutes later, pointing to the

355

dining table and setting two bowls of Thai chicken noodles down in front of them.

'Wow! This is delicious!' exclaimed Mands, taking a mouthful.

'Amazing!' added Lizzie.

'Quite the little housewife, aren't you?' said Mands.

I decided to take this as a compliment.

Dishes done I decided to head home reasonably early for once. It was my first day back in the office tomorrow and I wanted to be on form.

'What are you doing?' asked Mands.

'Going.'

'Where?'

'Home.'

'Why?' asked Lizzie, screwing her face up. 'It's not even ten o'clock.'

'I know, but I just want to get a good night's sleep before I start back at work. Don't worry, I'll see you both on Friday.'

'I hope all that country air hasn't made you soft, dolls,' said Mands.

'Quite the opposite,' I said, kissing them both goodbye.

That night I climbed into my lovely, comfortable, very expensive, un-lumpy and dip-free queen-sized bed. But, as tired as I was, I couldn't seem to get to sleep.

God, the noise! I thought to myself, as the third car alarm went off in the street outside. I got up to check the bedroom windows were closed. They were. And as I did I heard someone yell out 'You're a cunt Michael! A *fucking* cunt!' from the street below. You would've had to have been certifiably deaf not to hear it.

'I SAID A FUCKING CUUNNTT!'

Followed by the smashing of a glass bottle, presumably thrown. And then another.

Fabulous. I guess it'll take a while to get used to it again, I told myself. I would've given anything for five minutes of silence. Three hours later I finally drifted off, ear plugs in and a pillow over my head.

The next morning I woke to yet another car alarm. I tried to go back to sleep but then the rubbish collectors came along.

Might as well get up then, I thought. I showered, dressed, and drove into the office. It felt odd putting on a suit again. Odd and slightly uncomfortable. It was somewhat of a shock to my poor body which had been living in nothing but jeans and trainers for months. It was even stranger driving to the office without being chased by a convoy of four-wheel drives and motorbikes.

My arrival back at the office was well received to say the least. I was literally set upon. In my absence word had spread that a few of our major clients had been seen searching around for other agencies, much to Gareth's horror. It appeared that Erica hadn't done such a great job of keeping everything under wraps. Gareth was distraught and looked approximately ten years older than when I had left.

'It's OK,' I placated him. 'I'll get them back.'

My work was cut out for me, ringing around, assuring them of our commitment to their business, and setting up as many meetings as quickly as I could. I was kissing arses left, right and centre. Instead of publicly disintegrating a very sheepish Erica, as I would have relished and thoroughly enjoyed doing in the past, I included her in all aspects of the rescue mission. She had made mistakes and I wanted her to learn how to fix them, so they wouldn't happen again. Plus, I desperately needed the assistance and, as she rightly feared for her job, she was more than happy to help. By the end of the week I had met with all of the disgruntled clients, wooed them back, and averted any major catastrophes for the company, much to Gareth's relief. I was also absolutely exhausted. Dead on my feet.

How on earth did you used to manage this? I wondered to myself.

What I wouldn't have given for ten minutes with a pot of tea and a date scone.

There was something else that was bugging me too. While in the past I would have experienced a massive adrenaline rush and sense of satisfaction at working so close to the line and pulling it off, this time I didn't. I just felt tired.

It'll come back, I told myself. *Just give it time.* I certainly hoped so.

I had been avoiding Alistair since my return. He had left messages everywhere. On my home phone, work phone, and mobile. Lots of them. He knew I was back in town and quite obviously wanted to speak to me. It's not that I didn't want to speak to him. It's just that I wasn't ready for what might happen when I did. I had stopped being angry with him. I don't know when and I don't know how, I just had. I no longer wished him a long and drawn-out death from a painful and lingering STD. In fact, I no longer wished him any harm whatsoever. I just didn't feel ready to see him again. Not yet. I needed to concentrate on getting back into the swing of my life, at least for another couple of weeks, and think about what it was I wanted. What was right for me? And was that him?

One week after arriving back, as I sat in my office, I had a phone call from Elsie.

'Hiya luvvie. I hope I haven't caught you at a bad time?'

'Not at all.'

Truth be known I was running late for a meeting with Gareth. He could wait.

'How are you?' I asked, pleased to hear her familiar voice.

'Oh, OK love.'

She didn't sound OK.

'Well, truth be told, the arthritis is giving me a bit of grief lately.'

'Oh Elsie, I'm sorry.'

I could only imagine how bad it must be if she was actually admitting to it.

'Them's the breaks, love. Life isn't all beer and skittles.'

'How's Bob?' I asked.

'He's grand. He sends his love.'

'That's nice. Please send it back.'

'I saw Ethan this morning.'

'How is he?' I asked.

'He's fine. Just his same old lovely self.'

I was glad to hear he was fine.

'And thankfully that Josie girl's left town again. I knew she wouldn't stick round for long. Like honey to a bee that one.'

'Oh.'

This was a surprise. I was sure she'd be back again soon though. She had things to collect after all.

'He's got a bit of a sad walk on him though,' continued Elsie. 'Sort of stooped. I think he misses you, love.'

I think it was probably Josie that he missed, but I didn't say anything.

'How's the café going?' I asked, keen to change the subject.

'It's going OK, it's me that's not. It's getting a bit too much for me. I think the time has come to sell it.'

'Oh no! Really?'

'I've no other choice, love. No children to take it over.'

'Would anyone in the village buy it?' I asked.

'I don't think so. Everyone's a bit too stuck in their working ways here.'

Selling the café to a stranger would break Elsie's heart.

'Oh Elsie, I'm sorry.'

'Sweetie pie, don't be, it's the end of an era, that's all. Dogs bark and the caravan moves on. That place is crying out for a revamp and some new blood. Hell! Even I know how dated it is.'

I had to laugh. It might be dated, but it was also so very Elsie.

'Now, when are you coming back to visit us?' she asked.

'I'm not sure,' I sighed. 'I really want to but work's just so busy at the moment.'

'Well, we'll all be waiting here for you when you're ready love. Take your time.'

I felt as though her words had a double meaning, but I wasn't sure what it was.

'I will. I miss you.'

'We miss you too, Sam.'

I said goodbye and ambled along the corridor to the meeting I was almost half an hour late for. I couldn't be bothered running.

I was supposed to be going to a bar opening with Mands and Lizzie after work, I think it was another one of Darcy and Samuel's. But I was just too tired to make an effort. For some reason the idea of getting dolled up and going to a bar was, well, decidedly unappealling.

I rang Mands and made my excuses.

'Well, what exactly are you going to do?' she asked. 'Stay home and wash your hair?'

'Probably,' I replied, laughing.

'Are you sick?' she asked, sounding concerned.

'No,' I replied. 'I'm just a bit tired and I can't be arsed getting glam.'

I heard a sharp intake of breath. Followed by a long pause.

'You must be sick,' she replied. 'You should go to the doctor. Now.'

Mands tried every ploy in the book, but for once in my life I was unswayable.

I went home and I did wash my hair. And then I cooked myself some dinner. And then I decided to phone Ethan.

'Hi,' I greeted when he picked up the phone. 'It's Sam.'

'Hey stranger,' he replied, a smile in his familiar voice. 'Crushed any balls lately?'

'Oh, just a few,' I laughed.

'How are you?' he asked.

How was I? I wondered.

'I'm . . . OK,' I answered. 'It's good to be back but it feels, well, kinda strange at the same time.'

'Take your time,' he encouraged. 'You'll be back into the swing of things before you know it.'

I really hoped so.

'And how have you been?' I asked. 'What did you get up to today?'

'Oh, you know, stitched a dog's foot, put a horse to sleep, delivered a calf.'

'You delivered a calf without me?'

'Well, I was thinking about ringing you and asking you to drive back and help. I could have done with your expertise.'

'Very funny,' I laughed.

We chatted away together just like old times. We talked

about Elsie and Bob, about Mack and Abbie, about the farm, about Mands and Lizzie, about all kinds of stuff. Before I knew it we'd been chatting for over an hour.

'OK Sam,' he said. 'I'd better let you get some shut-eye before tomorrow.'

'OK then,' I agreed, although I didn't want to go.

'Lovely talking to you.'

'You too,' I replied. 'I'll give you a call again soon.'

'That'd be nice. Take care of yourself Sam.'

I put down the phone with a smile on my face. It was nice to know that even though he was far away Ethan was still the same old easy-going chatty person. And that even though I had left we were going to stay friends. His friendship was something I really didn't want to lose. Ever.

The following night, Mands, Lizzie and I went out to dinner at Prego. It was my long-awaited welcome-home dinner, and Manuel was making a special meal just for us. With strict instructions that it should not involve Tahitian vanilla beans, not in any way, shape or form. We sat at our usual table by the window. It was wonderful to be able to sit in a restaurant once again, in public, with my two best friends, without the fear of being harassed or recognised. Just like the good old days. It seemed the public had forgotten me as quickly as they had found me, and I was more than happy with my new-found anonyminity. Happy to be just another girl, sitting in a restaurant, with her two friends.

'Cheers girls,' said Mands, clinking our glasses of bubbles. 'Here's to the long-awaited return of Samantha Steel!'

'Here, here!' chorused Lizzie.

But before I had a chance to clink Lizzie's glass, her mobile, which was sitting on top of the table, began ringing.

'Lizzie speaking. Yes. That's right. Correct. Customs? Yes. I beg your pardon? You've what? You've got to be bloody joking! When? And what EXACTLY are you doing with it?'

The conversation did not appear to be going all that well. Lizzie had slammed down her glass of champers and was getting progressively redder in the face. She was now also standing up at the table and shouting into her phone. The people at the tables around us were listening in. Truth be told, they had no choice in the matter. In fact, the entire restaurant was listening. And staring. Mands and I looked across the table at each other and raised our eyebrows.

'And when EXACTLY are you planning on releasing it?' demanded Lizzie. 'TELL ME you are joking! No! YOU listen here,' she shouted. 'I don't think you UNDERSTAND. I am OVULATING! I said OVULATING! And I need that SPERM now! NOW! Do you HEAR me? I said NOW!'

Mands and I looked at each other again and smiled.

It was good to be back, I thought to myself, taking another sip of champers. *Oh, how I'd missed them.*

Two weeks later, after taking time to settle back into my apartment and job, I decided to phone Alistair. I still found it difficult to get to sleep at night with the noise outside, and I was still waiting for my career drive to return, but I knew I couldn't keep him waiting forever.

Epilogue

Exactly one year later I stood at the crest of the green grassy slope, looking down at the large cluster of people gathered under the willow trees by the stream.

'Oh for fucksake!' exclaimed Mands. 'Goddamn cow shit! What are the odds?'

It appeared she had once again managed to find herself a cowpat to stand in. She took her heel off and furiously rubbed it across the grass.

'Quite high round here, dolls,' replied Lizzie, as her hand gently circled the enormous belly poking out from under her beautiful mint-green frock.

She looked so radiant, there was a good chance her head might just glow itself right off.

'You ready, love?' asked Dad, smiling at me. 'Guess we better follow these two.'

'I guess so,' I replied, smiling back at him and taking his arm.

He looked so dashing in his navy suit. It was lovely to see him out of his apron for a change. We walked down the gentle slope, following Mands and Lizzie through the borders of forget-me-nots which had been laid out on the grass for us to follow.

I could see him standing beneath the tallest and greenest willow tree, facing away. I would recognise that tall stature and those broad shoulders anywhere. We walked through the cluster of people. Our friends, and family. There was Vicky holding little Max in her arms. The Steel female stronghold had finally been broken with his birth, much to my father's delight. There was Susie, smiling madly, a gorgeous new bloke on her arm. There were Darcy and Samuel, looking for all the world like two GQ models. There was Jenna, holding her small daughter's hand. There was Gareth, his two little boys at his feet, and his pretty new girlfriend at his side. There was stunning Jasmine, and her very foxy boyfriend James.

And there was my mother, or at least I thought it was my mother. Christ alive! She appeared to be wearing a frock! All my life I had been positive she would turn up at my wedding wearing army pants. I gave her a smile and she smiled back. She looked beautiful. Standing next to her and beside Bob, was Elsie, not that I could have missed her in the hot-pink suit she was wearing, with matching hat and handbag. She gave me a huge grin and a little wave. I waved back. She had so much more energy now she had sold the café. Her arthritis had even decided to give her a much-needed break. The new owner had kept the name, and the red-checked tablecloths, but had slowly changed nearly everything else. She had even put in a proper Italian coffee machine. It was now possible to get a decent coffee in Floodgate. All of Elsie's recipes remained, along with the ones the new owner had added.

'Change is as good as a holiday, love,' said Elsie, who still came in at least twice a week to give me a hand or to just have a chat. I was always glad for the help, although my cooking had come a long way and I could now make a date scone to rival even hers. Business was good. Floodgate had earned a bit of a reputation as a peaceful getaway over the past year and with more accommodation being built the visitor population had soared. I would never make as much money as I had in the city, but I made a living nonetheless. And there was something to be said for living, I decided. Plus, it was still virtually impossible to find any clothing, beauty treatments, or skincare products to hurl your notes at here.

And then we were there, Dad and I. Stopping. Dad gave me a kiss on the cheek and a smile and moved away.

'How're ya doing, little lady?' whispered Ethan. 'You look stunning.'

'Positively crapping myself,' I replied. 'But in a lovely way.'

He smiled down at me and I smiled back.

'Who would've thought?' he whispered.

'Yes,' I whispered back, smiling. 'Who would've?'

That night, while karaokeing to 'I Will Survive' with Mands and I, Lizzie's waters broke, exactly one week early.

'The child couldn't have picked a better song to arrive to,' observed Mands. 'It'll be well equipped with the lyrics.'

In light of the nearest hospital being one hundred kilometres away and the local doctor being one of the wedding guests and, in his own words, 'too tanked to be delivering any wee babies', Ethan was given the honour, with the drunk doctor's assistance.

'Sure, what's the difference between a cow and a woman?' said Ethan, much to Lizzie's horror.

But although he'd never delivered a baby before, he did it effortlessly and calmly. And although Lizzie had never given birth before, she was a natural. Heaving and pushing all through the night, as if it were just another day in court.

Mands and I left the technical stuff to Ethan and instead stood on either side of the bed, each holding one of Lizzie's hands, providing words of support and simultaneously managing to plough our way through three bottles of champers.

'Give me some!' demanded Lizzie, lunging for my glass. I gave it to her.

At quarter past six the next morning Lizzie was cradling her baby in her arms and crying her eyes out with happiness, of course. It was a gorgeous, perfect, beautiful little girl. Mands and I sat on the bed beside her crying our eyes out too, with happiness, mixed with a bit of drunkenness, me still in my white wedding gown and Mands in her mint-green bridesmaid's frock. We were a little the worse for wear after our all-night baby-booze-bender.

'Shease a woverly bebe,' said Mands, stroking the baby's head, perhaps a little too enthusiastically.

'Shease esh beautifulsh,' I agreed, holding one of her tiny hands in my own. And she was. Simply beautiful.

'Whashername?' I asked.

'Isobel,' replied Lizzie.

'Ah . . . Ishabelle,' sighed Mands and I.

'Get a load of these two,' said Lizzie, to the sleeping baby girl wrapped in a white cloth. 'These are your godmothers. God help you.'

Ethan appeared back in the doorway.

'How's my beautiful bride?' he asked.

'Bit pished,' I replied.

'Go on, get out of here,' instructed Lizzie, as Ethan came over to the bed and lifted me up into his strong arms.

'Let's get you to bed then,' he said, carrying me out of the room, and not even coming close to knocking my head on the doorframe.

But by the time he carried me down the hall and gently placed me onto our bed I was fast asleep. Or passed out, if you prefer. There would be no consummating of vows this morning. But what the hell? We had the rest of our lives to consummate to our hearts' content.

As for my slice of fame? Well, the odd media stalker has tracked me down over the past year. A few months ago there was a picture in the *Telegraph* of me line dancing with the caption 'Samantha Steel Getting Down on the Farm'. But this wasn't as exciting as shagging the captain of the national football team, so it was only on page six.

As for the captain of the national football team? Well, he and his wife went through a very public and messy divorce a couple of months back. She did quite well out of it, from what I'd heard. Although I didn't hear much because, quite frankly, I didn't care to. Alistair finally decided to leave me in the peace I had requested, although I still have the earrings to remind me of our public rendezvous (or rather Mands does, it's her turn). Whenever I've seen his picture in the paper, or in a magazine, it's always with a different woman hanging from his arm.

As for Tiny Tits? Well, she's just had her biography published, by none other than Alexander Carroll. I think it's called *The Sideline Wife*, or some such bollocks.